MISTRESS OF SOULS

CM HUTTON

MISTRESS OF SOULS

Copyright © 2023 by CM Hutton
All rights reserved.

No part of this book may be reproduced in any form or by any electronic or mechanical means, including information storage and retrieval systems, without written permission from the author, except for the use of brief quotations in a book review.

This is a work of fiction. Names, characters, business, events and incidents are the products of the author's imagination. Any resemblance to actual persons, living or dead, or actual events is purely coincidental.

Cover Character Art by: Ellie @mageonduty
Cover Design by: Rebecca L. Garcia

MISTRESS OF SOULS

CM HUTTON

Note from the Author

Please refer to the next page if you would like to view the complete list of trigger warnings before continuing.

However, if you thrive in the dark like me, venture on unaware and enjoy the ride. Don't be surprised if Mariax whispers commands in your ear or her tail slides around your throat.

TRIGGER WARNINGS

This is a dark paranormal romance and some of the material may be triggering for you. As a work of fiction, any portrayal of BDSM is not meant as a guide. The scenes depicted between any dominant and submissive does not necessarily constitute a healthy relationship.

Anxiety	Knife Play
BDSM	Mental Illness
Blood	Murder
Blood Play	Occult
Breath Play	Panic Attacks
Humiliation	Sexual Content
Death of a Minor Character	Sexual Violence
Degradation	Sex Without a Condom
Demons	Stalking
Dub-Con	Strangulation
Expressionism	Strong language
Gore	Torture
Grief	Violence

GLOSSARY

Inferuna: A version of what humans call "Hell".
Vancate: To travel through space and time. Disappear and reappear somewhere else.

PRONUNCIATIONS

Inferuna: In-fer-oo-na
Mariax: Mar-ee-ax
Primeval: Prime-ville

SCOTTISH DIALECT GLOSSARY

Aye: Yes
Bairn: Child/kid
Cannae: Cannot
Cheetie: Cat or kitten
Leannan: Sweetheart
Chugging: Jerking off
Dinnae- Did not
Nay: No
Neep head: Turnip head
Oorlich: Damp, chilly and utterly unpleasant.
Sae: So
Stramash: Disturbance, racket
Verra: Very
Wee: Little
Willnae: Will not
Ye: You
Yer: You are or your

PLAYLIST

This is the massive playlist I listened to while writing and editing Mistress of Souls. I suggest you put it on shuffle to fully embrace the entire vibe and my eclectic music tastes.

DEDICATION

For everyone who suffers from childhood trauma and now likes hand necklaces—this one's for you.

PROLOGUE

The Primeval

I hiss through clenched teeth, suppressing a groan as moist heat slips down my cock. Once again, I've been forced to release my body's constant ache since *she* left me.

I fist the immortal male's red hair, his scalp pulling with the ferocity of my grip. Shoving him down, my tip slips into his throat. Small jolts of pleasure radiate through my balls, but it's not truly satisfying.

To feel something right now other than physical release is beyond me. I just can't muster an emotional response.

I loosen my fingers, releasing his strands. With any luck, he understands now he is giving a pitiful blowjob.

The male continues to bob along my length. In a daze, I watch his horns move, curling my hands into fists at my side. Every time I see horns, I think of her. The leather of the couch gives as I settle back to try to enjoy this subpar blowjob.

At one time, I wished to feel nothing—to rid myself of the emotions building deep in the blackest part of my soul. But now… now I want them to return.

She ruined me.

When she left, more than half of me had left with her, leaving a gaping, festering wound in its place. At least I have my pain. Pain is always there, surrounding my very essence.

The agony I'm in now, however, after tasting feelings again, is a million times worse. I always knew I didn't want to give in to sharing my soul with another, to open myself up to emotions. I have lived for eons, and I still ignored the screaming inside my mind as my rational thoughts disintegrated. Emotions are dangerous, even for those who know of their capability for destruction.

I allowed another a permanent spot in my life.

My little one will never know why I committed those dark deeds she holds against me. I never got a chance to explain, a chance to tell her what went wrong. I never betrayed her, yet it is cemented in her mind that I did. She feels the certainty in her bones…in her blood. What I did was unforgivable, irredeemable in her eyes.

That day was the last time I ever saw her. It replays in my mind constantly.

I pick up my glass from the end table on my left and swirl the amber liquid around, sending the notes just under my nose before I take a large sip. I hold the glass with my fingertips and rest my head back on the couch, trying my best to enjoy the sensation of another pleasuring me, worshiping this glorious body, but I'm still lost.

I am everything all-powerful. The beginning and the end.

Yet I have been brought down by a simple four-letter word. How did I let this happen to myself? Bitterness churns in my gut, creating a burn that creeps up my throat. I feel ill even as the male between my legs continues to suck on my dick.

"Deeper," I command.

He attempts to oblige, but I am far too large for his pathetic mouth without assistance. My dick is barely tapping the back of his throat. He wraps a hand around my base, his lips meeting the fist he has wrapped around me.

My anger explodes at his lackluster efforts. Magic swirls deep within me. My shadows manifest around him and rip his hand away from my dick. Another shadow collects his other wrist before I wrench them both behind his back, causing his back to arch.

I take his sliver of control away from him entirely, grab his horns, and thrust my cock deep into the back of his throat. Shadows bind him, further keeping him immobile. My abs tighten and release as I thrust, the small hole of his throat forced wider and gripping me as I pump harder. Gagging echoes around my living space.

Many emotions tear through my heart. Just the thought of her brings resentment, love, hatred, anger, happiness, misery, desire…

Pushing her from my mind, I fuck the male's face faster and harder until my pubic bone is slamming against his nose. I look down to watch myself move in and out of his drooling lips, I know the outline of my cock head moving in his throat is visible. He tries to break free from the shadows binding his wrists, so I tighten them.

He is probably running out of air. I don't care when I feel an orgasm rising to the surface, but it's just out of reach.

I tighten my shadows around him, bringing another up to encircle his throat. My dick grazes my shadow from the inside as the skin on his neck stretches. Parting my lips, I groan loudly, while gagging continues to issue from the male.

My erection throbs with anticipation. I'm reaching for that sliver of feeling, that tiny bit of desire I'm chasing.

But it's never the same, no matter how many times I use

someone.

No matter how many times I pleasure myself imagining her curves and thick thighs…It's. Never. The. Same. I need *her*. Without her, pleasure is meaningless. I don't know if I want to throttle her or worship her. All I know is that one day, I will have my hands wrapped around her throat again. I'll be fucking her so deeply that she will never forget our reunion.

She is mine. She agreed. Whether it was eons ago or meer days, she made a vow. I intend to show her who she belongs to. Remind her who her daddy is. She can try to run, but I love the hunt.

I moan and arch my back as desperate tingles of pleasure ripple through my body. Thoughts of her collared and gasping as I fuck her breasts throw me into oblivion. My balls tighten as my pleasure releases. I come hard into the male's throat as I hold him on my cock, pulsing down his throat. I keep him there as I force him to swallow every drop.

When I let go of his horns, he pulls off of me, leaving a string of spit connecting us. I smack him in the cheek with my dick leaving an imprint in cum and slobber. He should be thanking me. Not everyone gets a chance to suck such a magnificent piece of male beauty.

He gasps in a deep breath, sitting back on his heels as the sting registers, and rests his hands on my knees. He's mistaken if he thinks I'm going to get him off now. I don't give a shit about his pleasure. I used him. That's all this was. I had a tiny moment of bliss, just enough to hold on to my sanity.

I raise my knee and push my bare foot against his chest, knocking him on his back. "Get out," I growl menacingly.

His glare turns haughty, and he looks like he is going to argue with me.

I come down on top of him and grab his throat in a bruising grip. Pure rage seeps from my pores, and my unstable mind allows too much power to seep into him.

"I said, get the fuck out."

His eyes widen in horror as the realization washes over him—he just sucked the dick of a monster, one far greater than him.

I release him, and he scrambles back before bolting up and sprinting out the door. A sinister smile graces my face as I continue to stare at the space in front of me.

With a sigh, I stand and make my way back to the couch. I sit, feeling the smooth leather caress my bare skin.

The empty feeling returns almost immediately.

I backhand my glass off of the end table into the far wall, sparkles of fine glass fill the air where it shatters. The dregs of my whisky slowly drip down the wall.

For a moment, my heart rate stammers. Blood glistens on the wall. Crimson streaks trail downward, creating a puddle on the floor. Screams fill my ears. I close my eyes as tightly as I can and then open them to stare at the same spot on the wall.

Whisky. It's just whisky.

I grab the bottle next to me by the neck since my glass is now gone, place my lips around the opening, and take several long pulls. I force myself to take deep lungfuls of air.

Another moment, another day, and the vicious cycle continues.

When I see her again, when I touch that gorgeous body and wrap her tail around my wrist, maybe I'll be whole again.

I had no choice but to stage the event she hates me for. It has become the catalyst for my life to dive into this constant downward spiral. Night after night, I sit in this opulent space, glass in hand, staring into the void that is my life.

Inferuna is not known for its entertainment, and I've lived here for a millennia.

Monsters of any and all breeds are found drinking, screwing, or buying a variety of rare illegal human items that can be found on the black market. For me, I end up watching reruns of *Friends* on an endless loop. I've even attempted to read the massive pile of books left forgotten on her nightstand…but the empty void inside me shudders at the thought of enjoying something that brought her pleasure.

Does she suffer the same way I do? Does she struggle with the constant agony, reliving every moment? Not the good times a pair of lovers have, but the gruesome, violent memories.

I fell for her while learning the art of torture, but it came at a heftier cost than even the art we were taught called for. Sanity. The mind-bending it took for us to accept madness burned all traits of whoever we were before out of us. Our personalities changed, reaching into the darker depths of ourselves.

I will never be the same again.

And all because I allowed myself to feel.

My life before her had been stagnant. I floated through eternity, not in time or space. Had no true physical form. I just existed. I was the villain, the unknown force. I was what my soul desired. Some realms I discovered had crumbling societies and weak systems of power. I took it upon myself to crumble them faster, destroying their worlds entirely.

There is no reason to leave a world slowly rotting when you can speed up the process and decimate the entirety of it. Put it out of its misery.

There have been other realms, on other planes, that have

intricate systems of power in place, but they could have actually used my help. And at those times, I played the hero. Many times, they wanted me to be their god, their king, their master. I always declined their requests, uninterested in that sort of life. Being set down in one place, in one realm, on one plane is not something I've ever desired. Until her.

I don't know when I'll see my Angel again. But I will see her one more time. I cannot remain this close to her, separated by meer realms, without her being in my arms.

Daddy doesn't share. She. Is. Mine.

CHAPTER 1

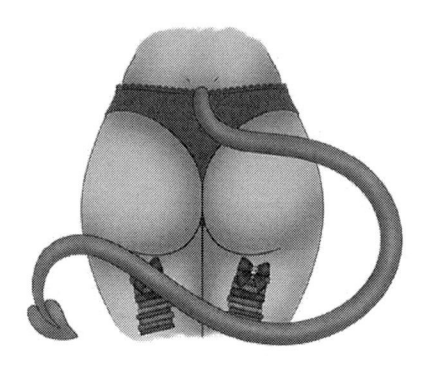

Mariax

Blood pools on the cement floor. The crimson liquid drips from the metal table above, adding to the widening puddle. The heels of my thigh-high black leather stiletto boots echo around the small space with my movements.

A crack ripples through the air when I use my tail to whip the male fae bound to my table. I trail my gaze along his body, assessing my work. His upper thighs, ass, and broad back glow with crisscrossing red stripes. Welts rise among the webs. The ball gag shoved into his mouth and secured behind his head mutes his moans and screams.

As I listen to his muffled pleading, I mentally recoil. Memories echo in my skull, burrowing from the places I keep the most painful ones locked away before I can stop them. I grit my teeth and squeeze my eyes shut. I have plenty of material to inspire me to finish this session. After spending over two thousand years in Inferuna, I don't need my own trauma to do that.

Inferuna... that is the true name of the place humans think of as hell.

I was created there and bred to become one of the best torture demons that has ever existed. There, my drive for torture was not out of joy like many before and after me, but to complete my time served and getting the fuck out. I'm not like the other demons that manifest from the creation fires…I never was. I don't know why, though, but something different happened when I was made.

I place my hand on the globe of his ass and move it in a light caress, debating if he's had enough yet.

Gripping my tail in one hand, I swing it in lazy circles as I stalk around my client. My tail, used for bringing pleasure and pain, is capable of shapeshifting into anything I desire, and it has been one of the most useful tools in my trade. Today, it resembles the humans' 'classic' version of a demon tail, long and thin with a spade-like point at the tip.

His wounds are healing, but slower than they would normally. Aurelia, a witch friend from New York, made me a spelled ointment. When the ointment is applied to flesh, it slows the quick healing ability of most supernaturals, making their sessions into what they need or want.

There are many reasons I am the best fem domme, known best for inflicting equal parts pleasure and pain. However, if I'm caught in a particularly manic mood, the delivery of pain can get a tad messy.

The trauma I endured while in torture training and beyond has ruined parts of me I will never get back, and a large portion of that trauma is from the toxic relationship with Him. I trusted him beyond reason, throwing myself into his offer of mind-numbing safety without a backward glance…until he betrayed my trust. In reality, I should have known better. In fact, I did know better, but the pull of his dangerous energy and indescribable dark power was too much.

He carved a hole for himself within me, a space that will forever be void. I fled Inferuna because of him. His actions had caused me to react impulsively. I should have stayed to confront him, but the danger was too great.

A flutter of movement catches my eye.

The fae's left hand is curling into a fist and releasing repeatedly. Acknowledging the sign that he needs to speak, I yank the ball gag out and bend at the waist to meet his gaze. His face is pressed against the cold metal table, flecks of blood color his pale face. His long black hair is in knots and shoved over the opposite side of the table, out of my way.

Once I get to his level, his eyes zero in on my chest, strapped tightly into a midnight-purple corset. I sigh internally. He's one client who consistently loses focus. I have to punish him often—though punishing a client is one of the more entertaining parts of my job.

My body and mind have been through so much since I was created. It's easy to find humor in another's pain when nothing I will ever do to them, with their consent, will cause permanent scarring of their psyche like mine is.

Unlike what He did to me. Unforgivable.

Laughing darkly, I tilt the fae's chin with a sharpened nail. A rivet of blood runs down my finger from the small wound as he meets my eyes.

"Are you at your limit, sub?" I ask in a sharp but seductive tone.

"Harder. Whip me harder." He groans, arousal burning in his cerulean eyes.

I grab the hollows of his cheeks and squeeze hard enough to turn the pads of my fingers white.

"Aren't you forgetting something?" I hiss. "You will address me as Mistress anytime you speak to me." I glare, digging the tips of my nails into his cheeks. "Do you think you get to make demands here? You will remember your place, or I will show you what true pain feels like."

This pathetic fae will never understand what it is like to reach the point of never-ending suffering—of torturing a soul so brutally that every moment of that gore-filled time fills me with horror at the monster I was made to be.

No, he will never know what I have gone through to get here.

His eyes harden with defiance and pure lust. I drop his cheeks, and the left side of his face slaps the table as I step out of his sight. I hear his heart take flight. He's clearly unsure what I will do to him now that he can't see me.

The key to instilling fear in these situations is continually disappearing from view. Adrenaline rushes in their veins anytime they catch the sight of my elbow or the tip of my bloody boots in their peripheral. The element of the unknown sets them on edge. This dickbag disrespected me. He knew what he was getting into when he signed his limits form and agreed to be submissive. He was going to get the maximum of the punishment levels he agreed to.

"You know, I think you're enjoying your punishment a bit too much. I've torn your back to shreds, and you're lying in a puddle of your own blood. Your pathetic dick is throbbing, trapped beneath you. Yet you demand I whip you harder." I scoff. "No. Fuck that and your demands. I have just the perfect toy in mind for you."

I walk toward the door and whip it open before he can speak again. Cool air from the hallway rushes in as I exit. The door clicks shut and locks behind me.

I walk down the hall quickly, passing the moans and screams of clients, my mistress-in-training executing my every command. I arrive at a door on my left. When I place my tail on the scanner, the door unlocks and swings inward. I stride over the threshold and into the room.

My private playroom is one of my favorite spaces in the Snuggle Pit. I eye my toys, searching for the one I have in mind for the belligerent fae. From the corner of my eye, I see a splotch of red. I follow the bloody prints from my boots to the entrance of the room.

My head spins at what they remind me of. My heart is beating so rapidly that I fear it'll break free of its bone cage. I rush to the two-way mirror on my left and place my forehead on the cool glass, my hands bracing on either side. The glass fogs underneath my sweaty palms.

Not again! I can't let my past continue to make me suffer.

With breaths beginning to saw in and out and my chest constricting, I strain to suck in even thin streams of air. Panic rushes in, and the edges of my vision waver with darkness.

The memory of drowning in my own blood, thick and hot, clogs my throat. I can't breathe. My lungs burn as they are slowly depleted of oxygen.

Bones snap and puncture my skin. Pain. Pain, like I know all too well, encases my body. Each of my fingers crunch and grind, as if a mallet was hammering them to nothing.

Searing heat roars from my nerve endings as a knife glides under my skin. My exposed muscles and tendons gleam with blood. The pain is endless. Wave after wave of agony washes over me. My limbs shake with shock.

Both freezing and on fire, sweat coats my skin, and a familiar unforgiving stainless steel table bites into my back. A blade appears in my sticky crimson hand. Sobbing and unable to stop, my breathing comes in quick, short pants.

My skin burns and sizzles. My throat is raw from gargling screams as a piece of searing metal plunges into the soft parts of my body again and again.

I close my eyes tightly. *Where is that screaming coming from?*

I blink my eyes open, and harsh lights from above shoot bursts of pain into my brain. A cold sweat covers my body. As I come to my senses, I force myself to take deep breaths…then realize the screaming is coming from me. I stop immediately and put my head between my bent knees.

As I regain control of my breathing, my body continues to calm. More awareness seeps into my mind as my breaths even out. I lift my head, finally realizing I had sunk to the floor and curled into myself during my panic attack. My tail is curled tightly around my waist like a security blanket.

When will this madness end?

I stand and rest my sweat-dampened palm against the glass to my left as I survey the room. My gaze skips over the bloody footprints, making a mental note to have mats installed in the hallway so I stop tracking blood everywhere. Those blood-soaked prints will no longer hold any power over me.

I speak my mantra over and over in my mind.

I escaped. No one can force their will on me again. I am the mistress of my own life. I am free.

I take a deep breath.

You are Mistress Mariax. You do not bow to anyone. Pull up your big girl panties and slap your mask on. NO ONE will see you broken ever again.

The sound of an echoing pleasure-filled scream from the hallway reminds me I have a client. Despite how drained I suddenly feel, I encompass my mistress energy, forcing myself to feel fierce and confident. Tap into that wondrous healing power that my makers imbued into me. It works wonders on the psyche as well as the body.

I stride back to the punishment room with my new toy.

The impatient fae is thoroughly pissed off and thrashing. His muscles bunch as he strains against his bindings. A wicked and slightly haunted smile twists my lips as his struggles renew my spirit.

Serves him right for being so disobedient.

I grabbed one of the more lethal toys in my arsenal.

My stainless-steel cane shines with bright-violet paint. Sharp studs about a quarter inch long begin at the top of the cane and are evenly placed. The studs gradually become larger as they near the black leather grip on the opposite end. There is almost a violent, ethereal beauty in my new toy, like a storm that hovers above, dark and menacing and biding its time for the perfect moment to strike. No imperfections mar its surface.

The heavy weight of the cane takes on a whole new meaning as I contemplate where to begin. I decide to exercise the ghosts of my past while teaching this asshole a lesson in manners.

Small splashes erupt beneath my boots as I stride through the slightly congealed blood to the table. Strong and confident, I assess each of his bindings. They are all holding, flawlessly executing the job I designed them for, to contain supernatural beings.

I pace behind the fae again, his head twists awkwardly in an attempt to see what I am doing.

A wave of memories ripple through my mind. I shove it away before it can dig its claws in as goosebumps skitter atop my shoulders and down my back.

The male curses in several languages, and I relish interrupting his tirade. "On the limits form you filled out, you circled, underlined, and verbally expressed your excitement about trying the toy I am about to use. You scored it as a five, very eager to explore, the highest option available. Both of us know you get off on pain. But what you don't realize is you only get off on pain when it is in your control to gauge the level," I state, bored, impassivity layered in my tone. "Now, do you remember your safe words?"

His body noticeably tenses as he contemplates defying me again, but he forces out a response through clenched teeth. "Yes, Mistress."

"What a good sub. It seems some of the words I left you with have sunk into that thick skull of yours."

I scent his anger, fear, and arousal swirling together in a potent cocktail. We'll see how much arousal is left by the time he uses his safe word. There will be no ball gag this time to dampen his screams.

I lean down to just behind his ear and whisper, "You have no experience with the pain you're about to endure. I look forward to the pleasure of your screams."

CHAPTER 2

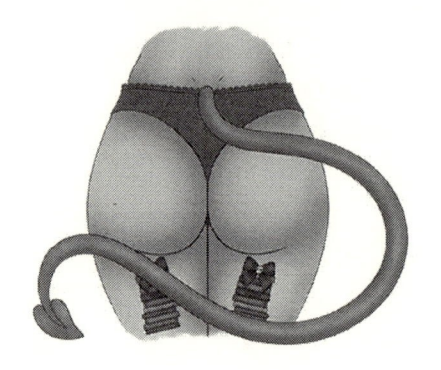

Mariax

Stepping out of the shower, I reach for a towel from the warmer. There is nothing better than wrapping up in a toasty towel. My skin is elated by its fluffiness.

The shadows in my wake seem to vibrate with agitation as I walk around my bedroom, deciding what I should do tonight. I could go to the bookstore, one of my main haunts, or even a bar. There is always something peaceful to be found at my favorite supernatural bookstore, Tightly Bound. The quiet atmosphere soothes my nerves, the warm lights, the sweet but musty smell of paper, the gentle music the storekeeper plays that really settles my spirit.

I am a true bibliophile.

The smell of the books is euphoric.

However, I can't drink at the bookstore. New business idea: a bookstore where patrons can drink and read at their leisure.

I grab a cotton T-shirt out of my dresser and slowly scrunch my long, bubble-gum pink wavy hair as I continue my internal debate.

After reliving my past today, I need mind-numbing liquid to saturate my body thoroughly. Alcohol is a must, so a bar wins. A human bar is out of the question. I cannot be around any being where I cannot be myself tonight, even if I must cloak my true form to get to my destination.

I will let my freak flag fly. Maybe I will even find someone to hook up with. I don't care what kind of being they are or their gender.

I have never understood why humans harp so much on whether their young are male or female. First, they come out looking like weird aliens or old men. Next, until they are a few years old at least, they just shit, eat, and sleep. That's it! What kind of idiot would choose that life? Not this bitch, that's for sure.

Demons can reproduce through screwing, but it is a mutual decision between partners if they want to be fertile. Plus, there is no need for a male and female pairing. Any couple can procreate. One being just has to carry the thing. Still not signing up for that any time soon, even if I'm not the host.

There are a few bars for supernaturals around Philly, but most are shitholes and full of pervy creeps. I deal with those types enough at the Snuggle Pit.

Feeling indecisive, I think about which bar to go to while I dress.

Sitting on the luxe stool in my walk-in closet, I slip an arched foot into each leg hole of the black jumpsuit before standing to lift the rest of the material over my body. Slits start on both sides of the ankles and move up to my hips. The top of the jumpsuit comes up over my medium-sized breasts and lays on my shoulders with two thick straps, which cross behind my back to loop around my waist and tie in a bow above my ass.

I love this jumpsuit. It's comfy on my curvy body, easy to move in for whatever strikes my fancy—pain, pleasure, or combat—and sexy as hell.

The result is stunning.

My inhuman light-pink skin, covered in tattoos, is on full display. The deep V of the top stops just above my belly button. The material is thin. It's not thin enough to be translucent, but it shows the outline of my nipple piercings. The back of the jumpsuit is mostly bare, except for the X and bow created by the straps.

Standing, I move in front of the full-length mirror to apply my war paint. Makeup is more than just a tool to enhance beauty, it is the true mask we don for strength. The mirror reflects my opalescent eyes as I line them with black liner. I wipe the smudge of lipstick off my lip ring and tweak the one in my left eyebrow.

Bending over, I slide on my black leather stiletto ankle boots. Even though I need to sharpen the stiletto heels into spikes regularly, the sides are as sharp as blades.

I enjoy employing them to keep my clients in their place. Running an underground sex dungeon, both metaphorically and literally, can be a headache. Each supernatural who comes through my door has a unique set of needs, strengths, skills, and, of course, kinks. The stranger, the better.

I stride to the mirror one last time and decide I look fine as hell.

Now that I'm glamourous and fully dressed, I exit The Snuggle Palace through the front door, as the snowy, winter breeze and magical barrier washes over me.

I truly enjoy that feeling because I know my business and subs are well protected. I love the witch who placed the stay-away wards on my property so much. I hope to see her again soon. She's seriously the sweetest being I've ever met, just don't piss her off.

My building is made up of several levels that are viewable to the public thanks to the nifty wards. There is the illusion of three stories above ground, with the real building having an additional four beneath it.

The only real above ground level floor is the main entrance to The Snuggle Palace's member's only club with viewing rooms and a stage. Once below ground, you have the pain and pleasure rooms and The Snuggle Pit with my personal playroom and office. The next level down is Lauren's apartment and a couple more for guests. To get to the final two levels, you would need the key, and there is no duplicating that, for my personal space, complete with a library, makes up Level Three. Real, functional dungeons take up the bottom level, warded for security and sound, even at that depth.

Once I clear the barrier, a familiar deep sense of dread and thoughts that have been plaguing me for months creep in. Any time I leave the Snuggle Pit, it's like a sharpened icy claw runs from the nape of my neck all the way down my spine. Something is watching, biding its time. Waiting.

I need to take the threat seriously at some point, but my current headspace screams booze and pleasure. I give in to my baser instincts and head in my chosen bar's direction.

Snowflakes collect in my hair, ice crunches beneath my feet, and my breaths fog, but I can't feel the cold at all.

There are ten blocks to walk to Get Fucked.

The name of the bar could not be more perfect, and it's one reason it is my favorite haunt. I take a deep breath to steel myself for a social outing, but the reek of the city hits me in full force. What a mistake this was. Piss, sweat, car exhaust, and hot dog water swirl together in an odoriferous fog that blankets the city.

Why do I live in this cesspit again?

The creeping dread agitates my senses, slithering along with me as I take quick strides along the street. I dodge humans, supernaturals glamoured as humans, bike messengers, and who the fuck knows what else. It is all bringing me closer to the brink of total rage. My mental stability can't handle the number of beings in this city. It reminds me too much of the claustrophobic atmosphere and stench of Inferuna.

This is why I rarely leave the comfort of my Snuggle Palace.

Looking ahead, I see the green haze that announces my arrival at Get Fucked. A magical signature takes on a color when a witch places wards, and the color depends on the witch using the magic and the owner of the property. The hue of the wards at Get Fucked is a putrid, muddy green. It doesn't shimmer like some of the other wards I've seen. More like a noxious fog from a fetid swamp.

Nothing says 'stay away' to a human like this ward.

The spell keeps humans out of the fray of imbibing supernaturals. It works most of the time, but occasionally, a human stumbles in and is invited to stay indefinitely.

The door creaks when I push it open with my shoulder. The usual mixing haze of smoke, stale beer, and sweet liquor coating the atmosphere hits me upon entry. Get Fucked isn't too busy tonight to my relief. With the floor sticking to the underside of my heels, I find my placement by hopping up on a bar stool in the corner by the wall. From this vantage point, I can see everything in the room and keep my back guarded.

Teddy, the bartender, floats over to grab my order.

He is an odd supe, a spirit, but not fully a ghost. He has just enough left of his body to use his limbs if he wants for more than making drinks. He named the bar Get Fucked because those were the words he'd shouted to the redcoats with his last dying breath. However, something went wrong in his transition to death. He never fully crossed the threshold to Inferuna.

He was as trapped as I felt. Maybe that was a good thing, since he had one of the best bars in town and could mix a mean cocktail.

"Mariax, you look like shit. The pervy bastards got you down?" Teddy asks as he makes me a frozen margarita.

I never order anything. Teddy just makes what he wants and knows I'll drink it.

"Um, yeah, you could say that. My ass is over this whole day."

I take a sip of my margarita. The salt and frozen mixture dance on my tongue. Yes, a margarita is just what I need tonight. Tequila, do your thing and bring me into delirium.

I let the bar soothe me. The whole thing has lulled me into a calm I was much in need of.

Since it is a weeknight, the jukebox is all the background music we've got and someone is liking the nineties dance country. At least it isn't 'my wife left me and took my truck and dog' shit kind of tune.

The dim, hanging lighting lets people fade into the deep booths if they want or stand out at the high top tables.

Even if it isn't busy tonight, there seems to be variety here. I'm pretty sure that one booth is hosting a vamp if the blonde fae stumbling out and to the bathroom with a hand on her neck is any indication. Some shifters are drunkenly trying to line dance with several other supes. Demons, angels, and more are sprinkled around.

The numbness of slush ice on my tongue and lips is refreshing, erasing the heat coming off everyone. I'm thankful no one approaches me, so I can just decompress.

By the time I am on margarita number three, nearing the end of the glass, a breeze drifts in from the bar entrance. One of the most alluring scents I have ever encountered ignites my senses.

My back straightens and I breathe deeply, with my eyes closing in bliss. The scent is unique: pines, fresh coffee, and wood smoke. It is comforting and woodsy. It reminds me of a cold winter night with a campfire crackling in the open woods. Crisp air and fresh snow on the ground with a large mug of rich coffee in my hands.

Opening my eyes, a smile plays around my lips. I need to know who that scent is coming from. It is damn delectable.

I swivel my head toward the door and spot a delicious creature.

The top of his head grazes the frame as he bends slightly to enter the bar. His dirty-blond hair is long and untamed, the waves going in all directions. A gorgeous smile spreads across his face as he scans the bar, looking for an open stool. I swear he could be a toothpaste model for one of those idiotic commercials that humans love. I don't know what caused the smile to grace his face, but damn, it sets my blood on fire.

The alcohol buzzing through my system has my senses in disarray. His scent and features alone make me overwhelmingly horny, and I can't stop staring at him. I don't usually find blonde, happy males attractive. However, this one might do for an epic night of fooling around.

I wasn't in the mood to partake in any kind of social interaction when I arrived at the bar unless a one and done tempted me. It's why I sat in my usual corner, with my back to the wall. Drinking so much is the best or worst decision I will make tonight. But all my plans have changed, as I feel my core tightening and moisture pooling between my thighs. This is the second time in my life I have felt this type of lust.

How am I so turned on by his smile and scent alone?

I wonder if he has a deep, gravelly voice to match that body.

He continues to smile while he leans one forearm on the bar while talking to Teddy. I notice he has slightly elongated canines.

What are you?

I need to get closer.

I do my best to elegantly slip off my stool, but I slightly stumble and make my way to his side of the bar. He didn't walk in with anyone, but that doesn't mean he isn't meeting a girlfriend or a date. Either way, I don't give a shit at this point because I have my eyes set on him. I have claimed him for the night. Maybe it's the tequila talking, but I don't care.

I lick my numb lips, leaving a slight glossy shine over them. *How much alcohol did Teddy put in my drinks?* Three margaritas should not knock me on my ass this quickly, especially with the speed of my immortal metabolism.

I continue making my way toward the beast of a male.

My tail knocks into other bar patrons as I swagger over. When drunk, I don't have nearly as much control over it, so it wanders mindlessly. Luckily, it hasn't become a grab-ass tonight, because that has gotten me into shit in the past.

My sight darkens on the devilishly handsome male who now has taken notice of me. His eyes trail down my body with an appreciated eye-fuck, and I see the heat banked in his moss-green eyes as he flicks them back to my own gray ones. There's also a slight shimmer to them that ebbs and flows.

Good. I need someone to play with; he looks like just the type I could take a bite out of. Shit, maybe I'd let him take a bite out of me too.

Those sharp canines of his would sink deeply into my flesh. A soft moan slips out of my mouth at the thought, and he sits up a little straighter in response.

The stools surrounding him are filled, but he knows my game.

He abruptly kicks the stool out from underneath the

chick sitting next to him, vying for his attention by twirling her hair, pushing her plump breasts up and touching anywhere she thinks she can get away with. He obviously had no interest in the bottle blonde attempting to get into his pants. Luckily for everyone, he took action, since I have confidence in spades and would have dragged her off that stool by her hair.

At least while I don my mask my confidence shines.

Nope, I'm not thinking about that right now.

I refocus on my task. There is a hot as fuck male unknowingly awaiting my presence.

As I near the bar, the blonde is in a pile on the grimy floor, glaring daggers at him. I cackle as I step over her but accidentally-on-purpose step on her pinky. I put my other foot on the bottom rung and attempt to climb onto the stool. I almost fall off, but I feel warm, large hands grab my waist and settle me securely on my ass.

I look up to see if that same gorgeous grin is on his face.

His eyes zero in on my parted lips as my tongue unconsciously plays with my lip ring. The tip of his tongue slips out, a piercing on it shining briefly when it flicks the middle part of his top lip just under his cupid's bow.

I've never seen anyone make that exact motion except in a porno, but it still sends powerful pulses directly to my clit.

Something about it makes me think about all the things he could do to me with that tongue, not forgetting about the bonus of his piercing. I swallow, trying to keep myself from fucking him right here on the bar.

With his long dirty blond hair wildly framing his face, I stare into his moss-green eyes and notice them swiftly change to black. I see something else in him through his dark orbs, something violent and destructive. It wants to play, and my own darkness acknowledges it. Shit, I think it's even attempting to call it to the forefront.

I feel my power rising to the surface, my tail curling sensuously around his calf. He lets out a startled breath, looking down at my tail, which is now rubbing itself on his leg over his pants. He raises a pierced brow and smirks slightly. His face is only a foot away from mine as we unconsciously lean closer.

Time itself does not exist. It is irrelevant. All that matters is the beasts that live within us, acknowledging each other.

Teddy slamming another margarita down in front of me shocks me out of our state of limbo. I glare at Teddy when he looks from me to the stranger, realizing he just fucked up and interrupted something intense. He raises his opaque hands and backs away. The odd gait of his half-ghostly body disappears in spots as he moves down the bar.

I then noticed the growl coming from the male next to me as he glares down the bar. He's watching Teddy, his eyes still black, with a gaze that promises violence. I touch his toned forearm, and he whips his eyes back toward me. I grip tighter, and his gaze slowly returns to green.

Warmth is building underneath my hand. The longer my skin is touching him, the more heat rises with it. Soon I feel a sharp pain, like his skin is burning mine. A magical pulse ripples between us. I know he feels it too, because his eyes widen. His bearded face morphs into a mask of amusement and fascination.

I pull my hand away, but he puts his large one over mine. The calluses on his palm scrape my knuckles.

He gruffly clears his throat. "I think we got off on the wrong foot, gorgeous."

I was right. His voice is gravelly, sexy, and so incredibly deep. And he has a Scottish accent.

A shameless grin appears on his face.

I throw out my hand. "My name is Mariax, not

gorgeous. And just who the fuck are you?" I ask cheekily.

His warm palm meets mine as we shake. "I'm Hunter, and the pleasure is yers I'm sure," he says, and winks.

Wow. He is the definition of an alpha-hole. With that thought, something tickles the back of my mind. Shifter. That's what the wild part of his scent is.

I tilt my head to the side, narrowing my eyes and analyzing him.

"What are you?" I ask firmly.

He laughs loudly and so hard tears trail down his face, waking up the entire bar to our conversation.

He continues laughing, wiping the tears from his eyes with the bottom of his T-shirt. I get a glimpse of his tan, toned abs and the top of his happy trail before his shirt falls back into place. My mouth waters. My attraction to him is unmistakable.

"Well fuck, lassie. I've had no one come right out and ask me that question. Usually, they feel my alpha vibes and either stay away or drop their pants," he says with a confident smirk. "I don't know what yer deal is, but I'm game to find out." He winks roguishly.

Proven by his pants-dropping statement, he has no problems getting laid and does so with ease. What is the fun in that?

"Don't you like the chase anymore?" I ask bluntly. "Also, seriously, what the hell are you? You say you're an alpha, but an alpha of what or whom?"

His grin widens across his face. "I'm a fucking lycan, baby. Chances are ye haven't had anything like me before," he says, leaning closer to me once again.

I raise my right eyebrow with clear disdain.

"A lycan?" I question.

"Aye, a lycan can shift at will and control said shift. A werewolf only shifts during the full moon and cannot contain the shift."

I laugh.

"First of all, Pup, thanks for the lesson in the intricacies of shifters, but I have met several shifters. You're not rare. I just couldn't place what you were in the food chain. I don't know what you think makes you more unique than the others of your ilk."

He lightly chuckles. "Might have something to do with me being an alpha. Gives me the right to be a little more high-handed than the rest you've bounced on."

I roll my eyes to feign annoyance, but I actually don't think I've been with an alpha shifter before. Sounds kind of fun. Would he be rougher and more dominating, perhaps even wilder?

Just the idea causes my pussy to clench in anticipation, but his smug attitude still gets the better of me.

"You're still a youngling compared to me. You are just coming out in this world, and I don't know what you think you can offer me that I haven't experienced already, alpha or not."

He looks at me incredulously, like I've grown a second head. Perhaps it was because I wasn't fawning over him like most women might have, but the look in his eyes says he's trying to figure out how old I am, since I look around thirty-two in human years.

"What does an alpha lycan even do? Do you have a pack, or do you just run around the slums like the rest of the lone wolves, calling yourself top dog?" As I volley questions at him, each one filling me with malicious humor, his annoyance rapidly shows on his face. "Also–

Hunter cuts me off with a growl so lethal it raises the fine hairs all over my body. Now that's a sound I could happily get used to in the bedroom.

"I can smell yer arousal from here, luckily for ye–" he breathes in deeply taking in my scent further, "–it is curbing my annoyance from yer rudeness." The growls rumbling from deep in his chest never cease, even as he speaks.

His interruption annoys the fuck out of *me*, so I continue where I left off. "You might be sexy as fuck, but you are still a pup."

In response to my purposeful attitude, Hunter's hands grip the counter firmly, the bones of his skeletal tattoos running the length of each finger appearing starker for a moment. Other features of his body tighten as well, but most curiously is the growing appendage in his jeans.

I tilt my head the other way when I notice the extra bulge around where the base of his dick is. I'm insanely curious about what kind of supernatural magical dick he's blessed with.

He rolls his shoulders back and sits up straighter, his resolve to be a respectable alpha evident in his posture.

"Well, since ye asked so pleasantly, I'll spill my guts then, aye?" he asks sarcastically, but his cocky smirk is sneaking back across his sexy mouth from my compliment.

Before I can answer him, he answers me.

"An alpha takes care of their pack. They see to the needs of everyone within it. I am in charge of all of their lives, every minor aspect. Nothing goes on within my pack that I don't know about. They live within my territory for safety, family, and…" He reaches across the space and grazes my earlobe with his index finger and thumb. "To seek pleasure."

He bites his lip and releases it, small white indentions from his teeth showing briefly. Murder moths flutter in my stomach with the endearing gesture. Butterflies are much too delicate to live within me, so I adopted the idea of murder moths, fierce creatures that bash my stomach lining and force me to feel things.

My cunt throbs as he strokes the pads of his fingers along the shell of my ear, massaging with just enough pressure. I close my eyes, attempting to regulate my breathing, surprised I'm allowing him to touch me like this so openly.

The floor gives a scraping sound as he pulls my stool to between his legs and replaces his fingers with his mouth, sucking and nipping my earlobe. His breath hot on my neck and wetted ear makes a shiver rush down my spine.

He pulls back slightly, and whispers gruffly, "lycans have a very healthy sexual appetite. So, I can be quite busy."

I knew he was sexy, but I didn't know he had a bit of humor mixed in with his total-alpha-hole personality. He's said all the right things, while flashing teasing grins, and I found them disarming the chaos that usually gets my back up and puts me on the defensive.

Leaning back, he grabs the beer that Teddy finally brought him, although Hunter hadn't ordered anything. He looks at me and lifts the bottle, his furrowing brows and eyes, saying, *What the fuck? I didn't order anything.*

Something deeper simmers between us.

"What do ye say, Cheetie? Do I drink a random beer?"

I wave him off and laugh. "Teddy has this thing, especially with me. I'm guessing he's including you now. He brings me what he thinks I'll like that night. Tonight, it's margaritas."

I raise my glass and gesture in a mock cheer. The tequila is making me feel nice. I've lost count of how many I've consumed.

He grins with a flash of teeth. "There's a reason they call it te-kill-ya. See if ye like his drink choice in the morning."

My thoughts are swirling around in my brain as if afloat

on the alcohol I've consumed. I ignore him as I suck in a big mouthful of icy, bitter sweetness.

"Wait! What in the actual fuck is a cheetie?" I ask, since he called me that earlier. It better not be some kind of insult, or he'll learn quickly that it's best not to disrespect me so brazenly.

Hunter laughs deeply and with a wink, responds, "Och, it means cat or kitten."

No one has ever called me a kitten before; something so soft and innocent, something that needed taking care of. Why did it make my heart shyly flutter and want to retract my claws so I could be petted?

Such a strange response, considering who I am and what I did for a living.

Hunter takes a swig of his beer and gestures toward me with the bottom of the bottle. "Now, so as to keep things fair, what are ye and what is it ye are, Mariax, and what do ye do?" He feigns a conversational, joking tone, but the gravel in his voice and his slight Scottish accent thicken as he purposely uses my name.

Shivers race down my spine. I love the way it sounds. I could listen to him say my name over and over.

What would it be like if he moaned my name?

I decide to give him a brief and confusing answer. Flirting with Hunter is too much fun. I haven't smiled like this since... my smile falls. Since Him.

I shake my head and focus on Hunter, hoping he doesn't notice the slip.

The muscles in his arms bulge and tighten as he grips the bottle, and I watch his veins rise to the surface. There is not an ounce of fat on him. His thick frame is corded with muscle. I can easily picture him raising a car over his head and howling at the moon.

I snort at the thought, but I ignore him as he looks at me

with questioning eyes. He finishes the last of his beer and slips the bottle through his fingers to settle on the bar top. Teddy swiftly replaces the bottle with a fresh one, and we continue our conversation.

"I'm a demon" I answer snarkily, gesturing to my tail and then horns, "in case you haven't noticed." I pause for dramatic effect, "And I own The Snuggle Palace. Maybe you've heard of it?"

"I've seen the sign, but I've never been inside. It's down in Fishtown in between two stores, aye?" Hunter inquires.

"Yep, it's between a liquor store and a gift shop. But," I say with a sly smile. "It's not the building that you need to be worried about. It's what's inside of it. Or under it, I should say."

"Aye, what's inside yer building?" The innuendo is thick in his tone. "Cannot be too frightful, considering it's got a wee lass like you inside it."

"A sex dungeon," I say bluntly, and take a large gulp of my margarita.

He chokes on his beer, and I reach out and slap him on the back before trailing a hand down his spine, saying, "Yep." I speak bluntly, popping the P at the end. "A sex dungeon."

He takes the towel Teddy flings at him as he goes past to serve another drink and wipes spilled beer from his fingers and the counter.

"Well, that's different," he says with amusement, before taking another swig of his beer.

He wouldn't be so full of amusement if I had him in one of my punishing rooms.

The image of me standing over him, running my bladed tail down those abs I glimpsed under his T-shirt… A trail of blood follows in my tail's wake, my gaze eating up his muscular naked form. The sight of his thick cock growing harder with the knife play…

I'm getting way ahead of myself. I don't normally think of my potential clients in this way. It's got to be the fucking alcohol.

Suddenly, panic blooms in my gut, gripping my throat as I remember Him bringing up the idea of teaching me how to be a dominant someday. He is the one who taught me everything, who taught me the importance and trust involved in a dom and sub relationship.

A cold sweat breaks out on my forehead, and I squeeze my eyes shut, trying not to let my panic overload my system.

I tell myself, *you're not in Inferuna. You got out. You've been out for over two hundred years.*

A large hand grips my thigh, and I open my eyes. Hunter's face is inches from mine, concern evident in his pinched brows. A little V appears between them.

"Are ye okay, Cheetie? Where did ye just go?" he asks with worry.

I pull up my mental shields, battling my panic attack. I throw my mask back in place, tilt my lips upward, and produce a small smile.

"Oh. Yeah, I'm fine. I was thinking of all the things we could do together. If you came to the Snuggle Pit, I mean. That's all."

I can tell by his expression that he's not buying it.

"I'm not sure if I'm into that, Cheetie." I would have been disappointed, if it wasn't for his sly grin and glinting eyes highlighting his mischievousness. "Guess you'll have to spend the night convincing me why I should trust you enough to even consider it."

The night continues as I talk with Hunter about random pieces of our lives. The buzz from my margaritas turns into a jumble of intensity, like the electricity that builds in the air before a storm, chaotic and unpredictable. Alcohol builds in my veins, zipping through my system.

The room spins, and I lay my head on the bar over my crossed arms, fixated on the Adam's apple bobbing in Hunter's throat as he continues to talk to me. I have no clue what he's saying, but the deep, resonating sound of his voice is soothing. I find myself comfortable with his voice, his presence…despite his high-handed attitude.

I like this one. He'll be fun to break, is my last coherent thought.

I reach over to find Hunter's hand, but it's gone. Damn it!

I roll my head on the bar, searching for a more comfortable position and close my eyes. I can hear Teddy in the background, speaking to someone over the phone.

"Yeah, she's passed out again." My head swims as silence radiates. Not even the music from earlier is playing, meaning everyone's gone home and I'm stuck here slumped over the counter. "Margaritas. Hey, don't yell at me! It was her choice to drink them, and she was having fun for once. I haven't seen her laugh that much in, well… ever."

More silence comes as someone responds through the phone, but I just turn my head with a groan as a wave of dizziness makes me and the room swirl on two different axis. I know Teddy puts more than alcohol in his drinks to stop his immortal patrons from healing through their buzzes too quickly, but it is rare I pass out like this.

I must have had way too much fun with Hunter. It's a shame I can't remember what was said between us, only his laughter and my own echoing. Fuck, and his damn sexy face constantly staring at me with heat. It should be a crime to be that attractive.

Where did that bastard go? I was expecting fun, and he promised me an epic lay.

"Look, she's safe here. She knows it," Teddy continued. "Mariax knows I would never let anything bad happen to her. The guy she was with even promised to take her home. Sure, he seemed sincere, but I'm not going to let some fucker take her just in case he turns out to be a prick."

If I could stand right now and if he wasn't a ghost, I would climb over the counter and slap the shit out of him for that. Hunter could have taken me home and had his wicked way with me, and I would not have given a shit. It would have been nice to feel something good, for once.

"Yeah. I've already closed up. I'll watch over her until you come and get her."

I waved my hand as if I'm shooing a fly, but it was sluggish. I wanted to be left alone. I was comfy, and a smile still pestered my lips as I tried to think about my wonderful night. The next time I jolt awake, it's with my arm being thrown over a slim shoulder, and Lauren berating me.

Where the fuck am I?

"And another thing, Mistress, you know better than to drink alone. Why didn't you take Tiffany or me with you?"

I don't answer. At least, I can't remember if I do.

All I know is cold air washes over me before I'm shoved into a vehicle. Cracked leather scrapes against my alcohol sensitized skin, and the shooting lights of the city nauseates me. I know I've annoyed both Lauren and the driver as I constantly press the up and down button of the window, one minute seeking cold fresh air, but a cascade of cold shivers forces me to close it.

I don't remember getting out as warmth envelopes me, but the stern voice above me continues to pound into my head like a sledgehammer.

"Stop talking, Lauren. Please, I want to go home and snuggle into my bed. My nice cozy blankets, fluffy pillows, soft mattress…"

"Mistress, you're already in your bed. I changed you out of your street clothes. I tried to put you in a nightgown, but you growled and promised a bloody death if I forced you to do anything else."

"Oh, sorry, Lauren. Thanks for always taking care of my pitiful ass." I love her. Lauren is such a gem and has always been there for me, as a friend and submissive. "Will you sleep here with me… please?"

"Yes, Mistress, of course." There's a rustle of cloth before Lauren slips under the covers and rolls over to face me.

My eyes slowly close as she reaches out to interlock our hands between us. The softness and warmth of it soothes me all the way to the pit of my being.

CHAPTER 3

Hunter

"Ye goddamn bitch!" I quickly shove my pointer finger into my mouth and suck on the small wound caused by the flames on my gas stove.

The tea pot shrieks in my ears. Steam billows around me as I yank the teakettle from the angry burner and place it on a trivet. Steam sends a sharp pain through my burn when I draw my hand back. I suck the digit back into my mouth, briefly wishing I was sucking on something more exciting.

Internally, I roll my eyes at myself. *Always thinking with yer wee head.*

I move to the cabinet, pick out a small tin of loose leaf Earl Gray tea, and scoop some into my steeper. Earl Gray is my absolute favorite, but the London Fog blend is also delicious.

My beta, Charlie, gives me so much shite because I like tea. Why he thinks drinking tea is for pussies is beyond me. I know he steals a sip from my mug when he thinks I'm not looking.

I pick up the chipped blue mug, relishing the warmth seeping into my calloused palms. This ritual viscerally soothes my soul, and not much can match that small moment of bliss I get when I inhale the warm fragrance of the tea and the leaves steeping.

I still haven't decided if I will accept Mariax's offer.

At the bar last week, my wee Cheetie was determined to show me how being a submissive could change my life.

It's not fully that I doubt the lass. It's that I don't see how my wolf would allow it. It's in my genes to lead and take control of all situations. However, I can't deny the giant carrot she dangled in front of me to be free from the shackles binding me to my responsibilities, if only for a while.

That is a dangerous thought. I will have to fight against my very nature if I truly want this, but maybe she is worth the battle scars.

I watch my crescent moon tea strainer dip and rise from the surface on a small wave. My moment of peace only lasts just that before my ex storms into my house, uninvited and unannounced, and shatters it.

I've never had a reason to lock my door until now. I definitely need to adopt the habit if he is going to be pulling this.

"What the hells are ye doing here?" I shout, practically shattering my favorite cup as I slam it down on the counter next to me.

I move to the door and slam it closed behind him. The neighbors don't need to hear any more than they are going to. The bastard still hasn't answered me as I pin him with my gaze. There's a smirk on his face, taunting me to smack the shite out of him.

The problem is we lived together for a couple of years, and this was our home. But the minute he ran his mouth about my business to anyone who would listen, I couldn't trust him. Since then, he hasn't been welcome in my space.

I kicked him out months ago, and I've only seen him in passing while other pack members are present, but I can't help but take in the powerful lines of his body.

A light red stubble peppers his cheeks. My fingers itch to run my hands through his short, shaggy locks like I used to. The smooth auburn strands cascading through my fingers.

I suck in a sharp breath when an all too vivid memory rises to the surface. Those same fingers pressed against the back of his head as he took me into his throat. Swallowing me down with ease, despite my large size. Him moaning as he bobbed along my length, the act alone giving him pleasure.

He was always exceptionally good at giving head and enjoyed it thoroughly too. My cock hardens against my will, and I lick my lips, glancing away.

I will not be pulled back into his web just because he decided to barge his way into my house. "Again, what the fuck are ye doing here?"

"What, I can't come to visit my alpha?" he says with a slightly sarcastic sneer.

I grit my teeth so hard I'm surprised they don't shatter, my irritation getting the best of me. "Ye know that if ye have a concern that needs my assistance, ye must reach out to Charlie first."

Patrick broke my heart. I shared a secret desire with him. And he traded for his own gain.

In my heart of hearts, I want to be a part of a throuple. To have both a male and a female to share my love with. To explore and play. Pleasure and love. I've never been someone that believes love is a one time deal. My love isn't only for one other soul. No, love truly cannot be defined, no matter how many times people try. And although I'd never show it on the outside, love is what drives me.

My purpose, my place on this earth, is for the love of my pack, the love of myself, and the love I desire to give others. A polyamorous relationship would be my ultimate dream.

I cannot choose, and I refuse to choose between a male and a female. Even though I'm required to mate, I refuse to be with only one gender. I've never gotten close to having that type of relationship, but I won't stop dreaming.

Patrick had trouble allowing me to be the dominant partner in the relationship, despite being one of the lowest ranking wolves in our pack hierarchy. I could feel him fighting my alpha dominance every time we were together. When I let him have a little power to soothe his fur, he would take a mile. Even before we got together, he always thought he was the most important being in the room; even more than me. I think that was what drew me to him, the idea of taming that.

Although I hate to admit it, I still care for him, but he broke my trust.

He also never really wanted a female in our relationship, even though he went along with my desires and even encouraged dates with a female and us. He just strung me along, year after year. And I finally had enough.

"Ye do not have the right to enter my house unannounced like ye own it. Get the fuck out."

He places his hands in his pockets, the picture of nonchalance, and begins strolling through the ground level of my small home.

"I don't think I will. I think I will stay right here and watch you war with yourself and your conflicting emotions about how much you want me. Don't think I didn't notice your pupils dilating earlier."

"Fuck ye, Patrick. The way my body responds to ye is instinctual and muscle memory. I can't just erase years of pleasure."

He sighs, making a great show of pretending to be distraught. "Baby, don't you think this has gone on long enough? It's been two months. It's time for me to come home."

He glances up at me, attempting to plead with me.

"Ye betrayed me. It's over. No second chances. We don't work. If ye don't want this to turn into something ugly, something that will become, let's say, awkward, at pack events, I suggest ye kindly get out."

He does the opposite and approaches me, stopping only a foot away. He ignores the color shifting in my eyes and the lengthening of my canines, slipping his hand down my body to cup my cock through my sweats.

I laugh uncontrollably. The nerve of this asshole.

The look on his face says that wasn't the reaction he thought I'd have, fucking narcissist. He thought he could walk back in here and reassert his claim. Stroll right back in my life. Hell, back in my heart. No. I've sucked his dick enough times that I've gotten sick of the flavor. Something I once loved, becoming grotesque and sour, is no longer appealing.

Once I get my laughter under control, I shove him hard in the chest, and he takes a step back.

"I don't see why you're being so unreasonable. It's unacceptable that you broke up with me because I told a couple of friends you're polyamorous. Pillow talk is not a secret."

"Why would ye think that something told to ye in a passionate moment could be turned into gossip and spread like a disease was dandy?"

"Hunter, listen, I didn't do it to hurt you, it was that I wanted to share a part of our lives with them. A part that you wanted to fulfill. A part that maybe someone could take if they only knew."

"Bullshit. Ye thought ye were important because ye were fucking the alpha." I scoff and shake my head. "Ye hid that ye were searching for a leg up and in doing so, showed yer true nature. Ye thought that spreading my private thoughts would get ye higher in the pecking order. And if someone was agreeable, ye could pick the person and be above them, control them and by extension, me. If I had known all this, I would never have made the mistake of getting close to ye in the first place."

An ugly flush creeps up his neck, anger causing his features to morph into a cruel, ugly visage.

I lean down next to his ear, continuing my assault. "Plus, ye were never anything special. An average lay with an average dick. Ye mean nothing to me anymore."

I step back, enjoying the view. His skin nearly matches the shade of his hair, and his wolf is seconds away from breaking free.

"Who do you think you are? I could ruin you, share your dirty secrets and watch you crumble," he sneers. "Do you think you can just get rid of me like a piece of trash?"

I cross my arms and sigh deeply. "What secrets? Ye already aired them. Ye sure turned yer coat quickly. One minute yer calling me baby and the next yer threatening me? This is why ye will never have any power or say in the pack. We both know ye couldn't handle it, anyway."

Patrick always caused problems in the pack, even since we were pups. We messed around on and off for years before our last stint in an actual relationship. But no more would I let his lies of innocence open that door for him.

I know now that I never really trusted Patrick because of all the shite he started in the past with others. He thrives on drama and lives to spread gossip.

The potential with Mariax, on the other hand, doesn't seem daunting. I want to trust her and have very little fear that she will cause me stress just for the hell of it, unlike Patrick.

Knowing he will never get it through his head, I resign

to using an alpha command to force him to leave. This won't end well, but he's left me no other choice. As I tap into my alpha cadence, I feel my magic rising and swirl around us both.

"Patrick, ye are no longer welcome on Appalachian pack lands. Ye are hereby forbidden from communicating with our family and allowing our gazes to land upon ye. All knowledge ye have of our pack is sealed and ye cannot communicate it in any way. Ye have two hours to pack yer shite and leave."

I take a few steps towards the front door and fling it open so hard it crashes into the wall. Turning, I glare at Patrick.

He stands there with wide eyes, shocked at my display of power. Growling, I stalk back to him and grab him by the throat. His eyes bulge as I squeeze. I shake my head in disgust before dragging him out of my house by the neck.

Once outside, I drop him in the mud at my feet.

There was no regret as I stare down at him, the sad, pitiful male I once called mine, that I just erased from the pack.

CHAPTER 4

Hunter

It's been two weeks since I had drinks at Get Fucked.

I'm trying to read, but I keep getting distracted by thoughts of Mariax. Her voice had changed to the cadence and pitch of Mistress Mariax as she tried to convince me that being submissive was a treat I needed to partake in. Her voice became slightly deeper, and a dangerous sultry lilt accompanied each word.

Her tantalizing offer still plagued me. Should I take her up on it?

Scooting to the edge of the papasan chair, I stretch out my legs and raise my arms above my head, nearly brushing the bookshelves crammed into my bedroom. I roll my neck from side to side and a satisfying crack follows. Curling back up, I resume reading, only to be interrupted a moment later by the rhythmic vibrating of my phone.

I glance up from my book, remembering I have no clue where my cell is. The hunt for my phone, which happens way too often, commences as I move about the room, tossing dirty laundry over my shoulder and tripping over piles of books.

Damn it, I need a proper library. Why do I do this to myself?

Without any luck, I search my comforter next.

Frustration heats my cheeks as the vibration of my phone continues, but my phone evades me. Whoever is blowing up my phone is going to regret it.

I thrust my hand beneath my bedsheets, probably wasting my time, but then my thumb grazes something solid.

"Fucking finally, ye dirty whore!" I shout at my phone as I untangle it from my sheets.

I squint at the suddenly bright screen in the dim lighting of the room. The scowl on my face quickly turns to a broad grin when I see a text from Mistress Cheetie in my notifications. I bet she was pissed when she realized I put my number in her contacts and texted myself while she was passed out at the bar. A laugh breaks free as I relive that part of the night.

She looked so innocent, sleep taking her away from me. Her mask had dropped, and I marveled as a new side of her emerged.

Her beauty defies sense, the slope of her button nose above her defined upper lip. The shape forming her cupid's bow was prominent, creating a slight permanent pout. I enjoyed memorizing all of her features without her psychoanalyzing me. Drunk or not, her mocking smile and quick wit were on the offense.

I ran a knuckle down her cheek as I whispered in her ear, "I'm putting my number in yer phone, Cheetie. Text me when ye remember the puddle of arousal I left ye in."

Then I slid two fingers into the pocket of her jumpsuit, where I could see the outline, and plucked her phone out. I held it up to her sleeping face, and luckily, it unlocked. I quickly texted myself and added my name to her contacts: Hunter, yer next lay.

My heart accelerates with anticipation as I look at my phone.

I read her message and laugh at her blunt but flirtatious message.

Cheetie: So, the Pup thinks he's clever. How the hell did you get into my phone?

Shaking my head, I respond with a grin still plastered to my face.

Hunter: That'll be my secret Cheetie *wink emoji*

Cheetie: Hmm, taking advantage of a helpless drunk demon.

Cheetie: Very chivalrous, dick.

Hunter: I never claimed to be a good guy.

I am definitely not a good guy. The thought of her sultry voice makes my cock twitch. She is a sexy challenge. I haven't heard anything from her in a bit, so I text her again.

Hunter: Och, ye miss me. Ye inviting me on a date?

Cheetie: First of all, yeah, right. You're the big bad alpha wolf. Shuddering in my little boots here. Second, fuck off.

Hunter: Seriously, lassie, if ye want to see me again, ye just have to ask.

Cheetie: I regret not deleting your number the second I found it.

I can hear the sass and sarcasm that fills her words even through the text. Her looks might've been what initially drew me in, but her personality and quick wit make me look forward to future conversations with her.

I flop on the couch next to the giant mountain of laundry I've yet to fold. A couple of random socks and pieces of clothes fall to the floor. Sighing, I reach down, pick them up, and fling them back onto the pile. Fuck it, I might as well chug it, a perfect way to delay the tedious chore of folding.

Lifting my hips a bit off the couch, I slide my sweats down to my ankles, not giving a shite that my bare arse is nestled on the cushions and my clean clothing. Legs free, I spread my knees wide and stroke my cock from the head to the base. My thumb runs along the barbells in my piercing with every languid movement, sending pleasure radiating through my bollocks.

Cheetie: Although... I wouldn't mind playing with your thick cock for a time or two.

Hunter: Aye? And what would ye do with it?

Cheetie: I could think of a few things... I'm getting so wet just thinking about them *wink face*

There is no way I am going to last with her sexting me like this, so I grab one of the short, worn cotton ropes from the laundry to my right and untangle it from a pair of black boxer briefs. I bind my bollocks with it to enhance the pleasure and drive off, coming too quickly.

I think of Mariax and all the filthy things I plan on doing to her. My cock is unbearably hard, and I throw my head back on the couch to take a moment before I come all over myself.

Hunter: Damn, Cheetie, ye can't tease a man like this. Tell me now, or I will drive over there and fuck ye raw.

Cheetie: mm hmm...

Cheetie: You have a lot to learn about control, Pup. BUT b/c you aren't my sub yet, I'll play with you...

My phone vibrates on my thigh. I look at it and curl my fingers around the rope. I curse viciously at the photo she sent me of two gorgeous, round tits trapped under a soaking-wet white crop top. Her nipples are hard as hell, the barbells poking through them making them that much hotter. The thin material hides nothing, but it feels like there is an air of unknown about them all the same.

I twist the loop tighter around the base of my bollocks, trail the tail end to cross over the top of my swollen knot and around my shaft, then circle back to capture the base of my knot. I tie an easy-release bow at the base of my shaft, facing me. My bollocks and knot look like two pairs of ripe cherries sitting atop one another: red, swollen, and begging to be tasted.

I switch my phone to my left hand and cup it as if it's my lifeline. I squeeze my cock with my right and pick up the pace with my movements, hissing through my teeth.

I can't stop picturing her flat on her back under me…my thighs on either side of her ribcage and my cock sliding between her oiled tits as she squeezes them together.

My phone vibrates again, but I don't stop jerking off. I make a slow corkscrew motion over the head, my thumb skimming the slit each time.

The incessant buzzing continues, and I am forced to answer it.

"Aye?" I put the phone on speaker and answer on a growl, not bothering to hide my lust coated voice.

"Hunter, are you too busy jerking off to my pic to text me back?"

I continue my methodic strokes, adding more pressure to my piercings. "Of course, I am, woman. Ye sent me a filthy pic of yer tits," I groan, my Scottish accent distinct with my arousal. "Plus, I know ye are wet at the thought of me hard and moaning yer name."

"It's not hard to make you want me, big boy," Mariax teases. "But the thought of you rubbing one out makes me wish you were here to titty fuck me and come all over my throat. Send me a pic and wrap your hand around your thick cock too," she commands, followed by a breathy moan.

I hang up and don't hesitate to do as she demands.

I love my incredible cock as is, but add in the ladder and light bondage…it's godsdamn irresistible. I take the pic, making sure the angle shows how raging my cock is, all of my rungs, and my knot and balls turning a deep reddish purple. I attach the pic and press send.

Hunter: Make sure ye scream my name when ye come, lass.

She doesn't respond for a while, and a bit of the need consuming me vanishes with my growing anxiety. I frown at my phone, willing her to text me back.

She sends another picture, and I'm speechless... The curves of her tits take up most of the frame, but beyond her gorgeous rack, I can make out her out-of-focus pink belly and tail between her thighs.

The view is so fucking hot, I cum without any buildup.

I give myself a few more hard strokes anyway, the rungs of my ladder creating extra pressure against my cock. The pleasure builds in my tortured bollocks before reaching a peak and forcing itself to every nerve ending in my body. I moan and curse in Gaelic as cum jets out in hot streams all over my hand and abs.

The dirty picture and idea of thrusting my cock between her tits plays on a loop in my head.

The woman knows how to get under my skin as no other has. Granted, I only ended my long-term relationship with Patrick recently. Plus, it's hard to get to know someone when yer cock is in their throat. I open my eyes and grab a T-shirt from the pile next to me to clean myself up.

We spend the rest of the day texting back and forth, sexting, and bickering as I continue with the necessary evil of house chores.

Despite my hatred for the endless pile of laundry on the couch next to me, I find myself high on Mariax. I can't remember the last time I've been this excited by the mere idea of how sex *will* be with someone. She already brings out my fun side like she has a direct line to my wolf's need to play and fuck.

Although our conversation takes a turn and demands my full attention when she challenges me. A tendril of anger wraps around my mind, my jaw ticking with irritation. Doesn't she know better than to challenge a Lycan?

Cheetie: I don't think you could handle it. It's better if you don't come.

Hunter: WTF?

Cheetie: Yeah, you're clearly not into the lifestyle. Tying up your balls is not even close to what I can do to you. It's cool. Not everyone can handle the pain.

Hunter: When

Cheetie: ????

Hunter: When the fuck do ye want me to be at yer wee sex pit?

Cheetie: *laughing face* Sex pit? It's called The Snuggle Pit. Come for the Snuggles. Stay for the Pain.

Cheetie: I don't blame you if you chicken out. It's okay. Maybe you need a few more decades to master your fear.

Hunter: Fuck off, woman. When should I be there, oh powerful Mistress Cheetie?

Cheetie: Well, we'll see if you have the balls to show up. A week from tomorrow at one pm. Don't be late, Pup. Only good boys get rewarded.

That last sentence went straight to my cock. I palm it again before giving it a couple of hard strokes through my third pair of sweats for the day. I can't believe I'm getting hard once again and if she keeps it up, I will be doing fucking laundry again.

This creature is driving me mad.

I've never been one for praise, but hearing it come from her…she's fucking with my mind. What is it about her that puts my cock in a permanent state? I swear I've jerked off more times than was appropriate, thinking about every inch of her exposed skin. The titillating image of her tits and throat covered in my cum will forever be in my spank bank. I roll my eyes. I need to get laid.

Determination floods through me while I think about

her taunts. Challenge accepted, Cheetie. We'll see who's laughing when I'm balls deep in her.

Her moans will be music to my ears.

CHAPTER 5

Hunter

The bright sunlight illuminates the sidewalk as I step out of the heavily forested park. I lift my tattooed forearm to shield my eyes.

I begin my trek through the few blocks it will take me to get to Mariax's wee sex club.

I agreed to this session with Mariax when the sexy bitch threw down one too many challenges. My wolf and I couldn't resist. Her fuckable mouth forming the words 'don't knock it until you try it, Pup' brought my cock to life in an epic way, immediately throbbing and seeking escape from my jeans.

I generally hate it when someone talks down to me and thinks they can assign me some pet name, but something about her makes my wolf stand up and take notice. He notices a challenge and is willing to fight for dominance. I push my wolf to the back of my mind.

It's one thing being a member of the Appalachian Pack. It's another being the alpha. I am responsible for dozens of wolves, pups, and their families. The daily stress associated with the job could easily suffocate me.

I have my core group of friends in the pack, especially

my beta, Charlie. But being intrigued by someone non-pack, not to mention a being of a different species, is new to me. I live for the pack. I will throw down my life to save my wolves. I've also fucked a lot of the pack members. Being the alpha has its perks, after all.

Maybe it's been too long since I got laid.

That could also be why Mariax has sunk her claws into me so deeply, scraping the bone.

I arrive at the Snuggle Palace, where the Snuggle Pit is hiding beneath its levels, surprised that it's actually in a decent part of town. I know no humans will enter this place or even know it exists.

Her wards appear solid. I can feel the stay-away vibes pulsing against my skin and making it itch. I don't enjoy wards, but they're a necessary evil because of all the shite that supernaturals and humans do to themselves and each other. I survey the three-story building, noticing a purple hue.

I crack a smile. I love how girly this lass is.

She's such a contradiction to her flaming personality and dark outlook on life. I could tell from the moment I met her she was going to be a test of my patience—an interesting one, but a challenge nonetheless.

Mariax is an alpha as well. We are meant to battle, and only one of us will come out on top. I'm curious to see what is in this building and what she thinks she can do for me. I don't have high hopes, though.

Maybe she's as crazy mentally as she is crazy hot.

Usually, crazy makes for some fun sex, and I've definitely had some insane full-moon sex. The moon pulls lust and magic out of all of us.

Maybe I should invite her to a full moon hunt and let her revel in the moon's glow beside me. I wonder if she'd be into it. Shaking my head, I realize I'm still staring at the building like a fucking twat.

My skin lights up like it's a separate entity. It feels like spiders are crawling under it as the wards assess my intent. I push past them after what feels like an hour of judgment, and the feeling under my skin passes once I'm on the other side.

I turn toward the wards at my back, glaring at its foreign magic. It's like looking through a haze into the city beyond, as if a cloudy piece of glass is on the other side of the barrier. The haze meets the glass, sliding up and around. It doesn't go in any one direction, but it's almost eerie to look at.

I walk down a few steps before turning right and coming face-to-face with the most ancient door I've ever seen. It stands at least eight feet tall and five feet wide. Runes have been sporadically carved into its surface and they thrum with protective magic. A band of pure gold was laid into the center of the door, making a perfect square.

I've always been interested in building architecture and random shite like that. I haven't done anything with it except for construction though, which is not architecture by any means. I built the cabin on my land in the Pocono Mountains. I enjoy going up there once a month. I probably would spend more time there if I had someone to take with me. But this hidden facade is fucking awesome.

I knock on the door twice with the side of my fist. I get the feeling this is what it was like to gain entrance to a speakeasy. I chuckle at the thought as a small rectangular window opens in the center of the door at the height of my chest.

Oh, shite. It is exactly like a speakeasy door!

I stoop slightly to peer into the window-like opening. The sight that greets me is nothing like I expected. The large, greenish face of a male orc fills the little rectangle. I stay bent and put on my most charming smile, even knowing orcs don't give a damn about niceties.

"State your business," the orc demands, his voice thick and grating on my nerves like the ward did.

"I have an appointment with Mariax."

The orc rolls his eyes. "Yeah, you and every client that comes here," he grumbles. "Name?"

The sound of papers shuffling reaches me through the small opening. My frustration at the gatekeeping makes me bristle.

"Hunter," I state briskly.

"Sorry, no Hunter on the list."

"Come again? She invited me personally."

"I don't give a fuck. You're not in the appointment book. Entrance denied," the orc declares, slamming the little window closed in my face.

I stand, trying to wrangle my temper.

What the actual fuck?

I will not give up so easily. I pound on the door with vigor, smirking when the window slides open again. This time, a different face appears. The hairs on the back of my neck stand in warning as my brain supplies that it's a werewolf.

"I thought he told you to leave. Now, run along with your tail between your legs like the little bitch you are, *Alpha*," the shifter commands with a sneer.

"Who the hells are ye?" I question.

The werewolf doesn't deign to give me a response before slamming the window once more. I stand there dumbfounded at my current predicament.

I'm saved from my thoughts when the heavy metal door starts sliding into a built-in channel.

Behind the door stands a short, curvy female with midnight purple wings. Her kinky purple hair swept back with a clip, just like how a stereotypical sexy librarian would wear... She even has black oversized cat eye framed glasses perched on her nose. But that is where the comparison to a librarian ends. Synched on her neck is a very prominent collar, complete with a big metal ring centered in the middle. It's a rich obsidian embroidered with moons and stars. In between the celestial beauties, sharp silver spikes repeat all the way around.

She wears an emerald green corset with gold trim, tight leather pants, but I'm thrown by the cozy gray full length sweater thrown over it.

She taps her stiletto impatiently, planting a hand on her cocked hip and glaring at me, her annoyance clear.

Maybe I interrupted her crossword puzzle or some shite.

The female with a serious case of resting bitch face stands boldly in the center of the foyer. The enormous male orc and the werewolf, who enjoyed barring my entrance far too much, lean against opposite walls with their arms crossed.

I eye the female, amused. She's like a wee guard dog, a ball of anger ready to attack.

I can't help the grin that spreads across my face. The toe of her shoe taps irritatingly as she waits for who knows what. She acts as though I disgust her with my presence alone.

Since she continues to stand there without inviting me in, I decide to jump on this grenade. I tuck my hands into my pockets, a picture of cool indifference.

"I'm here to see Mariax," I explain again.

They all stare at me, staying silent. It's as though they enjoy the minute amount of power they have, acting like gate keepers on a power trip.

"This is where ye use yer words and invite me inside," I say with a raised brow.

I wait a moment more before my patience gets the best of me. Screw it. I don't need this bullshit, especially from such a wee pest.

"Okay then, nice to meet ye too," I say, taking a step forward and attempting to push past the female.

Our standoff is interrupted when a cackle rings out from behind the beaded curtain on the other side of the welcome desk. Mariax struts into view on the tallest heels I have ever seen, all sexy swagger, pushing the curtain out of her way with a tinkle of the crystal beads.

All four of us turn in her direction. I raptly watch the swing of her hips and the bounce of her tits with each of her steps as my mouth waters.

Mariax is dressed in a tight black corset, her tits cradled in see-through lace cups. They're so full, they're practically spilling out. Her nipples tease me with the outline of their sharp points.

My eyes travel lower, taking in the rest of her. A bright-purple G-string, black fishnet stockings, and tall, thigh-high black leather boots are all that cover her lower half. Her seemingly random tattoos peek through the netting, begging me to tear them off and study them like she is an art exhibit.

She is perfect, so goddamn fuckable.

My cock stiffens, and my knot throbs lightly as she nears. I try to tame it down, but that's just not happening, especially as her scent reaches my nose: chocolate, petrichor, and hazelnut.

I rake my eyes over her body, practically salivating.

Does she dress like this for all her clients or just me?

The thought makes anger churn in my gut. Mariax is too sexy for her own good. Sex on a goddamn stick.

I can't believe I'm becoming territorial over a female I just met.

I mentally slap myself on the back of my head, reassuring myself that I only want her so I can fill her holes with my cum. The irrational anger I'm feeling toward how she is dressed makes no sense.

I already feel myself wanting to give in, if just for the chance to taste her cunt. My cock continues to lengthen and harden into a piece of granite, and my knot throbs and aches, making me groan. The weight of it presses against my jeans.

"Hunter, I see you had the courage to come after all."

"It doesn't require much courage to visit a gorgeous lass."

"You keep thinking that, when I have you chained to my table," she says with a wink.

Even her threats are a turn-on.

The werewolf and orc speak over one another as they fight to be the first to explain my presence. The intensity of their explanations growing in fervor.

I smirk and shake my head. Pathetic.

Mariax bites her lip and tries not to smile, her smoldering gaze landing on mine. She opens her mouth to say something but instead arches one adorable, shapely eyebrow and lowers her eyes down my body. Undressing and sizing me up, probably making her own assumptions about me and wondering if she can take me on.

I'll enjoy watching her try.

She zeroes in on the strain in my pants. The python-like appendage is hardened along my leg. I'm not exactly sure what will happen here, but there has to be sex involved, right? I was told she'd explain everything when I got here, whatever that means.

She drags her gaze back up my body and turns toward her wee bulldog. "Lauren, I'll be in P7 with the pup." She gestures toward me with a flip of her hand. "Absolutely no interruptions."

"Yes, Mistress."

I glance back at Lauren and wink.

"Fuck off," she hisses. I like her pluck.

Mariax then swivels on her gorgeous thigh-high boots without another word. She peeks over her shoulder and crooks a finger at me, beckoning me to follow her.

I almost refuse. I am not a puppy falling at her heels. Yet I find myself walking behind her.

I don't know what I expected the room to look like, maybe similar to a porn setup, but again, she surprises me. We stand in what is essentially a large concrete box. To my right is a giant mirror, which takes up the entire wall. A metal table is anchored to the floor in the center of the room. Thick chains hang from each corner, each with a leather cuff attached. There is a coil of rope lying on top of the table. No, that's not just rope. A colorless aura pulses around it, displacing the air just enough to be visible. Interesting.

I sweep myself around the rest of the room, noting the absence of anything else. There are no whips or any other kinky fuckery hanging on the walls.

Mariax leans against the mirror, running her hand along the length of her tail as she analyzes my every move. When my eyes meet hers again, she gives me a mind-blowing smile, her teeth gleaming from the lights overhead. Wee fangs shine along with her straight teeth. Hell, if she wants to bite me with those…

My cock and knot are swollen and throbbing, edging the line of pain and pleasure. I reach down to adjust myself, but she's in front of me between blinks.

Her tail wraps around my wrist and jerks it away. *The*

fuck?

She hisses. "Did I say you could touch yourself, Hunter?"

She can't be serious.

"If I want to touch my cock because yer arse is too sexy to ignore, I will."

She raises on the toes of her boots and plants a hand on my chest to grab the material of my shirt. As she settles back on her heels, she drags me down to her. My face is close to hers, but she doesn't seem bothered by it. If anything, it seems to empower her.

She brings her lips to my ear and whispers, "Pup, if you didn't realize, you're in my domain now. Do you understand what that means?"

The low rumble of my growl is the only answer I can make. She is testing my limits. I have no problem pinning her to the ground and showing her her place.

A slightly manic aura shines in her eyes.

"Are you sure you're the alpha of your pack?" she asks sarcastically. "You shifters are all fond of rules and territories. Well, I have my own set of rules. And you will *not* break them, or I will take it out on your ass. Maybe I'll even peg you with my tail as a punishment." Her seductive voice is at odds with her harsh, belittling words. "Although, I think you'd enjoy that."

The constant low hum of my growl is a warning; a warning she is choosing to ignore. A sudden sharp sting emanates from my lip. The wee bitch bit me. And hard enough to draw blood.

A warm drop of blood hits my neck just before her tits graze my chest. I inhale sharply as the pain centers and goes directly to my dick. *Fucking hell.* I am both angry and turned-on, to the point where my vision is blurred.

My wolf sneaks a glance at her as I lose focus.

Mariax watches the shift of my eyes with intrigue. A

small amount of blood remains on her plump lower lip. The tip of her tongue slips out to taste it. I did not know the intensity of an alpha female would be like this, especially a demon.

I've never spent much time around demons, so this is different.

Mariax turns away from me and moves toward the table. I try to think of a quick response to this weird situation, something smartass and meant to force her back into her place, but my mind remains a blank slate.

Clearing my throat, I grab Mariax's attention.

Her eyes zero in on me as she ties an intricate knot in the rope. She smiles, a mischievous glint growing in her eyes. She places the rope back on the table and plants her hands on her hips. Her stance and the swish of her pink tail scream brat. I'm usually into that, but I ignore my cock's line of thought.

I narrow my eyes. "I'm done with this shite. Why am I here, Cheetie? What's the point of all this?"

"You're going to do this because I command it. That's it, and that is your first lesson as a sub.

"Except I haven't agreed to be yer sub yet," I growl at her.

"That may be true, but in here you will listen to what I have to say, sub or not. I am Mistress Mariax in this space." She gestures around the room. "And when you're here for a future session, you don't have the privilege to give me shit like you just did, walking in that door like you are still in control. This is my territory, not yours."

"The next time I hear some cocky, dick-headed, no-filter dribble come out of your mouth, my tail will have its way with you. I'm tempted to make you misbehave so I can bask in the pleasure of my tail whipping across your flesh."

As she speaks, my cock jerks in my britches. In a

millisecond, I'm throbbing, my pulse making my head swell with every beat. But I refuse to be turned on by a wee bitch giving me orders. Fuck that.

I feel like I'm back in training to be an alpha and I'm floundering. I have not been belittled like this in decades. Rage heats my blood, a hot flush creeping up my neck. My wolf is readying himself to tear through my body and make his presence known.

No one should have this much control over parts of me that only I should be able to control. Maybe it's her age. I know some demons can be old and have unseen powers, but I am used to being the alpha in every scenario. I take. I conquer. I claim.

"I know you're about to say something really stupid. I dare you." Her lips curve into a taunting smile. "Go for it. See what happens. Today was only supposed to be an introduction, so I could tell you exactly what happens and the relationship between a mistress and her sub, but you are already pushing the boundaries."

She leans back and eyes me, and a growl tears from my chest. I wrap my hand around her throat as my control slips. "What do ye want, woman? Am I to grovel at yer feet and beg ye to punish me?" I shout. "That's not something I'll ever do."

"You need to tell me if you're okay with this. Because I'm not doing anything until you agree to the rules, and I only told you the first one. Consent is how a sub keeps their control, even as we test their boundaries.

"Screw this. Ye know, I was insanely curious about everything ye do here. But listening to that never-ending taunt and allowing ye to play with me like a fly caught in yer web? No. Only a wee brat like ye could severely piss off a male while wearing a sexy get-up." I'm seething, which thickens my accent. I lower my eyes to her prominent cleavage and come back up to meet her glare.

"This shite is over."

I make three steps toward the door before her tail wraps around my wrist, halting my progress.

I snap.

My vision becomes blurry as my wolf takes control. Fur erupts from the skin on my arms, quickly traveling up to my shoulders. Bones break and reorder themselves as I take the shape of my wolf. I'm halfway through the transition when I feel her sharpened nails dig into my forearms.

She kicks one of my legs out, dropping me to the floor and following me down. She's straddling me the next second and has her tail pressed against my neck.

My breath comes out in pants as my shift slows, but doesn't halt entirely. Excruciating pain pulses throughout every nerve in my body as I try to stop my shift.

Her tail is not just a tail anymore, it's a mother fucking blade. *Hells yes!* Usually I'm the one drawing blood, but I can work with this.

I refocus on her. The fury I felt moments before has vanished. The edge of her blade presses deeper into the skin of my throat. A drop of blood trails down my neck and into the little dip between my collarbones, pooling there.

It's unreal how she threw me around like that.

Supernaturals have not gotten our information about demons correctly, because she moved me around like I was a goddamn rag doll. It turns me on and pisses me off at the same time.

The moist heat of her pussy seeps through my jeans and boxer briefs. Only her excuse for panties and fishnets cover her. I imagine tearing them to shreds with my teeth…dipping my tongue into her dripping cunt and sucking her clit into my mouth.

The scent of her arousal makes me groan in frustration and need. I know she won't act on it, her and her godsdamn rules. Her braids have fallen forward, dangling over her shoulders and dangling down each side of my face. Her knife-bladed tail is still held against my throat, but she's not saying anything.

I push up on my elbows, cutting myself on the sharp edge of her tail. "Listen, Cheetie, I know this is yer domain, but I cannot submit. Ye can talk and explain all the rules ye want, but the thought of submitting when it's in my very nature to rule and give orders is just wrong. Weaker beings submit. Why should I willingly grovel or whatever a submissive does?"

Mariax sits back on her heels, inadvertently pressing her pussy deeper against my cock. I have no doubt she can feel the hardness under her, because she smiles. But this is not a smile I've seen before. This smile seems genuine. There's no calculation behind it, no other objective.

I'm struck by the thought that I want to grab her by those horns and kiss her stupid. I want to taste every inch of her beautiful, tattooed skin and trail my tongue between her breasts and down her stomach.

I place her braids back over her shoulder and remove her bladed tail from my neck. I groan, but it's not from relief. It's from the fact that I want the knife back on me to keep drawing blood through minor cuts.

Mariax takes a deep breath and says, "Why don't you be a good boy and listen to me? Because I really would love to show you why you need this."

Somehow, the praise calms me when it would have aggravated me from anyone else. Perhaps it's the distraction of her tail, how sharp and deadly it appeared, and yet her features were gentle and understanding.

"Fine. I'll listen to ye. Ye have five minutes."

She rolls her eyes at my command before drawing a claw under my chin to tilt my head back and meet her eyes better.

"It is going to change your life, and I'm positive you will learn to accept it. Hell, even enjoy it. Thinking you're going to control me, and do whatever else it is you think in your testosterone-laced mind you're going to do, is not happening right now." She taps the sharpened nail on my forehead. "You need to let go of the control. That is part of the reason. I think you would enjoy being submissive. Do you ever feel overwhelmed with all of the responsibility? Taking care of all those other wolves has got to be a lot on your shoulders. Don't you ever want to be in the moment? To not have to think and worry for a while? To expel all thoughts except to do what you're told? It is a freeing experience; I want to show you how and why you might love it."

I reply with a sound Scots can make to convey any number of feelings, and she doesn't stop me from leaving this time. Making my way out of the room and up to the exit I stew in my thoughts.

Maybe I do want to listen to her. I mean, I still don't like the thought of submitting, but she does make a good point.

I'm always on the clock, twenty-four-seven. I am the wolf everybody brings their shite to, from actual crises to basic pack problems. Most of it is minute bullshit issues that they could honestly solve themselves, but they don't have to because they have me. It's what I was bred for.

The whole point of a pack is for us to rely on each other, but I don't have a partner to share the burden. In traditional pack structure, there aren't two alphas, so I can't even have one to share this load. Even if I claimed a male as my spouse, the pack wouldn't acknowledge him as an alpha because two males cannot breed. But I've turned the construct on its head by staying single for a long time. Our pack continues to grow through the betas and members of our pack. I know I'm still expected to produce at least one heir. I just don't know if it'll ever happen.

I realize the stress of my life has been slowly smothering me. I never realized how bad it had gotten because I didn't allow myself to sit and think about it.

The tension in my neck and shoulders hardens my muscles painfully. A boulder nestles onto my back as my anxiety grows.

Maybe I do want to know what it's like not to worry over every decision I make. For all the bullshit and swagger she was throwing at me earlier, it seems like she's genuinely trying to help me… or at least she thinks she can.

I didn't even know I needed help, but I feel that her experiences have shown her I do. I don't want to admit it to myself though, so she's sure as fuck isn't going to hear it from me.

CHAPTER 6

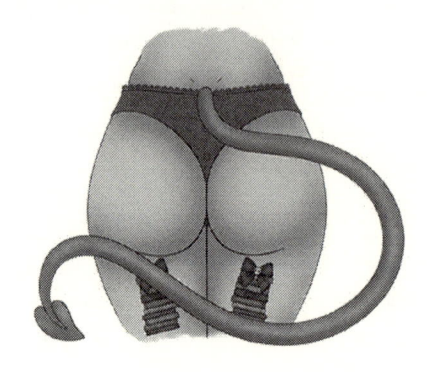

Mariax

I breathe in deeply, allowing the scent of books to lessen my ever-present anxiety. I blow the breath back out through my lips and wander down the small, packed aisles at Tightly Bound.

I pick up a book at random, breathing in deeply. The scent notes of cardamom, vanilla, cinnamon, and coffee always permeate the space. When I take a book home from this shop, the pages always hold onto a hint of the store's essence, and I love it.

This bookstore is unique in more ways than one. Its primary clientele are supernaturals, and it is owned by a witch named Morgan. I'm not sure if she is a light or dark witch, but I know she knows how to style the space.

The walls are painted a beautiful lavender with a black damask pattern on top of it. Across the ceiling flowering vines weave and interconnect, hanging down at random. There is no way to tell if something holds up the plants or if it is by magical intervention.

On occasion one of the flowering vines will drop down low enough to tickle a patron's ear or ruffle their hair, like they just want to play.

Bundles of herbs, plants, and flowers hang on every wall dispersed between bleached animal skulls. Candles sit on floating shelves and line the front window of the shop.

This is my favorite bookstore in Philly. It's a little hole-in-the-wall business, a diamond in the rough cesspool we call a city.

I don't hate Philadelphia itself, but crowds of humans, the constant loud noises, and the stench weigh heavily on me every day. Little bookstores like these bring me joy in an otherwise dismal world.

"Do you need help finding anything, ma'am?" the clerk asks me with a toothy smile.

"No, thanks. I'm meeting someone," I say to politely dismiss her. Plus, I wasn't lying. Hunter is due to arrive any minute, and I have a serious bone to pick with him.

Every werewolf I employed for security at the Snuggle Palace was replaced the other night. When I questioned the unknown lycan stationed by the front, arguing with Jeffry, my ogre doorman, he said his alpha ordered it so here he was. He then shrugged, as if I wouldn't go on a warpath for Hunter fucking around with my business.

My fury has only matured.

I sent him a deceptively nice text message a day later, to invite him to Tightly Bound. My Pup mentioned he's also a book lover, since I asked him about the bookshelves in the background of his dick pics; a weird thing I picked up on later when I went back through them. So, what an excellent way to invite him for a friendly afternoon of books and coffee before I remind him of the capacity I have for less-conventional punishments.

Continuing my perusal of the stacks, I wander down each aisle. One of the coolest parts about this store is they have a small coffee shop by the register *and* an entire display of books written by indie authors. The best books I have ever read were written by indie authors.

I was ecstatic to find several of my favorites displayed: H. D. Carlton, Rebecca L. Garcia, Kat Blackthorne, Avanne Michaels, Opal Reyne, Bea Paige…just to name a few.

"Hello! Welcome to Tightly Bound! Please let me know if there is anything I can do for you," an enthusiastic employee calls from the window display she is setting up.

"Aye, I'll do that."

Hearing the Scottish accent, I poke my head around the shelf I was entranced by and give Hunter a beaming smile, but I allow a bit of my ire to seep into my eyes.

Hunter tilts his head to the side in question, unsure how to decipher my expression.

Before giving him the time, I stomp toward him and bind his wrists behind his back with my tail. His eyes widen in surprise, but I feel the evidence of his arousal pressing between us.

It does nothing to quell my fury.

"You do not have the right to make any decisions about my business!" I shriek, causing the employee to gasp and cover her mouth with both hands.

Hunter growls at my outburst and shoves me backward with his shoulder, forcing me to retreat into the secluded aisle of bookshelves.

He crowds me into a bookshelf, the spines of hardback books digging into my shoulder blades. His hips pin me in place, curling over me as he leans down to get in my face. My lower back screams from the tension of my tail stretching to maintain its grip on his wrists.

"I don't know what ye are talking about, Cheetie," he snarls, his warm breath fanning my cheek.

"Mhm, of course," I say with attitude, rolling my eyes.

"Seriously, what is the deal woman?"

"I can't believe you're being so fucking obtuse," I hiss,

shoving him in the chest. "You fired all of my security and replaced them with members from your own pack!"

"Aye. What's the problem?"

"They were my employees, not yours. They weren't even in your pack."

His expression softens slightly, but the anger still simmers in his eyes. "I'm an alpha, and they are not. I told them to get the fuck out, so they did. They were rogue Weres, lassie. Without a pack, they can rarely be trusted. I will not have ye put yerself at risk when I can easily bolster yer protection," Hunter explains, like it's the most natural thing in the world to dive headfirst into protecting someone he just met.

I stare at him with pinched brows and narrow eyes. Could it really be that simple?

"When I came to this existence, I was rogue too, and on my own. My employees are my people, picked for a reason. Someone took a chance on me, so I took a chance on them." I stare at Hunter with pinched brows.

What are the chances he genuinely cares, and this was not a power play?

I free him from the confines of my tail, already missing the contact with his skin. He smirks while rubbing his tattooed wrists. Light indentations from the ribbing pattern of my tail ring both of his wrists.

I could get used to seeing those marks on his skin. They look good on him.

My clit throbs in agreement. I need to stay focused. *Ignore his yummy tattoos and piercings for now, Mariax. You can play with him later.*

"Seriously, Pup, that's not cool. You cannot just decide to replace members of my staff without consulting me."

He has the decency to look bashful for a moment. Hunter leans even closer, so his lips ghost mine as he speaks.

"Fine. I'm sorry, sometimes my alpha instincts don't take no for an answer, so I do without asking. Don't let this go to yer head, but yer right," he says with a resigned huff.

Our banter is interrupted when 'Down with the Sickness' by Disturbed plays loudly from Hunter's back pocket. His smile grows, and his eyes sparkle when he hears the song.

He reaches back and pulls out his smartphone, answering immediately without checking the caller ID.

Who the hell is making him so happy from a simple phone call?

"I'll be right back," Hunter tells me as he answers the call, walking a few paces away. "Hey, what's up?" he says, greeting the caller.

I wish I could hear the other side of the conversation.

"No, I can't today. I'm already spending time with a bonnie lass," he replies and winks at me.

Warmth blooms in my chest at his words, but it is quickly replaced by something ugly as his conversation progresses.

"Aye. That works for me." He listens for a beat longer. "Wear something sexy," he commands and ends the call.

I try my best to mask the jealousy surging through me, but I fail. Who is he talking to, asking them to wear something sexy? It's not my place to be jealous, far from it. Hunter is not mine. We are not in a relationship, and he hasn't even agreed yet to being my sub, these feelings need to back the fuck up to wherever they came from.

"Who was that?" I question, while I cross my arms, fully aware I sound like a petulant brat he thinks I am.

He smirks and responds, "Just one of the people I've been seeing. I recently put myself back into the dating pool."

"Oh," I say lamely, attempting to smother my demon

instincts to make it rain blood.

I wish I could reach through his phone and drag my bladed tail down the torso of the mystery caller, spill their guts and dance on their maimed corpse.

"Cheetie?" Hunter says gently, softly rubbing his thumb across my cheekbone.

I mentally shake myself out of my dark thoughts before I act on them. Reminding myself again that Hunter is not mine.

"Hmm?" I respond and flutter my eyelashes dramatically.

"Nothing. For a moment, I thought ye were planning my murder."

A startled laugh escapes me. If he only knew the depth of my depravity.

"Anyway. Coffee? How do ye take yers?"

I sigh in relief at the change in subject. "Cream and a little sugar. The coffee's color should resemble hickory wood. Oh, please also add a dusting of pumpkin spice."

He raises both brows. "Well, that's oddly specific. I've never met anyone who describes their ideal coffee by a type of wood."

I shrug. "I'm fancy like that."

Hunter leans down and speaks just low enough so I can hear him. "If ye can describe yer coffee with such detail, I'm curious how ye will describe my cum as it coats yer tongue."

With that, he casually walks to the coffee bar to order for us.

I'm speechless. My mind has momentarily forgotten how to function. Hunter has a dirty mouth, and I love it.

When he hands me my cup of coffee, I cradle it between my palms, soaking the warmth into my flesh. With every breath, I inhale the decadent aroma of my drink.

Perfect, it's just what I asked for.

CHAPTER 7

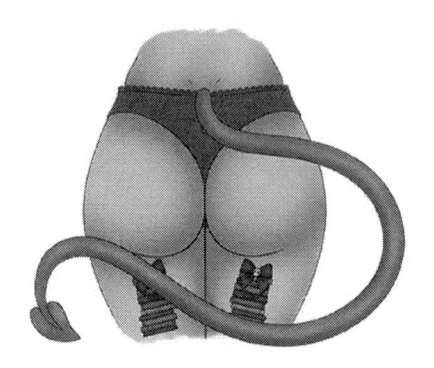

Mariax

With texting and the occasional calls, we chat for hours on end. Getting to know Hunter has been the most fun I've had in a while. I usually ask him complicated questions so I can just listen to his Scottish accent and melt for him.

My attraction to him grows daily. His passion for his pack and determination to be everything they need him to be is inspiring. The plans he has for his pack and the future show him to be nearly perfect.

It makes me wish someone would go through such difficult lengths to keep me warm, happy, and protected.

My stomach flutters with nerves and excitement when his name lights up my phone screen.

I also feel completely safe with him in a way I never have before. I'm comforted by the knowledge he is a good person and doesn't seek to hurt me.

Thinking about Hunter puts a little spring in my step as I walk through my home. I flick the switch to extinguish the lights, the shadows extending from the corners of the living room and toward the entryway. I exit my suite and lock the door behind me before sliding open the hidden door juxtaposed to mine.

When I step through the door at ground level, inky darkness envelops me. I make my way to the bar, using muscle memory to find my way. After flipping the switch behind the bar, long rows of liquor are illuminated by backlighting from floor to ceiling.

I stock the best liquors on the top shelf of my bar. And, not surprisingly, one of those is His favorite: Lagavulin. I wouldn't bother stocking it, except that the prominent members of the supernatural community would throw a total shit fit.

Even the scent of it wafting in the air reminds me of him.

We would drink, fuck, and fight almost every night when I lived in Inferuna. A small smile plays at the corner of my lips before my anger chases away my brief moment of joy. I'd never wanted to have soft feelings toward him, never wanted to let my guard down. But he worked his way in, unwilling to let my soul survive without a part of his embedded in its recesses.

I don't doubt for a second what he told me all that time ago. The memory of his whispered voice close to my ear as he held me and ran his hand down my back where I was stretched out on the bed is still fresh.

I will burn this place to the ground to keep you. I don't care who I have to kill, torture, kidnap... list any atrocity you want. I will do it if it means keeping you as mine.

However, that level of devotion comes at a cost.

He broke me. My body, mind, and soul fractured in irreparable shards. No one else is to blame besides me. Something is wrong with me, and it has been for my entire existence.

When I became his, it was like a portion of my dark essence melded with his. The safety, comfort, and pleasure he offered was a balm to my exposed nerves. It was the main reason I agreed to be his submissive, but when I fled, the organ in my chest stuttered. A chunk of it tore from my body, leaving a weeping wound, and nothing has filled that void of longing ever since.

I know something fundamental in my makeup is missing, an abnormality that could only have occurred when the ether forged my physical self. I haven't figured out what the difference is, but I always wondered if I could find out. I have a feeling he held the answers, but if he did, he never felt the need to divulge the information.

Bastard. He probably planned to lord it over me.

That's what he did. He was a manipulator. A narcissist. Withholding secrets until it benefited him to get what he wanted.

He was a terrible Dom, and everything I strive to be the opposite of. It's why consent, safety, and aftercare are so important to me.

It'd be nice if everyone showed me the same courtesy.

The bar was pretty cleaned out after the last full moon show.

This level of the club has only two entrances. One is for me and my trusted employees and the other is the curtained door. They have no access to the other levels of the club, especially the dungeon, and my personal living space; which is below ground level. If they want to visit The Pit, they need to go back to the lobby and get around my security there.

The entrance to the club consists of a lobby, bouncers, coat room, and elevator. The clients take an elevator directly to the Snuggle Pit directly below this floor. It opens out into a small foyer before they can enter the black gothic style large double doors. Those are always guarded, no matter what time of day or night.

I can't risk exposure in any way that would hurt me, my business, or my patrons. Otherwise, if someone wanted, they could sneak in here and do all kinds of evil, especially considering that most magic is hard to trace.

I had my witch specifically place a trip board on every level, so if anyone enters outside of business hours, it alerts me the instant that it happens.

I work through the list, noting which top-shelf liquors need replenishing, but when I get to the spot where the Lagavulin should be, I only find one bottle with a quarter of the amber liquid left.

What the fuck? There should be at least three bottles. They didn't drink that much at the last party. They were really into vodka.

Who is drinking my liquor?

Dread slithers along my skin, raising the fine hairs all over my body. A thundering pulse beats in my ears as my heart pounds harder.

I tear through the recycling bin, matching the liquor bottles to the empty stock list. Everything is accounted for except for the Lagavulin. My confusion turns to rage as realization dawns on me, and I bare my fangs at the space in front of me.

Someone was here. Someone not only drank my liquor but tried to hide the evidence, like I'm some imbecile who doesn't keep track of her stock.

I search behind the bar for the empties and find them stashed in a shadowed corner behind the cheap liquor. Grabbing one bottle, I glower at it, examining every inch as if looking at it would give me insight who the bastard is who's fucking with me. I'm willing to bet that whatever is stalking me through the city is also messing with my club now, and I'm tired of waiting for the creature to show up.

At this point, I'm ready. I dare them to show their face.

I close my eyes and grip the neck of the bottle tighter. Small fissures appear in the glass as I grip it like it's the neck of my mystery stalker. When I slam the bottle onto the bar top, it shatters into thousands of tiny pieces. I plant my hands on the bar, ignoring the sharp pieces of glass that cut into my palms, inwardly cursing myself.

I do not have time to worry about this shit.

I need to make sure the Snuggle Palace is ready for business tomorrow night. I swipe the back of my hand across my forehead, brushing my pink locks out of my eyes.

Owning my own business shouldn't be this much extra work, especially considering my past, but I give anyone who runs their own small business credit. This is not a cakewalk. Sometimes it is more of a hellscape.

When I open my eyes, I swear I see Him leaning against the doorframe in the corner of the room, a tumbler of whiskey dangling from his fingertips at his side.

I hear the slight *tink* of rocks tapping against the glass as he swirls it and stares at me with void-like eyes. That's impossible. It can't be him. He's in Inferuna right now.

Why is this illusion plaguing me?

With my next blink, it vanishes.

Just moments before, He was leaning against the wall with that irresistible smirk I hate so much gracing his features. The corner of his lips were slightly curled, and his dimples on display. Tears pool along my bottom lashes, and I have to rapidly blink them away, not allowing myself to succumb to the agony that thinking about him brings.

He doesn't deserve my pain. For someone who said they love me to bring me so much torture is irredeemable. Allowing love into my life was a mistake.

Never again. Love was for suckers, anyway. It was for humans, with their stupidly short lifespans while I go on, forever, with no end in sight. I'll clasp at my immortality for the lifeline it is. I can, and will survive, anything.

My mind refuses to believe that my past is just haunting me or stalking me with no chance of escape. No, someone is out there, fucking with me for their own fun. So, following my instincts, I check the entire floor and the surrounding view from the catwalk above.

Proceeding with my crusade to lessen my anxiety, I hurry into the main club room. This portion of the Snuggle Palace is triple the size of the showroom. The showroom is usually closed off, unless it is a night with a live sex show, which occurs twice a month.

When customers want to imbibe in their fantasies in a hands-on manner, they explore every kind of pleasure imaginable in this room. I set up the space like a typical nightclub, but there are a few kinky additions. The side rooms are a big draw with their themes, set with any toy you can imagine to bring your sexual fantasies to life.

In one room it is all about bondage, another breath play. The kinky themes of the rooms rotate because there are so many different fantasies to account for.

An enormous bar runs along the wall, perpendicular to the dance floor. Purple lights outline the mirror behind the display of liquor. The bartenders are nude and sometimes offer lap dances for extra tips, making their choice freely.

I would never make it a job requirement.

Anyone getting too handsy with one of my workers without permission either has their face scraped against the sidewalk as they're thrown out, or the worker gets the freedom to break their fingers. That's a favorite rule and concession of mine; one which makes my employees feel safe and allows them to tap into their vengeful side if they have one.

However, when consent is granted, we absolutely encourage open sexual exploration and socialization of all kinds. No kink is shamed, no matter how strange or perverse.

There are also several cages hanging from the ceiling, where professional dancers tease and pleasure themselves.

On any night, there could be vampires feeding from their favorite artery, while their meal moans and pants as they pleasure them simultaneously. Arousal and blood lust almost always go hand-in-hand.

Or you can find a demon giving out the pleasure of pain, wolves knotting their playmates, and all manner of public spectacles. And don't forget the themed rooms and all that can be done there from role playing to using the provided implements.

Lauren manages this aspect of my business, so I rarely have to deal with it. She maintains the schedule and hires employees to tend the bar, serve patrons, with bouncers and monitors to keep everyone safe.

I survey the room, noting anywhere someone or something could be lying in wait. I turn on all the lights and clear the space, leaving no shadow unchecked.

Once I'm satisfied that nothing is amiss in the main room, I head back to the showroom to complete my check of the nooks and crannies that someone could hide in. If someone is here, they would have had to get by me in the main room to get out or go down my private stairs and that has a coded scanner protecting it. No, the only place left for someone to hide is here. The reason I left the check of it to the end was to make sure no one was getting by me by hiding until my back was turned and I was busy in here.

There are six square rooms made of glass. Customers can change rooms, depending on his or her taste. With their consent, they can leave their glass clear for nearby voyeurs to enjoy the view. But if they desire privacy, with a tap of a button, a thick, smoke-like substance fills the glass, obscuring everything from view.

I walk in front of the rooms on both sides, tapping the glass and signaling the rooms to transform. The smokey walls slowly dissipate, my touch overriding the settings from within. Each room contains every level of comfort imaginable.

I can't be certain or calm my mind until I'm positive nothing hunts in the shadows. I take a deep breath through my nose and hold it in my expanded lungs. As I exhale, much like the smoke, my unsure thoughts and anxiety dissipate, allowing me to clear my thoughts of Him and shove them into the deepest corner of my mind.

The last room I check is on the left side of the stage.

Many would think it's the best seat in the house, as it's the one directly in front of the stage, but they would be incorrect.

The room to my left has the best view because it's perpendicular to the enormous bed on the stage. There's not always a bed. Sometimes there is a custom Saint Andrews cross, with manacles attached to chains, and other times it's bare. But the bed occupying the space now is no ordinary bed. There is a custom-made, under-the-bed restraint system built into the frame, complete with adjustments for most supernatural creatures.

My best friend, Tiffany, knows a guy who does modifications and hooked me up. During my live sessions, I often enjoy picking out one patron in the crowd to be my willing victim.

Volunteers are heavily vetted by Lauren and pulled from a never-ending list. Since we opened, we have only had a few patrons taking it too far.

Years ago, a female witch was spread out on the bed before me. As I tied her down, she reached her free arm into a secret pocket in her dress and revealed a knife, then attempted to stab me in the chest. My tail caught the knife by the blade and returned the favor, driving it so deeply into her heart that it sent a shudder through my muscles when it came into contact with a mattress spring.

Little did the bitch know it wouldn't have killed me

anyway. Far from it, actually. However, it was a giant nuisance, and I refuse to allow any fuckery like that to happen again.

It turned out she had recently been to Tempt Me, one of my competitors, and gotten a taste for the public bloodshed they deliver. It's classless and ignorant, since they foolishly let any creature in. The demons that run that club, a minuscule blip on my radar, allow any kind of fucked up shit, and worse. Someone there had to have set her up. I suspect it was to test my vetting process, which she got through, and now I'm not sure how that happened.

I'm beginning to suspect this feeling stalking me has been around for longer than I knew, messing with me on a deeper level.

Not in my club, however. She should have known better.

Since we're of a higher level than that bottom of the pile shit club, we have no shortage of immortal beings willing to partake or be publicly punished and pleasured. Plus, it is one of my kinks to display my dominant side for those longing to witness it. I might be fucked up on the inside, but I admit satisfaction fills me with the knowledge that I regularly terrify females and males alike.

When I embrace my dark essence, the level of power racing through my veins is indescribable, but it's nothing like His raw power skating along my skin and holding me hostage.

It'd once been intoxicating until it became suffocating.

He thrived off that suffocation, even if I hated it, and I vowed I would never allow my clients to feel the same vulnerability I did in those moments.

I tap the glass in the room I stand in before plunging it back into shadows. Smoke creeps up from the floor and up the walls. The inky interior is welcoming, a balm to my raw nerves, so I step farther in. I leave the door open and lie back on the chaise lounge, facing the entrance.

Thoughts of Hunter filter into the quiet space of my mind as I think of having him inside this room with me, overtaking those of Him that have trespassed.

The feral look he pinned me with once I explained some of the basic rules of submission is forever imprinted in my memories. He's unsure about being a submissive, and I am questioning if this is the right path for him. I might have gone a little overboard with the cocky attitude during his first session, but I know his wolf wouldn't respect me if I didn't challenge him in a memorable way.

Hunter is a big boy.

His muscles bulge and threaten to tear out of any clothes he wears. His scent also lures me further to him…but there was something about his aura that called to me, something that reached out and claimed something inside me.

I know he's still making his official, final decision, but I know he will be here regularly. Who knows what our relationship will look like in the future? I feel the urge to dive into his life and wrap my tail around him to keep him with me. I haven't been able to deny my attraction to him, and it only deepens each time we talk, text, or see each other.

It's not the first time I've had a client I've been attracted to, but this is different. It's been deeper and startlingly overwhelming since the beginning. I didn't feel the connection until I sobered up and relived what I could remember of that night at the bar, but he'd gotten under my skin and seems to be staying.

My body sinks further against the plush lounge as I relax, and my tension eases. I close my eyes, placing my hands behind my head.

Not to mention the way his panty-dropping Scottish accent caresses my ears. I could listen to him read a boring-as-hell car manual and wouldn't be surprised if I came from his voice alone. I have a place for him in my life no matter what, but I will be incredibly disappointed if he doesn't at least try my way.

He needs this release, even if he doesn't know it himself.

I never had a Daddy Dom until Him.

I didn't know how deeply I craved that connection to surrender myself. It was a fight at first. I never truly became a hundred percent submissive, since I'm a switch, but the times when I permitted myself to be in the moment are some of the best of my life. And it's not just about the pleasure, although that was fucking fantastic.

It was about being taken care of and shedding my anxieties and worries for at least the time I was in that mind space. At least, I *thought* I was being taken care of. I learned things about myself I wouldn't have otherwise explored, and learned what my boundaries are, as well as how quickly someone could violate them.

Which, for me, was startling to learn, considering I didn't think anything could bother me.

Hunter needs that just as much as I did. I might not be practicing torture or being tortured, at least not without consent, but I can see the struggle he lives with. His wolf will fight against me, but I will win it over, even if it needs me to run while he gives chase.

I need someone I can finally call mine, someone I can shape to what I need, while also giving back.

What would it be like to go on a date with Hunter?

Fleeing into the woods on our walk back to my home, stripping off all my clothes and allowing him to hunt me. The excitement and thrill of the idea awakens a primal part of me. It causes my nipples to tighten and rub against my tank top, as a pulse thrums in my clit. I run a hand over my chest, making small circles with my fingertips. The barbell through my nipples presses against my skin, but then I force myself back to the present.

I'm getting ahead of myself. I need to try to be his mistress first. I cannot give up this desire to have his needs satisfied in this way. He needs to experience and learn about being a submissive first.

When I think about it, it's probably why I've been seeing and thinking about Him so much lately. I never completely eradicated him from my thoughts, but they were slowly decreasing in frequency until recently.

What I need is a new distraction, and my eyes are already set on Hunter.

Let the games begin, Pup.

CHAPTER 8

Hunter

Once again, I find myself standing in the meeting house about to address my pack. It is my duty to notify them of changes to the pack structure.

Everyone knows Patrick and I broke up, but I need to inform them of the recent drastic turn of events.

I clear my throat loudly and make eye contact with Charlie. He releases an ear-splitting whistle, and the room quiets immediately.

"Thanks man," I say and smirk at him, before I turn to everyone else. "I know ye all have concerns and other issues ye need to discuss with me, but it'll have to wait a minute."

Grumbles ensue but silence quickly takes their place.

"I am officially informing ye that I banished Patrick from the Appalachian pack, our lands, and contacting us," I announce in a clear, firm voice.

No one says anything, but I hear several loud gasps.

"He was a disgrace to our pack and does not deserve yer sympathy. He's lucky I granted him the kindness of banishment and did not tear him apart slowly," I state darkly.

It's no secret that I am a formidable force. It's why my pack trusts me with their safety. However, it doesn't stop the occasional flash of fear when I make bloodthirsty comments like that. I don't enjoy their fright, but it's a necessary evil.

They all know what he did, so I tack on, "he was also instructed to not speak of the business of this pack in any form." I sigh, running my hands through the nest I call hair and wrangle it into a messy bun. "If ye see Patrick or if he contacts ye, report it to Charlie immediately."

"For anyone wondering if this was too harsh," Charlie chips in. "Remember that Patrick violated our alpha's trust and revealed secrets that weren't his to share. He showed he was untrustworthy. Who's to say he wouldn't have betrayed the pack if it benefited him?"

Just like Charlie, to always have my back.

"Exactly. Everyone's safety is my priority," I answer with a nod. "Now, onto regular business. Reform the line and we'll get started."

The line quickly forms, but the remainder of the room erupts into loud and comfortable socialization. The conversations of so many wolves in one place makes my ears ring. Wee bairns in wolf form race between the legs of adults as they nip and wrestle.

Most of those here were lycans like me, but we sometimes brought in lost and confused werewolves that needed sheltering and protection. Many, at first, were concerned by my choice, but their wolves were like ours – just chaotic and uncontrollable.

A wolf needs a pack.

As long as they were good people, how could I deny them? Plus, the bigger and stronger our pack was, the better. We had our territories to defend after all.

I clap my hands loudly to get the pack's attention. Whispered conversations continue, but it's not a concern.

Phil, a burly male with a barrel-shaped chest, stands at the front of the line. He speaks when I gesture for him to begin.

"Alpha," he says, nodding with respect. "The teenagers are stealing my cans again. I save those cans for months, and every time I get a good stash ready to turn into cash, my bags disappear. I also can't help but notice the new boots Noah is wearing today, yet he's never had a job, and I know his mama didn't buy them." He glares at a group of sixteen-year-olds yelling and laughing in the back of the room.

"That's unfortunate, Phil. But what exactly have ye done to solve the issue on yer own?" I ask him.

"Well, I've brought it up to the brats' parents, a fat lot of good that's done," he mumbles.

"And then ye slashed the tires on their bikes," I finish his mumbled statement for him.

I stare him down, knowing he has done very little other than break the law himself and complain loudly about the pups to anyone who will listen.

He continues, "I don't know what else to do, Alpha."

I sigh, deciding to take it easy on the old bugger. "Next, time—"

"Next time!?" He yells.

"Watch yer fuckin' tone, Phil," I growl, the weight of my alpha command heavy in my reprimand. "As I was saying, next time ye have an issue ye don't know how to solve, come to me and ask for guidance. This whole stramash could have been avoided."

His shoulders slump in resignation, but his scowl remains.

"Now, what would ye have me do to help make it right?"

"Punish them. Whip some sense into those ungrateful heathens," he growls.

I stare at him, unimpressed. "Ye know I won't harm the bairns, but I would be willing to find some extra community service opportunities for them to volunteer for every weekend for the next year. If yer cans still go missing after that punishment, we can revisit the beatings," I state, and wink at the teenagers, who now have their shocked expressions trained on me.

Obviously, they heard it all thanks to our incredible hearing.

I listen for literal hours as wolf after wolf complains about petty concerns or fights with their neighbor. The occasional request for a construction project piques my interest, but that happens rarely. The pack begs for help as if I don't already do everything in my power to fulfill everyone's needs.

I'm grateful I could solve most of the wolves' issues. However, a headache blooms and throbs behind my left eyebrow.

I really hope what Mariax said is true. I hope it offers even a wee bit of relief from these nagging duties I must suffer through daily. I'll kneel for her whenever she commands if she can help to soothe me and my wolf.

CHAPTER 9

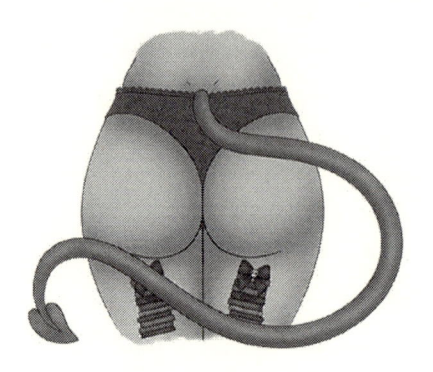

Mariax

"Mistress, you have a visitor," Lauren announces, walking into my miniature library.

My library is situated perpendicular to my suite but has a secret door that lets me into my home or the stairs that take me to the surface. I can avoid running into clients or employees on my way to eat some snacky-snacks, binge read, and snuggle in the softest blankets I own with it this far below the public floors.

I raise my eyes from the book in my lap and sigh. Lauren is the only one that searches me out here.

Lauren elaborates, "I know this is your personal time, but it's Hunter and he's not taking no for an answer. Plus, I thought you might get pissed if I maimed him a bit while forcing him to leave."

I giggle lightly at the thought of Lauren beating the shit out of Hunter and flying his ass out of the club.

"Fineee," I say, defeated, and then throw my blankets off of me onto the daybed.

I immediately feel the loss of comfort and warmth. Extracting myself from their cocoon is not welcome. However, the excitement of seeing Hunter again keeps me moving.

I arrive in the entryway and dismiss Lauren, Jeffry, and the latest guard Hunter stationed at the entrance for protection duty so we can have privacy. But Hunter grips my tattooed forearm tightly and drags me roughly into the coatroom to the right of the enormous doors.

The ambient lighting is at its lowest setting, creating an unintentionally romantic atmosphere. I bristle with the thought and take a step back from him, his hand dropping to his side.

"Care to explain?" I demand.

"I accept yer rules. I will be yer submissive, however—"

"Submissives do not have the privilege of making demands. You either accept my terms or you leave."

"Aye, but I was going to say—"

"Hunter, do you want to become my submissive or not?"

"Aye."

I pause, mentally slapping myself when I realize I was about to forgo all the proper etiquette involved in a new dom/sub relationship.

I am a good dominant. I must not fall into the shitty habits taught to me in my past relationship. I was treated poorly as a submissive, and I refuse to treat Hunter in the same manner.

"Good," I state, allowing a sexy smile to curve my lips.

"Good? No wee comment, or a bratty list of demands?"

"No Hunter, I will do everything in my power to be a responsible dominant and see to your needs," I explain, my fingers running through his thick beard as I caress his cheek, my tail quietly slipping around his waist to draw him closer to me.

"You are going to be so much fun to tame, Pet." I take in a deep breath, fighting my face for control to hold my smirk back. "However, first we must go over a few basics of the relationship between a dominant and submissive. I apologize for not going over them on your first visit."

Hunter's eyes fill with tenderness at my omission. "It's okay, Cheetie, we all make mistakes. The important thing is ye admitted ye made the wrong choice. That shows me a great deal of the type of mistress ye are."

He spreads his arms and wraps them around me, cuddling me into his warmth. "So, what are a few of the basics?"

I take a step back, but my upper body remains in place as Hunter refuses to let me go. "Where are ye goin'? Ye can answer me just where ye are."

A giggle escapes my lips, surprising me.

"Fine, you domineering bastard," I tease. "Well, there is safety for the dominant and submissive. I'll need a list of kinks that you would like for me to satisfy."

When his eyes slipped to the side in nervousness, I softened my gaze. "Nothing will be too far for me, Hunter. I want to be a safe place for you where you can rest not only your pleasure, but your worries. I won't judge you for any of it, in the same way I hope you don't judge me for any of mine."

"Yours?" he asks with his head tilting.

I laugh and reach up to gently pat the side of his face. "Aye, big boy. Don't think you're the only one being pleasured."

A lobsided grin fills his face. "I'm down for making you scream, Cheetie. I'll even make you purr for me. I've even been thinking about all the ways I'm going to—"

"Whoa, there!" I exclaim before he can go into some wicked sexy talk that's likely to have me lowering my panties before he's even finished. "We still have more to discuss. For instance, you'll need to pick safe words for different actions that have different meanings, and we need to delve into your hard and soft limits..." When his nose scrunches up like he doesn't really understand, I sigh. "I know it sounds complicated, but I promise I will be patient with you, Hunter. We can go slow. I can give you a list and material on things if you prefer."

"That all sounds verra professional. Ye must do this for a living, aye?" he jokes.

Rolling my eyes, I continue. "Now say, 'Yes, Mistress'."

Hunter battles to keep his face blank, his cheeks twitching from the effort of holding back a scowl or a smile.

"Must I?"

A grin creeps into my features. "Of course. It'll help you learn that I'm now the master of you, Pup. I'll make you say it over and over again until your tail wags every time you say it. It's one of my rules, and without your approval of it, this won't work."

He gave a huff, his cheeks darkening as he looked to the side again. "Fine, *Mistress*."

"Good boy," I croon, slipping my tail from his waist and trailing it down to his ass in a featherlight caress.

I shift my tail into a paddle and smack him hard on the ass, enjoying his groan and his scent intensifying with arousal. The pine, coffee, and wood smoke smell deepening and stroking my senses.

I've put so much of my blood and determination into my business, no one, aside from Tiffany, understands the lengths I go to.

I've been in the human realm for over two centuries and I've never allowed my feelings to control my business decisions.

Allowing Hunter to sub for me is a big risk, one I would not normally take.

And yet, I cannot deny his allure.

I just hope this doesn't blow up in my face.

CHAPTER 10

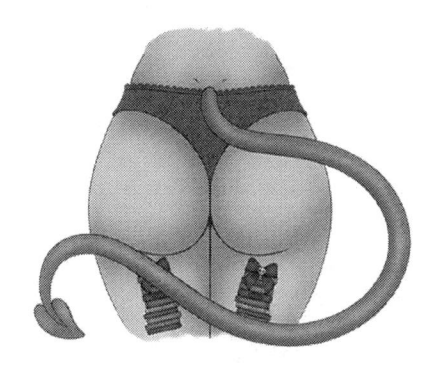

Mariax

1 Year later

My dreams still haunt me. I know they are dreams, I know they aren't happening now, but I cannot escape them once they latch on. They must play out it seems. The current one playing out in my mind is just the latest of the reel that loops when I close my eyes.

The skin is peeled from my flesh in strips exactly one inch wide. Manic laughter sounds around me, blending with a wet, tearing sound. *Fuck, is that my skin?* I'm not sure how much skin I have left at this point. It feels like my stupid djinn has been at it for hours, possibly even days. He is especially meticulous when it comes to flaying. The extreme heat of Inferuna only makes it worse.

I feel my body wanting to commence rotting, but I am still alive. Alive by pure will, demon regeneration, and this putrid-tasting concoction of what the higher-ups call Vitasmooth, 'it's got everything the body needs'. Fuck that shit. It's probably half arsenic, not that it would hurt me, but it would account for the taste.

I've lost count of how many times we have replayed this

scene in my dreams.

Sometimes it's me on the gurney, and sometimes it's him, my torture buddy. However, this version is not how it usually is. Yes, he is still splattered in my blood and bits of skin, but there is a presence behind his eyes that is unfiltered evil.

The male I knew was aware this was his job training and not to take too much pleasure in the task at hand, and yet his sadistic smile said he was loving it.

I long learned that my djinn was insane, but it was always his promises that he'd make everything up to me later that had me melting for him when I finally got my reward.

We have been taking turns peeling and flaying skin on each other for nearly a year. It is truly an art knowing just how taut to pull the skin without it ripping. By the end of the assigned task, there is a neat tray filled with one-inch strips of skin.

I force my head to lift a fraction to look down, my body screaming in agony at the tiniest movements. The light pink of my skin has been removed from nearly everywhere I can see. The only skin I have left is on my feet. I cry out in agony as I drop my head back down. I am sure I look like a pile of exposed muscles with hair attached to the top. He always leaves my scalp for last.

He hates to see my pink mane leave my skull.

He leans over the table, his harsh breath whispering across my exposed muscles. "Oh Mariax, it has been a long session, hasn't it? I could use a break." He picks up a bottle of Vitasmooth and chugs it like a strawberry milkshake. "Ahh, yes, that hits the spot. Would you like some?"

Before I manage more than a strangled groan, he pours the drink over my face. Yellow smoke wafts upward from my skin as I shake and drown on the table.

What is this? Is he seriously going to drown me in Vitasmooth? Suddenly a cloth is scrubbed harshly across my fleshless face.

I inhale my first breath after minutes, letting out a constant scream, my body convulsing on the metal table.

My eyes flash open, but I'm unable to take in the room around me. Sweat glistens across my brow, a bead making its way down my temple and into my hair. I attempt to raise my hand to push my hair away from my face, but my body refuses to comply. I'm trapped within my body. My mind spins out of control as fear clogs my throat.

Sweat has pooled beneath me during the intensity of my nightmare and the subsequent panic, but I can't shake the feeling that I am lying in a cooling puddle of blood. The icy temperature of the blade of the ulu ghosts against my back causing my muscles to seize. He bragged the first time he showed it to me he got it off some people on Earth that used it for skinning animals. I will my limbs to move, only my eyes willing to comply as paralysis takes full control.

Adrenaline spikes in my veins as pure terror claws at my heart with serrated blades. I can't move. I can't fucking move. *No, no, no, no!* The flawed organ in my chest will likely rip through my ribcage at any moment.

Blood pounds in my ears, blocking out all sounds. My vision swims before me, turning the ceiling above into turbulent waves.

As I think the panic will finally drown me in its dark depths, my tail twitches beneath me. With the movement, a little clarity comes back to my mind.

None of this is real. None of this is real. You got out. I am the mistress of my own life.

No one can control me anymore without my permission.

I force deep breaths into my lungs, expanding them to the point of pain, before releasing my breath. Oxygen surges through my blood and to my heart, slowly helping to decrease its rapid rhythm. My body slowly is coming back to me. My tail twitches beneath me, my hands curl into fists before I release them. I don't feel the soft bedding beneath me, only the slick, unforgiving metal of the torture table.

Movement is granted to my body as if something pushed a hand into my chest and jerked my body back to life.

I roll out of bed and land in a crouch on the floor. My motion detector night light comes on, but it's not enough to chase away all the shadows. It only illuminates a cold light from between the bed and side table.

My tail turns into a dagger, arching above me as I seek the looming threat.

Shadows creep across the floor. The trees on the street outside cast ghoulish shapes through the windows by my bed. They writhe and dance across the carpet.

I realize my right hand is slipping from underneath me, and I'm losing my grip as I fall to one knee.

My heart rate keeps steady, but it is still much too fast. My breath is coming out in pants as I warily track every shadow in the room, knowing that a threat draws nearer.

I still don't know what the threat is, but I know that something has me in its hold, something stronger than my mind is capable of creating all on its own. I slowly stand, careful not to make any noise. Clothed in only an old threadbare t-shirt, it's so thin the darkened peaks of my areolas are visible in the stripe of the night light.

Something heavy hits the floor in the kitchen. I twist my head violently to the left as dread coils deep within my gut.

Icy fingers slowly trace down my vertebrae again.

Keeping to the shadows, I crouch walk, using my hands on the ground to hold myself from falling into a crawl towards the sound. I probably look insane going through my own house like this, but only idiots in the immortal world don't take their paranoia as a serious indicator of danger.

I slowly stand from behind the short end of the kitchen island, eyeing the cracked hardwood floor beneath the toppled mortar and pestle. But then my gaze is grabbed by an unusual sight.

Every single one cabinet in the kitchen has its doors flung open. *Fuck me running.*

I make it a point to close cabinets after each use. Leaving cabinets open was one of His terrible habits. The daily frustration of having to practically breathe down his neck and nag him to close cabinets made a deep groove in my mind.

Panic still clouds my vision, refusing to release its grip. The nightmare is continuing.

My instincts take hold of my body when knocking sounds from the door. I growl in response, low and deep. Dashing into the nearest shadow, I press myself into the wall and my tail curves in front of me, blades thrashing with irritation.

Who the hells is at my door? I listen intently, trying desperately to hear past my thudding heart.

"Mistress?"

The doorknob twists, creating a slight rattle as a key is inserted into the locking mechanism.

I slide further around the next corner and behind the bookcase. I can still see the entrance to my suite through a gap between the bookcase and the wall. Light streams from the hallway as a silhouetted figure creeps into my suite and closes the door.

A wicked smile graces my lips as I growl loud enough that they hear their imminent death resound in their eardrums. The voice that called to me earlier sounded familiar, but they should know better. Everyone knows no one comes into my space uninvited... or your death warrant is signed.

Something whacks painfully against both of my ears, awakening my awareness and halting me from granting death's wishes.

Suddenly, I realize I'm staring down into wide blue eyes, pupils dilated with fear. My tail wrapped itself around their neck so tightly that no breath can escape. I hadn't even realized I'd moved.

As if the skin suddenly caught fire, I release my hold, and they drop to the ground. Lauren suddenly coughs and hacks as she breathes, the sudden intake of oxygen surprising her body. She rolls onto all fours, her wings rumpled from being pinned to the ground, and turns her gaze up, glaring at me, tears rimming her fearful eyes.

"Mistress..." Lauren says, but her eyes soften as she takes me in.

"I don't need your fucking pity. I told you never to come into my space without express permission. I gave you access for emergencies *only*," I snap at her, leveling her with borderline hatred at seeing me so weak.

"I heard you screaming...I know you get nightmares; I could hear you from my room. You were so loud."

"If you knew it was a nightmare, then you shouldn't have come."

"I didn't know if you were actually in trouble, though. I had to make sure you were okay. Fuck the consequences. You're my mistress, and it's my duty to be sure that you are safe," she sobs, tears of frustration sliding down her red cheeks.

She's crying. Not because of what I did to her, but for the pain she knows I harbor. My fists clench, hating the sympathy in her eyes.

I forcefully rein in my anger, softening my features. It's only because she cares. "Fine. Thank you. Now please leave."

"But Mistress, I ca—"

I cut her off before she could protest further. "Leave now. I'll talk to you later. I can't... I don't want to dissect my emotions with you right now."

"Mistress," she begs, and my anger flares. She needs to leave before I do something I will regret.

"You're my submissive and your master has given you an order. So, get the fuck out before I tie you down and whip you until your screams make your ears bleed."

She gulps and says quietly, "yes, Mistress."

She practically runs out of the door.

Breathing a deep sigh of relief and loss at the presence of another, I run a hand through my hair. My fingers get tangled in the sweat-dampened strands. I flinch from the slight pain in my scalp, only to be reminded again of him laughing maniacally.

Always saving the scalp for last.

I close my eyes as tight as I can until I see bursts of light shine like fireworks behind my eyelids. I remind myself that I got out.

I open my eyes on the next exhale, internally berating myself for the bullshit I allowed myself to go through. Why do I let the terror of my past control my present? They don't control me anymore. However, that doesn't stop me from being a prisoner in my mind.

I want nothing more than to obliterate these memories from my mind. Anytime I have a dream, whether he makes me bleed or consumes my body with pleasure, mixed emotions flood my system for days.

I fought hard. I'm losing the never-ending eternal war of admitting my true feelings for Him. A millennia was spent with him worshiping my body, torturing me with pleasure and pain.

Tears fill my eyes as the sudden loss strikes. I feel hollow. Empty. No purpose. No affection. No…love.

A searing pang of regret simmers in the back of my mind as I think of how I treated Lauren. I always go on the defensive when I'm overwhelmed, especially after a nightmare. I didn't mean to lash out at her. For fuck's sake, I almost killed her, and then I promptly ordered her from my presence. I didn't even ask her if she was alright.

What is wrong with me? I probably should remove her access code, but if there is an actual emergency… I don't know what to do anymore.

In the living room, I curl up in my snuggly circle chair. The soft fabric cocooning my body in an embrace. I pull a blanket over myself as I stare at the wall across from me. The trauma of my time in Inferuna replays on a clear, vivid, and brutal loop. My mind seeks an escape from the pain.

I always come back to Him for safety and comfort.

Why? Why do I still want him? Why do I need him?

He's still in Inferuna, where I left him. I'm sure he's moved on. He's lived for eons longer than me, so he has plenty of other creatures to think about than me. I thought he was my everything. I let him in. He became my daddy, dominating every aspect of my life within the bedroom and some out of it. I loved being his little one and pleasing him. The praise that would slip from his lips was a balm to my battered soul.

I wish he were as heartless as he pretended to be. I would be better off now. But he was never cruel to me. Although he never gave a fuck about anyone else. In fact, he openly threatened to destroy realms if it meant he could keep me, his Angel.

He was the only one who was allowed to call me that.

Tears cascade down my face as the dam breaks, finally faltering under the intensity of my emotions. Wracking sobs shake my body as I struggle to breathe.

I miss the feel of his body against mine. The warmth of his touch as his large palms cupped my breasts. Waking up to him between my thighs, eating my greedy cunt.

I touch my fingertips to my lips, remembering how silky the head of his cock was as it slid deep into my throat. The indescribable flavor of his release makes my mouth water, and my fingers shake. Arousal slowly begins its patient burn, eating up the lonely desolation I feel.

My trembling fingers glide down the column on my throat, pausing briefly to wrap my hand around the base. The ghost of his hand covers mine. The memory of him controlling my breath as he fucked me. If what he said is true, if he meant it—

I shriek loudly and fist my hair tightly with both hands as I stand, anger and loss swirling deep in my gut. If he loved me, he would never have done that to my best friend. He would not have hurt her.

If I ever see him again, I may just torture him for the vice-like grip he still has on my life—the hold his ghost refuses to relinquish.

But first, I will get an explanation.

The absolute gory display he put on caused me to flee, covered in blood. Without speaking a word, standing up for myself, or demanding answers, I ran like a pussy. Emotions are weaknesses, slowly causing atrophy until power is nothing but an illusion.

I stand at the foot of my bed. The potent mixture of grief and arousal is too much to handle. At least the latter emotion I can somewhat control. I can alleviate the ache, but it's never the same.

I haven't come as strong as I did when I was with Him. He awakened numerous kinks within me: age play, BDSM, bondage, breath play, hand necklaces, anal, blending pleasure with pain... you name it, we tried it.

He taught me how to command and be commanded.

Shoving my satin nightgown over my chest and down my body, I bare my tits and glistening pussy. Shadows from the soft glow of the lamp on my nightstand writhe across my skin in a sensual dance. My tail caresses my hip and slides up my torso until it reaches my right breast. I pleasure my nipples slowly, flicking the blade over them and taking turns with each of them. Smooth yet biting, causing me to draw in a sharp intake of breath.

I cup my other breast in my palm, needing the tender flesh and feeling the heavy weight of it as my nipple pebbles. The peaks harden and throb. My tail shifts into a short blade, leaving a thin trail of blood as it lightly slides down my sternum to my pubic bone.

It cuts through the neatly trimmed patch above my cunt before it shifts into a replica of a monster cock I read about in one of my dark romances. Hard ridges run along the top horizontally, and bumps line the underside. At the base, there is a large knot, not yet swollen.

Closing my eyes, I soak in the pleasure thrumming throughout my body. I feel almost high with the knowledge that I command my body and grant it release.

In the year I've known Hunter we haven't had sex, it's not that I don't want to, but I am trying my best to be a professional. However, the temptation to grab his fat pierced cock and ride is intense and growing by the day.

My teeth sink into my lip as I slide my tail further into my pussy. I rub slow, light circles on my clit, just enough pressure that the telltale inferno has begun to build in my core. Right now, it is just embers, stoking the need in me higher and higher. I moan and curse under my tail's administration.

In my mind's eye, I see Him fucking me, pounding into me as his potent power coats my skin. I aggressively shove the monster cock into my pussy, aiding my body in the torturous climb and meeting its demands. My tail continues, thrusting deeper and deeper with every stroke. The ridges on the top of the dildo rub on my g-spot, making me scream as I near my climax.

I'm massaging my clit in tight circles, increasing the white-hot burn within. The sparks ignite along my skin as pleasure radiates between my nerve endings. Bliss is near, but just out of reach. I can't help it, as the image of Him above me slips into my mind once more.

I stroke my clit faster, adding pressure with the pads of my fingers. I'm positively railing myself with my tail. My body, with the onslaught, moves up the bed with every thrust.

I'm ruining myself, but it's worth it to keep the memory of the pleasure, the ghost of his touch, the fleeting happiness I felt during that brief time I didn't ache with loss and need. The constant craving for a connection with another.

I envision him behind me, one hand wrapping around his wrist as his hand tightens on my throat. He thrusts into me harder and harder. My back bows as his cock hits the sensitive bundle of nerves in my cunt.

I almost come, but I hold it back. I'm not ready. I can hear him as if he is here with me now...

"Are you ready to come? Be a good girl for Daddy and come. I can feel your greedy pussy clamping down on my cock. I know you're close, little one. Let go."

I shake my head no.

"Just let go. You're not the one in control here. You need this. I need this."

The movements of my tail mimic the sounds of flesh on flesh perfectly. I mimic his thrusts the way he used to, just as I wish he still did. In that moment, I realize, even in the haze of pleasure, that I still want him. Despite everything, I need him.

I push the thought away. I'll think about why I am administering some self-assigned punishment later. Now is not the time or the place to analyze these feelings. This is my time to feel something other than devastation.

I make small circles with my tail, rolling my hips in tandem. I pinch my clit between my thumb and forefinger, rolling the hardened bud between them.

My bladder feels as though it will release against my will, but I know better. The first time I squirted it was with my tail and hand. I was alone in my suite in Inferuna exploring my new demon body when I found my G-spot, the slightly rough texture begging me to stroke harder.

I don't need a male to make me reach peaks of pleasure so intense my release roars from my body in strong, short bursts of slick.

His voice sounds again in my mind.

"That's a good girl." The gravel of his voice cascades down my spine and causes me to shiver. "Milk my cock. Seek your release. Take it. Take everything you need from me. Take it because as soon as you do, I'm taking your ass with my thick cock. Come for Daddy, now."

The pressure created by my swollen G-spot is blinding as it shrinks to an electric blue flame, all of my attention focused on it, before exploding outwards violently in a burst of pleasure so intense it borders on pain.

Euphoria erupts, washing away my lingering sadness. My release soaks me as I squirt over and over in powerful jets. My head thrashes from side to side as wave after wave of sensation spreads from my core to my limbs.

I'm soaring in bliss, ignorant of the inevitable plummet.

I scream into the silent space, calling his name against my will, and freefall willingly into the dark unknown, abandoning any pretense of who I am, that I even exist on this plane. I reach out, grasping for the nirvana hidden in the inky void. This is the only escape I know.

The waves of my release crest higher as my orgasm continues. I slow my tail, but the orgasm does not cease, as if some unknown force is guiding it.

I climb my way up to another orgasm before the first one has even abated. The spark is not a full forest fire. Moans and screams shred my throat as his name repeatedly leaves my lips. The orgasm builds and hits its peak. There's nowhere else for it to go but out.

I don't exist anymore.

No name.

No body.

Nothing but a bundle of pleasure remains. My toes go numb, and my breath comes in quick pants. Colors scatter across my vision like a kaleidoscope. I'm barely moving my tail anymore, but the knot at its base is fully seated inside of me.

My orgasm subsides. Reality returns and awareness practically bitch slaps me across the face. My eyes crack open, and I swear a shadow darts across the ceiling. I dismiss it as my post-orgasmic haze muffles my senses.

Rolling onto my side, I examine the truth. I admit to myself that I loved him. I loved him fiercely with everything my being possessed. If he never became my daddy and cared for me, I wouldn't have survived Inferuna. I love him even now, but I refuse to forgive and forget.

That was one of the most powerful orgasms I've ever had since coming to the human realm. It just clarifies why I haven't had any long-term relationships. The fact that I do love him terrifies me to my very essence. The epiphany is not welcome.

What the fuck am I going to do?

They say that time heals all wounds.

FUCK THAT.

Time doesn't heal shit.

All it does is give you more time to bury your pain or drown in the darkness.

He has always lived rent-free in my mind, but since the night I allowed weakness to crawl in again, thoughts of him have plagued me. The wound on the organ in my chest was ripped open anew.

These wounds are silent killers. From the outside, everything appears healed, but beneath the surface, the hurt festers and rots, poisoning the blood and spreading until it's too late.

It's impossible to forget the night he told me he loved me. I didn't and still don't believe I am meant to be loved. There is nothing about me that screams, 'amazing partner, will provide affection and endless patience'. Maybe he thought he loved me, but I find the reality of the situation severely depressing. However, his words are still branded into my memory, impossible to remove.

"Angel, this is not something I take lightly at all. It's been something I've wanted to tell you for years. I only recently realized the truth when it swam to my consciousness after a dream I cannot recall. I kept these thoughts to myself, which was selfish, but I thought I was protecting myself."

His downcast gaze raised the hairs on my arms. His guilt is misplaced, and I go to speak to tell him that, but he continues.

"I worship you. You don't realize what that means for me because I haven't told you much about myself and I probably never will divulge all of my secrets. However, I

will answer any question, even if it brings excruciating horror to my psyche. But you need to know this. You are my nirvana. You. Are. Mine. Whether realms, time, or existence separate us, you will always be mine. I laid claim to you the moment you became a presence in my life. I am a male possessed. I have thought about locking you in a cage and chaining you to a wall so you can never leave me."

"The words 'I love you' are too simple to encompass my feelings. They have been said so many times over the centuries that they are now a platitude that holds no power."

"I don't believe that love is something that you really can say with words. It's more than that. Love surpasses everything in reality. I will burn this fucking place to the ground to keep you. I don't care who I have to kill, torture, kidnap…list any atrocity you want. I will do it if it means keeping you as mine. You are my nirvana. You are my solace, what is keeping me sane in this shithole. If I didn't have you, I would have decimated this realm the second I placed a foot on the soil. Fuck any other being in this place. I don't give a shit about anything or anyone except you."

The memories of him never cease.

It is not often that I have been granted a reprieve since I fled Inferuna, that I have not had a nightmare or a panic attack sneak up on me. I lie on my bed, tangled in my sheets in the aftermath of my climax.

I clench my fists in frustration, the fog of pleasure dissipating too quickly. A flare of pain ignites in my right hand. I lift it into my field of vision, noticing for the first time the deep gash in my palm and blood smeared all over my hand and bedding.

It's then that I realize I hadn't just slipped from imbalance when I woke up in a panic. It was my blood that caused me to slip. I didn't feel the bite of the cut at the time.

I roll over until my head and neck hang down over the edge of the bed to search the floor. The edge of a blade lies within a smeared handprint, the books from my nightstand scattered around it. Awareness causes my heart to stutter.

I haven't laid eyes on that dagger in decades.

How did it end up next to my bed where I could step on it at any moment?

I vividly remember sealing it in a box and placing it underneath my bed in an attempt to forget it ever existed. I eye the dagger again and reach down and pick it up by the tip of the blade with my pointer finger and thumb. Rolling onto my back I scooch my ass further up the mattress so my pillow supports my head once more.

As I encircle the handle with my tacky fingers a different memory is triggered.

I stand at the kitchen counter in our suite about to put the hot mug of coffee to my lips when a hand covers my eyes, completely obscuring my vision. His scent washes over me and I relax into the body behind me. I grin like a fool and finish taking a sip of my coffee anyway, allowing the weight of his hand to remain in place.

A dark chuckle rumbles through his chest, tickling my back. "If you insist on wrapping your lips around something..."

I shake my head, smirking. I set my mug down and pry his hand away from my eyes.

He grips the counter on either side of me, caging me in. "I have something for you, little one."

A spark of joy fills my chest at his words.

He places a thin rectangular box on the counter in front of me. A sapphire silk ribbon is tied in a bow across the middle. I tug on one end of the ribbon, causing it to unravel before lifting the lid to the box and revealing my present. My joy remains, but curiosity takes precedence as I peer into the box.

"It's beautiful, but why would I need this?" I lift a detailed, hand-crafted dagger from the box and hold it across both of my palms.

He runs an index finger from the tip of the blade to the end of the handle and whispers in my ear, "Although you are more than capable of defending yourself. Too many scenarios exist where you may fall to harm despite your abilities."

He lifts the blade from my hands and trails the tip lightly over my collarbones and down my sternum. Goosebumps rise on my skin at the seductive bite of the metal.

"It cannot hurt to give yourself the upper hand against any adversary. If all else fails you, my blade will always heed your call."

I drop the dagger to the bed as if it seared my flesh. Covering my eyes with both hands, I shriek in frustration.

Will I ever be freed from the memories clawing at my psyche?

CHAPTER 11

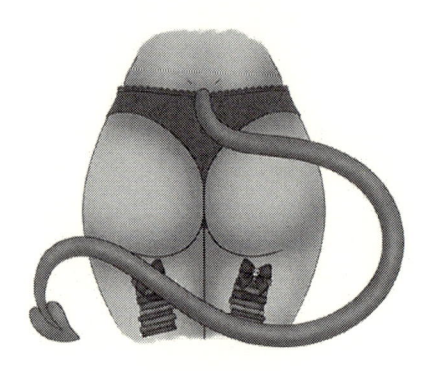

Mariax

"Mistress, please, may I touch ye?"

I stalk to the center of the chamber, my heel clicks echoing off the walls, and my tail swishing with every sway of my hips.

My Pup is bound with his arms above his head by a rope soaked in wolfsbane. The rope is anchored to the table by a thick chain that runs down to the floor directly beneath. He's not fully naked yet, but we'll get there in due time.

I run my hand over his jeans-clad thigh just so I can see him twitch. "Why would I do that, Pet? Have you been a good boy since your last session?"

"Aye! Aye, I have been sae good. I even restrained myself from chugging."

It took me a while to get a grip on his use of the Scottish dialect. Every once in a while, I had no clue what this massive brute was saying. But I could honestly listen to him talk about nothing all day and be soaking from the deep burr of his Scottish accent.

Chugging is a new one for me. I assume it means jerking off, but he is going to sweat under my ministrations while explaining.

I glance down at the visible bulge in his jeans, the outline of his knot pronounced along with his erection. I run a bright pink manicured nail down his naked tattooed torso and hum to myself. The black ink of his huge mountain range tattoo spanning from shoulder to shoulder is stark against his tan skin.

"What was that?" I let a bit of venom seep into my voice. "Correct me if I'm mistaken, but aren't you to address me as Mistress?" I pause a beat, really making sure he comprehends what's about to happen to him.

"Aye, Mistress. Sorry."

He's so quick to please me, and I have to hold back the smile that wants to spread across my glossy lips.

"And another thing, you know you are to explain to your mistress the meaning of your Scots' words so I can understand that gloriously capable mouth of yours. You better tell me, or you will not like what comes next. Pain is only the beginning."

Occasionally, I must remind my subs who is in control, especially when they are an alpha.

These big, strong alphas are desperate for release. However, they must be willing to train their minds to let go and naturally default to being submissive while in a scene with me. By putting someone else in control, they can reach new levels of pleasure. Meanwhile, I get to play with a different part of their psyche.

Hunter has been working for nearly a year to earn his collar, but he still has a lot to learn.

"Aye, Mistress," Hunter swallows, his Adam's apple bobbing. "Chugging means jerking off...to pleasure myself. I wish I could chug to my thoughts of ye, Mistress. The way yer tight arse fills out anything ye wear…"

Looking down at Hunter, I realize he got lost in a euphoric state. Subspace is a glorious place to be for those that reach it. I need to check in with him, and this warrants a reminder to use his safe words if he needs them. His pulse feathers beneath my finger as I tap a nail on his carotid artery.

Wrapping my hand around his throat, I lean down, pressing my lips close to his ear, and whisper, "Is there something you aren't telling me, Pet? Do you remember your safe words?"

For once, Hunter is silent. He is not the type to be speechless. Standing, I saunter over to my wall of pain, planting my hands on my hips. Looking over my array of toys, vehicles of pain and pleasure, I decide to go with a classic, so much pleasure that it becomes painful.

"What are your safe words?"

His eyes slowly refocus on me. "Green, yellow–" he stops to clear the gravel from his tone, but it's no good, "–and biscotti."

"And what is your color now?"

"Green. Definitely green."

I smile and my tail whips around from behind my back, transforming into a wicked blade and nicking him on the cheek.

"Oops, sorry, Pet. Sometimes my tail has a mind of its own."

I bend down and slowly lick the shallow cut. The taste of his rich, warm blood is delectable. Hunter moans loudly in appreciation. I slip my sharpened tail into the waistband of his jeans, nicking him once again.

His breathing hitches, but it isn't out of fear. Hunter loves danger and is an adrenaline junkie. In fact, he has begged me more than once to include knife play, but only with my tail. My tail turns him on, almost to the point where he is obsessed with it.

I cannot wait to use it for pegging him sometime soon.

I deftly flick the tip of my tail up, slicing through his

jeans and belt and down his pant leg. I rip the rest of the fabric free with my hands. Catching the edge of the fabric with my tail, I toss it to the floor. As my eyes slowly graze up Hunter's body, I am greeted with his fat, pierced cock jutting up straight from his body.

There is no way I am able to put his chastity cage on over that raging monster.

An idea springs into my consciousness and an evil grin creeps across my face. I wrap my tail around his length from base to tip with slow, practiced motions, tightening my hold with each coil. Just as he's getting comfortable and his breathing picks up, I transform my coiled tail into a pliable icicle, leeching any warmth from his cock.

His response is immediate and violent, even in subspace. Hunter tries to pull away from me, but he barely makes any progress before he starts swiveling his hips like a worm caught on a hook. The metal table underneath him and his bindings keep him from escaping like vulnerable prey.

The cold temperature does its job, and his dick softens enough for me to put his cage on.

I put the first piece of the cage on by carefully pushing each of his balls through the ring, followed by his now softer dick. I have to be careful I don't catch any of his skin on the post that sticks out of the top of the ring.

The ring is large enough to circle his entire package comfortably, including his knot. Tucking what I can of his cock head and shaft into the slightly curved metal. It is designed to be put on when he is completely soft, and in his semi erect state it is a challenge. I connect the shaft piece with the post on the circular one to trap him fully, locking the device.

Pleased with my handiwork, I take a moment to admire him. I tip my head to the side in a brief moment of amusement, and realization swirled with desire. Hunter's knot reminds me of my own toy when I shift the top of my tail into a monster cock replica.

Leaning over the table, I rest my breasts on his chest as his eyes dilate. "Are you in much pain? Is your little cage pinching or chafing anywhere?"

"Nay, Mistress." The rolling of his Rs and the deep burr of his Scot's accent sends a throb directly to my clit.

The lust wafting from Hunter is also heady, but I need to ensure he is being taken care of. The mistress-submissive dynamic only works if the mistress knows her submissive's needs, health, and breaking point.

I breathe deeply. Fuck, he smells amazing, the fresh coffee notes of his scent swirling in my thoughts. I would love to let him loose and ride his cock to oblivion, but I remind myself I have to remain a professional.

"Good, then you can wear your cage this entire session and maybe for the next. If you still have refrained from self-pleasure by then, I will free you from your cage. Today, as a reward for being a good boy, you may pleasure your mistress."

His pupils fully dilate, hardly any of the pale blue showing. Shifters are so much fun to work with. They could be loyal and obedient to a fault. I lean down further, placing my neck just above his mouth, and let him inhale my scent.

Backing up from the table, I bring my leg up and slice through the rope, binding his wrists to the table with my stiletto heel. He sits up quickly, but is careful not to move from the table. The welts on his wrists from the wolfsbane are already healing.

"How can I pleasure ye, Mistress?" Hunter rasps as he eyes the deep V of my jumpsuit.

I assess his growing arousal and decide he would like to taste what his cock is missing out on. This will remind him why he is in his cage and increase his torture. The harder he grows in his cage, the more it pulls on his balls. I won't get the image out of my head of his knot swelling, trapped by the cage, and his pre-come leaking all over the polished steel any time soon.

"Well, Pet, would you like to taste your mistress?"

I take a finger and slide it through the bars surrounding his swollen head, gathering the pre-come and bringing it to my mouth. I gently suck on the tip of my finger.

Hunter starts visibly shaking from holding himself on the table. "Aye, Mistress. Please, may I eat ye out? I can smell yer arousal from here. Ye smell so fuckin' good. Please, Mistress."

I tilt my head to the side, still gently sucking on my digit, deciding to let him play. "Come over here and get on your knees."

Hunter jumps off the table and lands in a crouch directly in front of me. His mouth is less than an inch away from my soaking pussy.

He doesn't realize I want this just as badly as he does.

Fuck, do I want this. I've wanted Hunter to pleasure me for the entire year we've been doing this together, but I wanted to remain distant for professional reasons as we got to know each other on this deep and intimate level.

Now seems like a good time to start. He's fully behaved for every session for the last six months and finally has fully sunken into the role as submissive.

He looks up at me through his thick lashes, his pupils are completely dilated.

"Good boy." I untie my romper as I watch the need pulsing from his body. The black fabric slides to the floor, and I kick it to the corner of the room. I stand before Hunter in just my black ankle boots. "Alright, Pet, take what I give you and make sure it's good. My displeasure results in your punishment," I order, as my bladed tail trails down his body

from shoulder to hip.
　　Blood slowly wells from the shallow cut.

CHAPTER 12

Hunter

Fuck! I love this lass.

I kneel on the floor in front of Mistress Mariax, hands gripping my thighs, head bowed in submission.

Finally, I get to taste her sweet cunt.

It's been over a year since I started coming to The Snuggle Pit. I know my mistress has been attracted to me since our first session when she whipped my arse with her tail for trying to shift. I could smell the arousal rolling off her in waves.

Every session since the first, her sweet scent becomes more fucking tempting.

She's fighting the attraction, but I know my sexy Cheetie will be a goner after I eat every inch of her sweet pussy. I will take all the pain of my cock being trapped in a cage gladly for a wee taste of her coming on my tongue.

"Good boy," she purrs, and the sound of her voice, and those two words, stab my groin with a fresh wave of need.

Her black outfit falls to the floor, and she kicks it into the corner. The lass stands before me in just her sexy as fuck boots, her curvy pink skin on display just for me.

The urge to bite her thigh and tear from the confines of

my submission is almost too strong.

I can see her large tattoos on her thighs and rounding towards her arse, plus the smaller ones smattered on the rest of her legs.

I can't wait until the day I'm shoving my cock into her tight arse and reveling in the sound of my name ripping from her throat.

The combination of soft curves and muscles on my demon is utterly mouthwatering. I thought I would only be attracted to her body, that I would loathe her dominating personality, but she surprises the fuck out of me every time we are together.

I fight the fierce urge to lift my head and devour her naked pussy that's just inches from my face before she's given her permission. I won't allow my impatient impulses to ruin this for me.

In my peripheral, her pussy piercing glints with her slick honey. The scent of her arousal hits me again, telling me I'm not the only one fighting the need to fuck. The dark, possessive part of my soul beats its chest, roaring *mine*.

"Alright, Pet, take what I give you and make sure it's good. Do not forget, my displeasure results in your punishment," she orders.

I inhale sharply as Mistress Mariax slowly drags her bladed tail from the base of my bowed neck down my spine, applying just enough pressure to break the skin but not maim.

My cock jolts in its cage, causing searing pain and pleasure to build in my ballocks to a nearly unbearable level. My knot slowly grows as the pain spurs it on. The way this cage is designed is pure torture, and I cannot fucking get enough.

She designed a custom metal cage just for me.

It is welded and re-enforced at any point of connection.

The harder my cock gets, the more my balls pull upwards. My knot squeezes in the metal O ring above my balls, but there isn't anywhere for it to go.

A low growl builds in my chest, my body thrumming with how goddamn turned on I am right now. I've wanted to ask her for knife play scenes more often, but we have only done a few so far.

Mistress grips my shaggy hair with both hands, her nails biting into my scalp, and yanks my head so I am looking up at her.

Her tail continues its slow, taunting trail up and down my spine. Warm drops of blood run over my arse cheeks and land on my upturned feet.

I need her pleasure. I need to give her everything until she is dripping down her thick thighs and my face is drenched in her desire.

Without any preamble, she shoves her cunt onto my face. Her taste and scent overwhelm me at once.

Holy shite. Fuck, fuck, fuck, dinnae come!

The pressure of my cage nearly borders on pain and my balls clutch like I might implode within seconds.

The urge to touch her with more than my tongue takes hold of my senses, and I grab her arse cheeks, my large hands nowhere near containing them. Driving my tongue into her hot core, I focus on my mistress' needs. Her arousal coats my tongue and it tastes like the most decadent hazelnut cream.

I could feast on her for days.

My breath is taken from me as her tail wraps tightly against my throat. I stare at her, her arousal coating my lips and beard.

She swallows and glares down at me.

"Did I give you permission to remove your hands from your knees?" she questions in a breathy voice.

Mind foggy with desire, I fight my mind for an answer.

"No, Mistress. But—"

Her tail tightens around my neck further. My Adam's Apple rubbing against it as I swallow and attempt to force air into my straining lungs.

"No excuses, Pet. You may touch me when I will it," she commands, her voice now clear and biting.

I can only nod in acceptance, black dots appearing in my vision and lungs burning.

She loosens the hold of her tail but doesn't remove it. "You may re—"

I lunge forward before she can finish her sentence. Running the flat of my tongue from the wee space above her arse all the way to her clit, I glide around her hardening bud, making sure my tongue piercing brushes against it, but not granting her what she wants.

"Oh gods!" she moans.

She's close to abandoning her mistress mask already.

I attack her clit, brutalizing it with my tongue piercing with every stroke.

She mutters in a language I've never heard, and I don't fucking care to define it right now. I risk a glance up, a couple of my hairs tearing with the slight movement. Her head is thrown back in pleasure, her long braid tapping her arse with each of my licks. Her pouty lips part slightly as her breathing becomes uneven, every muscle in her body taut.

I'm going to enjoy making her lose control. She will no longer think of me as just her submissive.

With that thought, the rungs of my ladder attempt to escape my skin as my cock throbs endlessly. I groan loudly into her cunt at the mixture of pleasure and pain.

She grinds into my face with abandon, her moans and curses floating to my ears. I alternate between nipping her lips and licking up every last drop she gives me.

My cock is so hard. I can't do this much longer before I blow my load like the fucking pup she dubbed me.

Growling, I bite her clit and then immediately start sucking on the hard bud while my beard rubs against her sensitive flesh.

"FUCK!" Mariax groans through clenched teeth. "Hunter, do not stop. If you do, I will slice your throat open."

She's now riding my face with total abandon. I don't take her threat idly. My Mariax is a dangerous creature.

She releases my hair and digs her nails into my shoulders for more balance.

I can hardly breathe with how hard she's forcing my face into her pussy with each swivel of her hips, but I dinnae give a fuck. If I die here, at least it'll be an epic story the pack can tell.

I know she's so close. I've been wanting to make her come since I first became a regular at Mariax's sex club. I circle her dripping cunt with two fingers, seeing if she'll stop me. When she only looks down momentarily to bite her lip at me, I slip two fingers into her pussy, fucking her in the only way I've been given permission.

"Hunter! I—bastard motherfucking cocksucker!" She shouts.

My wolf rises, wanting to bite and claim. She has no idea she's called me by my name multiple times, telling me that her little mistress' mask was slipping.

Shite, hearing my name on her lips is so fucking hot.

Jolts of pleasure race to my cock. Ahhh fuck! My cock tries to break out of the confines of my cage but pain races through my knot and balls. *FUCK!*

I double my efforts. My lassie *will* come on my face.

I growl and rub my beard aggressively directly against her clit. I add a third finger easily and curl them with every thrust. Stroking that elusive spot. She is so full and tight around my fingers, gripping them tighter as she nears her orgasm.

I have to see the look of pleasure on her face. I glance up to another fucking incredible sight that will be a permanent addition to my spank bank.

Mariax's eyes are closed as she pants and moans. Her tail, which left my neck at some point, is toying with her nipples, pulling on the barbells pierced through them. Her tattoos are glistening from the sweat beading on her pink skin.

Murder is in her eyes when she catches me watching her. Her mask is gone, but the fear of me coming before her is real.

"Don't sto—" A shriek interrupts her threats as I pull her clit piercing with my teeth, brandishing my tongue piercing like a weapon against it. But she is determined to remind me who is in control. "If you stop…" she takes a deep breath, "I will never let you out of that cage," she growls.

I lower my eyes, grinning against her pussy. I suck her clit and piercing back into my mouth, quickly flicking it with my tongue. Her pussy pulses on my fingers.

Adrenaline screams in my blood, knowing I am about to make her come all over my face.

I feel her clit swell under my tongue and then I'm granted the best surprise of my life. The purest form of female pleasure pours down my throat and I swallow—it's only fair—as she squirts and screams my name. She comes so fucking hard her knees buckle.

I grab her waist to steady her while I lick up all of her come. She twitches with every swipe. Her pussy is swollen and soaked, and it's the sweetest honey pot I've ever tasted.

I will do everything in my power to make her mine. Make my Mariax admit she desires to claim me, too. When she came on my tongue, she started a dangerous game.

I can no' wait until we finally fuck and she gets to play with *my* dominant side.

CHAPTER 13

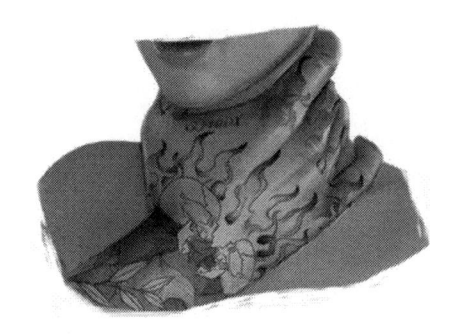

The Primeval

I get lost in thoughts of Mariax as I drink and lounge on my plush bedding. I never used to care for extra soft or over the top comfort in my bedding, but she made me see the error of my ways during the years we lived together.

She always had the sweetest smile on her face as she dreamed.

I often stayed awake well into the night just to watch the rhythmic rise and fall of her chest. Something as mundane as watching her sleep brought me peace, to see her calm and, for a moment, happy.

My lower body slowly relaxes into the mattress, the soft contours of the pillow top cradling my body, as my torso, shoulders, and head rest on the many fluffy pillows.

As I think of her, the notes of my whisky seem to change to her unique scent of chocolate, hazelnut, and petrichor blended together, lightly sweet and alluring. It is just as strong now as it was the first time we slept together, and I buried my face in her neck.

When she transformed her tail into a knife and pressed the sharp edge into my dick, I was so proud. I enjoyed testing her, leaning into the blade to see if she would remove the blade or allow it to cut me.

I miss her company. Just being in her presence was always a buoy for my spirits, lifting me out of my frequent dark moods, even if I was irritated with her, and her sassy remarks. Our constant bickering and teasing are the soundtrack of our days.

I'll never forget the look on her face when I gave in to my desire to have her, no longer holding back any of the feelings I wanted to unleash on her. To own her. To mark her as mine in as many ways as I could.

I demanded she submit to my will, but she fought me. Mariax was always a challenge, so strong willed and unafraid to deny me.

However, denying me came at a price. Defiance brewed in her eyes when I pressed my hand against her mouth and reminded her just what her brattiness would cost her.

"Only good girls get rewarded."

I smile and take another sip of my drink. I won in the end, it was inevitable.

Our joining was powerful, realm shattering even. I had never felt a passion like ours, and filling her with my cum was blissful and so rewarding.

She had many different types of smiles, and they always helped to clue me in on her thoughts. The sly smile when she was up to no good. The sexy smile that meant she wanted me and would have me, no matter what. The small, sad smile when she was being brave for my sake. And the smile that lit up her whole being, the smile that she saved only for me...until she took on a new submissive.

Hunter. The Alpha of the Appalachian Pack. What makes him so special that she bestows the smile meant for me on him?

Jealousy, an emotion I don't feel, often burns like poison in my veins. *She is mine.*

I watched them together. Dominant and submissive.

They were both so deep into the scene that they never noticed anything was amiss, not that they would have been able to feel my presence either way, cloaked as I was. But I missed nothing.

My little one's rapturous expression was a knife in my chest. She held his lips tight to her pussy by his long hair, riding his face to chase her release. Hunter's back steadily became a patchwork of shallow cuts as she continuously ran her sharpened tail all over it. His tattoos became nearly invisible from her ministrations.

Mariax's mistress mask not only dropped, but shattered in the moments he pleasured her.

I cannot dwell on seeing them together any longer. I won't. Because, at this rate, I'll vancate to him this instant and slit his throat.

A cruel grin lifts one side of my face before it falls.

No. If I do that, Mariax will hate me further for killing her little fucking mutt.

She is my obsession and has been for thousands of years. I will always desire her, but right now I crave her pain more. When we were together, our dark essences fused into one menacing force. And I will never satisfy my ache for our power to blend and stay entangled for eternity.

CHAPTER 14

Hunter

The damp earth and thick scent of pine are a welcome reprieve from the stench of the city. I trot through the woods in my wolf form, thoroughly enjoying the freedom to drop all of my barriers and be myself. Normally I run with Charlie, but he had something to do with his mate tonight.

This is the only time I feel free besides when I am subbing for Mistress Mariax.

I pick up the pace and run through the trees, dodging the trunks expertly. My canines glisten wetly as a wolfy grin spreads across my snout.

The woods and all of its tiny inhabitants welcoming me as I run for the sheer pleasure of it.

If I do not let my wolf out to play regularly, it's much harder to control my emotions. Everything is heightened, even in my human skin. Caging my wolf increases the risk of someone suffering their final death at my claws.

I enjoy running in the park, it's my favorite place close to the city. The full moon rises in three days, the anticipation of its call thrumming in my blood.

The wind shifts and I'm distracted by the enticing scent

of leather, bergamot, and wood smoke. I slow my movements as I approach the densest part of the woods. Staying hidden within the shadows of the trees, I silently hunt for the source of the mouthwatering smell.

The brilliant white orb hanging in the sky shines through the canopy, the branches forking across it appearing like skeletal limbs as I let my wolf's instincts take over. It wants to hunt, so I give it freedom to chase that scent.

My darker side loves admiring the silent beauty of the woods at this time of night. It's almost ethereal.

A male stands in a partial clearing. The canopy above is broken, allowing the moon to illuminate the space. He's so still he could be mistaken for a statue; the only indicator of life is the minute rising and falling of his chest.

He must have a death wish, wandering alone in the woods so close to the full moon.

I'm frozen in wonder as he suddenly sprints into the thicket of trees nearest to him.

Godsdamn, he's fast.

I give chase, my curiosity turning into a deadly hunger. The thought of tearing into his flesh is a little too enticing. Luckily, I have control of my wolf, so I don't plan to truly make a meal of him, but I can't deny that side of me that's human and wants to eat him in a very different way.

Whoever this male is, he's wandering as if he hasn't a care in the world.

Why is he here?

I thought I was getting closer to him, but with every beat of my paws against the forest floor, his shadow stretches further between us.

As I stare at his silhouette, he disappears.

My wolf slides to a stop, scraping the layer of dirt underneath the cover of leaves before bursting up in a cloud as my claws dig into the earth. I gaze around warily, the black eyes of my wolf allowing me to see as if it were daylight.

My heart increases to a rabid staccato.

The power of the male I was stalking unleashes in a burst, sliding over my skin like a heavy weight. There is no part of my coat that is not weighed down by the unimaginable force. I have no idea what type of creature is threatening me, but I refuse to let him win.

I am not defenseless, and I will tear him to bloody strips.

My wolf continues to scan the surroundings, getting impatient and unnerved. My wolf doesn't know where his back should be facing, wary of the vulnerability.

Quicker than he vanished, the male reappears only a foot or two in front of me.

He stands calmly, gazing down at me with his hands in his pockets. The material of his perfectly fitting shirt displays the curvature of his strength with every inhale as it tries to contain his impressive physique underneath.

He is all muscle, toned and cut, it is evident even through his black v-neck t-shirt. The moon's glow sets off the healthy pallor of his skin. It's not as dark as my tan "surfer boy" looks, as Charlie says, but he's not pale either.

However, the lighter tone of his skin serves to highlight his many tattoos. Of the skin showing outside of his clothes, only his face is untouched by ink.

My previous thoughts of how I'd like to eat him come back to the forefront of my mind, but I don't let them take over. He might be a threat, and I do not take that lightly.

The low menacing growl of my wolf shatters the eerie stillness of the night. He laughs, a deep, resonating laugh that turns to lust in my veins, his black shaggy hair falling into his eyes as he does so.

My eyes are drawn to the large, detailed black rose that covers his throat, it's so realistic I could count every petal.

"Is that your growl? That's fucking cute," he says, his

stunning violet eyes crinkling with deep-seated humor.

My rage wins out over lust.

How dare he imply that I'm not threatening, that he is not crossing the line into death by just being in my presence? I do not take kindly to beings that think they're better or stronger than me.

I bend my rear legs and launch myself off of the ground. I take him by surprise, hitting him square in the chest with my front paws. When his back meets the ground, I'm still on top of him.

His neck is vulnerable as his head cracks against the dirt. I take advantage of his weakness and aim for his tattooed throat with my fangs. He grabs my muzzle when I'm mere centimeters away from tearing out his jugular with my canines. I attempt to snap at his face, but he has both of his large, tattooed hands wrapped around my muzzle, holding me at bay. I press all my weight on his chest, and he doesn't even flinch.

He stopped laughing as soon as I took him down, but he's not struggling at all, and I cannot fathom how that's possible.

Lycans might not be the strongest supernatural creatures, but being the alpha of the Appalachian Pack gives me extra speed, strength, and virility. Shit, most consider me the most powerful wolf on this side of the country, and this dickbag thinks he can manhandle me?

His scent is trapped in my sensitive wolf nose, overpowering my thoughts and senses. My wolf's sense of smell is hundreds of times stronger than any human's. But as his power still ripples from underneath me, the trigger to shift back into my human form is intense.

I struggle to fight against it, but I can feel his magic forcing its way into me. Impossible. He shouldn't be able to do this.

Against my will, I shift.

Fully naked, my entire lower half is lying on the man below me. My hands pressed hard into the grass on either side of his head. His hands, which never left my muzzle, are firm on either side of my bearded face. One of his thumbs skates across my lower lip, and my breathing accelerates.

I try not to panic. This male forced my shift. The thought has me floored.

He's clearly above me in the food chain, yet I want to make him submit to me. It's unlikely, and I know it will be a battle, but I have to try.

"What the fuck are ye?" I ask, keeping my face passive.

The right side of his lip pulls up into a smirk as he gazes down my body, pressing his dark aura against me. "What I am is of no consequence. Just know I am bigger, stronger, and willing to devastate your entire existence," he says deadpan, but there is a manic gleam in his eyes.

His hands tighten along the sides of my face, scraping down my beard, the rasp of his nails loud in the quiet night. Goosebumps rise across my exposed flesh, and he removes his hands from my face.

I'm stubborn, not willing to let myself go down to this threat. *No way in hell.* Who the fuck does he think he is?

Some damn god?

I shove myself up from the ground and he follows suit, staring down at me, being only an inch or two taller than me in stature.

"How dare ye force my shift," I manage to spit out through growling. I get in his face fully aware that I'm naked and not giving a flying fuck.

The creature has the audacity to laugh in my face. Literally, I can feel his breath tickle my cheek because of how close we are standing.

I want to take a step back, to widen the space between

us in case I need to act quickly against him.

He finally stops laughing and smiles cockily, dimples showing in both of his cheeks.

Damn, if it isn't handsome. The realization just makes me dislike him more.

"Again, why would ye force my shift? That is a huge overstep. Have ye not heard of boundaries?"

"Because I can," he states smugly and winks.

"Ye are dangerously close to feeding the soil beneath your feet yer entrails. Why are ye in my forest?"

"Do you have some kind of claim on the dirt beneath your feet?"

"Answer the godsdamn question!" I yell, my hackles rising higher with every word that passes his lips.

He smiles a little too brightly and explains. "I've come to this forest my whole life, scruffy wolf. Just because you're the current Alpha, doesn't mean your kind has always owned it. We allow you to make it your territory."

"And who is we?"

"That is information you are not privy to for a reason." His tone darkens and a flash of something takes over his features, but it's gone too quickly for me to identify.

Something seems off about him being in *my* woods in the first place, let alone commanding my shift.

He steps closer, shrinking the space between us further. "I smell that you like to play."

"What do ye mean by that?"

He takes a deep breath in through his nose, pulling in the air surrounding us to fill his lungs. "You're drenched in my favorite scents, Scruffy," he says with a sly smile.

"And what would those be?" I ask, too curious not to.

"Leather, chains, lube… and someone powerful. These are all evidence of a very good time," he explains, reaching out to slowly run the back of his tattooed fingers down my lower abs and onto my happy trail.

Grabbing his wrist, I halt his progression south.

He ignores me and continues speaking, "However, you also reek of arousal, like you've been waiting days, perhaps weeks, to spend," He practically purrs, "is the person I scent on your skin not taking care of you properly?"

He needs to back off right the fuck now. I will not have him disrespecting Mariax.

"Enough questions. I'm not interested." I turn to leave, but something cool, yet silky, grabs my bicep. Looking down, I try to make sense of what is holding me in place.

The thing is filled with dark, powerful magic, somewhat see through but firm against my skin. Shadow magic? I turn back towards him, unnerved by the change in events.

The tendril of shadow releases me and seems to absorb back into his body.

"I see the look in your eyes. Inside you is a good little puppy who wants to trust someone so much that you'll let them lead you, collar you. I see it in alphas all the time. The weight of responsibilities over such a large group of people is heavy. I can help you with that burden."

Hunter chuckles, "saying he's too late, I've already got someone to handle all my needs."

"Why not two?" He questions be, raising his brow.

"Because that'll violate my contract with my domme. If ye are so familiar with the lifestyle to know all of that, how is it ye dinnae know that a submissive is loyal to their dominant?"

Something flashes across his face too quickly for me to decipher it. His composure was once more back in place. Did I just see that?

He smiles slyly, but his cheek ticks with annoyance. "Fine, what about a date, then? We can get to know each other. That's not a violation of your contract, is it?"

Although it's in our contract that we are both free to date

and fuck, it doesn't feel right to me to fall headfirst into anything with this strange male. However, I am very curious to learn what makes this male so intriguing. "If I agree to a date, don't ye think ye should introduce yourself first?"

He lightly palms his forehead. "Of course how rude of me. I get tackled by a werewolf–"

"Lycan," I correct him.

"Tackled by a lycan unexpectedly, but forget to introduce myself in the process," he teases. "You can call me Brad, and you are?"

"Hunter," I admit a little sourly.

CHAPTER 15

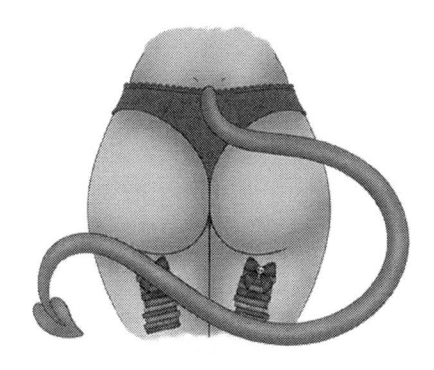

Mariax

Two thousand fifty-seven years in the past...

Walking into a literal replica of a high school, a human science classroom was not what I expected when I was told to report to Torture 101 for yet more training.

I scan the room, noting that only a few students have arrived and claimed their tables. The tables are wide enough for two bodies to sit at, side by side. However, there will be no way to sit comfortably on the backless stools.

Starting with torture early, I see.

I spot an empty chair in the far-right corner of the room and sit my pink ass down, grudgingly grateful that there is room for my tail on these idiotic stools. I glare around at the other initiates. Not everyone who enters torture training is forced to be here or is even a torture demon. Honestly, half of my training sessions have been filled with volunteers of all manner of beings. I even heard a rumor that a djinn will be in one of the sessions.

Now *that* I would love to see.

The instructor is taking forever to show up.

With a deep sigh, I lean on the table and rest my cheek

against my palm and slip into my few memories. I was crafted from the ether months ago and was given little time to acclimate to a functioning, self-aware being. And now, I have been thrown into training without a say in the matter.

I know it should excite me to learn all the ways to inflict pain on a soul...but truthfully, I don't really give a shit, even though I was literally made for this job. I will do what I need to survive in this place while serving my time.

The little free time I have to explore Inferuna is spent wandering the streets and mentally mapping every path that might lead to a viable exit. They have to have some way to leave this realm, and I'm determined to find it.

The odoriferous stench that accompanies the city comprises too many scents to pinpoint what all of them are. However, the scent of brimstone and fear hangs thick in the air, causing my stomach to clench.

Fear has a distinct scent. It's noxious, heavy, and oily, as if someone took years of fermenting noxious hot, unwashed sweat with a hint of urine ammonia and compacted it into vapor.

The streets that snake through broken-down buildings, shacks, and tents are comprised of shitty old brick. It makes me wonder how any of this is still here if the place is as old as they say, with it crumbling at our fingertips. All streets lead to one central point, making it the center of the wheel, and each street leading off from it, the spokes.

The streets are all unique in their own way.

One leads to the Potentate, another to the Amethyst District, which is where most medium to higher ranking Inferuna residents live. The Black Market stretches between three of the spokes. Last, Oleander Forest lies down the last spoke. Within a few steps of walking down the path it becomes gloomy and dark. Oleander flowers springing between the tangled roots of the trees.

I have yet to find anything but the inky darkness of the abyss surrounding the city. Far above the shithole we call a city, a perpetual, smokey red haze obscures the view of anything beyond it. Sometimes I stare at the drifting haze, wondering what the Potentate is concealing.

During one of my treks, I discovered the torture chambers. I now know they gave me immediate access to these chambers because of my torture-demon status. The rooms incinerate anyone that has not been granted permission when they try to cross the threshold.

I found the door cracked open and slipped inside, following the scent of rotting blood and fear. It surprised me to meet another demon who had mastered her resting bitch face just as well as I had, possibly even better. Once I witnessed her glorious scowl, I knew we had to be friends, whether or not she wanted me.

Tiffany is a pain demon. Feeding off the inflicted pain of souls, she has the ability to penetrate the mind to trick it into thinking what it is suffering is so much worse. It isn't just physical pain either that she feeds on, so the torture cells aren't her only cafeteria.

She is so godsdamn beautiful. Her light-blue skin stands out against her long, curly ultramarine-blue hair. Her horns begin at her hairline and curl down toward her ears. Her large, dark wings rest against her back, their blue hue so dark, they appear almost black.

Meeting Tiffany in the torture chambers was a surprise, but not as much as finding out about her job assignment.

She has one of the worst jobs a demon can have, tasked with cleaning the tools, bodily fluids, and anything else splattered in the torture chambers in exchange for allowing to feed.

Unlike me, she grew up in Inferuna and was born from the womb of her demon mother. I am grateful not to have a family. Hers is made up of some of the shittiest creatures in existence.

The worst being her father who sold her to an apex predator, the closest he could get to the top of the Inferuna hierarchy, to pay for the debts he was drowning in. That dick for brains threw away his daughter to be free of his greed.

Nope, I'm better off without someone to think they own me enough that I can be used for their advancing downfall.

Demons come in many subspecies, as proven by the creatures around. However, torture demons are something entirely different. The run-of-the-mill demon is still capable of decimating towns and wreaking havoc among the humans, but torture demons are created to do one thing: torture the souls of the damned with efficiency and detachment. We are not born into this realm or any other. We are forced into being. I was never a child, never learned as I grew or made friends.

I came to exist, fully formed and deadly.

I refocus as the prick of an instructor struts into the room like he's a peacock trying to find a mate.

He's an imp demon.

I've seen enough of these demons around Inferuna to know they usually have a massive complex. To make up for their short, stubby, ugly bodies and faces, they act like they are better than everyone else and at the top of the food chain. Little do they know how easily their lives could be snuffed out, thrown over the edge into the gaping abyss and wiped from existence. There are only a few ways to kill a demon, and the abyss is one of them.

Does this fucker expect us to be impressed by him?

He's stuck instructing beings on how to torture souls. How mundane and mind-numbing of a job that must be. Session after session, starting over with new minds to bend and break...infusing their brain matter with disturbing torture techniques and fueling their hunger to inflict pain.

I would feel sorry for the bastard, but he chose his path. Maybe when I'm done serving my time, I'll do him a service and sever his head from his stumpy body.

I smile and stifle a cackle at the imagery playing out in my mind.

Movement at the door causes my senses to ignite when a male abruptly halts his movement into the classroom. I can feel his eyes scan me, willing me to turn toward him like everyone else in the room.

I ignore the pull to meet his stare. Instead, I glare at the instructor. The new male smells incredible. Leather, bergamot, and wood smoke assault my nostrils.

Why is my body acting like this?

I feel the thrill of fear—no, not fear, a true threat—zip through my body.

Sensing this male is old, older than any being I have ever met, explains those feelings. He knows more than many of this plane has forgotten due to his age. That would explain the undercurrent of something not quite of this realm in his presence. The thrum of his power sets my body on alert like he could rip me in two without breaking a sweat, caressing my skin and seeking a way to infiltrate my senses further. There is no kindness to this creature. He would destroy me mentally, physically, and emotionally.

Despite the slow burn of fear, I feel my pussy getting wet from his scent alone.

My young body has known pleasure—nothing that was life-altering, but I had fun. I've messed around with some of the creatures down here, and I don't discriminate. Male, female, demon, or other, if it can give and receive pleasure, I am all in. But I have never reacted instantly to anyone before, which is pissing me off.

I don't like elements out of my control. Anger surges throughout my body, trying to surface, but stops just under my skin, simmering and ready to strike.

The enticing smelling male continues his swaggering gait through the rows of desks, sending out his dominant male aura through the room as he moves. He gracefully lowers his tall frame onto one of the horrid stools; the stool that was, until a moment ago, sitting vacant next to mine.

I need to focus on succeeding in this course. This is my purpose. If I fail torture training, I'll be recycled back into the ether. The male's scent is too distracting.

My mind whirls with disconnected thoughts, some full of lust and some an intense need to dive into his brain and sift through his being. *What is he?*

The slow instructor interrupts my thoughts by finally beginning the session.

"Welcome to Torture 101. I'm Instructor Lasandre. Sit down, shut the fuck up, and learn your craft. I have assigned you to become proficient in the art of torture. You must serve as a professional torturer for a minimum of two thousand years after your initial fifty-year training period."

He pauses to glance around the room, noting the emotions playing across the faces of those present.

"I don't know what you sorry fucks did to end up here. However, you will either fail your training and we get to snuff you back into non-existence or become something of a nightmare should you pass."

The instructor drones on about the importance of torturers and their place within the hierarchy of Inferuna. There will always be plentiful souls to torture. However, other beings here were sent to serve as punishment, and occasionally, some volunteered. There are many throughout Inferuna, as expected. Still, only a select few choose to do anything other than drink themselves into oblivion at one of the bars on Lamenting Street.

There are a few interesting supernatural creatures

throughout the classroom, such as a minotaur, siren, leprechaun, vampire, and a cyclops to name a few. It is way too easy to tell which ones volunteered, were forced, or were created to be here, like me.

The volunteers sit tall, shoulders back, and chin lifted with pride. Idiots. The forced ones are almost cowering, leaning back as far as they can without toppling off their stools. And the torture demons look, well, bored. It is not new what is expected of us. It is part of our makeup to crave giving pain. The only difference is we haven't honed the skills awakened in our brains. We lack the practical hands-on training that will see us not being recycled.

I feel eyes on me from my right, but I refuse to acknowledge his presence.

He has been staring at me and obnoxiously tapping his pen to no beat I've ever heard since he sat next to me twenty minutes ago. He also has an annoying habit of weaving a wisp of shadow between his fingers, the motion similar to one walking a coin across their knuckles.

I don't feel like entertaining this asshole's interest or playing fifty questions. He is clearly one of the imbecile volunteers. They have to be seriously psychotic to volunteer for this shit. Does he get off on torturing people and need a new avenue to slake his lust?

What is he, anyway? His presence is palpable, his dominating personality overwhelming. I don't think I could fully ignore him if I tried, and I *am* trying. The room feels smaller with him in it. The power he exudes thrums against my skin.

Why am I even thinking about him?

I focus back on the instructor to view the list of torture practices we will learn to employ. He turns toward the whiteboard and scribbles a list:

Bamboo shards

Poison

Waterboarding
Paper cut method
Boiling
Flaying flesh
Burning
The list continues endlessly.

About an hour later, I'm about ready to slam the instructor's skull into the whiteboard until his skull cracks. How can someone make something like literal torture techniques boring?

His voice has a nasal quality, a slightly high pitch, and a cadence that would make a goddamn sloth jealous. The only time he essentially reanimates is if someone interrupts his practiced speech.

A blur of color shifts in my peripheral when a demon turns in his seat to stare in my direction. I can just make out around my tablemate's large frame a gaze full of malice and it immediately puts me on edge. Is he looking at me or the dick next to me? He then grips the back of the neck of the demon to his right, causing it to slump forward onto the desk as if asleep.

Somehow, no one else noticed their brief exchange.

Swifter than even I can process, Instructor Lasandre lashes out. Claws as sharp as blades tear through the flesh of the unconscious demon sitting in the next row forward. I didn't even see the professor transform into the more lethal part of himself.

His face morphs into a permanent snarl, thin lips pulled

back to expose two rows of sharp, half rotten teeth. His arms elongate so far that his knuckles drag on the ground. Wicked claws replace his hands, with seven on the end of each arm. But his eyes are the creepiest aspect of this form. They are a muddied yellow with black spots of different sizes that cover his entire eyeball; they remind me of a banana peel well past ripe. There is no pupil to speak of and it is impossible to tell where his stare settles.

Huh, I guess that's why he teaches torture courses.

Blood sprays the front rows as the demon's head is severed from his neck. Some beings lean back, and others throw their arms above their head as if they can shield themselves from the expelling carnage. The entire front row of desks gets soaked in blood.

I muffle my snicker with my hand, my body trembling with the effort. Those poor bastards were in the splash zone. I roll my eyes at the sheer stupidity of everyone else's fear or concern. The demon will regenerate in due time, so it's just a minor punishment.

They had been learning about far worse things.

Demon blood is thick in the air with the scent of the brimstone that helps make us. The front rows of tables are dripping with the crimson liquid. The headless corpse of the demon slips off its stool and thuds on the floor.

"And that is why you don't fall asleep in my course." The instructor states simply, transforming into his normal, boring appearance, with the bonus of blood splatter on his cheap clothing.

"Everyone turn to the being sharing your desk. Meet your new torture buddy."

My body tenses, muscles rigid with the unwelcome announcement. Turning my body to the right, I face my new *buddy*, trying my best to impale him with the invisible daggers shooting from my eyes.

I'd guess he is close to a foot taller than me. His body is

well muscled and toned, but not thick or bulky. His inky hair is messy in an effortlessly sexy way. It's shaggy and would come down just past his ears if I were to pull a piece straight down.

And to my dismay, he seems to be covered in tattoos, at least from what I can see on his arms and throat. I make a conscious effort to keep my jaw from falling open as I spot the intricate black rose on his throat.

His shaggy hair matches the dark stubble covering the bottom half of his face. The facial hair accentuating his high cheekbones and shapely lips. They're far too pouty for a male, yet it works for him. His bottom lip is fuller than the top, a light imperfection that only serves to enhance his stunning but intense features.

As he assesses me in return, some of his hair falls over his forehead and partially blocks one of his intense purple eyes. No, purple is too ordinary of a shade to describe their hypnotizing depths; they're violet but bright and iridescent, like a tempting flame glows behind them beckoning me to dive into their perilous pools.

"Well shit, angel, it looks like we will be spending a lot of time together," he says cockily, his voice deep and gravely.

I narrow my eyes, intent on making my opinion of having a mandatory partner clear. "Who do you think you are, you piece of fuck? Don't call me angel again. Angels are nasty creatures that are made to look innocent and glorious. Have you ever met one? Douches, all of them." My voice is pitched low and quiet so as not to alert the instructor or other demons of our conversation.

"Oh, are we being conversational now? You've been ignoring me the entire lesson."

I snort a laugh. "Yeah, I noticed your pitiful attempts at gaining my notice. Do you know how hard it's been to listen with you tapping on the fucking desk? Are you that desperate for a scrap of attention?"

His dark eyebrows shoot up his forehead in disbelief.

Well? His tapping had been annoying! I was considering breaking his finger the entire lesson.

"Seems like you're practicing how to be a rude brat who doesn't know a superior being when she sees one."

"Wow. I'm a brat? Are you kidding me? If you're expecting a subservient torture buddy, you'll be sorely disappointed," I say, seething.

"It'd be best not to upset your new torture buddy. Otherwise, I can add a little more salt to your wounds." He leans forward with a broken grin that promises malice. "You know, while I'm delivering them."

"I could tell from the moment you walked in that you were a cocky bastard. Why do I get stuck with the biggest dick in the room? Go fuck yourself, Cupcake."

"Cupcake? Do I look like the type to allow pet names? How about you call me Daddy, and if you're a good girl, I'll allow you to taste my cock later."

I cackle, leaning closer to him.

"Yes, you sure as shit are a cupcake. A deliciously sinful treat that calls out for attention. Pretty on the outside, but is nothing more than a soft, quick treat that will never satisfy your craving fully. Something that'll do nothing but rot your teeth." I cross my arms in defiance, brat mode fully engaged. "I do not doubt you taste delectable, but hard pass."

My ears ring in agony when the instructor slowly grates his claws together, making an eerie screech. The students get quiet quickly, turning to face the instructor en masse.

"Okay, okay, shut the fuck up and let me finish my obligatory speech."

A few snickers sound from the right side of the room.

"Torture buddies are partners for everything from now

until your training is complete. You will eat, sleep, and train together. Everyone will be assigned suites with two bedrooms and a common space to share. When you are not in training, you are *not* allowed to harm your partner in any way, mentally or physically. You are also not allowed to fornicate. I fucking mean it. End of discussion. There are consequences for those who choose to ignore protocol."

His last statement is news to me. Why would they assign everyone torture buddies and then also room them together? They can't expect no one to screw.

The male next to me clears his throat. "Why are we not allowed to fuck our buddy? How can that possibly be an issue? We are here to learn how to torture flesh, but we cannot participate in the pleasures of it? *That* is a bunch of bullshit."

I groan and slump my head onto the desk. *Well, shit, aren't we off to a great start? Draw his attention to us you worthless fuck!*

"First of all, you don't get to question me. I don't give a flying shit that you're a djinn and older than Father Time's balls. Do it again, and I will take it out on your pretty new torture buddy, Mariax."

My desk mate must have a hearing problem because he interrupts again.

"I can and will question anyone I want. Your life is a blip compared to my grand existence. Why would I care if you take out your irritation on her? We are to torture each other anyway, correct?

A deep growly gurgle comes from the instructor's throat as he ignores my buddy and continues. "Second, sleeping together creates feelings that have no place in torture training. If you would have let me finish, you would have learned that the purpose of rooming the partners together is a practice in patience and resistance."

"What gives you the authority to–"

"I said to be silent. In my classroom you are my underling. If threats of harming Mariax don't assuage you to behave, maybe expelling you will?" The instructor questions with a glare before moving on. "Now, being a torturer is not an easy gig. You can become addicted to causing pain, enthralled by the very thought that you hold the power to stop the pain or create more. It also helps your mind make a connection to stay grounded and build an unshakable foundation within yourself to prevent the mind from going mad, thus making you as useless as you already are."

The room is silent, not even a retort from the annoying djinn next to me.

The instructor makes a shooing motion. "Once you're done meeting your buddy, get the fuck out.".

My personal space shrinks as he grazes his knee against mine, shifting towards me.

I cannot contain my irritation with him any longer, despite the smoldering emitting from his violet irises. "Are you a psychopath or what? You announced, like a giant bag of dicks, that you plan on screwing me in front of the entire room," I whisper yell.

The last thing I need is more attention.

"I won't deny it. Yes, I am a dick. However, you weren't curious why the Potentate would enforce such harsh rules?"

"No. I just want to be left alone, and that includes from you. Furthermore, I don't give a fuck if we are allowed to fuck. I am not a female who will throw her legs open for any male."

I arch a brow, daring him to challenge me.

He seizes my chin, slowly sliding his hand down my tattooed neck to rest it at the base. He applies slight pressure, my pulse races against the pads of his long tattooed fingers.

I really hope he cannot scent my body's interest in him.

He bares his teeth at me, and his face contorts as if battling some internal struggle. He applies more pressure against my throat, and I close my eyes to hide my growing attraction to his rough handling.

However, my eyes fly open when he speaks again so quietly I can barely hear him, even with my demon hearing.

"You don't know anything about me, little girl. I was interested in you before, but you just laid down a challenge I cannot resist."

"What challenge?" I whisper back, entirely bemused.

"Tell yourself all the lies you wish, but you desire me. I can read everything your body is telling me," he responds, leaning closer until our lips are inches from each other.

"I would never sleep with you, forced proximity or otherwise."

He ignores my rebuff and continues speaking quietly. Our lips are so close I swear I can feel the ghost of contact as his lips move.

"Screwing you before would've been fun. But now? Breaking you and making you submit to me will make the game much more thrilling. Can you resist the call of a male dominating you, ruining your pussy, and being your daddy?" He inhales audibly, seeming to take in my scent. "Come to think of it, you've probably never had a daddy, have you?"

That's it. I'm done with this shit.

His eyes widen in surprise when my tail whips out and shoves him in the chest. He lets go of my throat, falls off the stool, and tumbles onto his ass.

Everyone in the room turns to watch the drama unfolding.

He groans in pain and lays his head back on the floor.

I stand over him, my tail swishing in irritation, hands clenched into fists at my sides. Faster than he can process, I straddle him and hiss in his ear, "I will never be your submissive."

He scoffs, "Ah, but I know exactly what your body and mind need, even if you have yet to realize it."

I slowly pull back enough so he can see my expression, my hair now hiding us like a curtain as it hangs down around his face. "I look forward to torturing this pretty boy flesh. See you around, *buddy*."

I stand abruptly, my tail slapping him in the face in the process, and then storm from the room.

CHAPTER 16

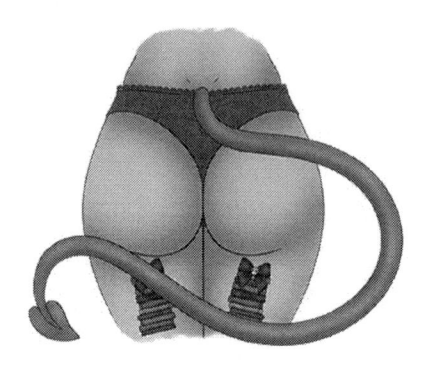

Mariax

Current day

You can do it, Mariax. Seriously, grab it by the balls and get to work.

Does it have balls?

On occasion, I have to give myself these pep talks. There are a few clients that, while in their true state, are fucking disgusting. No one has dreamed of anything like my current client, the Mayor of Philadelphia.

With his glamor applied, he is a handsome politician, silver streaks thread through his chestnut hair, and blue eyes hold the citizens in his snare. He looks just old enough to know the inner workings of politics, but is young enough to be sexy. Overall, an ideal image for most humans of the voting age.

I had to train for fifty years just to torture souls, and these humans are allowing what amounts to infants to make enormous life decisions? That concept is insane to me.

Anyway, the mayor is a horrifying mess of gray rolls, tentacles, eight eyes, and leaking orifices that look like assholes speckled all over his tentacles.

Inhaling deeply, I step into the room with grim determination.

Mayor Gloam is already lounging on the couch of his designated chamber, P3. His tentacles hang grotesquely over the back and sides.

In any other circumstance, I am pro-tentacle.

They're so sexy when not attached to a repulsive bag of dicks like the client in front of me, although my anger doesn't stem from what he is, but from what he's threatened me with.

This room has floor to ceiling and wall-to-wall rubber mats. The couch is covered in those plastic sheets that human grandmas used to cover their ugly ass floral furniture. The cover squeaks and creaks when you move and stick to any exposed skin.

"Mistress! Hello! I am so happy to see you again," he exclaims with true cheer.

I put on my best sultry look and try not to vomit in order to maintain my professionalism. "It's always a wonderful to see one of my best clients," I force myself to say with enthusiasm.

"No one knows how to pleasure me like you," he compliments. "I find the humans of this city easy to scare off if I am in the moment and…oops, forget my glamor."

He smiles with sharpened yellowed teeth.

I swallow the bile in my throat and cross the room to sit on the opposite armrest of the couch, placing my elbow on my thigh and resting my chin on my hand.

A key point about my oozy client that often has my spine tingling with annoyance and dread is that when Mayor Gloam comes, the entire room splatters with it.

No, he is not a being with one simple gland that releases cum. He has more than I can count.

The ooze he leaks is pre-cum, and it is a constant sluggish drip from his asshole-like orifices while he is at

The Snuggle Pit.

I have hit my max level of toleration. I am too old for this shit. This will be my last session with him. He can either have one of the trainee demons or move on.

Once I wore a face shield, thick plastic gloves to my elbow, a rubber apron, and a rubber bodysuit to his session. He did not take kindly to this, and threatened to make it known to the supe and paranormal community that my establishment wasn't willing to cater to ALL beings' needs and desires.

At the time, I couldn't afford any loss to my business. He knew it too; but that is no longer the case.

My outfit for Mayor Gloam now comprises a rubber halter top that exposes my midriff, skin-tight rubber pants, and black combat boots. I put my hair up in a long fishtail braid, beginning at my forehead and running down my back. If I must face a monster, I will face it like a mother fucking Viking warrior queen!

"So, Mayor Gloam," I say with a forced smile aching my face. "How can I pleasure you today? I know you're very busy and need to get back to business as soon as possible."

My smile turns into a grimace as he sits up and runs a slippery tentacle up my thigh. The sheen of his slime trailing in its wake.

"Oh, my dear, I am in no rush today. I want to explore all the pleasures you have to offer with that tail of yours."

Not my poor tail. It doesn't deserve this kind of offense. It's a beautiful tool, a weapon for the senses, and using it on him feels like I'd be defiling it.

"You have been teasing me for years about how it can bring the most intense pleasure…and pain. But I am still not sure about the pain aspect," he says with a gurgling laugh. "I would much rather just be pleasured by it."

This is one of the worst parts of my business.

Fuck this day. One more session, I tell myself.

I constantly feel the threat of vomit at the back of my throat. No matter what his request for drawn-out pleasure will be, I will get this session over with as soon as I fucking can.

Schooling my features, I purr, "Alright, I will wring pleasure from you with my tail as requested. But on one condition. You must restrain from touching me. This scene requires total trust on your part, and mine."

"Yes, Mistress. I do look forward to your ministrations."

I can tell, as pre-cum is creating a puddle around him on the couch, steadily dripping onto the floor.

"Well, just in case, I am going to bind your tentacles. It won't be painful unless you pull on your restraints. These are made for beings with your type of slick flesh, so you don't slip the restraints."

I stand and push the back of the couch he is laying on down. It is more of a futon, but he doesn't have to know that. The Mayor laughs as his folds of flesh ripple and roll from the movement.

I yank on three of the tentacles on the left side of his body and cuff them with the extra large spiny cuff I have permanently attached to this couch. There is one cuff in each corner. I make quick work of the rest of his tentacles.

I step back, feeling a slight release in my chest. He can't touch me. I can do this. Take this creature by the balls and get this over with. *Does he have balls?*

"Do you consent to the use of my tail to pleasure you as I see fit?"

"Yes, Mistress, do continue. I fear any more of your ministrations with those cuffs will have me coming before we know it."

Noted. The kinky fucker does like the slight pain of the spiny cuffs.

I whip my body around, closing my eyes for what must be done. I rub my tail and apologize for everything it is about to endure. Opening my eyes, I pivot on my heel, walking with purpose to the couch.

His gaze travels all over my flesh.

I shift my tail into a massive dildo. The length of it is almost my full tail. *Maybe he will hate this method of pleasure and never come back.* My tail starts shaking in quick movements, much like a vibrator, while I cradle it in my hands.

I risk a peek at the mayor and see his eyes–all eight of them–are honed in on the dildo. I reach my tail to the nearest piece of slippery flesh, continuing the shaking vibration.

Immediately, moans and gurgles issue from the top of the couch. I ignore them as I drag the dildo over each of his leaking holes. Precum continues to flow steadily, and I'm grateful for the grippy soles of my combat boots, the floor becoming increasingly slippery.

I dip the tip of the dildo into the hole closest to his cockapuss. I am not familiar with his foreign reproductive system. The Mayor's eyes have closed, but he is clearly trying not to rip his tentacles in half by the cuffs.

I piston in and out of the hole with my dildo tail.

The Mayor shakes, splashes of Pre-cum flying from him. Several splashes hit me in the face, and I hold back the curse and vomit, threatening to leave my throat.

Let's get this over with.

I pull the dildo out and insert it into the tip of his appendage. Really, it is the combination of a cock and a pussy, hence cockapuss. It is long and thick, but has a deep hole in the center. The pussy like hole is continuously opening and closing, clenching on the dildo.

"Mistress, oh Mistress, this is too much! I cannot handle

another second of this torment. Make me cum now!"

Normally, I wouldn't cater to this blatant disrespect of my title here, but I want this guy gone. He asked for it.

I close my eyes, preparing for impending doom. I pump my dildo tail into his cockapuss as fast as I can, vibrating on max.

Wet gurgles, moans, and groans are coming from the Mayor. He's lost the ability to speak. The cockapuss starts pulsing on my tail, and then, with one strangled gurgle and a vise-like grip on my tail, he erupts.

I shift my tail to normal, rip it out of his grip, and into a rudimentary shield. I hold my breath as a wave of oozy cum bathes the entire room, myself included. The mayor is wailing in ecstasy, but has ripped several tentacles out of his cuffs. He tries to grab for me, cum pouring out of him, eyes glossy.

I slip in the mess, backing away from him and landing on my ass.

"FUCK! I told you, no touching!" I scream so loudly, the mirror on the right side of the room shatters.

I didn't mean to act so unprofessionally, but a girl can only take so much before she wants to peel her own skin off and incinerate it.

I told him not to touch me, and with his threats of the past and his continued need to violate my personal space every time he's in this room, I can't take it anymore.

My boots slide around as I find my feet, using my tail to keep my balance as I careen out of PR3, leaving the convulsing mayor semi-restrained to the couch.

A repulsive shudder ripples down my back.

Sighing, I let the spray of my double-headed shower work the thick coating of cum out of my hair.

Fuck this day! Actually, fuck this week. I am so glad I am done with Mayor Gloam. When I end my day questioning if I was the one being tortured, something is seriously fucked.

Why do I insist on accepting clients like that?

CHAPTER 17

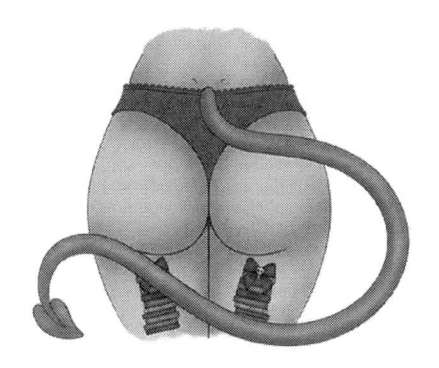

Mariax

I enter TT's, the tattoo shop belonging to my best friend Tiffany, and lean against the door frame, crossing one booted foot over the other.

TT's is small but cozy. From the doorway, I can see most of the building due to the open floor plan.

Directly in the entrance is a carpeted waiting room. A plush as hells royal blue velvet sectional commands most of the space. A round coffee table sits in the center, cluttered with binders of tattoo drawings for inspiration. An enormous flat screen TV rests on a low chest as a makeshift stand.

The scent of pumpkin emanates from countless candles on every available surface, screaming cozy fall vibes.

An ostentatious saltwater aquarium is built into the wall behind the clear case the register sits on. A yellow, blue ring octopus, which is one of the smallest but most deadly types of octopus there are, crawls through the eye of a cyclops skull planted into the seaweed and sea anemone with its own horde of clown fish in the spooky set up they call home.

However, the couch is by far my favorite part. It is

covered in big squishy pillows and throw blankets. I've spent more time than I can calculate hugging one of those pillows to my chest while reading, napping, or talking to Tiff as she works.

Directly behind the back of the sofa is the wall of the first booth of two. Each contains a padded adjustable tattoo chair, a small rolling stool, a stainless steel tray to put all of her equipment on, and a cabinet full of supplies. The walls that make up each booth are just tall enough to offer privacy, but even a shorter customer could look over them.

Tiffany looks like your everyday human tattoo artist when she is in her shielded form. But today she hides nothing.

Her true looks are heart-stoppingly fierce and gorgeous.

Her skin is a brilliant ultramarine blue. It's unfortunate she has to hide her tail, midnight blue wings, curving horns, and blue skin because of the humans. She's also got an ass that makes you want to bite it. I know from her bragging that some of her sexcapades involved just that.

Tiffany is a fellow demon gifted with a ton of powers, one of which is mind seduction. Yes, it works on me, too…when she wants it to. Anyone who can force their powers on my mind is undoubtedly insanely powerful.

Her client today is certainly a supernatural. The giveaway? The dude has huge golden wings. They're splayed and hanging down either side of the table to keep his backside uncovered.

I wonder if he would take me for a ride.

Tiffany is a work of art herself.

She's tall, curvy, and has a personality that draws everyone in immediately. Her dark curly hair is pulled back into a messy bun; surprisingly, she has very few tattoos. For someone who enjoys forcing ink into someone's skin with a needle moving about two thousand times per minute, she *loathes* having her flesh marred.

Why inflict pain on yourself when you get pleasure from giving pain to others?

The *tzz-tzz* of the tattoo machine is constant. Somehow, I find it soothing, like a lullaby.

Walking over to the nearest unoccupied tattoo chair, I slide down until I'm comfortable and close my eyes.

It has been a long week. Seriously, *fuck this week*.

My clients are causing me too much physical and mental anguish. As I enter the realm of dreams, the buzz of the tattoo machine cuts off, and I sneak a peek to find Tiffany staring at me like she's only just realized I was there. I close them again.

"Mariax! The fuck you doing here again? Your clients not behaving?" she asks as a smile spreads across her face and her lip ring, pierced through the middle of her bottom lip, glints from beneath her head-lamp.

Tiffany is the only tattoo artist I know who uses a headlamp to see every minuscule detail of her art. The results are astounding. I have seen tattooed portraits that could jump off the skin of their eternal wearer and have a true form, from a deer prancing through a meadow of wildflowers to seascapes that make me yearn to reach out and touch the choppy surf.

Not moving or opening my eyes, I respond, "Since when do my clients behave? Their definition of behaving and mine are two very different things. If I had it my way, 'behaving' would involve them acting badly on purpose so that I could torture their flesh through punishment. I want to torture something so badly that it aches. I never had to fight this need when I worked in Inferuna."

Sighing, I sit up and swivel to face her.

There has been some intense shit nagging me, and Tiffany is always up for a vent session.

I hop off the tattoo chair, coming closer to get a better

look at her art. She continues to tattoo the ass cheek of the huge, winged male.

He looks human except for the wings and the slightly luminous glow of his skin. On second glance, I think he may be an actual angel. Fucking angels, as I've said too many times in the past, never trust an angel.

They are douchebags. Every. Single. One.

Although it will be fun to watch this angel in pain in one of my playrooms.

Chuckling, I pull a padded chair out from under the desk and straddle it, facing Tiffany.

As I sit down, she glances up, blinding me with her headlamp. "Mar, what's got you so fucked up? Come on, spill the whisky."

She lowers her head and resumes her work, the male inhaling sharply as the needle pierces his flesh. The soothing *tzz.... tzzzz* is a perfect background for what humans call 'girl talk'.

Rolling my eyes at the idiotic term, I say, "well, guess whose day got fucked up by Mayor Gloam?"

Tiffany begins chair dancing to Harry Styles, serenading us with the background music of the shop. Chair dancing means she moves the lower half of her body on the stool with wheels in dance while her upper half stays stationary, not a twitch that would mar her flesh art.

"That motherfucker was there again? He's the most revolting piece of shit I've ever seen. I don't know why you still put up with that douche face."

"You know why. You were there when he threatened to ruin me and run me out of the city in the early days of The Snuggle Palace like I was the bad guy in one of those shitty Westerns."

"Yeah, but you're the badass boss of one of the best dungeons in town now."

"Actually, this was my last session. Thank fuck for that. I don't want to push him on one of the other trainee mistresses, but there is no way I will work with him again. Plus, there is a chance he won't come back..." a little cackle escapes as I explain.

"The fuck? What did you do?" she asks as she dry wipes the freshly tattooed skin before dipping her needle for more ink. "Don't get me wrong, congrats, girl! You deserve better. You're *the* Mistress of Philly. You don't bow down to slimy political bastards like him."

"Weeeeeeell, you know how he has those revolting tentacles that ooze? I strapped them to the couch with cuffs that would slice him if he pulled on them or tried to slip his tentacles out. Long story short, he begged me to pleasure him with my tail. I am still sorry I had to put it through that."

I scoop my tail up from behind me and pet it in apology. It has been limp since the episode like it is pouting or even traumatized. I might have to get it therapy even after what I just forced it to do.

Eyeing Tiffany as she tattoos away, I continue telling her what happened, including the moment I stormed out of PR3.

"Damn, that was a horseshit of a day. Seriously Mar, douche canoe Mayor Gloam needs to be banned from The Snuggle Pit. He's not worth the stress and nausea."

Mr. Angel groans in pain as Tiffany tattoos a particularly tender spot on his fine ass. Of course, he can't handle the pain. He's an angel and, therefore, a little bitch. I'd call him a pussy, but a pussy can handle pain, being used, stretched and filled beyond capacity – he wouldn't deserve such a wonderful title.

Mr. Angel interrupts our conversation. "Fucking hell, I can't take another moment of this!" He bellows, glaring at Tiffany over his shoulder.

She smiles sweetly at him, but I see the gleam of amusement in her eyes. "What would you like to do, Jamie? Do you want to call it quits for today and reschedule the rest of your session for another day?"

Jamie sighs deeply and nods.

He looks like he's had the worst day of his life. It's just an ass tattoo. I stand by what I've said about angels; I don't give a shit what anyone thinks. I will die on this hill.

Tiffany wraps up his scrumptious ass with Saniderm and reminds him of the care instructions.

As soon as she's finished, I spank him hard on his bare ass cheek, "Well, Jamie it's been fun. Pull up your panties and fly back home. Better mentally prepare yourself next time, wouldn't want to tap out again." I cackle.

He grumbles, pulling on gray sweats over his very naked body.

"See ya, Tiffany. I'll call to reschedule."

He smiles at her before whipping his head towards me and glaring. He tosses his long dark hair over his shoulder and stomps out of the shop.

Tiffany and I stare at each other. The door closes with a loud bang. We burst into laughter for several minutes. I laugh so hard tears are running down my face, and a cramp grips my side.

"Oh fuck, that was too funny. Please let me know when his next session is. I'd love to pay him a visit," I say as I wipe the tears from my face.

Tiffany smirks but shakes her head. "Oh no, Mar, that was fun, but I have a business to run. I will, however, take a picture of his face masked in agony for you AND tell him you've been asking about him."

"That'll do, Tiff." A couple more soft cackles escape me.

"Well, now that half of my day is free, why don't we

give you a celebratory tattoo? A big fuck you to Mayor Gloam. May his tentacles ooze anywhere but near The Snuggle Pit."

"Fuck yeah. I will never turn down the opportunity for a new tattoo. I've needed some self-care, anyway." My thoughts and emotions have been an utter mess.

Tiffany cleans up her station and wipes the chair before I hop on it. Settling into the smooth leather, I release a deep sigh. It feels like home, being in the tattoo chair, my best friend by my side. This is just what I needed after the clusterfuck of a week.

"What kind of tattoo did you want today, Mar? Are you feeling something tiny and cute, badass, color, or line work? You know I could go on forever with the options."

"I trust your artistic sensibilities. Surprise me. I'll take a nap while you zone out in your art," I say, yawning.

"Okay, you asked for it. When you wake up with a big dick tattooed on your ass, don't blame me," she sasses me and winks. "Take off your pants and lay on your left side."

"Yes, Mistress Tiffany," I purr.

She chuckles and demands, "Oh fuck off, just do what I said."

"What, I don't even get a *good girl*?"

Smiling, I shimmy in the seat and slide my black leggings off, leaving my thong firmly in place. I'm not making it easier for her to tattoo something on my ass. Tattoo naps are fucking epic. I will be dead to the world while she works.

I lay back down and turn over on my left side. Tiffany places a blanket under my head as a pillow. I listen to Tiffany shuffling around her workspace. The snap of clean gloves sliding on and the *tzz tzz* of the tattoo machine begins.

Getting tattoos feels different for everyone.

Some describe it as a lit match dragging along their skin;

others think it feels like their flesh is tearing. For me, tattoos are relaxation.

When someone has been through all the trauma and mind games I have, the act of getting a tattoo can be therapeutic. I can embrace the pain on my terms. I choose to have this pain, and I know it is temporary. The adrenaline coursing through my body from the initial prick of the needle makes me feel high, especially after a five to six-hour session.

As Tiffany continues her work, I feel my eyelids drooping. Warmth wraps around my body, and sleep tugs me under. The last thing I hear is Tiffany singing along with Harry.

I startle awake when a sharp pain pinches my ass cheek. Looking over my shoulder, I see Tiffany staring anywhere but at me. I continue to glare at her until her eyes swivel back to me, the picture of innocence.

"What? You were snoring so damn loud, Mar, I couldn't hear the music."

"I don't snore, bitch," I hiss.

"You do, but I also want you to tell me what else is up with you. You've been holding back on me."

"I just have been feeling anxious, like something is out there, maybe."

But I delay the moment she will begin the inquisition by admiring my new tattoo. As usual, she has made a fucking masterpiece. The tattoo spans from the side of my ass, reaching to just next to my knee.

She combined two of my favorite things: books and flowers. The design is broken up into two halves. When viewing it straight on in front of me, the design starts high on the outside of my right thigh.

I gasp in surprise when I view the portion on the left. This side contains Orpheus' skull and Faunus' ram horn. These two attributes pay a tribute to Opal Reyne's Duskwalker Brides series, one of my favorite monster romance series.

I skate my finger just above the image forever inked into my skin, but not touching the tender flesh. My eyes widen as I gaze at the half wolf skull with one brilliant purple orb, meeting the tattooed line running down the middle. The marks, like the rest, told a story. On the top of the skull, a ram horn curls, ending in a deadly point.

Love and happiness bloom in my chest, it's like having a piece of the book with me forever.

Pressing my lips tight, I brush my thumb along the virgin skin near the larkspur flowers leading away from the skull, meeting the other side of the tattoo in a geometric pattern.

Many do not know that these innocuous flowers are reapers disguised in delicate beauty, it's always the ones you least expect that can be the most deadly.

It finishes down into a point, with a crystal hanging from the middle line, dangling down to my knee.

I finally look up and meet Tiffany's eye, smiling wide enough to show my small fangs. "I adore it, Tiff! This might be my favorite tattoo so far," I say with true happiness.

Raising my arms, I attempt to pull her into a hug, but she places a hand on my chest, rejecting me. She eyes me with a look that screams worried. I can't help but expire a messy breath. There's no point in hiding anything from her. I should've known better than to try to delay the inevitable.

Tiffany would never judge me.

"I've had several dreams about that shitbag, and I hate that I'm still not over him. It's been over two hundred years since I've seen him. Plus, it feels horrible to still want him. He hurt you, and I can never forgive him for that."

"Mar, you know that's not your fault. You lived with the bastard for over a thousand years. Of course, he is going to be deeply embedded in your psyche. Plus, I told you, I didn't feel anything he did to me. Not that I'm giving him a pass, but he didn't have to make it painless."

"I know, but he betrayed me."

Like a reward, Tiffany presses the needle back in while we speak.

"I swore never to be claimed for that exact reason. He vowed to care for me and protect me. He fucked up everything we had. Whenever I think I'm moving forward towards getting over him, he slithers into my dreams. All the dreams aren't good, either. Some of them are nightmares, and I wake up drenched in sweat. I can't remember where I am, that I even made it out of Inferuna," I whisper. "While other dreams are like reliving my actual memories, some of the dirtiest, kinkiest, and hot as fuck sex I've ever had. The other night I woke up coming. I was fucking fingering myself as I dreamed of him. What the dick is wrong with me?"

"*Nothing*. Nothing is wrong with you. He was your first love. I know you don't like to admit it, but he was."

I wish I could hate her for being right, but I can't.

Tiffany reaches out and taps the angelfish tattoo on the upper right side of my chest. "Do you remember why you asked me to tattoo this on you a few years after we came to the human realm?"

"Because his pet name for me was Angel," I grumble.

"Exactly. You told me if you carried an angel on your

body, you would reclaim a piece of yourself. The best part was when you checked out the tattoo in the mirror after and declared her name is Lilith," Tiffany says with a laugh.

"Okay, fine, I will admit that naming her Lilith was a glorious moment. Damn, we should've told Mr. Grumpy-ass-angel her name. I would've loved to see the look on his disgustingly beautiful face," I sneer.

"I am not getting into a debate with you about angels again. Change of subject since I don't want you to dwell. Not all of your clients at The Snuggle Pit are that bad, right? I mean, there is that godsdamn gorgeous Scot, Hunter. Tell me more about him."

"Yeah, Hunter is one of my favorite clients. He is ALL alphahole outside of a scene, which is how I like it. I want him to challenge my alpha side. It's so fucking sexy. He's all growly and demanding. Plus, I love that he's finally accepted the relief it can be to sub. He's been trying to earn his collar. I know he wants me to claim him."

She gives me an incredulous look, like she can't believe the words that just came from my mouth. "You want to collar him?"

Gifting him a collar is a huge fucking deal, it would shift the status of our 'working' relationship to something more. I'm not sure if I'm ready to embrace all of the responsibility that comes with having a collared sub. Lauren is the only one I have ever collared.

"Tiff, what if I *want* him to claim me? To bite me and declare me as his. I miss the feeling of belonging to someone. I never thought I would after I discovered the power trip it was to be a mistress. There is something about Hunter, though. Maybe it's because he's so damn lickable?"

"Did my Mariax admit that she wants to sub again? Damn, you really have been diving deep into the memories and emotions. This is a good step. You'll always have

PTSD from Inferuna, but you are putting yourself together again, piece by piece."

Sighing, I run a hand through my hair, absently wrapping it around one horn.

"I think I'm holding Hunter back from his true potential as a sub. More often than I would like to admit. I find myself getting pussy flutters just from him walking into the room. It's becoming harder to remain professional with him in our sessions. Last week when he was at The Snuggle Pit, I may have had him eat me out as punishment…"

The tattoo machine cuts off abruptly as Tiffany flies up from her stool. Her blue hair whips around, some strands getting caught on her horns as she vibrates with excitement. Her headlamp dangles on one horn before falling to the floor with a clatter.

The tattoo machine still in hand, she points at me as she shouts, "You fucking SLUT! I knew it! I knew one day you two were going to fuck." She smirks, clearly proud of herself. Confusion crosses her face as she lowers her arm, a V forming between her brows as she contemplates the scenario. "Wait, how is eating you out a punishment?"

Sitting up and resting on my elbows, I raise an eyebrow.

"First, we didn't fuck. Second, it was a punishment for him, not me. By giving him a taste of what he's been craving for months and not letting him come, it caused him a massive number of blue balls. Plus, he was in a cock cage. Shit, I guess it even borders on torture," I claim matter-of-factly with mock horror. "The brute of a Scot can handle it, but I don't know if my pussy can."

Sitting back down, Tiffany sets her tattoo machine aside, and then folds her gloved hands on the chair and rests her chin on them. "It sounds to me like a sexy little demon is catching the feels…or maybe more?" she murmurs, her eyes flicking up to me and still full of mischief.

"Honestly, Tiff, I think I'm falling for him. Falling fucking hard, slip in a puddle of blood, and bruise your ass, hard," I say dramatically and sigh. I raise my right arm over my eyes. "I don't know what the hell to do. He's a client. I can't date him, can I? I tried that in the past, and it never worked out. Jealous partners and being the Mistress of a sex dungeon don't mix."

"I know just what you should do," Tiffany states as she continues her work on my tattoo. "Why don't you just fuck him? Maybe it's something you need to get out of your system. The male is fucking hot, so hot. I think my panties melted off when you showed me his picture."

Fuck him? I think, as I bite my lip. Tiff's here telling me I should go for it, and I really, really want to take her advice.

CHAPTER 18

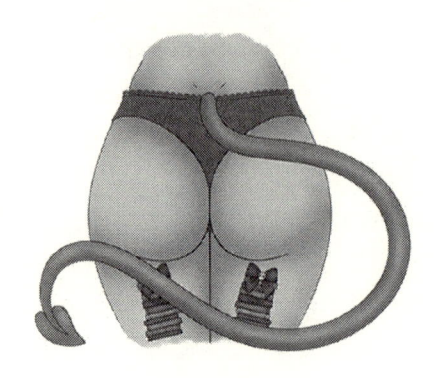

MARIAX

Hunter has texted me at least two times a month asking me out since he agreed to be my submissive. However, I made it clear from the start that I don't get involved with my clients, and up until now I have kept my promise.

Hunter has never felt like just a client no matter what I tell myself, though. He has learned to be a good submissive, but I am drawn to him in every way.

Well, I finally let him convince me to go on a date with him. It didn't take much after my talk with Tiffany a few days ago.

Hunter's personality draws me in, not to mention his wide, muscular body and untamed hair. I've dreamed of running my hands through it since I met him at the bar. And that evocative scent of his of pine, fresh coffee, and wood smoke surrounds me whenever he is near. The combination makes my mouth water and my palms itch to learn every inch of his defined body.

Our date has been great. I've laughed and smiled more than I have in decades.

Hunter has a vibrant energy that is exceedingly addictive. He took me ax throwing, surprising me with something other than dinner and a movie. He rented out the entire venue so it would be just us. We drank craft beer and threw numerous axes.

Hunter has excellent aim, but it is too easy to distract him.

When I circled his waist from behind and ran my nails down the length of his abs, following his happy trail, the ax he intended to throw went wide and embedded itself into the flatscreen TV mounted to our left.

On our walk back to my place below the Pit, we took a detour into the park, Hunter's favorite place in Philly.

"I'm so glad you agreed to be my submissive," I tell Hunter, accepting his hand as he laces his fingers with mine.

"Aye? And why would that be, then?" He asks, fishing for compliments.

"I like having you in my life. Punishing you is a bonus," I laugh.

Then I finally bring up the topic I've been thinking about during every one of Hunter's sessions. "So, Pup, I've been with shifters before."

"Been with?" He raises his eyebrows in mock confusion.

"Fine. I've fucked shifters before," I state bluntly as I side-eye him.

"Aye, continue."

Rolling my eyes, I do.

"Well, I've never been knotted with any of my partners. I want to know what it's like, from both sides, and if it means something more than just another part of fucking since none did it," I let out in a rush.

Hunter laughs warmly, twirling a lock of my hair around his finger as he speaks. "How long have ye been wanting to ask me that?"

"Um, let's just say a while. Will you tell me?"

"Hmmm, it's a hard ask, Cheetie," he teases.

"I'll throw in a pleasure spanking if you tell me," I say in a singsong voice.

"Now that is an offer I cannae refuse," Hunter says, winking. "First, only lycans can knot. It's a biological thing that we're born with that isn't the same for other shifters."

"Do other shifters have their own...fancy dick stuff?"

His eyes glint with humor. "I heard certain feline shifters have barbs, so yer lucky ye didnae fuck one of them."

I purse my lips to the side in thought.

"What about werewolves then?"

"Well, since werewolves were humans turned shifter, they don't naturally have that physiological makeup. Although all lycans can knot, alphas have the best chance of passing on the strongest traits through their seed, therefore bettering the pack with each new batch of pups."

"Okay, but what about–"

"Be patient, lassie." Hunter growls playfully before continuing. "Next, the whole point of a knot is to keep all of the precious swimmers from escaping. The knot swells when we are aroused and continues to grow all throughout."

"I kinda noticed that," I say with a snort of laughter, causing his lids to lower in annoyance.

"Yeah, but what ye don't know, is that the act of knotting is when a lycan's knot is nearly swollen to the max and then shoving it in a tight cunt to swell further, literally locking them into place. Every drop of cum is trapped, hoping for the best chance of pups."

"Wait, so the whole point is just to keep excessive amounts of cum in a body? What about pleasure? Your knot is always so sensitive when I play with it."

Hunter groans and palms the bulge in his pants. "Please

dinnae mention playing with my knot right now. I'm already turned on enough by this conversation."

I give him a sheepish smile. "Knotting only sounds fun for the guy, right now. You're not making it sound very fun for the partner."

He rolls his eyes before continuing, "There is pleasure, and a lot of it for both partners. From what I've been told, since I've never done it, the pleasure is just as intense on the one being knotted. We swell against tender spots and rock to stimulate our partner. The lycan comes again and again from the small thrusts their body allows, and each new jet of hot cum sets off another orgasm. See? A happy partner is one that doesn't scramble away and instead opens their legs for more in their pussy or ass."

"Oookay," I say with a hum. "So how come you've never done it then?"

"Knotting means something different to each person," he answers with his hand over his heart. "A lot of lycans are driven by the need to mate and make as many pups as they can. Others, crave the connection you get when being locked with someone for an unknown amount of time."

"What about you, though? I'm not really interested in what anyone else feels, to be honest."

"For me, knotting means so much more. When I knot someone, it means I trust them, mind, body, and soul. I crave that deep connection and will only ever knot someone if I know they're it for me. It's also a form of claiming, knotting paired with a bite is essentially a lycan version of handfasting or marking them as their mate."

I fold my arms across my chest, and then unlink an arm so I can tap my forefinger against my lips. I don't really know how I feel about that.

"I was kind of excited to know what it would feel like," I answer with a laugh and turning to the side. "I guess I won't be?"

Hunter gently grabs my chin to turn me back around and lifts it so I'm facing him. His mossy green eyes glint a certain kind of wickedness at me.

"Imagine my knot thrust into yer wee cunt, stretching yer walls farther than they ever have been before. My hot cum filling ye up over and over. We would be locked together for hours until my knot went down," Hunter growls out, his voice deep and raw. "If ye play yer cards right, someday I will give yer body a live demonstration of what knotting is like."

My pussy clenches, even as uncertainty tightens around my heart.

It's been a very long time since I've been in a relationship with that intense level of commitment. I'm not sure what to make of my feelings at the moment. Thoughts of the past and the very long-term relationship I was in eat at me.

A warm hand cups my cheek, his hand spanning the entire width of my jaw, his fingers curling beneath my chin. I lift my gaze to his and give him a small smile.

"What's on yer mind, lassie?" Hunter asks gently.

"Nothing important. I'm reflecting on how I got here."

"Do ye want to talk about it?" he asks as his thumb smooths over my bottom lip.

I nuzzle my face farther into his palm and he secures his other hand on my hip. "No. Yes. I... It's long and complicated."

"Start from the beginning?"

How far could I go with him? How far did I want to go back with Hunter? I knew in that moment that I trusted him more than I did most.

I sigh deeply, reliving my creation as I describe my experience to Hunter as if it's happening before him.

"It begins in darkness. A spark blossoms into an inferno,

bending the outlines of existence to its will, creation set into unstoppable motion. Twisted shapes move in the inky depths. Flashes of light creep in to dance with the shadows like wraiths. Only the strongest survive creation, for creation is to be torn from the ether and smashed into reality."

I lift my eyes to see him staring at me in wonder.

"I gain awareness near the end of my manifestation. Flames now dance not only around me, but within me. They wrap around my soul and cocoon it in their warmth. I'm not sure where the flames begin, and I end. We are one substance. One terrifying force, born for ruin and destruction. I do not know what I am, but I know I am real. Tangible. Living. The flames extinguish with a hiss as my physical form surfaces from the ashes."

Unfathomable emotions course through my body. They strike through me as I push away the memories.

I described to Hunter the basics of Inferuna, my creation, what my job was, and being forced to exist in a state of constant darkness and nothingness.

He can tell that my mood has shifted drastically. I'm not sure how he plans to handle this situation, but there's a gleam in his eye that piques my curiosity and also leaves me feeling weary.

He still hasn't responded to my truth, and my anxiety is soaring.

Maybe I'm too much baggage for him. He's so young and doesn't need my trauma screwing him over for the rest of his life. I'm going to tell him I made a mistake accepting his invitation to our date.

I shouldn't have agreed to this. I shouldn't have said anything.

Before I get a chance to make my excuses and trudge home, he's ripping the shirt off over his head, pulling it up from the back in the way that most males do that can melt panties.

"What the fuck are you doing? You know we're in the middle of a public park, right?" I hiss, my self-loathing morphing into irritation as he ignores what I share. How can he listen to me spill my guts and then start stripping?

Wait, why is he stripping as we stand on the walking path?

He grins at me mischievously and then winks before walking off the path into the woods without a word. I stomp after him, annoyed but curious.

We get far enough away from the path that I can barely see it anymore. He turns around suddenly, and I crush my nose into the hard planes of his chest while still mumbling to myself about men and their immaturity levels when it comes to the deep stuff. His chuckle comes out like rolling gravel; the sound is like a siren's call to my libido.

"Ye are worse off than I thought. Hmm. Good thing I have the cure. How would ye feel about a wee game?"

"What do you mean 'worse off than you thought'?" I glare, my words dripping with venom.

"Ye are stuck in yer head. I can see it written all over yer face that sharing yer past with me has triggered a lot of fucked up self-loathing. Ye usually stand tall and proud, the baddest bitch in any space ye occupy. But as ye spoke, ye curled into yerself, speaking quieter with each sentence and looking anywhere but at me."

How can Hunter read me this easily? I know my permanent mask hadn't dropped, but he still saw past it.

His features soften. "I won't ask about yer past again if it pains ye this badly. But I also won't ignore the signs that ye need a distraction desperately."

I work hard to keep my breathing even, and my face blank while my mind is reeling. I force my eyes up to his and plaster on my best fake smile. "What kind of game?

One that involves me getting naked and you in your wolf form?" I raise an eyebrow in curiosity.

"The kind that yer nipples become painfully hard, and it's not from the chill in the air."

I inhale sharply, and he takes the opportunity to softly press his lips to mine. It's the first time we've kissed, and he's quick to deepen it by slipping his tongue past my lips. I greet his tongue enthusiastically, moaning at the feel of his tongue piercing, creating a desperate need within me, desire heating my core. His hands shift down to my ass. I move my arms up around his neck, gripping his man bun and pulling him down and closer.

Our kiss is passionate. A soft, wet clash of lips that are hungry to nibble at each other's.

We're surrounded by tall evergreens, his pine, fresh coffee, and wood smoke scent complementing them perfectly. The woods are deserted by all life minus the forest creatures, and it couldn't be more insanely perfect. I know he was trying to make me feel better, but this is *more*. This is something unprecedented, and I'm surprised by my intense reaction.

He's hardening between us, and I want to climb on top of him and ride him like he's an untamable forest beast.

His hands shift up to the back of my head.

One caresses my horns, smoothing down the back of my hair as we kiss. He grips one of my horns near its thick base to bring me flush against his body. It feels fantastic to have him touching me so intimately. His palm sends waves of heat coursing through the length of it and onto my scalp.

He tilts my chin and head back to deepen the kiss. I've never been kissed so passionately that I felt dizzy before.

He pulls back, and I feel immediate longing and loss, but he quickly pops back down and plants a quick kiss on my lips, making me smile a little.

I look at him and smirk, "So, I thought this involved you

being naked?"

He laughs, and the sound of his belt buckle clinking fills my ears. His pants drop to the ground, and he kicks them, along with his boots, over to lie with his shirt, creating a pile on the forest floor.

My arousal is becoming tangible, my clit throbbing with my heartbeat.

He steps closer nude, proud, his hard-on bobbing with the movement. He grabs my ass in both hands and holds me against his erection while he explains his plans.

In a deep, commanding, quiet voice, he whispers against my ear, "I want to shift into my Wolf, and I want ye to run. If I catch ye, I'm going to have sex with ye right here in the woods so that all the forest creatures know my name."

His eyes are alight with mischief and lust. The thought of hunting me must bring something primal to the surface. I'm not used to being the prey, but I'll do my best to act the part for him.

And who knows, maybe I'll enjoy it.

"I will destroy ye in the best ways. I can't wait to chase ye and taste yer fear in the air."

I go to speak, but he puts his finger to my lips.

His warm breath washes over the side of my neck as he says, "and if ye win, I'll let ye use yer tail to do whatever ye want to me. Anything. No hard limits. No safe words. I'm yers."

My eyes widen as he pulls back and brushes his nose against mine. He can be so sweet. Sometimes sweet and cocky is a strange mixture, but it works for him. He cares deeply, too deeply, I admit. But I can't deny he's all in with everything he does.

It reminds me of a quote from one of the characters I saw on an American TV show at one of Tiffany's random parties. Ron Swanson, this grumpy old hard-ass male, says, "never half-ass two things, whole ass one thing." I believe Hunter could make that quote his motto.

I giggle at the thought.

He smiles broadly. "What's so funny, wee Cheetie? The idea of being hunted is funny to ye?"

I bite my lip and shake my head. "You reminded me of someone. I'll tell you about it another time."

"Okay, so do ye want to play, then?"

I don't hesitate before nodding and start stripping in front of him. I smirk saucily and begin making a show of it, shimmying my hips a little extra when I pull my combat boots and leggings off. Smoothing a hand down my stomach slowly, I grip the hem of my tank and rid myself of it. I rarely wear a bra or any panties, so I'm nude before him quickly, even with the brief strip tease. I enjoy the effect I have on him.

His jaw has dropped open, and a hand paused in running along his bearded jaw. His pupils are fully dilated, and any remaining color is now black, his wolf on the prowl. He stands there nude and frozen to the spot.

I take advantage of his momentary distraction, sprinting into the trees.

It feels odd to run completely bare, but it's exhilarating. I'm already so turned on, and he's only kissed me. Thinking of him hunting me sends a bolt of excitement directly to my clit, my arousal already beginning to slip between my thighs as I run.

The sticks and rocks have no effect on my shoeless feet. Out of my peripheral, I notice a streak of fur barreling towards me on my left side.

I wait until Hunter gets close enough, and then I grab his thick coat, using his own momentum to fling myself in the opposite direction and force him off balance.

His claws dig into the dirt as he tries to right himself, but I'm long gone.

My heart is beating wildly with anticipation.

I barely broke a sweat running this far. My demon blood was fully made for Hunter's game, the thrill and anticipation of a hunt instinctual. I have no doubts that I will win, and my victory will be so damn sweet. All the wicked ways I can use my tail on him.

I plan in the back of my mind as I use my instincts to guide me quickly and quietly throughout the woods. I run as swiftly as I can, minute after minute, using all the tricks I know to mask my trail.

My tail becomes what resembles a pine branch, the leafy needles working to smooth my tracks as my tail swishes the ground. My scent was a bit trickier to hide, but staying above the wind should help considerably.

It's then that I hear the crack of a large branch. I skid to a stop and crouch.

The wind blows gently from my left, and with it comes a feeling I know all too well. Trepidation. I fight my back from arching as a phantom claw scrapes down my spine.

My heart bashes against my ribs, and goosebumps cover my flesh. My breathing speeds up, white puffs forming in the chilly late fall air. I'm far from The Snuggle Pit's protection wards and the safety they offer.

Another branch snaps, sounding closer than before, and I know it's not Hunter. He would never be so careless as to make a sound. It is not attempting to be quiet, and that does not bode well for me.

I swallow my pride and run in the opposite direction.

I'm fighting my instincts to eviscerate this unknown creature, knowing that I need to survive at all costs to satiate my need for revenge against what has been stalking me. My lip curls in a snarl.

Its end will not be quick. It does not deserve a quick death after haunting me into near madness.

I'm so fucking tired of running. Running from anything that might trigger me, from my past, towards a future just as bleak as the one before it. This dreadful sensation I've felt since I came to the human realm is the bane of my existence.

I take off in a new direction, dodging between trees and climbing random ones, to jump to the next and mix up my path. But I hear it getting closer. Terror floods my system, and I panic. I thought I could face this alone, but I'm in over my head.

Whatever it is, it's fast, way faster than I anticipated.

I drop back down on the ground from another tree and run into something hard, my cheeks smashing against it as I fall back on my ass. I look up and find Hunter shifted back into his human form, now staring at me with wild eyes. His hair in complete chaos, filled with knots and frizz.

He holds out a hand, and he pulls me up when I accept it. He watches me constantly check my surroundings in the woods.

"What's wrong? Mariax, are ye okay? I was on yer trail for a while there. But then, all of a sudden, yer movements became erratic."

"There was something chasing me. I think it is what has been stalking me for years, and I don't know how to handle it," I explain, my frustration mounting.

He immediately goes on the offensive.

His muscles tighten in his neck. He lightly pushes me away and says, "I'll take care of it."

Before I can speak another word, his wolf seems to tear from his body. A gigantic, beautiful creature where Hunter was standing. His furry shoulder reaches just past mine, while still having all four of his paws on the ground. His coat is made of fine grayish-silver fur.

I long to rub my face against him and snuggle into his warm animal heat.

His scent doesn't change, but he's fully an animal. He turns his head towards me and examines me with intelligent eyes. I know he's still present in there somewhere, but his wolf has taken command. He takes off in the direction I came from, backtracking to find any sign of the creature.

I doubt it will take him long.

I hear my own heartbeat in the quiet night, feeling uncomfortable and alone in the small clearing of trees. A howl rips through the air, and what sounds like a fight in the distance. I don't know how fast his wolf can run, but he's far enough away that those are the only sounds that I'm hearing.

Suddenly, everything goes quiet, and I'm concerned that he is hurt, but then the shaggy wolf breaching the edge of the trees surrounding the clearing calms me.

He speeds over to me and shifts, returning to his human form, kneeling on the ground in front of me. Hunter stands and places his hands on my cheeks, silently communicating his concern.

"I don't know what it was. But it was something unnatural and evil. It pulsed with an energy that made my coat feel like it was covered in oil. Vile, nasty thing… I can't even properly describe it. I tried to grab it a couple of times, but it was like it existed and then, at the same time, didn't. It didn't really have a physical body, just an incorporeal form."

He looks a little shaken but mostly pissed he did not get to unleash his wrath on the creature.

I stand on my tiptoes and kiss him on the lips. "Thank you. You didn't have to go after it. You didn't even know what you were up against."

"I know, but I did it for ye. Yer the only thing that matters. It's gone now. Do ye have an idea of what it is?"

"I don't know, but not long after I came to the human realm, things began happening that I couldn't explain, and anytime I stepped out of The Snuggle Pit's wards, I felt eyes on me. I was, no, I *am* being stalked by whatever that creature is. It's like icy fingers of awareness and dread scrape down my spine whenever it's near. I'm on high alert all the time. I don't know what it wants from me." I continue, my cheek resting against Hunter's sculpted pecs, "However, there have been times that even in The Snuggle Pit, something is causing disturbances. My cabinets are left open. Things moved around. Different rooms within my building have been rearranged. The other day, a dagger I hadn't seen in years was on the floor peeking out from underneath my bed, blade first. I know I had it stashed away in a box, but somehow it was meticulously placed to cut me. Whatever it wants, we'll find out soon because it's escalating. I need to get rid of it. Wipe it from the face of this realm because I've had enough of this shit."

Angry tears well along my lash line, but I will not let them fall. Hunter is looking at me with a mixture of fierce pride and barely leashed fury that something dared do this to me.

"Let me walk ye back. I'm sorry our date has to end, but I don't feel comfortable with ye running in the woods on yer own. Hunting ye was so godsdamn hot, watching yer pink arse jiggle as ye ran. I couldn't wait to win, but yer safety is more important," he grumbles, a frown marring his features.

We walk back to where we disrobed to dress.

I wrap my tail around his waist and pull him to my side. As we walk, he throws a heavy, tattooed arm over my shoulders. The warmth he omits is comforting, a balm to my frayed nerves.

We're a block from The Snuggle Pit when he stops by a streetlamp. I lean against it, all of my energy evaporating.

"I have a cabin in the Poconos that I go to whenever there's a full moon. It helps me fully connect with my wolf when the moon's influence is strong, so I don't have to worry about terrorizing the innocents of my surroundings. Ye are welcome to come with me. I'd love to show ye the mountains and a few special favorite places of mine," his voice is gravely.

He stops pacing and turns towards me. My tail reaches out for him, so he walks until he's standing between my thighs, my ass planted on the concrete anchor of the lamppost. My tail slowly drags up and down his spine, and he shudders with pleasure.

I sigh. "I'd love to, but I can't just abandon Lauren. I have to give her some notice and cancel some sessions so she can handle all the mistress' duties on her own. But next time, we can plan ahead." I can't keep my smile in place, the thrill of the evening long gone. "There's also the concern of whatever that creature is that's stalking me."

He grows in frustration and kisses the top of my head before resting there. Then, he says one of the sweetest things anyone has ever said to me.

"I will always protect ye. Nothing will come near ye that ye don't desire. Ye have been through too much to deserve this, and I will see it gone. I will set all I can on it and find out what is causing ye distress. Anything unknown is a threat to my pack, and I will not tolerate any harm coming to them. If anything happens while I'm gone, please text me or call. I need to know that ye are safe."

I don't want to go, but staying out in the open is a risk I cannot afford right now.

We continue walking, his arm around my shoulders, and soon we're at my door.

Sadness sweeps over me, and I find myself not wanting to let him go.

I want to invite him to my place.

I want him to stay with me, but he has a look that says he wants to start his mission to protect me immediately, and I won't take that away from him.

CHAPTER 19

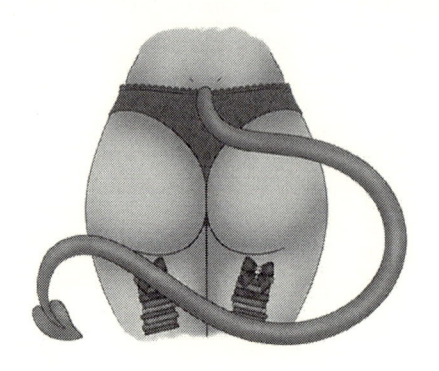

Mariax

Twisting my wrist to the right, I tighten the screw of the new soft hinges I'm installing on every cabinet. Finding my cabinets open constantly, caused by who knows what, is driving me insane. Hopefully, these self-close hinges will help.

Moving on to the next, I'm interrupted by a knock on my door.

I growl in frustration, muttering curses under my breath. Why am I constantly interrupted, especially on my time off? Can't get a goddamn minute to myself, and it's infuriating. I stomp to my front door and rip it open without checking who's behind it first.

To my surprise, Hunter stands there looking slightly sheepish, but there is still a roguish smirk on his bearded face. His wild hair is pulled back into a loose bun at the nape of his neck. Curly strands escape its confines and stick out randomly. One of his tattooed forearms rests against the doorframe. The other reaches up to grip the top of the frame, making the tendons and muscles in his arms and shoulders bulge in a mouthwatering way.

I continue my open perusal along the planes of his body.

A dark blue plaid flannel stretches across his shoulders, rolled up to about halfway up his biceps in the style that those human Marines do. It is the sexiest thing I've ever seen. I want to run my tongue between the roll of the shirt and his skin.

He clears his throat in an attempt to get my attention. I glare at him, my eyebrows pinching together, as I plant my hands firmly on my hips.

He laughs deeply and makes that sound that only a Scotsman could make. The sound could mean anything from an acknowledgment to indignation, but this one is potent with something I can't quite name. There is definitely humor, but it's laced with something unusual.

"Are ye going to keep staring at me, wee cheetie, or are ye going to invite me in?"

"You invited yourself here. I did not command your presence. Why should I let you in? You're supposed to be in the Poconos, anyway. Why are you here?"

He looks over his shoulder, turning his head both ways to see if the hallway is clear. I know he's concerned about leaving his back exposed. His wolf instincts are riding him hard, but it's not fear, just cautiousness. However, I stand my ground.

"Aye, I came home early from my cabin. The full moon passed, and I wanted to stay a couple of days further, but I couldn't stand being away from ye a moment longer."

Little flutters of anticipation take flight in my stomach. "Well, that's sweet, but—"

He cuts me off by putting his large, warm palm on my chest above my breasts, then firmly, but gently, he pushes me back. I allow it even though I have the power to stay like a brick wall all day if I want to.

I step backward, moving with the pressure of his palm until he clears the entryway. His leg snakes out, grabbing the side of the door and kicking it closed.

That move was so hot. What is wrong with me when I become aroused by his simplest actions?

But I must admit, maybe Tiffany was right. Maybe I do need to fuck him and get it over with, get him out of my system, and move on, especially because only one other being has made me feel like this, and I refuse to fall for that again.

He sees the moment of hesitation in my eyes.

He's quick to intervene, grabbing my sides, his fingers grazing the underside of my breasts before moving to lift so I can wrap my legs around his hips. I make a sound in protest, but quickly change my mind when I feel the wake of his heavy dick pressing against me through his jeans.

His massive erection is barely contained by his jeans, his entire cock head showing above his jean's waistline. The friction of the zipper and pressure from his stone-like hardness feels incredible between us.

I involuntarily grind into him and crash my lips into his.

He greedily kisses me back, his tongue probing the seam of my lips, parting them as he slams my back into the nearest wall. His tongue piercing clinks against my teeth, the smooth ball running down the center of my tongue. He moves his hips to hold me in place.

The action causes him to press his member directly against my sex, the thin barrier of just leggings doing very little to shield me.

His unexpected show of dominance is a massive turn-on.

Heat pools in my core, and my clit pulses with need. We battle with our tongues, spearing into each other's mouths. A sharp sting radiates from the tip of my tongue when I lick his canines. We groan simultaneously as my blood dances in my veins. The heat of our lust builds to an inferno.

He grips my breasts so firmly that I know there will be

bruises.

My tail screams in agony as it is crushed further behind me, the momentary distraction unwelcome. I grab my tail in my right hand close to the base and yank it free with a whimper into Hunter's mouth. He lets out a spew of profanity as my tail slips into the back of his jeans and squeezes a cheek.

He hardens further and grunts in achy need.

He replicates the gesture, filling his palms with my ass cheeks and lifting me away from the wall. Walking with determined strides, he heads into my bedroom like he knows the place, which is weird because he's never been inside my suite.

I screech a little when he throws me onto the plush, half-made bed. The soft, deep purple comforter is thrown over the mess of sheets and blankets underneath. He drops on top of me in a practiced move, his weight like a drug to my system.

This moment feels incredible, allowing me to take and feel instead of being in control. I am always in control. I've been in control since I left Him, and I'm not anticipating the feeling of nerves ricocheting through my blood.

I'm not scared of Hunter, but allowing another to take up space in my life is terrifying. Even though I've grown to know Hunter over the last year and desire him as a friend or maybe even a partner, I cannot allow our first joining to be on his terms. His conflicting emotions are clear in the pools of his expressive eyes.

I squish my hands between us and shove him backward, forcing him to kneel between my legs. I tuck in a leg and roll out from under him to stand next to the bed.

Both his eyebrows lift in confusion, and a set of fine wrinkles appear near his hairline as he does so. The expression would be almost comical if not for his lust still glazing his orbs. But there is also determination and a slight bit of concern present.

I point down to my previous spot on the bed.

"If you want to play, you better lie down because you're not dominating me," I command.

His eyes narrow, an appalled expression slashing across his features before morphing into a mask of indifference. The sight sends goosebumps cascading over my flesh.

The expression is not one I have ever seen on Hunter.

Maybe I don't really know him at all.

Or maybe I've pissed him off. We're not in a session right now, so technically, he doesn't have to comply, and I don't have to explain myself. However, he lies down, and a moment later, he's placing his fingers behind his head, eyeing me expectantly.

I position myself on top of him, straddling his hips with my thighs. I need to make quick work of his clothes, or I might combust on the spot. The tension between us is strung too tight.

I run the sharp edge of my transformed tail along the front of his body, down his torso until it meets the bottom of his shirt between my legs. A small expanse of golden skin and the dusting of his blond happy trail begins a few inches above his jeans.

The blade comes close to nicking the top of his shaft, and he inhales with excitement as he watches, but I veer the blade away from his flesh and cut through the fabric cleanly.

He hisses as I spin around quickly before I present him with my ass and begin rubbing it against his jeans. The tip of his engorged cock rubs against me. His hot breath kisses the back of my ear as he presses into my back.

"This arse might be the death of me, woman. I want ye so badly. My knot is practically begging me to impale ye."

Cool air kisses my back as Hunter rips the tank top from

my torso. My leggings and thong swiftly follow. I'm having difficulty controlling myself, my frenzied movements matching Hunter's.

I'm finally getting to do something about my attraction to Hunter. It's been too long. My denial of the level of attraction I have for him was torture. In fact, it only got worse when I commanded him to eat me.

A memory I've used way too many times to masturbate.

Neither of us says anything, the air thick with the scent of our need. Our heavy breathing is the only sound filling the room.

Goosebumps rise on his flesh, and though I've made it clear, he isn't in charge here. He still rocks against me and groans in pleasure.

His knot is becoming more pronounced the harder he becomes.

It fascinates me. I've been with shifters just never knotted and I can't wait to experience it swelling within me.

He flops back to the bed and fondles my ass cheeks before kneading them with his calloused palms. The sensation of his rough, unforgiving hands on my soft flesh envelopes me. It feels so good. Who knew a booty massage could feel so pleasurable?

A small smile curves across my lips. I'm grateful he can't see my expression.

Once his jeans are fully removed, I pry off his boots and peel off his socks one at a time, tossing them to the floor without care.

I swivel around again to face him, grinding on his erection. He's naked before me. I have never been so grateful that someone had forgone underwear. Hunter growls, and the vibration races to my cunt, pressing against his skin. He throws his head back in pleasure, baring his neck to me.

Suddenly, he seizes my waist and shoves me down on him repeatedly, my arousal causing me to slide against him every time. Thoughts about his lack of underwear situation vanish from my head with the building pressure and the intensity of my oncoming climax.

How I'm about to come so quickly with barely any build up is beyond me.

I wrap his wrists with my tail, binding them together and shoving them against his chest. I take over and continue moving against him without him controlling my movements. He lifts his hips in tandem with mine, aiding in getting me off within moments. The crescendo of my efforts sends zinging pleasure to the tips of my toes. I'm climbing higher and higher.

I need this. I need him.

His ladder fits perfectly between my pussy lips, quickly sending me spiraling into pure ecstasy. His face is an angry mask, but I can tell he wants me to come as well.

I reach between my thighs and rub his knot in small circles. It's swollen so much in the last few minutes I can see his veins under the stretched skin.

He moans huskily in pleasure from my ministrations.

It's so sexy seeing him this way. Abandoning his submissive persona I usually encounter during a session and just freely feeling is oddly empowering.

I jump over the peak into a sea of bliss, detonating. Squirting and coming all over his dick. My release runs down my thighs and all over his abs and hips, pooling in the dips between his muscles.

When I open my eyes and meet his, a bit of awe has replaced some of his anger, but it's still there. A piece of me wonders what he's so angry about, but I don't care enough to ask.

I close my eyes again and breathe deeply, my breath

fanning against his blond chest hair. "Fuck Hunter, that was—"

He sits up. One of my nipple barbells clinks against his. His bound wrists are caught between my breasts.

I open my eyes in shock, and a vicious glare greets me.

He's never been so forward, showing the more dominant side of himself that I haven't seen since he first came to The Snuggle Pit.

I release his wrists and simultaneously reposition myself over his waiting package. Before I can fill myself with him, I'm pinned beneath the weight of his chest. Squashing my tits between us is painful, but not so painful that it overtakes my pleasure. He's demanding and dominant, and I didn't realize I would like this side of him.

I'm struggling to release my desire to control the situation, but a deep sense of concern for the organ in my chest still lingers.

He attempts to slide his pierced cock through my folds, but I grab his throat with my tail and jerk his neck to the left, slipping on my cum that's all over us.

I lean on his chest with one hand while the other reaches to swipe a finger through my heat before bringing it to my lips.

I slowly suck it into my mouth, enjoying the sight of his pupils so dilated that I can hardly see the color of his irises. I taste fucking amazing, and my clit throbs as if in agreement. I'm situated perfectly to impale myself on his cock, tail still holding him firmly.

Pain spikes across my scalp when he shoves his fingers deep into my wavy hair and then seizes a fistful. I cry out when a few strands rip out, as he yanks my head back and places his other hand around my throat. The muscular tattooed forearm of the hand in my hair is pressed along my spine. The other arm runs from his hand around my neck, between my breasts and along my sternum.

He holds me there just above his member and speaks in a menacing timbre.

"Do ye think I would lie here compliant and let ye fuck me? I've been waiting for what feels like centuries to be inside ye. I have dreams about thrusting between yer bound breasts, spilling my release all over yer pretty face and neck." He leans down to run his prominent nose over my jugular lightly, causing me to shiver and my mouth to part, making the shape of an O. "Plus, ye came before me like a filthy little slut."

I start feeling lightheaded as he increases the pressure on my neck, truly choking me. It feels as if only a pin prick size hole is left to sip a sliver of air into my starving lungs with each breath. The way my head is forcibly held, I can't look at him, but I feel his burning gaze on me.

I've lost the ability to communicate as we sit choking each other. I curl my tail tighter around his windpipe, cutting off his ability to speak to me, and hope he gets on with it. However, he holds me there, just a hair's breadth above his swollen cockhead, hanging in limbo.

He forces his index and middle finger between his neck and my tail in a demand to be released and growls against my neck, scraping his beard and teeth along the sensitive flesh between my shoulder and neck.

Before I can process what's happening, he uses pure muscle to lift me up a little higher without moving his hands. I squirm in protest, but he slams me onto his cock.

Any air I have left in my lungs rushes through my moist lips. Even though it was a quick movement, I felt every one of his five ladder rungs as he entered me. The weight and rub of the barbell heads feel heavy and electrifying as they rub against my walls. I'm stretched around him in a blend of pain and pleasure.

I have never felt anything like it in my existence. It's a

truly indescribable feeling, and honestly, it's a shame every male doesn't pierce their equipment.

I'm soon lost to pleasure, becoming mindless as he lifts me repeatedly and forces me back down on his engorged dick. He does this a few more times before releasing my hair, leaving his other hand firmly on my throat. I remove my tail and finally allow him to take over.

I trust him to bring all the pleasure I need from him, but the frantic, desperate beating of the organ in my chest is near audible. I want to trust Hunter fully, but I worry how I will survive it if he abuses that privilege.

Anxiety is an ever present monster. Even when your body is fully distracted it will settle in to poison your happiness with worries from long past.

There are no more words between us as he becomes unhinged, thrusting with animalistic fervor as he squeezes my throat and slams into me, pounding me into the mattress so hard I slide up the cotton sheets.

My head is coming dangerously close to the headboard as my vision blackens.

As if he senses this, he loosens his hold, allowing me to take a few breaths before tightening around my throat again, restricting the airflow. Breath play is so fucking hot and unexpected from him. I wonder who he learned it from. I never knew he had this darker side in him.

He brings his forehead down to mine and begins whispering all the dirty things he plans to do to me, and it doesn't sound like these plans are short term. It sounds like he's been planning for a very long time. And now will be spending just as much time, if not more, fulfilling his fantasies.

I find myself in a desperate state, aching and pulsing all over my body. My skin is on fire, and my nipples are tight with arousal.

He eases his grip and removes his hand from my throat

before shoving my legs until they are arranged to his liking. They're now vertical and reaching toward the ceiling.

He resumes decimating my body, attacking it with bestial and violent touches. The wiry hairs of his beard erotically scrape my calves. I want him to fill me with his cum.

I try to look at his face but can't see past my legs. All I can see from this angle are my legs, his fingers digging into my ankles, and his massive frame.

For some reason, this bothers me, like maybe it's not Hunter fucking me.

I don't know who else it would be, but panic erupts within me. He feels the moment my magic sizzles in the air. He doesn't stop but parts my legs and places my feet on either side of his head.

"Are ye concerned I'm not going to let ye come? That I won't fill yer greedy pussy with my cum? Maybe ye are just a whore who only wants my dick. I know yer need matches my own. I intend to make ye come over and over until ye plead with me to stop. I won't. I've needed this for too long."

He lets go of my ankles and fondles my breasts. The sensation is a little jarring after they were bobbing around for so long with his thrusts. They're still against his palms, the sensitive peeks urgently pressing into his hands. The barbells feel like sheer torture as they cause more need to grow in my center. He grabs my hip with his other hand.

"Keep yer legs around my neck, or I will spank ye," his eyes fully dilate with the command, and I can see that he's losing control. His need for release is all-consuming. "Do ye understand me? So wet and needy for me. Wanting to take it all for yerself and leave nothing for anyone else."

I don't answer him, but his words are enough to scramble my senses. I arch my back off the bed, hands digging into the mattress on either side of my body.

Hunter places his thumb and index finger on the barbell of one of my piercings and twists. The pain is excruciating, but it borders on a pleasure-pain combo.

Wanton pleasure flies to my clit, and I scream.

"That's right. Scream for me. Scream all ye want. No one will hear ye."

He reaches out with his other hand and repeats his movements, wrenching my nipple and twisting. He still hasn't released the first nipple, and I'm in agony.

My head thrashes from side to side as pain and pleasure ripple out from my nipples. I can't control the needy feeling consuming me. I need to come, and I need to come now.

"Oh fuck. Hunter!" I scream."

"Did I say ye could speak, little one?"

I barely hear his words, thick with his Scottish burr, my pulse thudding in my ears.

"Rub on yer clit."

He releases my nipples and grabs my tail, holding it against my tight bundle of nerves, and I don't fight him. I make fast, small circles with my tail, my cum the perfect lubricant. He cups my wrists and pulls them above my head in one of his hands.

I'm so close to coming, and his brutish behavior is making it worse. He leans down until his lips are just above mine and skates his tongue along the seam of my lips.

"Ye don't come until I allow it," he barks.

I do as I'm told and continue rubbing myself in a battle not to come. My small bundle of nerves is hard and sensitive. My ecstasy is climbing higher and higher until I'm not sure what is up and what is down. I barely even know my name.

My legs are still firmly around his neck, but he's pulled back up enough that he's not squishing my lungs with his weight. He continues to spew filthy, naughty words laced with venom and desire. My eyes are closed from the onslaught, and I feel like a melting puddle of pleasure.

"Look at me." His command makes my eyes snap open. "I want to watch ye take me. How do ye like my ladder? Do ye feel it as I ruin ye pussy? Do ye feel each rung?"

His movements grow slower, and he purposely slips in one rung at a time. The race to my release slows, and I snap.

"Just fuck me already, asshole!" I forced through gritted teeth, seething at his audacity. "Shove your knot into me. Fuck me. Fill me. I need you to knot me, Hunter!" I half demand, half beg.

His expression darkens and he slows his pace further.

"I told ye not to speak," he states bluntly. "Ye will not be getting my knot thanks to not following the fucking rules," he says as he slowly pumps into me.

Hunter keeps his slow and steady pace, my body the instrument he uses to seek his own pleasure. He lifts a hand and gently runs the backs of his fingers down my cheek before lightly gripping my chin enough to make my eyes meet his.

"Ye want the pleasure of my hot cum filling that needy pussy? To paint yer insides, marking you so others know I was here? Ye need to earn it first, lassie," Hunter declares, biting my lower lip, then licking the blood that wells up as he groans into my mouth.

He abruptly pulls his face back and then slaps my breast, causing a sharp sting. I moan with desire.

He's not wrong. Every single time he drives into me, I feel the rungs of his ladder, and they might be my new favorite thing. His erection is as hard as a stone, but his skin is soft. In contrast, the metal barbells are unyielding as they make my flesh bend to their will.

And soon, permission or not, because I don't give a fuck, I call out as my body hits the peak he has been driving me towards, "I'm coming!"

He's lost to the rhythm he's set, my head now banging against the headboard repeatedly. He pulls out before flipping me over onto my stomach, reentering me and stopping my spiral towards oblivion. It's deeper at this angle. His breaths come in shorter and faster. His movements are jerky and less measured.

The absolute brutality of our joining is startling and shoves me over the mountain top. The intoxicated bliss is short-lived as he pulls out. I feel the immediate loss of him, my core feeling too empty.

But then I feel hot jets of cum on my ass and lower back as he groans and growls, milking himself onto me, a display of ownership that has me turned on but also infuriated.

He leans into the mess he created, whispering in my ear, "Next time, you will listen when I tell ye not to come, and then ye might get more. Good girls get to have cum filling their holes, not little sluts who can't follow the rules."

Despite Hunter refusing to knot me and pulling out, I feel elated. I finally feel connected to Hunter in a way we haven't been before.

I understand his refusal to knot me, but I'm still disappointed he doesn't trust me enough to be comfortable with the act yet.

We lay sprawled on my bed, a tangle of sweaty limbs. A piece of Hunter's hair tickles my cheek as I catch my breath and snuggle into his side. My nose is pressed against a tattoo of a full moon, but the moon has a shadow of a skull taking over its surface.

I idly trace the craters in the moon with the pad of my finger.

He leans over and grabs a few of the books that ended up on the floor from our sexcapades. Lying back onto the pillows, he places the small stack on his chest, reading the title of each one before turning to me with a raised brow.

"Haunting Adeline, The Beta Trilogy, Heartless Heathens, Order of Scorpions, A Soul to Keep, Heart of a Witch…" Hunter lists some of the titles. "Dark romance, hm? Some things never change."

"They're my comfort reads."

"Ye'd think ye would have had enough darkness in yer life, without the need to still read this smut."

"That's exactly why I read dark romance. The characters live in way more fucked up situations than mine. I can escape, if only for a moment. Let my demons see that theirs are so much worse. My trauma doesn't look as bad when I compare it to these fantasies," I explain, as I resume tracing his tattoos, this time the mountain range on his chest that spans shoulder to shoulder.

"Not to mention, I've learned a few tricks from those books. They can get quite filthy," I say with a small laugh, the expelled air from my lungs dusting his chest.

I watch as his pierced nipples harden in response, drawing me in for a taste.

CHAPTER 20

Hunter

There have been many strange happenings going on with Mariax and her club, things that cannot be explained but must have a reason. I pressured her to tell me everything now that the full moon wasn't breathing down my neck.

I don't believe in coincidences.

The fates know everything happens for a reason, and I will be damned if I don't figure out what exactly those reasons are.

I will not allow Mariax or her business to suffer any further.

To the average person, they may seem like simple inconveniences, but in the long run, they will take their toll. Small disturbances, missing liquor, not to mention whatever that thing was in the park. It cannot happen to her again. If I wasn't there… I honestly don't know what would have happened. Mariax could hold her own, but that creature terrified her. I'd never seen her in such a state before, which was unnerving.

I feel the desperate need to protect her at all costs.

However, something has been weighing on Charlie, my beta, for days and it's time he spills the tea.

I invited Charlie to my house, and we lounge on the couch sorting through the latest pack drama.

When he doesn't take the incentive to start it, I'm not shy to.

"What's been up with ye, Charlie? Something has been eating at ye and I don't like that ye haven't felt comfortable talking with me about it."

Charlie scrubs a hand down his face and slumps further into the couch. He places his cool beer bottle to his forehead and then clears his throat.

"I was at Get Fucked the other night when I was approached by a demon. I don't know anything else about them except they smelled heavily of sulfur and fear. They didn't say anything, just threw a crumpled piece of paper in front of me and bolted from the bar."

"Do ye at least know if it was a male or female? Did they have any identifiable traits?"

"Listen, man, I was already deep into my cups by then and in no state to give chase. I stepped down from my stool but caught my foot on the lower rung and nearly face planted on the disgusting floor."

"Wait, what the fuck was on the paper?" I ask, a bad feeling blooming in my gut.

"That's the thing. It's just a list of locations. They're all in a seedy part of the city and most likely abandoned. I don't know if we should look into it or not. It could be a trap. But what if it is important?"

My mind is racing as I think of all the possibilities as to why this mystery person would go out of their way to deliver this list to Charlie. Someone could be using this to get to me or the pack. The fact he mentioned that the creature was a demon, most likely fresh from Inferuna due to their scent, is a little discerning.

"I told ye about the problems Mariax is having. Do ye

think this could be connected to her?" I deliberate.

"Do you truly believe Mariax's issues will become a problem for the pack? It seems a little far-fetched to make that leap. The evidence is circumstantial at best," Charlie explains.

"I told ye, Char, I was there in the woods when it hunted her. It was pure evil, and a creature like that does not have a conscience. I am now another obstacle in its way to get to Mariax. What better way to get me out of the picture than to threaten those I protect?"

"Hunter, this is all just speculation. Plus, this list," Charlie says as he brings a folded but crumpled piece of paper out of his pocket. "Might be meant as a distraction for any number of things."

I growl deeply in my chest. My mind stuck on the thought that this has something to do with Mariax and the danger she is in.

Charlie continues, "It's my job to look at everything from all angles. I'm worried you're too close to the situation because of Mariax."

"I can't explain it, I say with a shake of my head. Call it a gut feeling, but something is coming for us all…and it may be bigger than just this vindictive spirit."

Charlie heaves a resigned sigh. "Okay, Hunt. Let's call the pack to the meeting house. We can explain the situation, what we know, and really nail the point home that you are concerned for their safety."

Charlie and I stand towards the front of the meeting room, greeting the wolves as they make their way into the room.

Two wolves break away from the group, chatting by the stacks of chairs to the side of the room, heading for Charlie and I. I recognize Zane and his best friend Indy. They've been stationed at The Snuggle Pit on my orders. Other than Charlie, I trust Zane and Indy the most of the gathered wolves.

"Alpha," they say in unison, bowing their heads slightly in respect. "What's this emergency meeting about?"

"I can't speak candidly here, but meet Charlie and I back at my place after the meeting and we'll explain further."

I must warn my pack and make certain every wolf is aware of the potential threat. The atmosphere is becoming thick with anxiety and tension and my pack feeds on the emotions I am unwillingly throwing into the room.

Charlie, who is standing to my left, clears his throat and nudges me with his shoulder to bring my attention back to the present.

Squaring my shoulders and standing up to my full height, I command the room with my alpha presence. The pack needs to know how serious I am about this, and I will not allow them to question my orders.

I clap my hands loudly in front of me, which grabs everyone's attention in the room, and the silence is immediate. A couple of people in the back always want to keep a small conversation going, but tonight, they are all avid listeners.

"Listen well, wolves. I will not go over this more than once. There is a great threat brewing in our territory. I cannot share too much information about it, but the potential for it to affect our pack is high."

Grumbles and slight murmurs arise, buzzing like an agitated beehive.

I continue, throwing my alpha tenor into my tone to silence them, "Our pack will remain safe, and in order to do that, Charlie and I are implementing some extra safety measures. Starting tonight, a curfew will be in place from ten at night until six in the morning. Every single wolf in this pack is to remain within their dwellings during those hours."

"Alpha," one of the teens in the back of the room interrupts. "Why would you keep us caged like this and not explain the situation further?"

"Yeah! What about patrol duties, and socialization?" another wolf questions.

Soon everyone is speaking over one another, and Charlie takes a menacing step towards the crowd. I notice his mate Clarice in the crowd, beaming at Charlie with pride for his assertiveness.

"You will listen to your Alpha, or you will answer to me. He will keep you safe, even if it means implementing safety measures you may not agree with. No one interrupts him again, or you will be put through the full Beta training drills at zero-four hundred for the next month, *and* you'll be excluded from the next full moon run," Charlie commands.

I nod at my second, and then continue. "Before I answer any questions, I will finish what I was saying before being interrupted. There is an unknown force threatening a small business in Philadelphia. Several events have occurred, and they appear to be escalating and spreading the reach of devastation into our pack lands.

"I have seen this creature for myself and hunted it through the woods closest to Fishtown. I was not able to keep pace with it and it did not hold one distinguishable shape to its form. This creature is not of this realm. The closest comparison to this being is what the humans call a poltergeist. It has an incorporeal form, unmitigated speed, and an aura of malice and hate. I do not know what it is capable of. I do not like that it is now acting out in a more public fashion."

I do not let them know that it was my hunting this creature that has me concerned that I have been marked for interfering with it, therefore putting my pack in its sights. Guilt surges through me at the potential danger I have put everyone in.

I know my pack will heed my warning. The drive to keep our lands and their families safe runs deep.

CHAPTER 21

Hunter

My fingertips scrape lightly at the white tablecloth covering the table in front of me as I drum my fingers and wait for Brad.

My nerves are shot, and I feel like I might puke. To everyone else, I look calm and composed, but on the inside, I'm a mess. Although Brad and I have already been intimate — very intimate, I feel like I have a horde of butterflies in my stomach.

What is a group of butterflies called, anyway?

Sighing, I focus on the words on the page in front of me. My hair hangs around my face, creating a curtain, allowing me to further dive deeper into this incredible fantasy world. This book is a slow burn, and the angst is killing me, but I love it. It's a fantasy romance and the world building is a genius. Rebecca L. Garcia is a brilliant author. I have a theory that she's a supernatural herself or she's had close encounters with the supernatural world.

She knows way too much about it to be just yer average human.

The main characters are just about to have their first kiss when the lightest cold, yet soft touch grazes my bearded jaw. I look up from my book and my mouth drops open, taking Brad in.

The shadow tips my chin up even further to meet my gaze. A cocky smirk tugs at the corner of his lips. "What are you reading, Scruffy?" he asks in a dark but teasing tone.

"Spellbound," I respond, closing my finger on the page and holding it up for him to see the cover.

He hums deeply, taking in the cover and then my face.

"It looks like it is a good read. I can make out the flush on your skin even through the tattoos and beard."

I blush further, the red on my cheeks and neck warm with slight embarrassment.

"Aye, it's fantastic. Maybe I'll read it to ye sometime." I wink to help cover it.

I open my book back up and look around for my bookmark. *Dammit, where the fuck is my bookmark?* I swear they must possess some kind of cloaking magic. Every time I find a new bookmark to use, they up and vanish within moments of taking them out of the pages.

Brad chuckles as he manifests one of the most beautiful bookmarks I've ever seen at his fingertips. He slides it slowly between the spread pages. That shouldn't be sexy, but it is.

He cages me in from behind and whispers in my ear, "You can read to me, but you'll be doing it naked in my bed."

I barely stifle my groan as my heart rate picks up speed. Brad stands and walks casually to the other side of the table, pulling out his chair and sitting. That smirk is ever present on his face, causing his dimple to deepen.

My attraction to him grows by the moment.

I attempt to draw my focus away from my cock. This is not why we're here. We're here to get to know one another.

Hunter, get yer shit together, man.

"So...What brought ye to Philly?" I ask Brad.

His smirk remains, but something shutters behind his eyes, hiding his genuine answer.

"I came here on business," he responds quickly.

"What kind of business?" I inquire.

"The kind that I cannot share with just anyone. It is dangerous and someone could get hurt if I spill the wrong secrets."

I can't blame him for that. I have pack secrets I need to keep close, so it wouldn't be fair of me to get upset over his inability to answer.

"When ye are not at the office, what do ye do for fun?"

"You've already experienced what I like to do for fun, Scruffy," Brad says and winks, taking a sip of the white wine in front of him before grimacing. "This wine is fucking terrible."

As though he drew her to us with telekinesis, our server skips to our table.

"Sir, do you need something?" she questions, twirling a strand of hair around her finger in a shameless show of flirtation.

It doesn't bother me. Why should it? Even if she didn't also flash me the same cute smile, Brad barely pays her any notice. I've also never needed to compete with anyone, and I'm not going to start today.

Brad doesn't miss a beat. "Yes. This wine is abhorrent. Bring me Lagavulin, neat. If you don't have any, find someone to procure it. I am not drinking this swill," he says as he hands her his wine glass.

Her mouth pulls into a frown. "Yes, sir, not a problem. I'll get right on that," she says, and quickly scampers away.

"Really?" I asked Brad. He just stares at me with a blank expression. "Did ye have to be such an arsehole to her?" My annoyance with him causing my accent to thicken.

Brad responds, "No, but I wanted to. You'll learn I do what I want when I want."

Okay then, time to change the topic.

"So yer a whiskey man, we have that in common."

Before I can ask him more questions about himself, he leans his elbows on the table and rests his chin on his calloused palms.

"What is it you do, Hunter?"

"I own a construction company. I also maintain a lot of the houses on my pack lands."

"Interesting," he states, brushing up his pointer finger over his luscious mouth.

I cannot draw my eyes away from the meticulous, slow drag of his finger. It's almost hypnotizing. I close my eyes for a moment to get my head and my cock back in the game.

"Fair is fair," he continues, "what do you do other than manage your business?"

I feel no shame as I proudly announce, "Well, I spend most of my time reading and going to The Snuggle Pit."

I watch his face closely for his reaction. This will go one of two ways, bloody terrible or he'll be accepting. I don't miss the subtle brightness of his uniquely violet eyes. His onyx eyelashes, long and beautiful, fan his cheeks every time he blinks.

"The Snuggle Pit," he says deadpan.

"Aye, it's a sex club," I respond nonchalantly, shrugging and grinning.

His eyebrows almost reach his hairline as he ponders this, but his forehead quickly smooths out as he reaches a decision.

Something cool and not quite solid grazes my calf, startling me, before he kicks my legs further apart under the table. A shadow slowly trails up the seam of my pants, catching on the fabric lightly, straight to my straining erection.

"Tell me more about this sex club. What is it you do there? Do you go there to sleep with beings? Do you like to watch?"

I completely forget about all my other questions for him and fully dive into my description of The Snuggle Pit.

"Actually, I have no had sex there," I laugh.

The whole time I'm speaking, he continues to massage around my groin, teasing me with this torturous method.

"No, I'm going there to sub for my mistress."

His movements still, "Your mistress… doesn't she have a problem with you being out on a date with me?"

I laugh too loudly for the quiet restaurant. "No. Mistress Mariax and I are not exclusive. We both understand that. However, I consider her one of my closest friends, well, other than Charlie."

The server is back again, interrupting me.

"Your whiskey, Sir," she announces, placing it in front of Brad.

Her hand shakes a little as she pulls away from the glass.

"That will be all," he says, dismissing her with a flick of his wrist.

I watch all of this silently, not sure I like this side of him. The controlling, dominating force is sexy as hell, but the rudeness is intolerable. That lassie did nothing to warrant his abrupt behavior.

"Seriously, please do not treat people like that. She did nothing wrong."

Brad's shadow resumes its ministrations as he sips on his whiskey and ignores my reprimand, swirling it slowly under his nose to inhale the bloom of scents.

I continue from earlier as I was saying, "I am Mistress Mariax's submissive, but we hang out outside of the club as well—"

He interrupts me. "You seem very fond of this Mariax," he states coldly.

Why does he care about my fondness for my Cheetie?

"Tell me more about The Snuggle Pit," he demands.

"There's not much more to tell. Ye really have to go there if ye want to experience at all," I explain.

"Is there any kind of security? How does she stop random humans from entering the premises? I've never seen a sign advertising a sex club," he says to explain his prying questions.

"Yeeeah, I'm not going to tell ye that right now." I say with a flirtatious smile.

His blank façade briefly turns into a glare before smoothing out. He holds up his hands in mock submission.

"You're right, I should not be prying so much. I am just intrigued."

"It's okay, baby," I tell him. "I had hundreds of questions when I first heard about her sex club. But actually, I'm more involved in just being a submissive there. Several of my wolves are stationed there as bouncers."

A smile slowly spreads across his face, but it doesn't quite reach his eyes. "So you have an inside track to The Snuggle Pit."

"I suppose, but I really only ordered them to be there for her safety."

The shadow slides away, and I feel the loss of his teasing strokes immediately.

"What is your mistress like? Tell me more about her. You are clearly enamored with her."

"Oh, I don't know. I guess she's like any fem domme. Her presence fills the entire room with her unique energy. Although, when she's not at the club, she seems to shrink into herself a bit. Like she doesn't trust the outside world."

A slight gasp leaves Brad, like that surprises him.

"Anyway, that's one of the reasons that I station my wolves there. She might be my dominant, but she has a softer side deep down, even if she doesn't want it to show. Although I know she can handle herself, it makes me feel better to have members of my pack watching over her. Ye will have to meet her sometime. Maybe we can go to one of her live shows."

This time when he smiles, it reaches his eyes, crinkling the corner slightly. "That sounds like an excellent idea for a date night," he replies with enthusiasm.

I reach across the table and capture his hand, smoothing my fingers across his knuckles. The noise in the restaurant dims until it's all white noise and all I can hear is our breathing.

There is a spark. Much like the one between me and Mariax, and I need to know where this is going. Even if we talked more about my mistress than each other. "So, when can I see ye again?"

The spark between us has never extinguished since that first night in the woods, and I wonder if it ever will.

CHAPTER 22

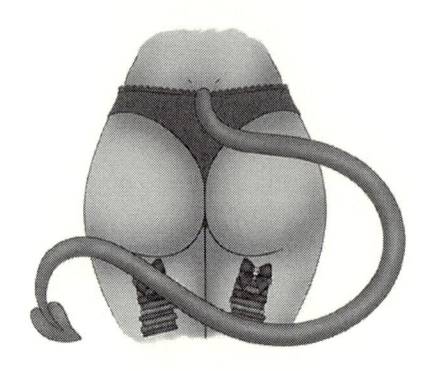

Mariax

It has been one long week. I swear my clients' requests are getting stranger and there are way more complaints.

Truly, all I desire is to torture something. I don't care if it is human, paranormal, spirit, or a fuckin pixie.

I never thought I would yearn for my job as a torturer, but some of my clients make me almost miss the good ol' days.

I really should take Hunter up on his offer to visit his cabin in the Pocono Mountains. He always leaves the city for at least a week during the full moon. Obviously, he cannot shift and run around eating people, can he? I wouldn't care, but the humans get squeamish about that sort of thing.

Maybe it would allow me the reprieve from my thoughts, distract me in a way only Hunter can.

I sit up, running my hands down my face. As I breathe in a sigh, I look down at the paperwork strewn across my desk and groan at how little I have gotten done before my mind has wandered to Hunter and, consequently, *him*. If he hadn't ruined everything between us, things could have been so different.

I'm here in the human realm, falling for Hunter, but too terrified to analyze my emotions.

I never had trouble expressing myself before Him.

I left my soul open for that bastard, and it has never been the same since His violent touch poisoned it.

Needing a distraction, I stomp out of my suite and into the hall. The familiar scents of pleasure, lavender, and vanilla assault my senses. I head down the hall, looking for my playroom.

My playroom is one of the best rooms in The Snuggle Pit. Seriously, it has the best toys, and I maintain them religiously. I transform my tail into the one of a kind key to unlock my playroom.

A series of clicks sound as the row of locks behind the door open. I push the panel open and step into the room, closing it behind me.

To my left, the two-way window to the adjacent room reflects a glossy black. With a flick of a button, I can activate the mirror and see everything in the room next door. Besides being my private playroom, I can observe clients or monitor mistresses-in-training like Lauren, thanks to that window.

The wall in front of me holds every punishing device available- canes, whips, chains, belts, skinning knives, ropes, tape, zip ties, wire, handcuffs. I could go on for days.

A spanking bench takes up residence in the right corner. It is one of my favorite tools. I had it hand-crafted by a fae, and it's spelled to weaken the user enough that breaking free is impossible. The right wall is made up of a giant metal grid. There are hooks and carabiners hooked up in even increments to allow me to position my client subs in any manner I choose.

Gliding over to the grid, I grab a cloth from the clean up bin next to the couch to my right. Usually, the bin is used for cleaning up bodily fluids, but the clothes work fine for polishing too. I polish the hooks.

Wouldn't want my beauty to get tarnished now, would we?

My mind wanders again, and I swear I hear grunts of pleasure coming from somewhere close. Those dreams have seriously fucked me up.

Maybe I'm feeling a little off today because I know Hunter is out on a date. He doesn't share information on those he goes out with, and I try my best not to pry, but I'm finding lately that I just want to sink my claws into him so that no one else can have him.

But that's not how our relationship works.

At least, not yet. I want him to be mine. I want to let him claim me. I want to have sex with him again so badly, but I haven't tried since he hasn't approached me about it. I was hoping he'd pop up at my home and fuck my brains out again, but nope.

Instead, he's out on a silly fucking date while I'm here wanting to get my pussy railed by a big, knotted cock, but instead I'm cleaning hooks.

I grunt. Jealousy isn't a good color on you, Mar!

Shaking my head and slapping myself upside the back of the head with my tail, I continue my work.

CHAPTER 23

THE PRIMEVAL

Hunter's small home on his pack lands is more spacious inside than I thought. It has an open floor plan and a cozy cabin feel. I don't enjoy idle moments, but being with him allows my brain enough distraction to be present.

Currently, he's in the kitchen grilling steaks and sipping whisky. He holds a tumbler in his left hand and uses his right to man the small grill built into his stovetop.

My hands shake slightly with minute tremors of unease. All of my plans are coming to fruition tonight. I know what must be done to rectify my relationship with Mariax. I must destroy her to save her, but it's not just for her. I'm a selfish bastard. I've been jaded and unsure of myself and despise these weak feelings.

I stood on that stage covered in gore for her. My implements of torture were neatly arranged beside me as I caused pain to another instead of her. I would do it again in a heartbeat if that meant she never again had to feel the edge of a knife against her heart, scorching iron melting into her flesh, or bamboo shoots jutting from her body.

In her limited experience with life and other beings, she did not perceive our relationship as dangerous, and as devastating as the fallout was, I would still choose to make her mine.

She was marked by the Potentate of Inferuna, although she didn't know it. She marked Mariax as a problem, a problem that needed to be solved quickly and efficiently.

Had I allowed the Potentate to act on her plan, Mariax's mind would have been lost to me forever.

I refocus on the present, observing Hunter in his domestic ways. He's very secure with who he is in life and what he wants. It makes me vaguely envious that he completes these basic household tasks with a soft smile. Each time he tastes his whisky, he makes a small, pleased sound that goes right to my cock. I'm so absorbed in watching him that I don't realize he's speaking to me.

Which only confuses me, as desire wasn't why I originally crammed myself into his life.

"Brad? Where'd ye go, baby?" he asks huskily.

"Just thinking about a surprise I have for you." I wink, taking a large sip of the amber liquid from my tumbler.

He sets the tongs down, turning to face the couch. "Aye?"

"Finish cooking, and then maybe I'll tell you what it is," I respond mischievously.

Hunter returns to his task. It smells divine, the grease from the steaks popping and sizzling on the griddle somehow comforting. Hunter uses tongs to plate the rare steaks and then adds baked potatoes already dressed from the oven.

We finish eating, and I help clean up the kitchen. It all feels very domestic, and I'm not sure how I feel about that.

I don't dwell on it too long before Hunter wraps his thick arms around my chest from behind.

He's only shorter than me by an inch but surpasses me in bulk. His wide chest expands past either side of my back.

He is corded with thick, defined muscles everywhere.

Being in Hunter's presence makes me miss my little one even more. I've been watching from afar and waiting, allowing myself the perfect moment to enter back into her life fully.

A few times, I let her get a whiff of my scent or catch the sight of shadows moving unnaturally. I relished the torment and indecision every time her heart raced, and she thought the strange occurrence might be me. Her utter dismay and fury, like a fine whisky, is to be savored and slowly taken in.

When I would allow her to taste my presence, she would become aroused. I could scent it from miles away. It is embedded in my psyche in a way that will never be removed. Her never-ending need for me plagues her to no end, and nothing could make me more satisfied. Being here on this plane for as long as I have been without her realizing it is telling.

She might hate me, but she craves me all the same.

As Hunter moves about the kitchen, his muscles tense and ripple with the slightest movement, causing a large, tattooed quote in simple script to draw my eye.

"Some books are lies frae end to end,
And some great lies were never penn'd..."

I believe that quote is by the famous Scot, Robert Burns. It tells me a great deal about Hunter in two simple lines. It's very evident that he is passionate about books, even negating several tattoos he has in their honor.

One I find fascinating is a stack of books that runs down the left side of his ribs. The books are worn and unevenly stacked like it could topple at any moment. Pages hang out of some books, and the spines are a muted rainbow of color.

I've had ample opportunity to explore his entire body, especially his torso, because he rarely wears a shirt. I tease him about it relentlessly, but Hunter just rolls with it, claiming his wolf's blood demands to display his physique twenty-four/seven.

I roll my eyes at his youthful nature.

His curly, chaotic beard tickles my neck as he leans close. "So, what's this surprise, then?"

"A little impatient, aren't we, Scruffy?" I say, letting a little irritation into my voice intentionally.

I enjoy his reaction to conflict and commands, and it's as easy as flipping a switch to arouse him. He doesn't respond but squeezes me tighter, almost to the point of pain.

Laughing darkly, I reach a tattooed hand behind me to grab a fist full of his hair. He hisses and shoves me away, but I keep his hair in my grasp, knowing the pain will radiate all over his scalp.

Not releasing him, I turn and glare down at him.

"I would watch what you do if you don't want to meet the end of my belt."

A bright flush covers his neck and creeps up to his cheekbones, anger and lust battling in his peat moss-colored orbs.

I release his hair and wrap my arms around him before vancating us to The Snuggle Pit.

He blinks a few times rapidly before stepping away from me. Being vancated can be disarming if you aren't used to it and I did give him no warning I was going to do it.

"Why the fuck would ye bring me here?" He questions me, his outrage evident.

"I thought it would be a fun space for us to pleasure each other. You already love coming here and you talk about it frequently."

"Aye, and? This feels like a betrayal to Mistress Mariax. This is her space, not yers."

"So it is," I say, attempting to keep the jealousy and bitterness out of my tone.

"I willnae play with ye here," Hunter says gruffly, walking to the opposite side of the room and crossing his arms. "I've told ye enough times that ye should have it branded on yer brain by now. I already have a dom and I willnae break our contract."

I glide over to him with soundless steps. Cupping his bearded face, I lean down and lightly kiss his soft, full lips.

"Shhhh, Scruffy, I never said anything about being your dom here. I just wanted us to have some fun," I explain between peppering light kisses along his jaw and down to his neck.

"Ye are not trying to dominate me?"

"No. Is this okay? I can vancate us back to your place if you want me to?"

"Nae, it is really verra sweet. Ye planned this all out for me. We can stay. But, I mean it when I say no dom and sub play, we are just Brad and Hunter."

"Understood, Alpha," I tease.

Enough talking. I crash my lips into his, kissing him deeply and passionately.

Our kiss consumes nearly my entire mind. I can feel Mariax's presence somewhere in the building, but it's faint. A trickle of excited energy builds within me. I swear that empty space she took with her when she left me throbs as if in knowing.

Before Mariax, I had never settled anywhere, and I was numb.

It took me a lot longer than I wish to admit that with feelings and emotions came good and bad, but chasing that high of a positive emotion to feel happiness and joy was worth all the pain. I didn't agree with that sentiment when I was drinking my way through the liquor and Inferuna, but now I'm back in the human plane. I've been building this relationship with Hunter and watching my Mariax from afar.

Hunter kisses me back, saving me from my dark, internal musings. I moan into his mouth as he runs his fingers into my hair and grips it, using it to pull my body flush against his.

His tongue stud is a thrilling addition to the kiss. The added element sends shivers of pleasure through me. With a thought, I remove my own shirt, as well as Hunter's jeans and boxers, storing everything in the ether for now. Reaching out, I twist one of his hardened, pierced nipples.

Hunter hisses and knocks my hand away. To help distract him from the pain, I back him into the nearest wall, never breaking the kiss. I startle him when I slam my hands next to his head, caging him in. There is a look in his eyes I can't place.

"Are you okay?" I ask him genuinely.

It takes a moment for him to catch his breath before answering. "Aye. Dinnae stop."

Hunter grips my shoulders and maneuvers us so my back is against the wall now. He kneels quickly and looks up to flash a beaming smile at me before leaning in, pressing his nose to my jean clad groin and inhaling deeply.

Hunter growls low in approval of my scent and begins tearing at my belt buckle, almost frenzied. I chuckle deeply, removing my belt with one quick tug. Folding it in half, I lightly strike his back with it several times. His breath quickens audibly.

I hold on to the belt in a tight grip, my other hand tangles in his thick, curly hair. The moist heat from his exhalations searing through the fabric of my jeans. I allow him to pull my dick and balls from their confines, but stop him from removing my jeans entirely.

He presses aggressive nipping kisses all over my pubic

bone, his sharp lycan fangs making tiny scrapes and punctures with each one.

I grow frustrated, looking down to watch as he circles the appendage in need, now engorged and throbbing. He palms his own fat dick as he pleasures me. My cock occasionally taps his shoulder or face as he changes locations on my body, the sensation causing him to groan.

Taking the belt I still hold, I wrap it around his throat and cinch it as tight as it will go on his thick tattooed neck. I yank it back so he will look at me.

I gaze into his eyes, pupils blown so wide there is hardly any of the moss green left. The confusion he displayed earlier seems more prominent. I'm slightly concerned with where his head is at, but I do not have time to worry over it when the game is in play.

Mariax could walk in at any moment.

I cannot have her see me having a tender moment with *her* submissive. Hunter has made it very clear he is *only* hers, but that he is free to date and fuck as he pleases. I need to make an impact, make them both feel some of the pain I have been submerged in the past few centuries.

"Are you done being a tease, Scruffy? Or do I need to fuck your face to show you how much I want you?" I question, my voice thick with desire.

It takes him a moment to register I am speaking to him.

"What did ye say?"

"Shall I fuck your face? Shove my cock so deeply down your throat you'll likely pass out, my cum spilling from your lips."

Again, he is a bit slow to answer, his voice gravelly and somehow tired sounding. "Aye. Bury yer long, tattooed cock into my throat. Use me."

I remove the belt, tossing it to the side before I lift him. Gripping his muscled waist, I force him to walk to the metal table with the ominous drain in the floor beneath it.

I have to give Mariax credit for how she arranged this space.

There is no element of comfort. Nothing here would indicate what happens in this room, the mind creating worse terrors because of the unknown. No matter, my shadows will do plenty to aid me.

Lowering my lips, I kiss his neck, making sure to suck hard enough to leave a hickey. It will heal quickly, but the satisfaction of marking something that belongs to Mariax makes my darkness sing.

"Climb onto the table and lie down on your back with your head hanging over the edge here," I say, pointing to the space directly in front of my groin. "Do not fucking move once you are in position."

Immediately complying with my command, Hunter does as he is told. My large skull tattoo on my abs meets his glassy gaze as he situates himself.

Usually, he is far too large for most 'normal sized' furniture. I have the same problem, but it appears that Mariax has considered this with the construction of her tables.

I walk in slow circles around Hunter, admiring his rugged beauty. I knew taking him to The Snuggle Pit was the right choice. He seems to be enjoying himself, but still, something feels off. Dismissing the thought, I come back around to stand in front of his head hanging off the table.

I've been planning this moment since before I introduced myself to Hunter. Stalking, analyzing, biding my time until I found the right moment to strike.

However, I did not plan on developing feelings for him. My emotions for him must be ignored, but that won't stop me from leaving the top button open and the zipper down, the seat of them revealing the top curve of my ass. I roll my neck, and it cracks loudly.

I line myself up and grip his cheeks to prompt him to open his jaw, which he does, even sticking his tongue out, like he is just waiting for my pre-cum to spread on it.

I slap his tongue with the head of my dick, grinning when he shivers.

"Open wider, Little Wolf," I demand in a tone that demands to be followed. My eyes rove over his naked body, each of his tattoos and piercings on display for my eyes to feast on.

His fat cock stands straight, pre-cum leaking continuously from the head.

"Take a deep breath, it will be the last one you have for a while," I command huskily, and then immediately I shove my long cock into the warmth of his mouth, wasting no time before his upside-down nose is blocked by my heavy balls.

This table sits at the perfect height as I thrust deeply into his throat. Hunter tries to grab my thighs to steady himself, so I bring shadows out to bind his arms to the side of the table.

When his defined chest seems to seize, I pull out enough for him to take one deep breath before shoving right back in.

"Swallow me, little wolf. Take me into your throat and massage my dick."

He growls, and the sensation is unreal. The deep rumble of it vibrating around my cock. Apparently, he doesn't need to breathe to growl because he doesn't stop. The base of my spine tingles and my lower abs draw in tight, signaling my impending bliss.

All of my plans will be ruined if I come too soon.

I step back, ripping my cock out of his mouth and coating his nose and chin with saliva and pre-cum. Hunter sucks in a breath, trying to lift his head, but he can't by how tightly my shadows bind him to the table. I step back over to him and cradle his head in my palms before releasing my shadows.

I shift my hands to his shoulders and use the aid of my shadows to support his back as I help him sit upright. His head falls back onto my shoulder, and for a moment, I think he passed out. But no, his eyes are open, staring at the ceiling, a small smile plays on his lips.

I once again use my shadows to lift his body completely from the table and slowly turn him before lowering him flat onto his back again, but this time his feet are closest to me. He doesn't struggle, just seems to be zoned out.

I let my power flow into the room, using shadows to bind his wrists above his head and secure them to the magically enhanced chain bolted to the table. My shadows yank his body down hard, drawing his ass almost to the bottom of the table, his legs now dangling off of it.

Next, shadows snake around his forearms and press them flat against the table, but allowing his hands room to grip the edge if he wishes. Another one lashes across his forehead to hold his gaze towards the ceiling, more shadows curl around his neck, and slither across the top of his hipbones. I leave his legs free of bindings, for now, but grip his tattooed calves to lift his legs, bending his knees so his feet lay flat on the steel, his heels close to his cheeks.

I lean between his spread legs and slam one of my hands on the table next to his head. The power I'm emanating, magically and physically, overwhelms him, just as I planned.

"Good boy. You look delicious, bound and at my mercy."

I flex the shadows holding him, and he grunts in response.

Lifting my hand from the metal surface, standing to my full height between his legs. My heart rate slows as I relax and enjoy the sight of him bound with my shadows. However, I do not forget why I chose the room closest to Mariax's playroom.

Being in a relationship with a being like me caused her endless problems. Being in love with me, which I know to be true, even if she doesn't know herself, has been the root of every negative occurrence in her life.

I told her before that I don't enjoy using the words 'I love you' because they are so often used carelessly, but it is love that I feel for her? However, I'm beginning to feel the same for the wolf my shadows hold.

She opened me up to feeling emotions, and without them both, I'd be lost, aimlessly wandering the realms.

I refuse to ever be without them again. Even if the moments of happiness are fleeting, I'll take them gladly. However, even though the damage Mariax inflicted wasn't physical, and it wasn't intentional, she caused irreparable damage, and for that, she must be punished.

Anxiety crawls up my throat with the thought. I do not care how furious she is with me; I enjoy seeing her pain as long as it's me causing it.

She can cry and scream while I lick the tears from her face and swallow her cries with my tongue. She needs a reminder of who she belongs to. Who she willingly gave her body over to because whether or not she's forgotten, she is mine and has been the entire time.

I cannot wait to see the look on her face. After centuries of dreaming of her, centuries of longing and pain, I will finally show her the consequences of her actions.

She has no idea what's coming for her.

She belongs to me, always has, and now I also have Hunter. I cannot deny that he has become mine, too. He might have been solely hers first, but now they're both mine. The organ in my chest strains against my ribcage as I think about Mariax in the same room as me.

I draw a packet of lube from my pocket and lather up my dick with it. I watch his expression as I rim the edge of his tight hole with my two fingers and plunge them in.

He groans loudly and starts cursing in Gaelic. Another wisp of shadow covers his mouth, gagging him. I leave just his nose free to breathe, for now. His muted grunts and murmurs are like a balm to my frayed mind. I love having this level of power and control over everything.

All beings will fall to their knees before me. It's just a matter of time before they break.

I add more lubrication as his muscle relaxes, pumping my fingers into him until he's loose enough to add a third. I splay my fingers as much as possible, drizzling the rest into his tight channel. Not long after, he's ready to welcome my size, but I'm losing my patience.

The thrill of getting caught by Mariax floods my system as I thrust inside with one quick movement.

Hunter screams against his shadow gag, his ass clenching my length, and it feels exquisite. I take pity on him and give him a moment to relax again.

I rest my hips on the edge of the table, only the head of my dick completely immersed. Soon his body will realize it has no choice but to open for me.

I've waited long enough. I slip into his warmth easily now that he's well-lubricated, welcoming me into the space.

Hunter's knot swells further and pre-come leaks from the tip of his dick as I massage his prostate. His cheeks clench with pleasure around me. The farther my dick slides into him, the louder his muted groans and screams grow through the shadow gag.

I drive my tattooed fingers into the hair behind his head, pulling it aggressively before wrapping the length of it around my wrist.

"Shut the fuck up and take that dick like a good boy," I command, my lips whispering against his and my shadow gagging him.

The feeling is intensely erotic and I pulse within him. I continue to move my hips in a steady rhythm, using the rope of his thick hair as a handle.

He's immobile as I wring pleasure from his body.

His pierced dick stands proud, bouncing with gravity as his hips meet mine in a seductive rhythm. I move my hands from the side of the table and grab the outside of his legs. Butterflying his muscular thighs open, they pull on the tendons painfully like his bound arms are being pulled on above his head by my shadows. The muscles in his torso, shoulders, and arms straining seductively.

I lift his hips slightly off the table and squeeze his cheeks in my hands as I pound into him furiously faster and faster, for a moment forgetting where I am and why I'm here. But it quickly comes back to me as I hear a slight noise coming from the room beyond.

He is oblivious to what is happening around him, other than the movement of my dick in his ass.

There's a shift in the energy surrounding me, letting me know my angel is close.

This is the closest I've been to her, without being disguised or shifted in some way, in centuries. Soon she will gaze upon my body once more, bringing how much she truly missed me to the forefront of her mind.

I haven't changed much in the centuries since we last saw each other, but now I have acquired more body art, covering me almost entirely.

There's a special spot on my ribs where if you stabbed a dagger into my flesh, it would pierce my heart. The hole is forever a void of nothingness. It can't be filled. Even with my dark seeping agony, I feel every moment of every day. I look forward to showing her exactly how it feels.

And, it is for that reason I have that void of untattooed skin.

Keeping my mind on the task, I tilt my head and continue listening to the room beyond. While my rhythm is smooth and even, my hips snap forward and work at a punishing pace.

I lean forward and wrap a hand around Hunter's throat while the other slams down onto the metal near his head, creating a loud sound. His eyes fly open as I slowly tighten my grip and siphon oxygen from his body. I carefully make my face blank, but if he's looking into my eyes, he will see the truth.

My truth of why we're here, and the more frightening the truth of my feelings for him. Mariax was the one to bring out these strong emotions in me originally. But he's too young to be able to recognize a lost and depraved soul in his presence.

He sees me, but only in a physical nature.

He doesn't understand what it truly means to be a god among men, to have your very existence plague you, everything that you've done etched upon the recordings of time but lost in your vast memories.

His face turns a deep red, and his lips are shaded to a beautiful blue. The last of his oxygen is depleted. Muscles are straining and fighting for air.

When he's about to pass out, I ease the pressure on his neck. However, I don't remove it, just enough that a sliver of air slips into his lungs to re-inflate them, and the small sip of air brings color back to his lips.

His eyes are full of mischief as he grins at me, only the slight upward turn of his lips showing, his eyes brightening, giving him away. The smile quickly turns to untamed lust. He tries to arch his back and hips off the table as I hit that special bundle of nerves.

Through his gag, I can make out snippets of him begging me, begging me to stroke him and make him come, begging me for release, but I'm not done playing with him yet.

I enjoy the sight of his debilitating need as much as the sight of him at my mercy. Both are empowering and deadly.

I cannot be defined, but I have never claimed to be anything but a monster. A monster with very little in this life to love or cherish, and Mariax is one of them too. I will, and always have, done anything for her to bring even the slightest smile to her face. But at the same time, I wish to ruin her for the pain she brings into my life.

When she left, a part of me broke. It was sheared off and bound to her. I didn't realize it at the time and I know she doesn't realize that we have been connected since then.

One reason Hunter and I came to The Snuggle Pit today is so that I could see if he would sub for me in his space, so I would be near her in hopes of getting caught. It was a calculated move to see if she felt me, just as much as I felt her presence.

I don't often speak of souls because I'm not convinced I have one. I know of other djinn that contained souls, but I am not convinced. On the other hand, Mariax is an entirely new creature. She is something that scratches the surface of depravity, and I cannot wait to dive in with fervor.

I remove the hand still gripping Hunter's neck and pull out of him. A touch of sadness shadows his face at the sudden loss.

I place my hand next to his head, so I am caging him in, inches away from his lips. He isn't empty long before I fill him with something new, a tendril of my shadow that acts much like a flexible tentacle.

Hunter sucks in a sharp breath at the intrusion.

He attempts to lift his head to kiss me, and I allow it, meeting his lush lips halfway. I groan into his mouth as our tongues languidly dance, reveling in the pleasure of my dick being stroked with one of my shadows.

His erection pulses against the groove between the sets of my abs, and his knot rubs against my Adonis belt, massaging us both. He grunts against my lips. His eyes roll back in his head when I press my weight onto him, making his pleasure soar. He is so swollen and painful with need.

I cannot wait to see the look on her face when she sees me with him, the male she has been a mistress to.

The game started ages ago, but now it's time to see who will win.

I must make her feel even a sliver of the suffering that I felt. I crave to see her jealous. I want to see her enraged beauty. I know how she feels. Seeing it on her face almost brings me to the brink of climax.

Returning my attention to Hunter, I notice his eyes are closed again. His body is slightly trembling. Pre-come is covering his abdomen, and he's mumbling incoherently in Scottish. I remove his shadow gag to hear him at full volume.

A gasp escapes him as he opens his eyes again. "Shite, it feels so good. Don't stop, Brad."

"Do not speak. I only removed your gag so I could enjoy your moans and grunts. Those are the only acceptable noises to make from your whorish lips," I snap at him.

I stop the movement of my hips and he growls deeply in frustration. I raise an eyebrow and throw all my daddy dom disapproval his way.

I snatch his ankles and bend his knees, pressing his feet flat on the table. His toes just meet the edge. I manifest more shadows and bind him to the table to keep him in this position. I grip the sides of the table on the outside of his legs. It's time to end this and embrace both of our pleasures.

But it's then that I sense something more from the room next to us. Somehow, my angel has figured out that there is a game in play when there shouldn't be anyone here. I can feel the change in the human technology that will allow her to see me, us. There might even be a bit of magic involved.

I turn my head to the side slightly, continuing to thrust into Hunter and relishing in the fact that my Angel is watching. In fact, she will be wishing it was her beneath me, even though she despises the very idea.

Whether tech or magic, my power overrides it and I can see into the other room. I cannot fully describe the look on her face, as it is a mixture of so many emotions, but the overall effect is stunning.

Color rises high on her pale pink cheeks, making them flush darker. I succeeded in surprising her.

Her lips are open in a soft O shape as she stares.

One palm is pressed flat on the mirror, and the other is threaded through her gorgeous pink tresses, pulling on her scalp in fury. The sight of her fingers brings the thought of my hands being in place of hers, grabbing a thick section of hair in my fist.

CHAPTER 24

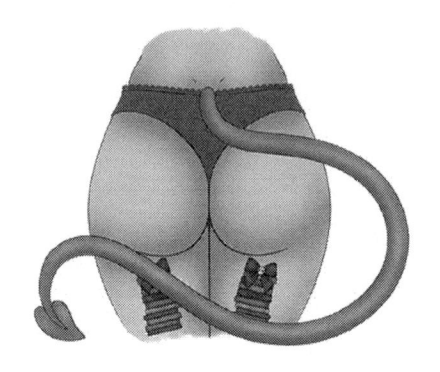

MARIAX

MY Hunter.

Mine.

Everything seems to be happening in slow motion. My feet are grounded to the spot.

Raising my eyes, I meet Hunter's lust-glazed ones.

He lies on the sterile metal table in the adjacent room. Head turned towards the mirror watching what Ian is doing to him in the reflective surface, his back flattened to the surface. His hands are bound above his head with shadows. His howls of pleasure fill the room. My mind is taking too long to process what is happening.

My eyes dilate, and a hot flush rises to my cheeks as I finally take in the whole scene. A male is standing between Hunter's muscular thighs, rhythmically thrusting into him.

I don't want to feel the heat pooling between my thighs. Why am I aroused by watching someone I hate fuck my lycan? My sub?

If there's anything I learned about my ex-daddy over the course of our relationship, it's that he's dangerously possessive, and that's putting it mildly.

If another being touched me without his permission, he

threatened to cane me until my body failed to hold me up and then lock me naked in a cage at the foot of his bed for a week. One time, he slowly drained the lifeblood from a demon in the streets of Inferuna for staring at me as we passed. The dirt below him turned to mud as the blood leaked from the puncture in his throat.

It took a lot of time and effort to get him to see that Tiffany was just my best friend. That she never had any intention of being with me sexually. He eventually ceded to this understanding, but not before he made it clear just how painful he would make her death if I ever had a reason to hurt because of her.

So, to come to my place and create this spectacle just to be caught…is unusual. He was always a bit mad, but I never expected him to be with another in front of me.

I can't catalog the range of emotions coursing through me, but some of the distinct ones are jealousy, hatred, arousal, fury.

With that thought, I stalk over to the rack with my canes and seize one before swinging it in an arch and slamming it into the two-way mirror repeatedly. Finally, there is a big enough opening into the adjacent room. I toss the cane to the side and analyze the scene before me, but nothing has improved. He is still inside Hunter but moving slower as they both stare at me.

Hunter's wide eyes are dilated, but he doesn't truly see me, so deep into subspace his surroundings are essentially numb. Yet, he is bound by those resilient and unbreakable shadows. Once they have you in their grasp, you do not move until their master allows it.

My rage grows when I shift my gaze to him. My vision tunnels as wrath consumes me.

I step through onto the decimated remains of the glass, crunching and grinding under my boots. I storm over to him while simultaneously wrapping my tail around his throat and fisting his tousled dark hair.

I rip him out of Hunter, and we slam into the wall behind him; I enjoy the sickening crack of his head as it smashes back. The tip of my tail becomes a blade while still choking him. I release his hair briefly and bend to snatch the dagger from my boot, swiftly digging it into the space between his erection and balls.

I glance up when his hiss becomes a groan of pleasure, the vibration of the sound traveling through my tail like a direct line to my clit.

My breath falters as he speaks a bit breathlessly, "Hello, Angel."

His voice nearly causes me to moan, so gravely, deep, familiar, and filled with dark promises.

"That dagger feels very familiar."

I stand quickly and seize a fistful of his hair again, my tail remains choking and slightly cutting his neck.

"What the fuck are you doing here, Ian?" I seethe, pulling on his hair and digging my sharpened nails into his scalp, the dagger in my other hand pressing harder into his sensitive flesh.

Warm blood trails onto my fingers from the slice.

"You didn't miss me?" he says and smirks, his hands rising to rest on my waist before drawing me against him. "Damn, I love knife play. You've never used two blades at once before," he punctuates his comment with a few strokes of his hips, driving himself onto the blade and groaning loudly.

Feeling his half naked body against mine is overwhelming. The combination of his hard dick and zipper below it slowly rubbing against the thin layer of cloth covering my pussy is erotic, the sensation creating an inferno of heat to flood my core.

I squeeze my eyes closed, refusing to forget my loathing

for this male and everything he has done to me. Breathing deeply, I become bombarded with his scent, mixed with sex.

It's a heady combination and I feel momentarily drunk on it.

"Fuck this!" I dig the blade at his neck deeper, rivets of blood run down Ian's throat and drip onto his naked tattoo covered chest. "You do not have permission to appear out of nowhere, like you're making some grand entrance. I have no doubt you planned out every detail…"

He brings an arm up between us, grabbing my tail just before the sharp end, dragging it down sharply to slice my own flesh.

Pain lances through me, blood welling and flowing down the lacerations. I loosen my hold during the momentary distraction.

Ian uses that time to grab my other wrist that is holding the dagger and squeeze. Bones crunch and grind together before I'm forced to let the weapon fall. While I'm blinded by the pain, he shoves me backward and uses his momentum to spin out of my hold.

He's now a few feet away as we square off.

I know the only reason Hunter hasn't barreled his way into this fight is because he remains bound and gagged by shadows.

"You're going to regret coming back into my life," I growl, every word dripping with venom.

I don't know why I'm surprised when his deep laughter resonates from within his chest. I slowly stalk towards him. For every step I take, he takes one back. Ian hasn't changed at all since I last saw him. He's still the tyrant who demands obedience from everyone around him.

And now after everything he's already taken from me, everything I still suffer through, he wants my Pup too?

Never.

For a moment, he actually looks pained by my words and his voice softens, "Angel, I never left."

He stands there sexier than he ever had a right to, with his still hard dick standing above his unzippered jeans. I grin at his arrogance when I realize where he stopped backing up and his head tilts slightly in confusion.

I'm no longer the same lost little demon, and he is going to find out just how different I am.

CHAPTER 25

Ian

Mariax sprints forward, throwing all of her power into her legs. I only have time to brace myself as she crashes into my chest, knocking the air from my lungs, and we plummet through the jagged remains of the mirror.

I roll away from her into a crouching position. Before I manage to stand, a sharp sting registers across the entire right side of my face as she slaps me with her tail.

I grab her tail and wrap it around my wrist, lashing out with a shadow to snatch her long braid. My shadow yanks her head back and I step up close to her, unleashing nearly my full well of power. Her eyes dilate and her body shivers as wave after wave of dark energy skims her flesh.

Blood drips from my wrist when she shifts her tail into something akin to barbed wire. On instinct, I release my hold and she pulls her tail back quickly, causing the little barbs to deepen the lacerations as they tear out of my skin.

I hiss through clenched teeth, trying to rein in the pain she caused, gripping her hair tighter with my shadows.

She spins in my grasp, twisting her body and ripping out several strands of hair in the process. She faces the wall that was previously at her back, donkey kicking me straight in the chest, forcing me to relent and step back a few paces.

I don't know where she learned more in the art of fighting, but she has improved greatly since I began her training.

We collide again and again, making contact with the other's flesh in a blur of movement, moving across the room with each strike.

I press Mariax against the wall with a restraint web, wrapping a hand around her throat. Shadow limbs creep up her thigh while she's held in place, screaming with the fury of a Valkyrie.

I hold her in place and slowly remove my jeans. They were becoming a nuisance and hindering my range of movement since they were already halfway down my ass as I fucked Hunter.

She lowers her head in an attempt to headbutt me when I step out of my jeans. I squeeze her airway tighter and lean back to watch her flawless skin change colors as she loses oxygen.

So beautiful.

She uses my obsession with her against me, kneeing me in the balls while I am enraptured. I release her throat to cup my balls, but circle her ankle with a shadow limb.

She quickly spins to my left so she's behind me and shoves me into the wall. She cackles when my body thuds against the cement and metal grid, my forehead bashes against it as well.

This is becoming tiresome. I will remind her who I am and what I am capable of.

I whip shadows from the ether and capture Mariax's wrists, binding them together in front of her. I turn her slowly to face me as she tries to struggle free, shoulders jerking and muscles straining, momentarily panicked by the confines. However, I watch as her resolve strengthens.

She dashes forward and throws her bound arms over my neck. Hoisting herself up to circle her legs around my waist, she arches her back, causing me to palm her ass for something to regain my balance. However, my attempt at staying upright fails and we crumble like a house of cards.

We're a tangled mess of limbs, but her horns seem to glimmer in the light, like a beacon begging to be used. I grab the base of her horns where they connect to her skull and throw her over my head and onto her back.

I stand, admiring the view.

Her skin is flushed, our blood covers her flesh and the remnants of her clothing. Her top is now cut to ribbons, one of her nipples toying with me as it peeks in and out of a tear.

I flex my shadows and drag her toward the spanking bench in the corner. I'll immobilize her and then spank the shit out of her ass for her disrespect and ignorance of the pain she caused me all these centuries.

In a surprise move, she manages to get her feet under her and runs backward until her back is flush with my side.

CHAPTER 26

Hunter

What the fuck is happening? He knows Mariax? Is he one of her clients?

Questions swirl in my mind rapidly, practically smashing into the next before the initial question formed.

There is a cacophony of sounds coming from the other room. It's like a damn war has broken out in The Snuggle Pit. Confusion and pure rage war with each other inside my mind. My muscles shake with the effort to free myself from my binds, but they have no give.

I refuse to be left here like some forgotten fuck boy.

How do they know each other?

Floating in a cloud of impending bliss caused me to miss most of their brief conversation, but I know Mariax called him Ian.

Has this Ian been parading around as Brad to use me?

I grip the edge of the table hard enough that I hear metal protesting and pull my body upward with my abdominal muscles. I gain less than a centimeter of space between my lower back and the table.

Mariax's screams, much like a highlander's war cry, blast into the room. Brad's shadows, NO, godsdamn Ian's shadows dissolve as their fighting intensifies, and he loses his connection with them.

Fucking finally!

I sit up slowly, my mind swimming with the movement, and my disorientation worsens for a moment. Exhaustion sweeps over me in waves. My mind is warring with itself. One half is content to remain disconnected in subspace, while the other half needs to witness what is happening in the other room.

I swivel my legs over the edge of the table and hop off. Stumbling completely nude over to the broken window to take in the carnage, I ignore the way my feet are cut to pieces. Glass cuts into my palms as I press them to either side of the opening and watch the scene unfolding before me.

Lust overtakes me as I watch them attacking each other again and again. I lean into the jagged glass, hissing as the shards dig into my shoulder deeply, and palm my still hard cock in one hand and gently massage my knot in the other, attempting to alleviate some of the deep ache.

Having a swollen knot is so much worse than blue balls.

I run my thumb over my piercings and groan. Why couldn't they have waited to battle until I came? My ass feels empty after being used, aching to be full again.

How did I not realize the shite he was slinging was all lies? He never even told me his name, I practically strangle my cock with the realization. How can I still care about what happens to him when he used me so heartlessly?

Mariax slashes her tail wickedly, blood sprays from the back of Ian's knee as she slices to the bone.

He falls heavily to one injured knee as it gives out and he crashes into the spanking bench with the rest of his body. He groans loudly, the wood and metal making up the bench splinters under his weight. Mariax launches on top of his bowed back and tears at his neck with her wee fangs.

He rears back and headbutts her in the face, but their combined weight defeats the structure of the spanking bench fully and it collapses.

Mariax screams like a banshee when her nose breaks from the impact of Ian's skull and the fine hairs all over my body stand on end. She is vengeance reincarnate, and she has never looked more wild and beautiful. Blood gushes from her nostrils, and her clothing barely exists anymore. Thin strips of fabric cling to her form, large patches of skin showing in between.

I grip the edges of the mirror tighter as I fight my instincts and my wolf to intervene. Two beings I care for deeply are tearing each other apart. I am losing the battle to keep my sanity as my anger, confusion, lust, and pride ripple over me in waves.

I honestly don't know who will win, and that thought terrifies me. Are they fighting to the death, or just aiming to seriously harm and maim? Mariax and Ian are giving all of themselves to this fight, careless to the injuries on their person or each other.

The tension between them grows the longer the fight continues.

Watching them, I come to the conclusion that this is necessary.

This is more than just hate, the emotions from them both so thick in the air, I can practically taste them. Whatever it is they have to work out between them will eventually be fought in words, so it is better they dish out the physical violence before they even try to really speak to each other.

I'm concerned they will seriously damage each other, but my arousal is a lust crazed beast. Everything in my groin is swollen and watching them roll on the floor and connect flesh to flesh endlessly has me feeling like I might burst.

I stroke myself as I watch them, bitter at being forgotten but aroused to the point of no return. My length jerks in my hand as my thumb runs over the slit in my head.

Ian picks up the remainder of the spanking bench, heaves it above his head, and then launches it across the room with a roar. It splinters into a million wood fragments, bursting out like the shards after a grenade has exploded.

They block their faces with their forearms simultaneously, as if they practiced for this exact moment. But the fight still doesn't cease. They haven't said anything this entire time, it's just grunting, panting, and groans of pain.

They face off, chests heaving, and hands clenched in the fists at their sides.

CHAPTER 27

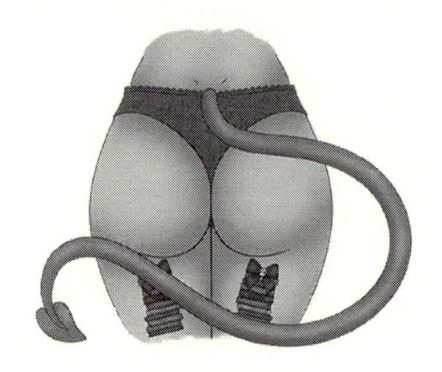

MARIAX

Ian and I face each other, sweat, and blood splatters the concrete below us. Everything he does has me on edge, from his pompous attitude to his tempting body.

He blows a puff of air out of the side of his mouth to get a piece of hair out of his eye, before running a bloodied hand along his jaw, the light stubble creating a soft rasp against his palm. Blood drips down the massive skull tattooed across his abdomen, the trail in their wake resembling tears.

Why did he have to add more tattoos?

Tattoos and piercings are like crack to me. I cannot resist once I've had a hit. I'm frustrated and pissed off that I still have feelings for him, and now I'm going to swoon over his bloody and tattooed ripped body?

I ignore my body, urging me to run my tongue down his throat and swirl it on the black rose tattooed onto the hollow of his throat and listen to my brain.

He sighs deeply, as if in contemplation of what to do with me now, so I answer the question for him. I rush him, knowing he will easily sidestep me. When my path is clear, I mean to parkour the shit out of the wall in front of me, but as my foot collides with the wall and I rebound, Ian is right behind me.

My slowly healing nose bashes against his chest, breaking anew. Pain lances through my face, and I shove myself away from him. He becomes slightly unbalanced, so I use it to my advantage, dropping and kicking his legs out from under him.

We are close enough now to the giant X in the center of my restraint grid on the wall with the arm and leg restraints attached to chains. I stretch my arm as far as it will go, reaching for one, but he seizes my wrist in his, pulling it down in a way that would break a mortal's bones. My tendons and bones protest, but it does not snap as he intended.

I hate that he knows what I'm trying to do.

Elbowing him in the face with my free arm, I feel it sink into the soft flesh of his eye socket. He cuts off my airway by digging his forearm into my throat. We scramble along the floor in front of the Saint Andrew's cross for an immeasurable amount of time before I feel his shadows wrap around my torso, drawing me towards him.

Pressing another shadow onto my spine, he forces me to arch and raise my ass. I don't get a chance to protest before he is raining blows across both cheeks. The burn from the blows is intense, and I already feel hand-shaped welts rising to the surface.

His hard-on presses into the back of my thighs, and it's too much. Warmth floods my sex and slowly drips down my thighs. I know he can smell my arousal.

His shadows tighten in response, and he grinds against me, the shredded leggings doing little as a barrier between us.

He tears a new hole in the fabric at the apex of my thighs, essentially transforming them into the shortest mini skirt I've ever seen. But that isn't enough. Ian's hands and more shadows work with frenzied movements to rid me of the fabric. All that remains is the elastic at the waist and a strip hanging down one side.

"Get the fuck off me!" I screech before I let my lust take over my senses and beg him to fuck me.

"Just remember you asked for this," he responds cryptically, his voice hoarse and deep.

Ian's power pulses around me, and I'm flying across the room back to where the remnants of the two-way mirror lay scattered when his shadows act as a slingshot.

I hit the ground hard and roll, fresh cuts and bruises forming as he hunts me. He is incredibly sexy, sprayed in blood, his tattoos hardly visible in some areas from the gore. A large cut runs across his cheekbone, and his bottom lip is split, making me want to bite it and suck the warm essence into my mouth even though I hate him as much as I do.

He goes for brute force again, and I dance away, using my knowledge of the room to my advantage. Jumping up, I grab the grid across the ceiling and wrap my legs around his neck. He grips them, trying to pry them off of him. I'm holding him so tightly between my thighs that I know he can't breathe.

I let go of the rungs above when he looks like he's about to pass out. We drop, and his back meets the floor. I land on top of him, sprawled out on top of his chest. My knees crack against the concrete when I fall, pain radiates throughout my body. I'm sure they're fractured.

I scooch back a little on his hard chest, enjoying the dazed look on his face. No doubt temporarily concussed when his head met the concrete. He'll heal in a moment, so I take him in while I can. I can feel his growing erection behind the base of my tail, even if his brain is scrambled.

I bite my lip, trying to hide the grin forming on my face

when I get an idea.

There was never a better way to get back at Ian than taking away his power in the bedroom. Even when he was teaching me how to be a dominant and he would play submissive, he was still mostly in control of the scene. However, there were times when I took full control, and so with that inspiration in mind; my tail becomes a wicked blade behind my back.

I trail it down his inner thigh from the tender skin below his balls to his knee. He groans, and I cover his mouth with my palm. His eyes are now aware, and they flash with anger and heat.

He grips the outside of my thighs with his hands and his shadows grip my calves, but they don't force me off him as I expected. Instead, he holds me down and moves his hips with need.

I turn my head to look over my shoulder, the desperate need to reacquaint myself with the dick I knew so well, overtaking the anger. I stare at his length. Runes tattooed in thin, delicate lines cover his shaft. I gasp in a breath at these new additions, wondering what would possess him to add them to his body.

I become distracted when he gently kisses my inner thigh and then bites it viciously. Pain blends with pleasure as his teeth sink into my flesh. I scream and grab his stubbled jaw, squeezing it open and forcing him to release me.

Focusing on his face, I resume my exploration with my tail.

It shifts to its normal form, latching onto his dick in a coil of undulating flesh. I move it up and down, using the blood on his body as lubrication.

Slipping my hands into my tank, I pull the cloth tight and rip the majority of it from my body. Only a small piece of the top is left covering part of one breast, but the other is exposed completely. I palm my covered tit while the nipple ring in the exposed one glimmers in the light above.

Ian's head, thrown back in pleasure, lifts as his sight zeros in on my piercing, but before he can move, I climb onto his face.

Ian gets over the shock of seeing me partially bare real fast. Grabbing my thighs, he attacks my core with vigor, biting and sucking on my lips and ghosting my clit with his tongue. He might have claimed to hate my body mods, but he could never help himself when they were in his face, the evidence of it continuing to grow harder within the coil of my tail.

Just as I wish he were buried inside me, he transforms his tongue into one that's long, with tiny bumps all over one side.

I buck against the intrusion, reminded about all the times in our past he used to enjoy torturing me with a new tongue. He rarely used the same one twice, and it always left me shattered into a million pieces when I came. Ian is employing the same methods now, the swirling of the abnormal appendage mind-altering.

A blend of a growl and grunts draws my attention to the left. In the cataclysmic events that followed, finding Ian, I completely forgot about Hunter. How did he get free from the shadows?

Fuck! Guilt consumes me, nearly snuffing out my desire.

But then I realize, although I cannot fix the current situation, I can put on a show to help Hunter find the release he deserves.

I nearly beg Hunter to join us, but just then, Ian sucks on my clit with strong, sharp pulses.

I massage my tits with my hands, flicking my pierced nipples with my thumbs intermittently, watching Hunter's glazed over eyes. My tail still works behind me, and it slides along Ian's length easily, with the copious pre-come trailing down from the head, pink now that is mixed with the blood.

Hunter strokes himself with one hand while massaging his knot with the other. His knot is so swollen and begging for release.

He's leaning heavily on the edge of the sharp glass mirror, causing blood to drip down his right arm. His feet are still in the room beyond, but his torso tilts slightly forward, as if drawn to us by an invisible tether. Hunter is practically panting as he jerks himself off, keeping his eyes locked with mine. His pace matches both my hips and tail.

Each bar of his ladder adds to his building bliss.

I don't look away from him for a second as I ride Ian's mouth with abandon, reveling in the feeling of him eating me out with his monster tongue. I continue gyrating my hips and force Ian and Hunter to groan with my increased pace.

It feels incredible to watch Hunter and soak in my own pleasure.

His tattooed chest flexes with his ministrations, causing his nipple piercings to wink in the light. I ache to run my tongue over all of his piercings. To feel them match my body temperature as I consume them with my mouth and cunt, and my tail's grasp jerks faster and harder in response to my thoughts.

Hunter is close, and he's also in deep sub-space. I fight my own lust filled thoughts as I focus on what Hunter needs, and right now he needs his mistress.

I continue riding Ian's face as I speak to Hunter. "Come for me, Pet. Show your mistress how much you enjoy watching her get eaten out."

Hunter moans at the sound of my command, his strokes uncontrolled

"Lift your heavy balls into your palm and pull gently. You're such a good boy. Come now," I direct him firmly, barely able to hang onto coherent thoughts.

"Mistress…Mar… Fuuuuuuuck!"

Hunter's head tips back as he covers himself in cum, shooting it all over his stomach, covering his fist before spilling into a puddle on the floor. Hunter always releases copious amounts of cum, but it's so much hotter watching him come from afar.

Like his orgasm drained the strength from his muscular legs, he wobbles as if he's inebriated, catching himself on the sharp mirror again.

I'm about to call off this whole thing when he smiles softly and nods as if to say keep goin' lassie, somehow looking restful, leaning on shards of pain.

Unlike Hunter's smile, nothing about this reunion of sorts is slow and gentle. It's quick, violent, and dirty. Quicker than I'd like. I'm reaching the precipice.

Bracing my hands on the ground, I thrust my pussy onto Ian's face as hard as possible. My toes are going numb, signaling my impending orgasm.

Ecstasy blooms in my core, the razor's edge I'm balancing on tilts and I freefall willingly into Nirvana.

I drive forward with my hips, my pubic bone smashing into Ian's nose, breaking it. More blood pools beneath me as Ian fights for breath. Warm ropes of cum jet onto my back, his nails and shadows digging into my thighs as he finishes with me.

I climb off of him and then stand above him.

"You owe me a new spanking bench, Cupcake," I state with an air of authority before turning on my heel and stomping to the door.

CHAPTER 28

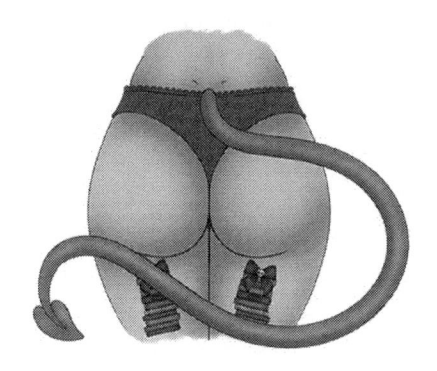

MARIAX

I stomp into the hallway completely bare, slamming the door behind me with enough force to send a crack across the outside edge...I couldn't care less. I pace in front of the door, shoving my fingers into the now absolute bird's nest I call my hair and pulling hard.

I don't know how to handle the emotions boiling in my gut.

Dadd—Ian is here. Ian has violently shattered my reality in seconds.

And then there's Hunter. I want to feel angry with him for being with Ian, but the dominant part of me recognizes he was deep in sub-space and hasn't had proper aftercare.

I saw the look on both of their faces when they were having sex. There is a deep connection between them. Ian is fighting it, but Hunter is already addicted, locked into Ian's gravitational pull...just like I was.

I need space to decompress and reevaluate my life's choices.

And that's when I notice Lauren.

She stands completely still in the hallway, her muscles tense with the sight of me, eyes wide and mouth popped open in shock.

There is color high on her cheeks, and I can see the tips of her wings above her head in the doorway. She holds a whip in one hand, dangling down by her thigh. She's just finishing up with a new client session.

She finally regains her voice. "Holy shit, Mistress, what—"

"Long story, but I need you to go to my playroom, collect Hunter and the other male, and place them in separate quarters."

"Wait, what's happened?" Lauren asks with concern.

"I don't have the physical or mental capacity to explain right now. But be gentle with Hunter. He is just coming out of subspace."

"Mistress, you didn't have a session with Hunter today and I didn't see him arrive."

I run a hand through my pink nest I call hair, my fingers getting caught in something sticky.

"It's complicated. Please, just follow my instructions. Hunter needs all the aftercare you can give him. Have him shower or take a bath, treat any unhealed wounds, and tuck him into one of the snuggliest apartments we have." I blow out a long breath and continue as I rub my temples. "Actually, grab the softest throw from my bed too so he can be wrapped in my scent since I can't be there," I add, my voice cracking on the last word.

I'm visibly losing my composure, and thankfully, Lauren doesn't question me.

Her eyes are full of concern as she appraises me. "Yes, Mistress. I'll tend to them."

I can tell she wants a further explanation, and to console me, but she holds her tongue she runs off to do as I told her.

What the fuck am I going to do with them?

CHAPTER 29

Hunter

I've run my hands through my hair for the hundredth time, cursing viciously under my breath in Gaelic and pacing back and forth in front of the huge pine tree in front of me.

Mariax hasn't spoken to either of us since it happened, and this is the first time in days I've been outside of The Snuggle Pit. I had no desire to leave her with her memories or *him*, but my wolf demanded we head to the woods.

I cannot fathom how I didn't realize Brad wasn't who he claimed to be. He's not who I thought I was falling in love with. Fuck, I've fallen for them both. This explains why I've cut everyone else off sexually and didn't know why.

I don't even know if he wants me for me or if I was just a means to an end. Either way, he used me, and that cannot stand. I feel like such an asshole laying there being pleasured as she looked on in horror.

I should have known better, I should have had Ian...Brad, whatever the fuck his name is, take me home instantly. And then I take it a step further and chug my cock in front of them while I watch them after their fight.

I don't know what to do with these feelings.

It frustrates me that I'm falling hard for Ian. I don't know if I can come back from that after everything that recently happened with Patrick. But I also love Mariax and will do anything I can to be with her.

Ian fucking used me to ease his path back into Mariax's life. I can see that now that sex isn't clouding my brain.

Something was off about him since the night I met him in the woods. Why couldn't I see this before? He was far too interested in Mariax and her sex club, and I was blind to it all.

But the fact that I was just a pawn in his twisted game makes my fangs ache.

Ian needs to explain everything, especially why he would lie to us. Whatever he did was a betrayal. I will know the whole story. Next time I see him, I will have my answers one way or another.

I'm done with being a doormat.

No one is going to walk all over me ever again. I'm a fucking alpha lycan!

CHAPTER 30

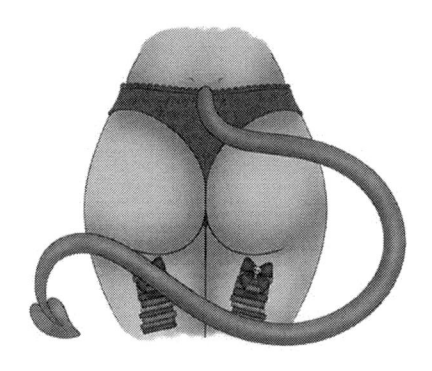

Mariax

For several weeks after Ian rudely popped up into my world again, he showed up everywhere.

I told Hunter and Ian to leave after I separated them into different apartments in The Snuggle Pit. I refused to speak to either of them and saw no point in keeping them there.

Confusion and guilt swirl in my chest when I think of Hunter. He didn't ask to be in the middle of Ian and me. I don't even know why he suddenly decided to show himself.

I have noticed that whenever Ian is around, not as many odd things are happening. It could be a coincidence. However, that is very unlikely.

One of two things is possible.

Either Ian is somehow causing these disturbances, or he is the reason that they're not happening, like whatever is stalking me is afraid of him. I still have no idea what is causing my cupboards to be left open or my dishes spread out in weird patterns.

Now, obviously, I'm a torture demon. Those kinds of things don't scare me. But enough is enough. I need whatever is happening to stop, not out of fear, but for my mental state. And thanks to Ian, that crumbling wall is fast falling.

I don't know how much more I can take.

But in reality, I've been feeling something watching me for longer than he says he's been vancating into the human realm, longer than I even realized.

That aching dread that is coiled deep in my core has receded lately. It's now noticeable, and my mind festers with the constant reminder that something was there and now isn't and it is just as unnerving.

I've been having more flashbacks and nightmares, and my lack of confidence is soaring. This is not how I intended to run my business. I cannot be Mistress Mariax if I'm constantly looking over my shoulder, worried about what, or who, is lurking in the shadows.

I don't know what I need to do. But one thing is for certain. I need to get more information out of Ian, and I have the perfect way.

I know torturing the information out of him won't work. And I'm assuming he hasn't been tortured himself recently. Although if he's been in Inferuna all the time I've been in the human realm, it is still possible.

I digress.

Torture won't work. So, I will create jealousy, need, and arousal so painful that his dick will feel like it is about to explode.

But I won't let him come. Not yet. Not anytime soon. I don't trust him. He keeps attempting to tell me what happened, and that he didn't betray me. But I cannot trust him. He tortured my best fucking friend.

I'm going out of my damn mind. Anyway, I intend to get answers. Tonight. Hunter and Ian are due here in a few hours, and I need to prepare.

The game is on motherfucker.

CHAPTER 31

Hunter

Ian holds open the door for me as we enter Mariax's suite.

I tromp into the room, my heavy boots leaving mud all over the entryway. I am not about to bring her wrath down upon me. So I toe them off. Plus, I know the kind of punishment she can inflict, not that I don't enjoy most of it.

I've wanted to try all the dark, taboo kinks with her. I have a feeling if the three of us can make this work, there are endless possibilities.

We would make a perfect throuple.

My dreams don't seem as far off now as they once were. My heart beats wildly at the thought. So many scenarios come to mind. I groan and reach down to rearrange my junk, not giving a shite that I'm noticeably adjusting myself.

Ian's leaning on the doorway into her bedroom, back against the frame, to watch Mariax and me simultaneously.

I raise an eyebrow at him, nonverbally asking, *What the fuck do we do now? This is yer shitshow arsehole.*

He stares at me with a bored expression, ignoring my question.

The two of them being in the same room is overwhelming. Their power fills the space and feels like it's seeping into my skin. I can't wait to see what these two can teach me.

I understand that Ian is dominant, mostly for the power play. He needs control just as much as Mariax and I do. However, he has the power and means to be the alpha of both of us. I've only known Ian for a few months, but I know he is a good male, despite how he portrays himself.

How he looks at her speaks of deep devotion, or maybe its obsession. It's possibly a bit of both. Ian is still deeply in love with Mariax, whether he wants to admit it or not. I'm enjoying him watching her, and it's a new side of him I didn't expect to see.

His pupils dilate as his arousal grows, the pulse in his jaw fluttering, a telltale sign that he's trying to hold himself back.

I slowly rake my eyes down his muscular body, the hard planes looking ready to escape his clothing. Even dressed simply in a black T-shirt and snug jeans, he is sexy as sin. His neck tattoos and full sleeves are on display, the ink creating living art that never seems fully natural. They always seem to be pulsing with his power.

The outline of his cock is clear as he hardens along his thigh.

I thought I was big, but I have nothing on Ian. The first time we were sixty-nining, I nearly choked to death from asphyxiation. I passed out right as I came down his throat, his hands clenching my arse cheeks as he swallowed me down, and it was incredible.

His bottom lip is pulled under his top teeth, his hands in his pockets, and his breathing is slow and even, but his emotions are written on his face, and the tension in his shoulders. He eyes her like a hawk as we all stand here awkwardly.

"Are we all just going to stand here all day?" Mariax asks, raising her eyebrows.

"Ye are the one who invited us here, Cheetie," I respond, a small smile pulling up at the corner of my right lip.

"Fine. What the fuck happened?" she questions us with anger and annoyance.

"Angel, you will have to be more specific than that. Too many events have occurred to decipher which exact one you are speaking of," Ian says pompously, eager to stoke her temper.

Taking his bait, Mariax stomps over, hands balled into tight fists, and glares up at him. "Maybe you appearing out of nowhere and fucking Hunter in front of me?"

Ian smirks and leans down until she is forced to bow her spine or meet his lips with hers.

She fists the material of his t-shirt with her tail and grabs his shoulders to keep herself upright. "If you believe Hunter is yours, then he is mine as well because I own you," Ian whispers darkly.

"He's mine," she hisses harshly, her lips nearly grazing Ian's. "You thought you could just waltz in and claim him for yourself? I don't fucking think so." Her voice is rising in pitch as her anger consumes her control.

I can do nothing but stare at the scene before me. They have no idea how much they are drawn to one another. If they would have the courtesy to ask me themselves, I would've already told them I belong with both of them. I am theirs just as much as they are mine.

Mariax shoves Ian in the chest and turns on her heel, muttering curses and barely veiled threats as she walks towards her living room, Ian and I trailing behind her like well-trained dogs.

She sighs deeply and sits on the right side of her love

seat, curling her legs into her chest and wrapping her arms around her shins. She looks so tiny like this, her wee form curled into a ball. Her expression is mostly blank, but a slight pinching of her features tells of the emotions she barely contains within.

I take the seat next to Mariax and Ian seats himself in the papasan chair. He looks out of place in this cozy environment. He tries to sit with his back straight, but the rounded shape of the chair is at odds with his posture. He's forced to lean forward, resting his elbows on his bent knees, his index fingers steepled in front of his inviting mouth.

I take in the space; soft lighting comes from a reading lamp on the end table between the couch and the chair Ian is occupying. A gas fire with fake logs burns soundlessly in the small fireplace directly across from the couch. A large bookshelf dominates the space, running along the wall to my left.

Every space on the bookshelf is filled from floor to ceiling. Books are stacked, slipped in sideways, and even stacked on the floor surrounding it.

Her interest in dark romance piques my curiosity. My fingers itch to graze their spines and listen to their whispered secrets. I rise halfway off of the couch, intending to dive into her cozy wee library, but her tail wraps around my hips and pulls me back down to the couch.

I grin at her and stroke the end of her tail that's still wrapped around me, the heart shape spade at the tip curling around my hand. Mariax shivers next to me. She's so responsive to my touch.

She clears her throat and I turn towards her at the sound. Mistress Mariax is now taking command of the room, all pretenses of friendly nature gone. She rips her tail out of my gentle hold and begins what sounds like a well-practiced speech.

"You didn't answer my first question, Cupcake. Why are you here? What was the purpose of showing up in my club unannounced?" she intones with anger and annoyance.

"Because I wanted to test your connection to me, to see if you still feel the pull of our bond. To listen to your pulse race as you took in everything you left behind," Ian explains seriously. "I also wanted to watch the veil of jealousy cloud your features."

"Really? Why do you have to be such an asshole?" I question him.

"You thought you could leave me and there would not be repercussions?" Ian fires back in response.

"He's just made that way, Cheetie," I chuckle, sinking deeper into the couch cushions and resting my arms across the back.

I don't miss the way Mariax tenses and then sighs as my arm grazes her shoulders.

She slowly turns her head to glare at me, and then returns her ire back to Ian before she continues, "Fine, I will play along like a good girl for now. But know this." Her voice lowers an octave, sounding like a deadly purr.

Ian interrupts her, living up to the arsehole status she accused him of. "Let me save us all a frivolous discussion and educate you on current matters."

Mariax leans back on my arm and huffs, but waves at Ian to continue.

"What you truly desire to know is why I tortured Tiffany in Inferuna. However, there is a more dire topic we must discuss first. I will not be interrupted by either of you."

Mariax and I glance at each other, too curious now to disobey.

"My reason for arriving in the human realm was simple.

Find you, relay what information I have, and then claim you over and over until you remember without question who you belong to."

"I. Am. Not. Yours. Get that through your thick djinn brain. We had a relationship centuries ago. You have no claim over me."

A low rumble comes from Ian's chest the more she denies him. The primal side of him is waking up and a dangerous gleam glints in his eyes.

"That is where you're wrong. You do not have a choice in this matter. You gave yourself to me freely, invoking an irrevocable bond that spans lifetimes," he proclaims, his upper lip curling.

"You thought that moving to a new realm would end my desire for you? Never," he growls possessively, the sound waking my body up.

Ian is a dangerous creature. That knowledge causes my wolf to wake up. The fine hairs all over my body stand on end as it takes in the tension about to suffocate us all.

Mariax's lips set into a firm line, her eyes narrowing, their opal-gray hue shining brighter with her emotions, is her only response.

Ian leans further forward on his forearms. "I came to warn you. The Potentate whispered his secrets too closely to the wrong shadow. I learned of a new plot to end your life. A creature was made in the fires of Inferuna, one unlike anything we have ever seen."

The room is silent except for our breathing and the beating of our hearts. Anxiety blooms in my gut at the memory of hunting the creature in the woods. I was right in what I thought it was, and that is not a good thing. It seeks to harm her. I will do everything in my power to assure it never touches her.

"I hate to burst your bubble Ian, but I've known something is hunting me for years."

He growls deeply with displeasure before responding, "Why have you done nothing to rid it from your life?"

"Until very recently, it was just a nuisance. I had no reason to worry over it because I barely left the Snuggle Pit as it is."

"Only to go get pissed at Get Fucked, aye?" I interject cheekily.

Mariax's tail squeezes between us and pokes me in the ribs. I chuckle at her small display of bratty playfulness and scoot closer to her on the couch. She ignores my question and responds to Ian.

"Seriously, I don't need you to vancate here just to tell me what I already know. The only thing you accomplished is disrupting my life," she responds haughtily, crossing her arms over her chest, causing her tits to sit higher in her thin tank top.

Ian and I both zero in on her chest, our predatory nature zinging through our bodies.

Ian stands and crosses the space to lean on the frame of Mariax's bedroom doorway, struggling to contain his building power washing over Mariax and I.

Every muscle in my body stiffens as his magic seems to have a direct line to my cock, the dark power kissing my skin.

Mariax rubs her thighs together, brushing mine in the process. She's probably feeling the desire his magic causes as well.

"I do not care if you want me in your life or not. You are mine, little one. You can choose to ignore the fact that your life is hanging precariously by the tip of this creature's claws." One of his shadows appears behind her back and pulls her hair sharply so that she must look directly at Ian. Another squeezes her jaw to force her eyes to his. "But I will not. Your life means more to me than my own. I will see that you are protected. Always."

Mariax's lips are slightly pursed from the shadow's tight hold, and she breathes through her nose in irritation.

After a few moments, he releases her from his magic, and she stands abruptly.

"I've had enough of this bullshit for today," she huffs and rolls her eyes.

Walking with determination into her bedroom, shoulder-checking Ian, who couldn't be bothered to move, on the way inside.

"Both of you, in my bedroom, now," she commands from within.

Ian sighs deeply but stays where he is planted.

I don't like him disrespecting her. I will only allow so much before I tear into him. He has no right to come into her home and act like a dick.

I stalk towards him, the thick carpet masking any sound from my steps, and grab him by the back of the neck, dragging him into her bedroom. A shadow whips around my wrist and pries me off him. He faces me with violence, the air around him practically shivers.

"How dare you grab me like one of your mangy wolves? DO NOT ever treat me with such disrespect again," he seethes, his violet eyes glowing with unchecked fury.

I match his glare, my own eyes becoming obsidian as my ire rises.

"Disrespect ye? How about how ye disrespected Mariax? We were invited to her home to talk about everything yer dumb arse instigated. What makes ye think she is going to be willing to listen if ye continue to act like a fucking neep-head?" My Scottish accent is becoming clearer with every sentence. I cannot help but roll my Rs and use slang no one in this room understands but me.

"Enough!" she hisses, pushing between us before shoving us with the heel of her palm to each of our sternums.

My body shakes with fury and my wolf is seconds from making an appearance, close enough that I can feel my claws waiting and ready to gouge and maim. Ian doesn't look much better. I don't know what happens when he loses his temper, but I'm feeling just manic enough now to want to find out.

She holds us there for several minutes, standing between us, knowing we won't risk harming her to attack each other. Mariax takes a deep breath in through her nose and out through her slightly parted glossy lips.

She briefly reaches up to cup my bearded cheek with her tail, and I nuzzle into it. I love that she has this extra appendage to play with. It's very pliable, similar to a cheetie's, but in place of fur is silky skin with hard, yet soft, ridges running down its length. A small smile creeps onto my face as I realize how perfectly her nickname suits her.

However, Mariax is going to have to learn that unless it's just her and me in a session or scene, I will not play her submissive.

I'm not against us all being together. In fact, I'm obsessed with the idea. My desire to have two partners is just out of reach. I know I must work my way back into her good graces.

Although, I know there will be no mending the rift between them unless they sit down and have a rational discussion. Emotional and sexual tension hangs in the air around us thickly, so thick I'm inhaling with every breath.

Mariax stops in the middle of her room and eyes me, mischief and determination in her gaze.

"Pup, you've been awful quiet for someone who's so loud when you're getting fucked by him," she says with a sarcastic attitude, gesturing to Ian.

A slight heat courses up my neck, but I shake it off,

shrugging one shoulder and smirking at her.

We should never have fucked in one of her pain rooms. That is not how Mariax deserved to find out about Ian and my relationship. She's pissed, and rightfully so. I know better. I should have put him off until permission was asked from my Mistress, as well as using her play space. He is just so…fucking irresistible, like her.

I've thought about how I would feel if I walked in on two males being intimate who I had been in a relationship with.

What the hell would I even do? Probably what Mariax did to Ian. Fuck my arse up and then throw me in a locked room.

Damn, I love that lass.

She strides quickly forward and snaps in my face, "Hello? Hunter? I'm speaking to you. Do you remember that I'm your mistress?"

My head rears back in shock at her rude gesture.

"Aye, I'm verra aware of who ye are to me," I growl, both pissed and obsessed with this bonnie lass.

She surprises me again by grabbing me by the cock through my pants, and I unleash a mix between a groan and a growl, fisting my hands at my sides.

"Oh, I see you're already here to play, good. I need something from you. Is that clear?"

"Aye, Mistress," I say automatically.

A choking sound comes from Ian as he hears me address Mariax as my mistress and show her the respect she earned from me.

I glance over my shoulder. Eyeing him as he coughs and splutters, holding a glass of whiskey that he manifested out of nowhere. Well, half a glass of whiskey. The rest seems to be dribbled all down his front. I am seeing a completely different side of him. It is magnificent watching Mariax break down his stoic and cold demeanor.

"Aye, Mistress," I say again, but I pitch my voice lower, grabbing her by the throat and surprising her. "However, I am not yer submissive when we are out of a session. Ye are not my mistress right now. Do *I* make myself clear?"

I release her throat, enjoying seeing Mariax so ruffled.

Her eyes are comically wide, her mouth hanging open.

I reach out a hand, gently lifting her chin, closing her mouth. This seems to bring her back to herself as she tries to shove me in the chest. But I don't budge. She didn't try that hard. I would have been flying across the room with her demonic power if she chose to wield it.

Her eyes bounce between us as if she can't quite choose who to set her sight on.

"So, Angel, what exactly are your intentions with us? It seems like your carefully calculated plan is falling apart. Some mistress you turned out to—"

Ian's lecture is brought to an abrupt halt when Mariax gags him with her tail, completely covering his mouth and encircling his head.

She saunters closer to him, as if this is an everyday occurrence, and stares daggers up at him. Folding her arms across her chest in anger only serves to accentuate her breasts and deepen her cleavage for us once more.

Ian's pupils dilate as he zeros in on her chest. Mariax uses her tail, keeping him gagged, and drags his face down mere inches from hers.

"And what the hell would you know about being a good dominant, Cupcake? Good dominants don't betray their submissive, and you, Daddy," she sneers, "are going to find that out the hard way."

Ian stays within her hold, allowing it for some reason. Maybe my words about respect opened his eyes a wee bit to the changes in Mariax. I didn't know her back then, but I've seen who she is now in the year and a half I've known her.

I cock my head to the side and cross my arms across my chest, barely holding in the laughter bubbling, mildly amused at the situation we find ourselves in.

She continues to gag Ian, who's towering over her, with her tail, as that dagger I first saw during their fight makes a reappearance at his throat. He groans as his blood slips free, but it's not a pain-filled groan, it's lust. He wants her.

Ian's pleasure filled utterance causes all of our breathing to speed up, the sound seeming to throb in my ears.

Jealousy heats my skin for a second due to their close embrace. Violence brews between them, but I feel excluded from the moment until she turns her face to me.

"Pup, I agree just to be Mariax if we are not in a session. However, I am not willingly going to just submit so easily. I don't submit to anyone," she says, running a hand through her hair and speaking quietly, as if suddenly unsure.

I make my way closer to her until my chest is flush with the left side of her body.

"That's interesting, my wee Cheetie. Please explain to me again how amazing it is to submit. How freeing it is to be taken care of and have every need satisfied. To rid yerself of the control that ails ye so that ye don't have to worry anymore," I whisper her own words back at her, causing her eyes to widen in surprise.

Mariax turns her body to face me a bit more, but still holding her blade to Ian, her right arm outstretched to keep it in place.

"Hunter." She rolls her eyes – bratty and sighing in exasperation. "This situation is vastly different, I–"

"Now, how would ye know if ye have never submitted to any creature? Ye were clearly submissive to someone, and if I had to guess by how ye two eye each other, I would bet it was Ian."

I take advantage of her attempt at a retort, dipping my

pointer and middle finger into her mouth, hooking them behind her bottom teeth. I use my hold to pull her to me. Her tail stretches to its full length still keeping Ian within her grasp.

Ian lets out a muffled grunt, and I briefly look over Mariax's head to see the cause of it. Her dagger sliced shallowly through his shirt and down his side with the force of my tug. His life's essence seeps into the fabric and trickles over the intricately layered metal of the blade. Ian's eyes blaze with a challenging come hither look.

Mariax tries to turn back to Ian, but my fingers prevent her from doing so. My thumb captures her chin, causing Mariax to go mute. I feel my wolf watching along with me, the predator assessing their prey.

"Did ye submit to him, Mariax? Were ye his good girl?" I whisper darkly, conveying how much I don't believe her bullshit.

I remove my fingers, having said my piece.

She doesn't answer, but shivers when my warm breath caresses her neck.

"If ye can handle being his…" I pause dramatically. "Ye can sure as fuck be mine." I step back and walk over into her line of sight.

She raises a brow, anger rising to the surface, causing a flush to flare up high on her chest. *Beautiful.* My tongue skates out, my piercing softly clicking against a fang, and slips across my lower lip. Her eyes track the movement, but she keeps her focus between holding Ian at knifepoint and me. Mariax is out of her element.

I grin widely, displaying my fangs at how much it pleases me to see her like this.

"Fuck off, Hunter!"

Her mask doesn't know which way is up. It keeps flickering between her mistress persona, desperate fury, wanting to flee, and wanting to throw us all down and fuck until we're satisfied. All of this is pictured on her face through her fractured mask.

She releases Ian and shoves him into a chair at the foot of the bed. As he tries to get up, she grins manically, and rope floats up from the ground as if reacting to her thoughts. It ties around his wrists, ankles, neck, and chest, crossing and tying itself in complex knots.

It's just rope. There is no way it will hold him.

Ian snarls, and I move towards him, but Mariax holds a hand up, motioning for me to stay. Now that Ian is secured, she turns on her heel to face me fully.

"Take off your clothes and lie on the bed."

I tilt my neck back to stare at the ceiling and scoff, "Sure, woman. I'll just strip and lay on the bed and do what ye say."

"Do you want to come tonight? Because I do and I want to make him watch," she points a sharpened nail at Ian. "So, take your goddamn clothes off, lie down, and shut the fuck up."

My attitude changes while I listen to her reasoning. I know when to keep my mouth shut.

I strip off my clothes slowly as I watch them again. Her evil grin is back in place, pleased with *my choice* to listen to her command. It feels invigorating being free from the submissive role and the possibility of sex with Mariax dangling in front of me.

She slowly paces in front of Ian, her tail grazing across his body with every pass she makes in front of him. He is livid. I don't know why he hasn't broken his bonds, but something is preventing him. I'm guessing that's why he hissed in pain. I reach behind me, gathering my shirt as I pull it over my head, standing there in just my jeans and socks.

Mariax stops in front of him and leans down, giving me

a tantalizing view of her peach of an arse.

"Christ," I mumble, and my knot throbs painfully as if in agreement.

Her tail sways in a tantalizing motion just above her arse. Her wee plaid skirt is so short that when she bends at the waist, it displays her lack of underwear. Her bare core almost brings me to my knees, her pussy lips begging to be tasted and burning from the scrape of my beard.

This female is trying to kill me.

I want to go over there and smack her on the arse so hard. Wrap her tail around my wrist and rail her until she's screaming my name in benediction.

I'll be her good boy whenever she wants in The Snuggle Pit or a scene, but right now, I'm going to enjoy everything being an alpha entails.

Mariax rakes a nail through the stubble on Ian's cheek, causing a line of blood to follow in her wake. It heals fairly quickly, but not as quickly as it usually would. Hmm.

She then does something that makes my breath catch in my throat. She bends a wee bit to be directly in his line of sight.

She doesn't have to change her position much because he is almost at her eye level while seated. Ian's eyes bounce back and forth as if he can't get enough of her being this close to him. Mariax takes a violet painted sharpened nail, which is more like a claw, and runs it down the front of his shirt, but as she's about to tear the fabric apart on the thin cut, Ian speaks, and she freezes with both hands fisted in the front of his black t-shirt.

He inhales deeply through his nose, inhaling her intoxicating scent into his lungs.

"I miss the way your entire body lit up with excitement when I called you a good girl. It brought me joy, an emotion I had not felt in eons," he declares. "I taught your mind and body about dark, urgent, and primal desires. That will never change. You are Mistress Mariax now, but you are still mine. You are mine for eternity,"

Mariax's triceps flex, and she renders his shirt to pieces. There are wee bits of cloth stuck under the rope in some places, and what remains of his shirt hangs by the back legs of the chair.

Mariax ignores his declaration and speaks, picking back up where she left off. "Since you remember the past so well, perhaps you remember this. My daddy would teach me things about bondage and what a good girl does to please her daddy."

In response, he rattles off a snarky comment, but Mariax smashes a palm across his lips.

"Oh, I'm sorry, I wasn't done speaking. No, actually, I'm not sorry. You can shut the fuck up, too," she admonishes.

Her attitude has transformed her very essence since we walked into her suite. She is strong, sexy, and on a path to vengeance.

"As I was saying," she continues, her tone cocky but conversational, "I was learning to be a good girl from my daddy, who was supposed to protect and care for me. He promised never to hurt me. But you know what he did?" Mariax punctuates her question by straddling his lap. "My daddy betrayed me," she states calmly, portraying mock innocence. The heart shaped spaded tip of her tail pushes his shiny onyx hair gently away from his eyes, and then leans her chest closer to brush his. Then, her voice pitches low and seductive. "All the little tricks I learned will be your undoing."

In the moment it took her to climb off of his lap, leaving the evidence of her arousal and pantiless state on the fly of his jeans, Ian's eyes changed. His purple orbs seem to pulse with dark energy, promising violence.

Mariax cocks her hip and gestures with one hand.

"Those ropes are magically enchanted, just like you taught me. Djinns are all powerful beings, but with the right spell, a powerful witch, and some magical finesse…" She curls her hand around her left ear as if listening for an answer, twisting her torso slightly so I'm in her sights. "I have one of those on call just in case." She winks mischievously at me before whipping her head back to Ian. "So yeah, fucker. You're trapped until I say otherwise. For once, you are at my mercy. And after what you did to me, you'll be lucky if you leave here with your balls attached."

I find myself standing with one pant leg off and the other halfway down my thigh. I was so fixated on everything she was revealing I became frozen to the spot.

I finish undressing, slipping my jeans off my legs. My boxer briefs soon follow. I toss my socks over my shoulder, where they rebound against the wall. I move to sit on the bed and lean back against the headboard, crossing my hands behind my head and continue to watch the show.

I am definitely being a good boy because she is in a mood, and I have a feeling this will be rough and dirty, just how I like it.

She takes her tail away from Ian's mouth, and he immediately growls deep, menacing, and hot as all hell. That primal urge to flee from a dangerous beast is the ultimate turn-on when you know it's coming from someone who would play with you before they kill you.

The three of us together would tear each other to pieces. I want to slip my entire length into Mariax's cunt and have Ian deep in my arse. Ian effectively fucking us both with each thrust.

I run my fingers over my head and down my ladder, releasing a small amount of pre-come and sighing in relief. Mariax whips her head over her shoulder, her mouth opening to give me an order, but quickly changes her mind as her expression fills with understanding.

She must finally realize that I, too, need to be dominant on occasion and with her, I need it even more. Especially right now in front of Ian... I will not submit to her here, especially with all of this tension and energy.

Ian seems at a loss for words, normally so eloquently spoken. He just growls and stares. If those ropes weren't tied around him, she would be flat on her back with both of his hands clamped around her throat again.

"What do you have to say for yourself, Cupcake?"

Ian responds, but I can hear his molars grinding with the effort not to unleash his anger on her.

"I already explained this. I didn't betray you, Mar. I loved you... I still love you," his voice breaks on the last word. His inner madness begins seeping into his vision. "You left me in Inferuna. So why the fuck are you mad? You think you have the right to be angry at me? Fuck you. You didn't spend the last century in that cesspit. Consorting and dealing with all those archaic imbeciles." He lets out an audible breath through his mouth, gearing up for another round. "I didn't betray you," he says again through clenched teeth.

Mariax taps a purple-painted nail against her lips.

"It's too bad I don't believe you. I watched you. I saw Tiffany's pain, her anguish, her tears... I witnessed it all. And the reason I left without you is because of that. Why would I stay to be with you when you're capable of inflicting those wounds on my best friend, someone I love unconditionally?" she questions, her voice warbling slightly. "Why, she sometimes tells me you're a good male, I have no godsdamn clue. But until you showed up here, I think I was finally starting to steer her away from that dangerous line of thought."

The corners of Ian's mouth twitch, acknowledging that

her best friend is not totally team Mariax, and she hates it.

CHAPTER 32

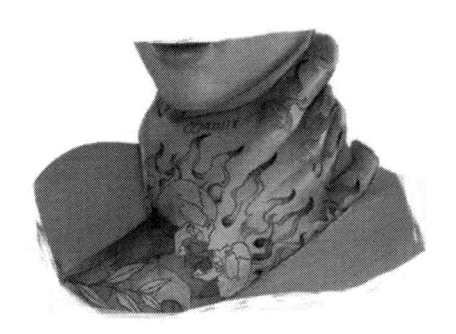

Ian

I breathe deeply, attempting to soothe my raging anger, the vitriol I want to spew from my lips, evidence I would enjoy choking the life from her and decimating her body with my cock all at once. I'm beyond livid that I'm slightly proud of her for showing this new confidence, but I'm also a hundred percent certain that most of it is a mask.

Her eyes show her sorrow. The madness in those depths matches mine.

Inferuna changed us both irrevocably, and I fully blame the circumstances of our relationship terminating on those changes, but she's in denial if she thinks she will ever dominate me. I do not submit to anyone, and she very well knows that.

She doesn't need to know that I pined for her and still love her. I need to convince her to trust me again.

As soon as I saw her, the wealth of emotions deep in my gut bubbled, and something inside me awoke in her presence to override some of that hate and jealousy I harbored.

I squeeze my eyes shut and shake my head, throwing all those thoughts out. This is not the track I need to be on right now. We are still discussing why she chose to leave me in misery for years. So what if I tortured her fucking best friend? Tiffany was nothing.

I saved Mariax, and I didn't even get a chance to tell her why before she was gone without a trace. I expected her to be upset, but not to flee. I don't even know how she left Inferuna. A regular torture demon should not be able to flee. And if I could find her, even if it took me a couple hundred years, the Potentate won't have any trouble either.

Her tail grazes my chest each time she turns at the foot of the bed. The pacing she is doing is driving me insane.

When I entered her home today, her petrichor, chocolate, and hazelnut scent enveloped me completely. It was like both drowning and taking that first breath of air.

Whenever I am near her, I am both dying and filled with life at the same time. That is the beauty of my Angel. She is both my savior and my punisher, my salvation and torturer.

"Mariax, open your ears and listen to me. Your life is in danger. I came to the human realm to protect you and warn you of what lurks."

"Even though I know it, you're just telling me this now? Getting your dick wet was obviously higher on your priority list," she sneers.

I ignore the jab.

"I know you are aware of a haunting, unknown force stalking you, but what you don't realize is I've already vanquished them twice, and they keep coming back," I explain seriously. "You are not safe here in the wards you trust so much. If I can break them, what else can pass through without your notice?"

"If this is your pathetic attempt to get me to stop fucking Hunter, it isn't going to work," she says seriously.

"I am not lying. How would fabricating a story such as

this benefit me?"

She points a finger at my chest.

"By weakening my defenses and letting you slip seamlessly back into my life. To play the hero and rescue the damsel in distress," she scoffs. "I am not in need of rescuing. I can take care of myself, asshole. Plus, I did not need rescuing. I have Hunter."

The cold feeling of rejection slices into the organ in my chest, quickly followed by outrage and jealousy.

I drive these useless emotions to the back of my mind, making my face blank and free of any indication of how I feel.

"I never claimed to be a hero," I state coldly, every muscle in my body rigid with tension.

Without another word, Mariax turns her back on me and starts stripping off her clothes. Does she really think she's going to take him in front of me? Oh, fuck no.

"Mariax," I growl, the threat clear, but she chooses to ignore me. "Angel, put your clothes back on so we can finish our discussion. I thought you wanted to know what happened in Inferuna. The sooner you learn of my motives, the sooner you will see the severity of the situation you're in now."

Mariax continues to undress, her tank top landing in a pile with Hunter's clothes on the floor. Now that I have no choice but to focus on her, I see what was just a blur as we fought.

She has me on her back, or at least a rendition of me.

Deep shadows with tendrils that look like mine come from a deep pool of ink. Horns grow from its head, making it more of a devil than a djinn, and I'm sure she thinks of me that way now. The only void in the smoky tones of gray and black are the voids where its eyes should be. Her pink skin being the color of the orbs.

It is beautiful and speaks to me on a primal level that she

would have me inked onto her skin.

She flips her thick pink strands of hair over her shoulder and glares at me, not taking anything of what I said seriously.

"Oh, I do, and we will finish that conversation. But right now, all this energy filled with hate and loathing needs to be relieved. I think Hunter is just the good boy that I need to satisfy that craving."

She bares her teeth at me and then slowly crawls up the bed towards Hunter, where he wears nothing but a shit-eating grin.

He will also pay for this whether or not he intended it. He is now part of her ploy and will be punished accordingly. I will have them both tied up and will use every magical ability to remind them who I am.

The little voice that is the embodiment of my madness breaks free, whispering darkly seductive thoughts to me. *You need to punish her. Free yourself from these ropes and ruin her. She left you alone for centuries.*

I grind my teeth so hard that I fear I'll shatter my molars.

"May I help you, Cupcake?" She questions me sweetly.

Still facing away from me and straddling Hunter's lap, she flicks her wrist, and a piece of the ropes slithers up my body and covers my mouth like a gag.

My eyes go wide, but every time I inhale, more of the magical essence embedded in the rope seeps into my system, clouding my magic and my mind further. I am becoming weaker by the second, and I will not be able to stop this atrocity from playing out.

I would love to watch Hunter have sex with someone, but I do not know if I can survive that person being Mariax.

My thoughts trail off as I refocus on the scene before me. Mariax is astride Hunter, her legs spread and placed on either side of his wide hips. His large, calloused hands are wrapped around her hips possessively.

I yell obscenities through the gag, but it comes out unintelligible. My eyes are unable to leave the scene in front of me. It's like one of those human car crashes, and you have to watch with morbid curiosity even though you cannot stop what's happening.

He tightens his fingers on her curvy hips, lifts her, and impales her down onto his hard, pierced cock. Her shrieks reverberate off the ceiling, much like my shock and intense arousal.

Why is this so hot? Why does my body enjoy this? She. Is. Mine.

Mariax is attempting to be in control and ride Hunter, but he is not having it. He was serious when he said he would dominate her, and I have no doubt he will. However, if she wanted to overpower him, she could do so easily.

Hunter sits up, bending at the waist with Mariax still on top, shifting his legs so they are now behind him instead of in front of him, and comes down on top of her.

Mariax releases a wild gasp, gripping his shoulders, and then he takes her once more. His movements are aggressive, claiming, and dominating. All the built-up frustrations he held onto are being consumed with their passionate joining.

I cannot handle this. My entire body is strung tight, my muscles flexing and straining as I attempt to free myself uselessly from my restraints. More blood rushes into my already excruciatingly hard dick.

I close my eyes in an attempt to block out their coupling, but it is no use. Somehow, the sounds they are making are even lewder.

Mariax gains leverage just for him to throw her on her back again. They're in a constant battle of wills, and it reminds me of the first time Mariax and I fucked, of how we ended up destroying most of the surfaces in our suite.

That's what happens when two alphas fuck, one of them has to submit or it will be an endless battle.

I growl and scream more garbled words through this wretched rope, fury blazing in my chest. If I had access to my power, I would reach out my shadows and rip them apart, pinning them down and freeing myself to punish them both. Or perhaps shout into their minds so loudly they would crumble and separate, parting from the pain.

How dare they screw in front of me?

The stirrings of an orgasm race through my body, the incessant ache deepening in my core and balls.

I am not about to come in my pants like some adolescent child!

Watching them is altering something in the makeup of my mind. I realize I want them. *Mine.* My madness speaks in agreement.

Mariax is back on top again.

I groan, holding back an orgasm, just barely. I always have complete control over my body, but it betrays me as the wealth of my emotions coalesces into a tight ball. My hips lift off the chair as I thrust my groin repeatedly into empty space, seeking friction, desperate to feel the release cascading across my body.

I moan so loudly that some of my cries break through the rope. Mariax is now facing me, riding Hunter in the reverse cowgirl position, watching me in my anguish. Her eyes are unfocused as she trails her eyes lower to stare at my undulating groin.

She must ease the ache she created.

I'm holding onto control by a thread, but I can't be bothered to care as I fight the euphoria that seeks to blind me.

When did she become such a vixen?

With that thought and Mariax watching my every move,

I release my hold and barrel into bliss. My balls tighten and throb, sensation shooting from them to all of my extremities. My toes go numb, and my body shakes from the force of my orgasm. Cum jets in powerful bursts into the seam of my jeans as I orgasm.

"Fuck! Mariax!" I shout into the rope, throwing my head back and letting the sensation take me.

My breath comes in heavy pants as I try to make sense of what just happened. I bring my chin back down and find her intense gaze on me still. She's grinding on Hunter, her tits swaying and bouncing with their erotic display. She's using his body to slake her need, fueling her lust by watching me watch them.

I am forced to admit that I crave more of this, more of her being taken aggressively by Hunter. More of her wielding her dominance over him as well.

A small smile slowly appears on her face as she rubs her clit on the top of his huge knot. Hunter barks a curse, and his body jerks as she massages him with her cunt. Her clit hood piercing grazes his knot at the bottom of every downstroke.

"Fuuuuuuck," Hunter growls, "If ye keep doin' that leannan I'm no' goin' to last."

I've never heard his accent so thick with overwhelming passion before. The tips of his fingers turn white with the force of his grip on her ass. Mariax yelps and bites her lip as he thrusts up harder and faster, breaking her rhythm and fucking her from below.

I cannot take my eyes away from them. Hunter's dick briefly shows each time he lifts her to his tip, his shaft coated in her arousal. I force my eyes shut, only to open them again a moment later.

It's as if my mind enjoys the torture they're inflicting.

Although I just came moments ago, I already feel myself growing firmer in my damp jeans, my cum making the material uncomfortable against my sensitive flesh.

Her playful side breaks through her layers of trauma as she revels in torturing me. Right now, she is using Hunter as her personal form of therapy, as if he is her lifeline to this plane.

"I want to be your lifeline as well," I whisper, scraping my lips against the rope's rough fibers. This experience has shown me a cold truth. I've always been a jealous male, to the point where I will do anything to keep what is mine.

It's evident that although I want to tear Hunter's limbs from his body and render them useless, I'm affected by him being able to touch what is mine. I fall prey to rapture while watching them.

If I want her to accept me back in her life, I must show her the events in Inferuna from my mind's eye.

I am aware that I hurt her by torturing Tiffany, but everything I did was to protect her. If I chose not to protect what was mine, she would be removed from life. She would be somewhere in the inky depths of the Abyss, forever mist among the ether, and I would not be able to recover her.

When Mariax screams, I know her orgasm is nearing.

Hunter lifts her off of him and sits up to change his position. She lets out a yelp when he grabs her tail and drags her back to him, but now lying on her front. Her chest is flattened to the mattress as he mounts her from behind. He lifts her ass in the air and then drives into her mercilessly.

Hunter grabs one of her horns in each fist, making her arch into him and support herself with her arm strength.

They're both facing me now, but Mariax's eyes are closed. However, Hunter trails a lavish and lust-filled gaze over me as he plows into her. He purposely keeps eye contact, and his pupils fully dilate as his arousal clouds his senses. He bares his teeth at me in a display of powerful dominance.

He has never been more attractive to me, and I hate it.

I watch her tail escape from between them and sneak behind his back. Her tail wraps around a section of his long hair and yanks it violently. Hunter growls, and his canines lengthen just a bit as his wolf peeks out. His eyes change to an unusual black, so dark they seem to swallow the light.

My dick twitches sharply when he bites her shoulder. Mariax hisses and releases her tail, only for it to swish in excitement across the bedsheets.

"Hunter, please!" she begs. "Knot me. I need you to stretch me, fill me," she manages to say through her stream of moans and whimpers.

Hunter slaps her ass hard multiple times, causing Mariax to swear and beg harder.

"No, my wee slut. I already told ye there would be no knotting until ye are mine in every sense," he punctuates his statement with more stinging spanks across both cheeks, never stopping his hips from pumping.

Mariax whimpers at his rejection, and my need to destroy him wages war with my desire to throw him down and reward him for his dominant behavior with her.

This feels right, the three of us bound to one another, a possible eventuality.

Mariax's orgasm takes that opportunity to strike, relieving her of disappointment. Her back arches into him, and her moans turn into screams.

"Hu- Hunter! Fuck, yesss," she repeatedly chants like it's a prayer.

Her magic seeps into the room with her release coating everything in it. Pleasure ripples down her body, causing her to tremble.

Hunter is not far behind her. He growls deep in his chest and bites her neck viciously. Blood trickles down her tattooed shoulder, and her arm that is stretched out on the sheet before her.

"Fuck me, that feels amazing," Hunter moans, her blood lingering on his tongue and teeth. "That's it, lass. Ye are such a good girl," his Scottish accent thick with his desire.

Mariax mewls and practically melts at his praise.

He picks up speed, ramming into her precisely three more times as he wraps his hand around her throat from behind and pulls her back flush against his chest.

They kneel on the bed before me, watching me as I watch Hunter come inside Mariax. His length disappears into her messy cunt just enough to refrain from knotting her but filling her with his cum.

He tightens his hold on her throat, cutting off her airway, as he challenges me with his stare over Mariax's head. Mariax moans and tries to move along his length, but he growls in warning and holds her still as his dick swells and throbs within her.

Hunter's energy fades. He collapses back against the pillows, dragging Mariax with him as he is still inside her.

I cannot sort through the sea of emotions I'm weathering, each one cresting and overwhelming my senses. What I just witnessed was incredible. I enjoyed it, and I want more. I want both of them. I need to be inside them both while we revel in bliss together.

I know this was a punishment that I begrudgingly and forcefully was made to take, but it will not happen again, not with restraints or against my will.

Only good girls get rewarded, but right now, Mariax is being a very bad girl.

CHAPTER 33

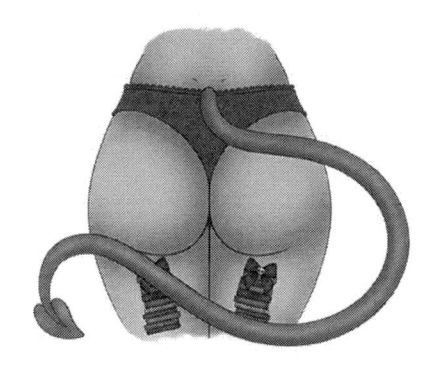

Mariax

Most people who have ever gotten a tattoo will tell you the same thing. It's painful.

I, however, want to know the lengths a body can go while withstanding the pain from the tattoo machine. Most human males, hell males from almost *all* species, cry or can't even handle the needle and quit before their tattoo is finished.

Tiffany told me once she had to order special numbing cream for this biker getting a pin up on his bicep.

The whole pain from tattoos gave me a new idea for punishment. My clients must still give consent to what is essentially my personal brand being permanently etched into their flesh.

"You stop by when Mariax is done with you, sweet cheeks!" Jeffry, my orc doorman, says, flirting with Tiffany as we walk away.

"Dude, leave her alone. Can't you tell she's interested in tasting a wolf, not an obnoxious ass hat like you?"

"Fuck off, Alec," Jeffry replies.

The sounds of their bickering fading as we leave the entryway of The Snuggle Pit and move down the hall.

"Mar, why in the hell am I here with my tattoo equipment?" Tiffany calls over her shoulder as she walks ahead of me.

My heels echo off the walls as I follow her, quietly cackling. She will know soon enough why she's here. If it goes well, this may become a regular occurrence.

"Stop at room P6," I tell Tiffany.

Holding my finger up to the pad on the door, a light scans my print. No one has permission to access this room but me, not even Lauren. I wait for the click, nudge the door with my boot, and hold it open for Tiffany to pass through first.

Tiffany stops dead in the doorway. "Uh, Mariax?"

"Yes, bestie?"

"Did you wrap me up a new toy to play with?"

"Absofuckinglutely."

In the center of the room, a very naked vampire grins at us.

He has the looks of a Viking: tall, broad shoulders, bulging muscles, shoulder-length blonde hair, panty melting cornflower blue eyes, ashen skin…not to mention the enormous hard on he is rocking.

Apparently, the silver chains wrapped around his throat, wrists, and ankles are no deterrent for his mirth.

"Ladies," he says with a dip of his chin.

The motion causes his skin to sizzle, and he hisses out a sharp breath. It's good to see he isn't totally unaffected; he is here for punishment after-all.

Tiffany glances at me but I shake my head to ignore him, motioning her to the worktable and padded stool I set up across from my submissive.

"Sub, you will address me as Mistress or I will bring out the silver cane and turn that gorgeous ass of yours into a bleeding, blistering mess."

"Yes, Mistress," he responds.

"Good boy," I praise.

"I have a new method of torture to try out and I thought you would be the perfect submissive to test it on. Do you want to know what it is, pet?" I question, slapping my tail against my palm like a cane.

"Yes, Mistress."

"Perfect, you don't have a choice either way," I croon as I circle the vampire, running a sharp nail down his chest and over his nipple.

The vampire gasps and his head falls back between his bound arms.

I decide to prolong my explanation, letting the anticipation and need for answers build to a crescendo. Ignoring my client, I turn my attention to my best friend.

I hug Tiffany from behind as she sets up the table. I squeeze her tightly, her soft, leathery wings pressed against my cheek. Her tail wraps around the back of my legs as she returns the embrace.

I loosen my hold and survey her supplies. "Do you have everything you need? Did you remember the custom order ink?" I question softly.

"Yep, I'm surprised it's so readily available."

I shrug. "What can I say? People love their pain kinks and body modifications."

It's quiet for a moment as Tiffany and I bask in the company of each other. Some days, I just need to be in close proximity to her to feel better.

"Is Jeffry single?" she asks out of the blue.

I smother a laugh with my hand. "Um, no sorry. He has a wife, and like ten kids," I explain, my voice laced with unfulfilled laughter.

"Damn. I bet he would be fun to ride. You know what they say about orc dick," she says seriously.

I arch a brow at her statement. "Actually, no, please

enlighten me."

"Once you go orc, you'll never forget the torque," she says completely serious.

"Wow, classy Tiff," I say with a snort.

She just shrugs and holds up two needles of different widths, as if examining them to determine which will be the most effective.

"Did Lauren finish setting up that new spreadsheet I suggested? For your client roster?"

I growl and mutter under my breath, "Yes, no thanks to you. I hate digital lists. It's confusing and I can never remember how to operate the program. We spent *days* in my office sorting it out."

"Pfft, it's easy! That's what I use to keep track of my tattoo clients," she elaborates.

"I just prefer the way things used to be, pen and paper, the sound of a quill scratching against parchment. You can't beat that," I sigh, casting my gaze to the ceiling.

"Okay, grandma. But for real, that huge fucking pile of pretty notebooks in your office closet is not going to help you keep your clients and their specific kinks organized."

"Ughhhh. But I don—"

The vampire groans, his hips thrusting into the air, desperate for friction. Tiffany stills as she watches my sub with rapt attention as he continues to hump the air. Small streams of smoke drift from any part of his skin where the silver makes contact, swirling gently through the air before disappearing. The more he moves, the more the chains burn him, building his desire to painful levels.

"Tiff?" I ask.

She continues to stare at him with her pupils rapidly dilating. I smack Tiffany's ass with my tail.

She growls and levels a glare at me. "What the fuck was that for?"

My brows pinch together, displaying my annoyance. Both of our tails swish back and forth in agitation.

"You were eye-fucking the shit out of him. He is here to be punished, not lavished by your attention." I snap my eyes back to my sub.

Tiffany rolls her eyes and huffs, mumbling under her breath as she lays out her tools on the temporary workspace. "Fucking cock block, pussy block... hells, orgasm block. Some best friend."

I slink over, my tail sliding up to push her hair past her ear. "I heard that, and that is why I fucking love you."

She turns around and swats my tail away, grinning. "I fucking love you too."

I glide over to Aiden, tail shifting into a sharp pinned wheel and running it over his right and then left nipple, watching them as they begin to harden into buds. I continue my slow balance of pleasure and pain while I chat with Tiffany.

"Do you think it's even possible to maintain a long-term relationship with two alpha-holes?"

"Three, including you," she corrects me.

I scoff, but ignore her jab. "Seriously, what would that even look like?"

"First of all, have you even come to terms with the fact that Ian is in your life again? I know you see him almost every day, but that doesn't mean you've accepted that he's really back. Have you spoken with him about Inferuna?" she asks in a rare display of gentleness.

"Um, no. Why would I? I don't need to hear any more of his lies," I seethe.

Blood wells from the tiny puncture wounds on Aiden's nipple when I pressed too hard in my agitation. *Fuck. Focus Mariax.*

I abandon titillating my sub and sit on the corner of the table. I wrap a lock of hair around one of my horns before letting it fall and repeating the motion. When my anxiety shows its despicable face, I fidget unconsciously.

"I don't want to talk about this right now, okay? I need booze before I even consider unpacking that heap of bullshit," I explain, none too patiently.

"Fair enough. What now?" Tiffany asks as she turns her gloved hands palms up in question.

"Now, I get his consent and you get to work," I say, smiling evilly.

"You're creepy. I like it," Tiffany declares, waggling her manicured eyebrows.

I walk over and grab the tail end of the chain, yanking hard. His muscles strain further and his breathing is labored.

"Now, as you can see, Aiden is a very bad boy and is punished often, so he requires a new form of punishment to keep things fresh. I thought to myself, 'What better way to punish a vampire than to brand him with a tattoo'?"

The vampire smirks. I can already tell what he's thinking, that any tattoo etched onto him will just heal the second Tiffany moves on to a fresh piece of flesh.

"You remembered the silver laced ink, right Tiff?" I ask Tiffany, referring to the special order ink.

"Yeppers," she states with a pop of her lips.

Moans reverberate off the walls along with the *tzz...tzzzzz* of the tattoo machine as Tiffany and I continue our conversation.

"Although, if you do decide to become a throuple, think of all the sexy possibilities that come with having two cocks at your beck and call whenever you want," she says as she squeezes more black ink into a tiny disposable cup.

I'll be in danger of arousal sliding down my thighs if I think about it too long.

As if on cue, Aiden speaks, making out the words

between pants, "Mistress, I can smell your need. It's driving me to lunacy. You want these males you're discussing. Fuck the what ifs and go for it."

I respect his bravery for speaking about my personal life so brazenly, but that won't save him.

"Thanks for your unsolicited advice, sub. How many lashings do you deserve for speaking without permission, do you think?"

He doesn't answer me as lust overtakes him. I continue questioning him, regardless.

"Describe to Tiffany how it feels as her needle pierces your flesh faster than your vampire speed allows you to run, forcing the silver laced ink into your skin."

The only response I get from Aiden is a strangled moan as he rocks his hips and tilts his head back, searing his neck on the silver chains.

Tiffany glances up at me from her kneeling position between his legs. Her eyes are level with the sub's glorious cock. She had been tattooing the inner thigh of Aiden.

"Uhhh, Mar? I don't think the vamp finds this method of 'torture' quite as painful as you had hoped."

His cock throbs, pre-cum glistening on the tip. Tiffany licks her lips.

"For fucks sake, that is very clear from the endless streams of moans and praise you are getting in…old Swedish?" I arch a brow in wonder.

Tiffany abruptly stands.

"Why don't we call it a loss, and go to *Get Fucked* instead? We can get drunk and discuss your love life without this one," she jabs a gloved thumb over her shoulder, "offering his input."

"You know, that sounds amazing. Plus, I haven't seen Teddy in a while. I wonder what drinks he'll make us," I say with a grin.

"Only one way to find out," she says.

I hold out my arm and she laces her elbow with mine as we head towards the door.

Tiffany stops and looks at Aiden over her shoulder, smiling seductively.

"I'll be back for *you* later," she purrs and winks.

CHAPTER 34

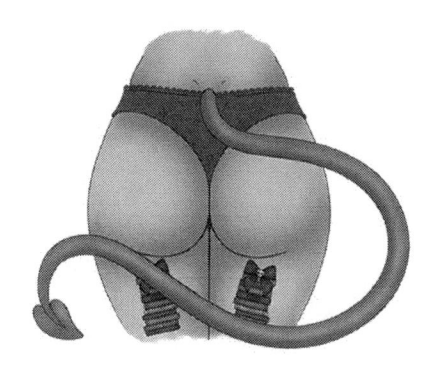

Mariax

I'm on the ground level of my building in the Snuggle Palace, attempting to create space between myself, Hunter, and Ian. I can't think when they are in close proximity.

I can't stop stewing in my never-ending thoughts.

Part of me wants to jump in headfirst, throw myself willingly into a relationship with them, and not look back.

However, my trust in Ian is not infallible. It hasn't been the same since Inferuna. He also disclosed that he's been stalking me for who knows how long. I admit the darker side of myself loves his possessiveness and obsession with me to the point he needs to stalk me.

I would have no issues dating Hunter, but after seeing him with Ian, some of my building desire for him has shifted. It's not that I don't want Hunter; I do. But what if entering a relationship with only one causes me to lose the other?

An emotion I have only felt a handful of times causes me to curl my fists up at my sides. Jealousy. I'm jealous of their relationship.

For fuck's sake, really, Mariax?

They have been together for months without me,

exploring each other sexually and emotionally. Plus, Hunter saw Ian before I did when he returned to the human realm. My feelings are irrational and idiotic, but I'm having a difficult time stopping the thought loops from reoccurring.

The employee entrance at the back of the club opens, the door smashing against the wall. The upper part of the door separates from the hinges, and it hangs by just the hinge left at the bottom. I don't startle from the noise, but it does immediately piss me off that something is broken in my club.

"Who the—?" I don't get to finish my sentence because Lauren is skidding into the doorway.

I've never seen her look like this before. She's pale, anger and worry mar her features. This is the angriest I've ever seen her. Her small frame shakes slightly with a continuous tremble in her limbs.

"Mistress!" she shouts. "You need to come upstairs now. There is a situation in one of the pleasure rooms," she explains.

"What kind of situation?" I reply curtly.

"You need to see it for yourself," she states.

With that ominous note, she turns on her heel and stalks back up the stairs.

Again, another unusual behavior for Lauren. She's always very respectful, but I'll let it slide because of how shaken she looks. I follow her up the stairs, quickly catching up to her but keeping enough distance between us.

We come out of the stairwell onto the apartment level and then swiftly make our way to the room in question on the level above.

I clutch the sides of my head and stare into the room with wide eyes while I look through the door Lauren holds open. Rage so potent it distorts my vision sweeps over me, and I scream to release some of the pressure digging its claws into my brain.

Hunter and Ian come out of nowhere, and now they're standing too close to me. Neither of them say anything. They just try to comfort me with their presence. Ian's power lashes out when he bears witness to the destruction, and I know he is just as livid as I am.

Hunter steps closer to both of us, ever the protector. He is unsure about what further reactions Ian and I will have and is more concerned about us than the actual scene in front of us.

It looks like something from the human show *Dexter*.

All I see is red, and it covers every inch of the room. There is enough blood that it could have easily come from twelve or more bodies. There's no way to tell right away if it's human or supernatural.

I don't have a clue how this could happen so close to me. Hell, so close to Ian. He was more likely to feel a disturbance between the two of us.

Ian is the first to speak, his voice cold and detached. "How did someone get past your wards without either of us feeling it?"

He aims the question at me, but he stands with arms folded over his chest in the doorway facing the room in question. His face is blank of any expression, and he tips his head to the side as if deep in thought.

"Exactly, Ian. How the fuck did someone get into my building?" I question firmly.

I run through my mental list of clients, employees, and maintenance personnel. Everyone who I employ is thoroughly vetted and none of them have the power or knowledge to infiltrate my defenses.

"There must be something bigger at play here. Someone with power, or someone with a powerful witch who practices dark magic in their pocket, is the most likely possibility," I explain my theory, my brows pinching in frustration.

My witch Ellie is strong, and I've never had a problem with the wards until now. Maybe Ian is right after all. Damn, I might need his help if I am to survive.

I look up at the ceiling in the massacred room, watching as thick drops of blood rain down.

"Why would someone do this? And who or what does all this blood belong to?" I ask no one in particular.

Aside from the constant drip, the only sound to be heard is our breathing.

Is this meant to hurt me personally or my business?

I feel attacked and violated. I'm getting way too old for all of this bullshit that keeps happening. *It needs to end. Now.* Clearly, things are escalating if The Snuggle Pit is no longer my safe haven.

Hunter and Ian both go to speak at the same time, their words tripping over each other. Ian grips my shoulders and turns me to walk a few paces away.

Now that the destruction is out of sight, I can think more clearly.

Ian places his thumb and index finger around my chin, tipping my face up to his. He's bent slightly at the waist to be at my eye level.

"Right now, Mariax, you are not safe. I cannot see you in danger. I need to protect you."

I scoff and roll my eyes. "Yeah, you did a really good job protecting me in Inferuna, didn't you?"

"Yes, I did. The Potentate's plans for you would make even your skin crawl," he states seriously. "I never questioned what I must do to keep you protected. I let those violent acts play out against Tiffany so you, my angel, wouldn't suffer a fate worse than death."

All the breath leaves my lungs at his declaration. Little

by little, Ian is showing me his true self.

Hunter comes up behind me and wraps his arms around my waist to support me. He's so big his tattooed forearms overlap above my pelvis. I lean my head back against his shoulder, sagging into him. Hunter shuffles us further down the hall, seeking more privacy.

We don't know who can be trusted.

Lauren takes over to deal with the room and calls the cleanup crew. Luckily, the room is mostly made of concrete or stainless steel, so there shouldn't be that much lasting damage, but there is a concern for the blood leaving permanent stains.

I don't care at this point. I'll board up the door, and it'll be that weird room no one talks about.

Hunter leans his back against the wall. I turn in his arms to press my face into his chest. He tightens his hold, pulling me tighter against him. I snuggle into him, wrapping my arms around his back. Ian stands off to the side, facing the direction we came from so that he can watch both Hunter and me and keep an eye on the room behind us.

Shadows run down my hair from my crown, softly petting me. Ian is soothing me in his own way.

"We can't stay here until this issue is resolved, Angel. I don't know where we will go, but I will figure out something."

Hunter's chest rumbles against my cheek as he speaks.

"Why don't we go to my cabin? It's smaller and easier to defend than here. Plus, it's out of the city. I'll have my wolves set up a perimeter and—"

Hunter tilts his head down to listen when I place my hand on his forearm and squeeze gently. He cups my face in his warm palm, running his thumb over my lower lip. My tongue can't help but slip out to play with my piercing in an unconscious motion.

"Hunter, please don't get ahead of yourself. It's a good

plan, but I can't just leave without making some arrangements," I say, kissing the pad of his thumb gently. "And right now, I can't wrap my head around that."

I can't dwell on the fact that Ian, Hunter, and I are having a calm conversation. There are no arguments or snide remarks.

The combination of their scents settles my anxiety as Ian walks over to us and wraps an arm around mine and Hunter's ribs, pulling us firmly against his embrace.

For the moment, I get a taste of what my life would look like as their partner, and an undeniable craving for them emerges.

CHAPTER 35

Hunter

A fire lit under my arse after The Snuggle Pit was infiltrated. So, I checked in on the progress my wolves are making.

Charlie and I walk a couple of blocks to get to the next location. We have already checked several, and this is the second to last on the list. It's a gigantic warehouse that takes up at least two city blocks or more. It's rundown, falling apart, and abandoned.

There are several abandoned warehouses around here, and a lot of crime and drugs are constant.

It's on the human police force's radar, if you name it, it happens here, but there's not much they can do. Abandoned buildings are just left vacant. Sure, they can hold raids and clean out each one, but the scum keeps coming back like cockroaches.

My pack is not above crime. In fact, we have several side gigs that are less than legal. But our main business, which is legit, is in construction. Not many members of the pack know about our side businesses. Not everyone can be trusted, and I'm glad I followed my gut on that.

Charlie places a hand on my shoulder and shakes me

roughly. I glare at him as he laughs deeply and hands me a Starbucks coffee.

Oh, sweet caffeine, how I missed ye.

I take a mouthful of the lifesaving liquid and hold the warm cup between my hands. My breath fogs in the air as it's early February and deep into the winter months.

I wish I were in the mountains smelling of fresh pine and the crisp scent of snow instead of this mishmash of rotting garbage, piss, sweat, and other putrid smells.

Making sure not to draw any eyes to us as more than necessary, Charlie and I try to blend into the scenery, but it's a challenge when our lycan genes make us taller and overall larger than the average human.

We sip our coffee and chat about nothing.

By human standards, we dress the part.

I wear jeans with a rip in one knee, a plain black hoodie, and work boots. Charlie's wearing an outfit similar to mine. Once our coffees are finished, I grab both cups, smash them together, and shove them into my pants pocket, not about to add more litter to this shit fest.

I sighed deeply, gripping the back of my neck with both hands, arching my spine to stretch. My hoodie rides up, and I feel the cool air dance on the hairs of my happy trail.

"Come on, Hunter. Let's get this shit over with so we can go the fuck home," Charlie says.

"Aye, I know. Ye have better things to do than scout around the city in the oorlich weather with yer best friend," I reply with mock dejection.

He rolls his eyes and scoffs like he loves nothing better, but I know he wants to get home to his mate.

Not surprisingly, the building is not locked or secured in any way, and we walk through the door on the side of the building without any complications.

The building is so rundown I'm wary a piece of the

metal roof will crash down on our heads at any moment. Old machinery is strewn haphazardly, like a tornado swirled everything about in its tunnel and they were never moved from where they landed.

The warehouse reeks of mildew and rat carcasses. Trash is sprinkled throughout every nook and cranny.

In the center of the space there is a perfect circular patch with nothing in it. Murky light peeks through a crack in the roof high above to shine in a thin beam of light. The dust disturbed by our search glitter and twirl in the beam, casting beauty to this otherwise dreadful place.

It's quiet, dark, and foreboding, likely holding nothing of promise. It's eerie that the only sound to be heard is the creaking from chains attached to some kind of pulley or hoist system attached to the metal grates on the second story and the metal beams that support the structure.

Charlie and I stay together as we search the building for any evidence of why this particular location is on the list.

Once the ground level is searched, we hike up the rusty stairs, our boots rattling the metal grates under us. There is even less up here, and it only takes a minute to check out the whole area.

However, the higher the climb, the more the fine hairs on the back of my neck stand up. I cannae pinpoint what is causing this reaction from my body. My wolf fights for control to perceive the threat before it attacks us, making my skin feel tight.

"Do ye feel that, Char?" I whisper.

"Feel what?" he questions.

"I cannae say, but something feels off about this place. It got worse as I got up here."

Charlie doesn't seem bothered as he leans against the rickety railing, stretching his arms out to hold himself up.

"Maybe you're just spooked, Alpha," he jokes.

But I am in no mood to linger or be mocked.

"Let's go, there is nothing here for us," I bite back, walking to the stairs.

I place my foot down on the top step before whipping my head back to him so quickly I hit myself in the face with my loose hair.

"Or, ye could stay and search more thoroughly. Beta, see if ye can do better on yer own," I snarl, and stomp down the stairs.

Charlie is quick to follow, but stays far enough back to be out of biting distance.

I decide we'll head back to the pack lands and get out of this damn cold, hitting the last location tomorrow. Even with my supernatural genes I can't take this biting weather. It's colder than a witch's arse out here.

Snuggling up in front of my fireplace and getting sucked into a book sounds amazing right now.

CHAPTER 36

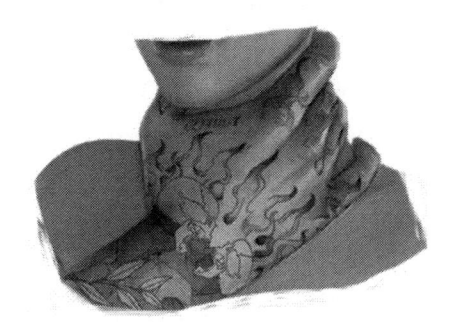

Ian

I lie on the bed in my guest apartment on level three of Mariax's building, my legs dangling off the end. Settling my hands over on my torso, I frown in thought.

Hunter and I have remained here to be close to Mariax. We cannot protect her if we aren't near when danger strikes. But this is as close as she will let us get. She flat out refused us access to her rooms or even the floor her suite is located on.

My brain aches from fighting the memories trying to tug me under. Before they can stick their claws into me, I hear the bathroom door open.

Hunter exits with a towel wrapped around his waist. The muscles covering every inch of his upper body bunch and flex as he casually walks over to the bed. I trail my gaze down his abdomen to his Adonis belt that leads straight to the visible outline of his dick under the towel.

"Like what ye see?" Hunter growls, lowering the tenor of his voice intentionally.

"I would like it even more without the towel. Why don't you be a good boy and show me what I'm supposed to like so much," I state.

"No, yer not going to distract me with promises of pleasure. Tell me everything there is to know about the relationship between ye and Mariax. Then, if ye are honest, I'll consider playing after," he scolds.

I sigh deeply. "What do you want to know, Scruffy?" I ask, rubbing the back of my neck.

I knew this was coming at some point.

"Every time I've seen ye two together, there is an incredible amount of tension between ye, and there's definitely deep hurt on both yer parts. I don't like seeing either of ye this way," he murmurs so quietly that I barely hear him.

"Hunter?" I ask a bit cautiously.

With barely a breath in between, he rapidly lists a stream of questions. "How long have ye known each other? How old are ye? When did ye first meet her? Were ye her daddy? Are ye interested in being in a throuple with Mariax and me?"

"Slow the fuck down and breathe for a moment. How long have you been waiting to unpack all of that?"

He bends at the waist, dropping his hands to the mattress on the other side of my body, and leaning his hips on the bed. At this angle, his rugged bearded face is suspended perpendicular to mine.

"A fair bit of time," he admits, his breath brushing my cheek. His wet hair hangs around his face, caging me in.

I chuckle. Young lycans can be so unpredictable at times.

I watch as a bead of water builds on the end of an errant strand hanging from his forehead. The small bubble of water slowly builds until gravity takes it and it splashes onto the hollow of my throat.

Blinking rapidly a few times to shake myself out of the trance-like state, looking into his eyes and speaking before my wolf has a chance to.

"We have a very complicated past. It cannot be described as easily as you wish. But I can show you if you're open to it. I don't want to lie to either of you. However, not all of my knowledge is for anyone but myself."

Hunter leans on his left hand, lowering his head to lick up the water resting on my throat. His soft lips and rough facial hair create a mind blowing contrast, causing my body to still.

"Mmm, a tempting offer to be sure," he acknowledges, speaking against my skin.

I gather a section of hair from the crown of his head, clearing it away from his face, so I can pull him up a bit to meet my eyes. The rest of his wet hair glides against my skin as his tattooed neck arches slightly.

He pushes himself up to his full height, blowing out his cheeks with a deep breath, rubbing the side of his whiskered face, deep in thought. His head is tilted towards the floor.

I don't invade his privacy by listening to his thoughts, even though it would be an easy way to dissect his feelings. I know when he comes to a decision because he lifts his gaze and his eyes bore into mine, the seriousness of the situation and all the information he wants conveyed in this expression.

"What exactly do ye have to do to 'show me'," he makes air quotes, "about yer relationship with Mariax?"

I stand and step forward, lightly grazing the back of my knuckles over his cheekbone. With my other hand, I push a stray lock of his clean, wet hair behind his ear.

"I don't have to do much. All I need to do is press my hand here." I lightly press my fingertips against his temple. "You'll be pulled into the memories I deem relevant. You should not have any lasting effects from the transfer since you are blessed with the genetics for faster healing. A human would be a puddle of brain jelly."

Hunter tries to remain calm, but his carotid artery flutters rapidly.

"It can be quite shocking to the system to have that much of my power flowing directly into your mind. But it's the easiest and most thorough way I can show you exactly what you want."

I cup his cheeks, the coarse and curly texture of his beard tickling my palms. I lean in, placing a firm kiss on the corner of his mouth.

He still looks pensive, but he finally agrees, throwing his hands up dramatically before running both hands through his ill-mannered locks. "Fine. Do what ye need to do, Ian, but I dinnae trust ye. The shite that ye pulled is tinged with madness."

We stare at each other for a moment before I utter, "I know."

I link my mind with his, sifting through my memories. Hunter's eyes are unseeing as he checks out of reality. His knees weaken once I am deep in his mind, but I'm prepared. I catch him in my arms and lay him on the bed.

I play back everything that I can from my time in Inferuna, how I met Mariax, how she has always been *mine*, how I *claimed* her.

I get sucked into a particular memory of the first time we slept together. It was such a pivotal moment in our relationship that I want to examine it further. I realize and acknowledge that Hunter is along for the ride, but I do not care.

It's not anything he hasn't seen before, and surprisingly my possessive nature is only simmering while we watch her with me.

I lie on my side flush with his thick bicep, absently

tracing the distended veins through his intricately tattooed muscles, watching every minute shift or twitch of his face.

His eyes are open, and they have shifted to an endless obsidian sea. His wolf is alert even if his unconscious mind is not. Mind sharing is a drop of my power, and I do not have to focus on it to keep the memories playing for him.

He's learned almost everything there is to know about Mariax and me. He looks exhausted by the influx of memories I shared with him. The sheer knowledge that I was able to transfer to him will take time to settle.

I plan on showing Mariax my side of what she calls 'my betrayal' in the same manner. The void she created within me remains barren, but it does not pulse aggressively in agony anymore. She is my entire existence; I will not live without her again.

Hunter stirs, throwing a thick leg over my waist lazily and cuddling his face into my chest.

He's finally becoming coherent enough to engage in conversation, but his words carry the cadence of one waking from a deep sleep, and he does not realize he keeps slipping between his thick and lighter accent.

"Do ye even think ye could stand seeing her with me regularly…and sharing her? Because from everything I saw in those memories, ye do not share or have any interest in sharing," he states pointedly, letting out a huff. "Ye fuckin' ripped a guy into pieces for merely touching her shoulder in the classroom. What makes ye think ye are going to be able to handle the two of us at once?"

I grit my teeth as I contemplate my answer, thankful I do not have to show him my face as I deliberate. It's not an easy thing to describe my feelings or the influence Mariax and Hunter have on me.

"I don't know how a relationship between us would be, but I know without a doubt that she is mine. She has always been mine and always will be mine," I declare, my hands clenching into fists at the thought of her with anyone else.

I blow out a sharp breath through my nose and turn to lie flat on my back. I place my hands behind my head, flaring my elbows wide and brushing Hunter's hair. That's half dried and even more untamed than usual.

"If that means sharing, I have no compunctions to being daddy to you both." I add, my craving to possess them growing with each word I utter. "As much as I am loath to admit it, it's not just about Mariax anymore. Although my obsession with her is still the sole reason I remain on this plane."

He chuckles deeply, surprising me. "Does it pain ye that much to admit I've gotten under yer skin?"

"Yes," I admit, deadpan, staring at the ceiling.

"Did ye use me as a way to get close to her again?" he asks, a bit of his rejection making his voice trail off.

"Initially, it was just about your presence and proximity to her…" I stop and clear my throat. "But I started feeling emotions again when I was with you. Emotions that I have not felt in hundreds of years. The first time I felt them was with Mariax. I believed myself to be cursed when she awakened emotions within me, setting me on a path of self-destruction. But now I cannot live without them. When I become numb to them, only the darkness resides within me, and that's not something that I wish to make acquaintances with again."

He turns on his side of the bed to face me and places his palm on the side of my face, my stubble making a noticeable scrape as he gently turns my head to look at him. I allow it. I need to know how he feels just as much as he seeks the same reassurance from me.

He's surprisingly calm, face set in a gentle smile, his eyes lightly shimmering.

"When we met in the park, ye lied about everything.

However, my wolf was uncharacteristically silent and was interested in ye from the beginning. And although I am not okay with everything, I understand ye and Mariax a hell of a lot better after seeing yer memories. Yer devotion and determination to keep her dinnae compare to any love I've known. If ye believe that ye are ready to share her with me, and if yer possessive arse can try not to rip my head from my shoulders, then we should give it a go."

He finishes speaking and bites his lip hard, the pink flesh turning white under the pressure of his teeth.

"However," he continues. "We must discuss everything with Mariax. I am not leaving her in the dark about anything *ever again*. We need to have every secret laid bare between us. Aye?"

I nod my head in affirmation, but do not speak. I swallow, my gaze becoming steely with resolve.

He's right. My devotion to Mariax is unmatched, and now I've decided I want them both. There is nothing that will come between us now. I know there will be challenges, but I can't deny the desire to possess them both.

I look forward to seeing Mariax's softer side that she shares only with Hunter. Mariax has changed since living in the human realm. She is no longer the demon fresh from the creation fires. She is confident and strong but is still able to embrace her playful side.

However, after seeing her struggle with her inner darkness, I know she needs both of us to thrive.

CHAPTER 37

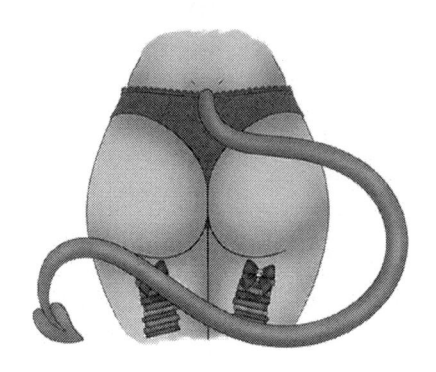

Mariax

I happen to be walking up the hallway of my floor to find Lauren to help me with the cluster fuck in my kitchen when the door at the end of the hall shakes vigorously. I jog closer, now hearing a murmured conversation on the other side of the door.

I lay my hand on the door to lean closer, turning my ear towards the door. Even with my demonic hearing, all the safety measures I've put into place dampen their conversation quite a bit, but I can just make it out.

"No, you cannot just waltz into Mariax's personal floor. If she wanted to, you have access anytime you wanted, jackass, she'd have given you the code," Lauren screeches at someone.

There's a scuffle and then Ian speaks.

"Little one, open the door. Your–"

"Wee guard dog," Hunter interjects.

"...is baring our entrance and taunting Hunter's wolf. It would be a shame if I had to remove her tongue for impolite behavior."

My breath stalls for a moment. I don't think Ian would actually harm Lauren, but you truly never know with him.

"Ugh," I grumble to myself, while unlocking the door with my tail. "What a shittasticly glorious day this is turning out to be," I finish sarcastically, pulling the door open.

Hunter pushes through the opening first, followed by Ian. Lauren attempts to follow, but I stop her with a hand on her shoulder. "It's okay, I can handle it."

"But Mistress–" Lauren protests.

"Seriously, go grab a coffee and a new book on me," I offer with a smile.

"A book?" she questions. The look of happiness that crosses her face at being able to pick out something to read gives my heart a little extra patter knowing I caused it.

"Fine, a manga, whatever," I say, gently pushing her back through the entrance and closing the door.

I turn to face the hulking males. "Why are you here? Tell me right the fuck now," I demand, stomping my foot.

They both smirk in response, but Hunter takes a step toward me.

"Ian shook me awake and insisted we dash down here, which ended up causing the stramash in the stairwell, because 'it's time we settle this and move onto the fun part'." Hunter explains broodily before tucking a strand of hair behind my ear and kissing my forehead.

Whatever thoughts I had about Ian's reasoning for seeking me out vanish at Hunter's touch.

My murder moths flutter in my stomach. I hug myself, not knowing what to do with my reaction to his loving gesture.

I push past him and rush back to my suite, unlocking it and entering. Ian steps a foot over the threshold, but Hunter bars his entrance with a tattooed forearm.

Ian rolls his eyes dramatically and vancates into my living room. Hunter sighs and rubs his forehead. "Can we come in, Cheetie? We also had something to speak with you about," Hunter asks politely.

I move to the side, gesturing that he should enter.

He surprises me again by gracefully sliding his muscular chest past mine before closing the door and locking it behind him. His need to protect me and my need to feel safe achieved all in one simple task.

Hunter, Ian, and I stand in my kitchen. Ian is making us all coffee at the marble counter behind me. They're both dressed casually in fitted t-shirts, Hunter's bordering on tearing from trying to contain his muscular body.

I'm clad in flannel PJ shorts and Hunter's Drexel University hoodie, which Hunter insisted I wear, pulling it down until my head popped through the neck hole, because I was distracting him with my night wear. I'm swamped in it, but I am possessed by the idea of stealing it and basking in his scent whenever I want.

Ian and I don't speak but we keep glancing at one another and looking away when the other notices.

Hunter grumbles in Gaelic before switching back to English. "Fine, if the two of ye can't be mature about this, I will."

Damn, flustered Hunter is sexy.

"What do we need to discuss?" I jut my chin in Ian and Hunter's directions.

Hunter replies, "First, knock off the attitude. I have had enough of both of yer shite today." He closes his eyes for a few moments to regain his composure. Opening his eyes, Hunter glances between Ian and me. "One of the reasons we came over this morning was to talk to ye about us."

"Us? There is no us," I rebut.

"Not yet, but…"

"Oh, no," I start. "I am not ready for this. Nope, not fucking happening."

"Lassie, it's time ye shut yer mouth, or I will give it

something better to do. It is my time to talk. Ian and I have spoken at length about becoming a throuple with ye. We agree that we want to explore being partners. Do ye want to give us a shot, wee Cheetie?"

"Hold on. You planned out an entire relationship that involves me without discussing it with me first?" I question Hunter angrily.

"To be fair, everything spiraled after ye staged yer little revenge fuck in front of Ian. He will never willingly admit this to ye, but he has been battling his emotions, confused why he enjoyed watching ye with me. There's only one way to find out if we can make this work," Hunter says seriously.

Hunter leans against the counter by the stainless-steel fridge with his ankles crossed, a smirk firmly in place. My eyes trace his naked flesh, sliding along each line of his tattoos and bouncing back to take in his nipple piercings.

I have never wanted to lavish attention on those tiny buds more in my life. He flexes his pecs when I keep staring.

Ian finishes with the espresso machine and wipes down the counter briskly before hanging the cloth on the hook next to the cabinets.

I cannot contain my nerves as I pace in front of the kitchen island.

Ian's chest brushes my back as he places a large steaming latte on the island. The latte's warm and comforting scent mixes with Ian and Hunter's, creating an evocative perfume. I picture stormy nights, cozied up with them with a book and a fluffy blanket. I wish the scent alone could transport me to the vision in my head.

I feel Ian's heat behind me again as I lift my bare foot to turn around at the end of the island.

He grips my horns tightly at their bases as he speaks against my ear, his breath fans against my lobe. "If you don't stop fucking pacing, Daddy and Hunter will be forced to punish you. Hunter will bind your breasts tightly with rope for me, and then I'll fuck them until I give you a pearl necklace."

"Perhaps I'll fuck yer face with my fat cock at the same time. Both of us using yer body at once for our pleasure, not yers," Hunter elaborates, his voice deep and sensual.

Their threats travel straight to my clit, making it swell with wanton need.

Ian backs up, forcing me to walk backward with him. If I refuse, he will drag me. Although, any time he's touched my horns forcibly like this…

I shove the thoughts away to ponder another time.

Ian releases me and rounds the island to sit on a bar stool across from me. I brace both hands on the island top, narrowing my eyes at him.

"Do not touch me again. You lost that privilege a long time ago," I sneer.

Ian doesn't respond, only steeples his fingers in front of himself, slowly tracing his bottom lip with his index fingers as he watches me with mild interest. There's a hunger in his stare as a shadow wraps around my mug and gently nudges it closer to me, encouraging me to drink.

I comply, but only because Ian makes the best coffee I've ever tasted. I welcome the warm scent into my body with a deep inhale. The first sip is always the best, the temperature is perfect, and all the flavors swirl together on your tongue.

Coffee is my lifeblood; my body craves it, and I'm always looking for my next hit.

I savor my coffee. If it didn't boost his ego to unmanageable heights, I would compliment Ian. I miss the simple ritual of waking up next to a warm body, early morning snuggles, and coffee in bed.

My heart gives a pang of sorrow.

Maybe he will bring Hunter and me coffee in bed. I can already picture expanding Hunter's cabin and adding a massive bed. Cold winter nights with only the fireplace to see by. The shadows dance on our skin as we explore and taste each other.

What the fuck, Mariax? You are not in a relationship with them. Stop fantasizing and handle your shit.

"Cheetie, where did ye go?" Hunter asks.

I realize I'm leaning on one elbow, cupping my cheek, and the other holds my mug halfway to my lips.

The daydream was a tempting treat laced with arsenic. One bite and the poison will overtake me.

A lack of trust and trauma skews my outlook on life. I'm fucked up, and I've come to terms with that. There is no future with them. My darkness seeks solitude and feeds on loneliness.

I blush, not sure how I feel about these revelations.

Ian enjoyed watching us? That is not how I expected him to react. I don't know who this soft creature is that blushes and simpers for a few kind words. Honestly, I should just tell him to go to hell and wash my hands of both of them.

But then Hunter says something that shocks me to my core.

"Plain and simple – we want ye, Mariax, and ye want us. Ye can try to keep hiding from the truth, but ye will be ours eventually. Do ye accept to embrace the shades of gray with us and explore the possibilities with a coupling like ours?"

Hunter gestures a hand between himself and Ian, the movement causing his muscles in his chest and arm to flex and bunch, his tattoos rippling, and the barbells in his nipples press against the cotton of his shirt, daring me to play with them.

I groan and shove my head into my hands.

"I can't keep my mind straight around you two and remember, I'm pissed at you both." I turn my gaze towards Ian. "I don't want to care about you anymore…to get jealous of thinking about you with another."

I look up when the hairs on my neck stand on end.

Ian is eyeing me like the predator he is. He tilts his head slowly, as if curious if I will flee. Violence brews between us. He calmly places his cup down, and shadows start dancing across his skin with his fury.

"I have had enough of this, little one. I am done playing games. You have attempted to evade my presence, and it is time you surrender yourself to me."

Ian vancates and reappears behind me. He leans against me, pressing my hips painfully into the edge of the island top.

Hunter takes a large step towards us like he's going to intervene and then thinks better of it, settling back and picking up his mug to take a sip of his coffee and hooking his thumb through one of his belt loops.

The fact that Hunter doesn't intervene is greatly telling.

Does he trust Ian? How is that possible?

I turn in the tight cage of Ian's arms so I can face him. Once my face is an inch away from his bare, tattooed chest, he takes the opportunity to grab one of my horns in a tattooed hand and cranes my head back. He wraps his other hand around my throat, his forearm pressing on my sternum.

My tail is pinned behind me, thrashing uselessly to free itself. My pussy is soaked, and I'm panting from his territorial onslaught.

Ian leans forward and inhales my scent at the space between my shoulder and neck, breathing a deep exhale across the same area. My nipples harden in response, and I bite my tongue to stifle my moan.

His chest rumbles against me as he speaks, his voice steely and hostile.

"I could talk all day, plead with you to believe me, and still fail. I don't have the patience for such a waste of time," he states coldly. "I will save us both the headache and show you my memories in the same manner I have shown Hunter. I will show you exactly what happened in Inferuna without the risk of you accusing me of fabricating lies. You are mine, and I will no longer allow you to throw accusations around like a little brat."

He wraps a shadow across my mouth like a piece of extra strength duct tape before I can spit out my retort. My eyebrows snap together in irritation. That is one thing I for sure did not miss from our time together, being silenced against my will. I was never a perfect submissive and had to work incredibly hard to please him.

But in moments like this, I can't help but rebel.

The truth is so close, but I'm terrified of losing the anger I've nurtured all these years. The anger that has fueled my passion to discover who I am, not who the Potentate or Ian thought I should be.

I struggle in his grasp, and he only tightens his hold further, adding more shadows to wind around my body. One comes up and yanks my hair back, and another wraps around my throat, applying pressure and has me caged between his arms. His body is pressed against the length of mine from the hips up. He has me bowed so far back on the island top.

Shadows hold me firmly in place as he runs a finger over the seam of my lips, over my jaw, up my cheek, and rests his fingertips on my temple last.

"We've done this before to clear up issues and prove I'm right, but this will be a little different, as it's a full memory of mine, not just a snippet to prove my point.

Brace yourself, Angel."

Without another moment of hesitation, my mind is plunged into his memories.

I see everything through his eyes on one of the worst days of my life.

I don't want to be here. I'm nauseated, and my anxiety tightens in my chest, but I can't stop looking. My eyes aren't open to the real world. Even if I tried to close my eyes, nothing would happen because he was controlling this hellscape.

I can't hear anything, and there's a strange pressure and ringing in my ears from the lack of sound.

I've experienced this sensation before when I sought solace in the woods north of the city. Without the blaring sounds of Philadelphia, my ears tried to cope with the silence.

It's like I stepped into a void or simply fell asleep. I feel his hand on my lower back, guiding my corporeal body forward. But when I turn, he's not there.

I hate having no control over my own body.

As I am led up the steps by the light pressure on my lower back, I realize we are arriving at Tiffany's second-floor apartment. It's then that the memory of Ian appears ahead of me. He knocks on the door with three loud bangs, ignoring the small, illuminated doorbell to the left.

Tiffany yells something disconcerting from inside, and then the door flings open, revealing one of her latest orgies.

Ian doesn't bother to take in the scene before uttering, "get out," in a deep, commanding voice. He is notorious in Inferuna, and all the creatures who live within this shitty realm know better than to cross the djinn.

Half-dressed bodies shrink against the doorframe as they slip past Ian, not daring to touch him. Once they're all gone, he steps into the apartment and closes the door firmly behind him.

Tiffany stands a few feet away with her hands on her hips, glaring. Irritation is scrawled across her features. Her ultramarine hair is in a messy bun, probably thrown up in haste. She only wears a corset over a pale pink lace G-string.

My ire rises as she boldly stands there, barely dressed, in front of my daddy. I bare my teeth, tension radiating through my shoulders, but an unseen hand moves to my throat and places enough pressure on my windpipe to remind me that I trust Tiffany with every fiber of my being.

"What?" she bites with hostility. "I'm fucking busy, and you've just thrown out all of my entertainment."

Her light blue skin easily shows the angry flush on her chest.

Ian doesn't move further into the apartment, but holds his hand up to stop her from speaking. A wave of power erupts from him, spreading throughout the apartment.

"Hey, asshole," she throws at Ian. "What the fuck do you want?"

"Enough," he says deeply, and I feel the command cover my skin with the authority in his voice.

The deep well of his power rises to the surface. Shadows form in a haze around him, and more writhe under his skin. His tattoos seem to come to life.

Tiffany's eyes widen, and her wings flare out behind her at the threat. Her tail thrashes in irritation. She narrows her eyes, causing a v to form between her brows but tips her chin down in slight indifference. She knows to respect the power he holds.

She relaxes her stance, but her wings remain open behind her. They're similar to bat wings in shape, tipped with claws, blue veins so dark they almost appear black run under the thin membranes. Her magic pulses around her in a warning.

Being within Ian's memories clearly shows me that he is so much more. I thought I had a grasp on who Ian was after two thousand years but seeing him in the presence of others without me is a whole new perspective.

He moves towards Tiffany, and she stands her ground.

"I require your assistance."

She goes to speak, but he silences her with a warning snarl.

"You can either choose to listen, or I will force you. I'm attempting to make this less painful for you, for Mariax's sake. But let me make myself clear. I do not care if you suffer or what pathetic emotions you may feel; I only care about her. She. Is. Mine. I will spare her any emotional damage that I can."

Tiffany tips her head to the side in interest and motions her hand for him to keep going.

"The only reason I'm willing to entertain anything is for Mariax. I don't like you, and that's putting it lightly. You're no good for her and never will be," Tiffany huffs.

"She is mine, just as much as I am hers. You will do this for me. It has come to my attention that the Potentate knows that Mariax and I have been seeing each other this entire time. They do not allow assigned partners to become more than that, especially ones that have worked as closely as we have. They fear that it will impact our ability to torture souls maliciously," he says with a snort of derision. "As if we could suffer any more than we do from what they put us through. They've made most of those demons mindless machines, following orders and doling out punishments. No other thoughts enter their heads besides malice and greed. They are vile, evil creatures. But Mariax is another creature entirely. Something about her is…other, and she is not like those other braindead creatures."

"No, she might have been created the same way, but she

is like no other torture demon I've met," Tiffany agrees.

Ian keeps speaking as though Tiffany's half of the conversation is irrelevant.

"I digress. They found out that we have been together for quite some time. Although, I don't think they know the specifics. One of your friends that you had at the party to watch that idiotic human show has turned on us. You should watch your back, and I suggest vetting your inner circle better. I would say trust no one but yourself from here on out," he advises while staring down his nose at her with superiority.

She narrows her eyes at him and begins pacing, her wings shivering with her anxiety. "So, what do you need me to do? What are they going to do to her?"

"All irrelevant, because you are taking her place."

She turns abruptly and faces him.

"Taking her place? How? Won't they know the difference?" Tiffany asks, gesturing wildly with her hands. "What does that even mean? Why do you always have to be so godsdamn cryptic?" She glares at Ian, demanding an answer. "Say what you need. Use your words a—"

Ian interrupts her.

"I will torture you in front of all of Inferuna. I will demonstrate all the skills I have been taught and how I am a good little mindless torturer. It is the only way to distract them long enough to inform Mariax of the situation. From there, we will leave and finally be free of this suffocating reality. Her term is up and she can be released from her contract."

"How the hell would you even leave?"

"That is none of your concern. However," Ian states and briefly closes his eyes in an effort to compose himself, "I will come back to collect you when I deem it safe enough."

Tiffany waves him off.

"I only have another hundred years of servitude, and I

certainly won't be needing your help. The thought of asking you for anything makes me want to vomit all over your tailored shoes."

She sighs deeply and grabs her horns in frustration. Her messy bun has fallen out, and her long hair is to the middle of her back, the bright blue strands curling in all directions.

After a few minutes of contemplation, she releases her horns and throws her hands out to the sides of her body.

"There's a reason I never volunteered for their bullshit torture school. I'm not too afraid to admit that it terrifies me."

"Would it ease your mind if I ensure you do not feel any pain? I will also personally heal you of the wounds I inflict," Ian offers.

"Can you take the memories away too? Is that one of your many powers?" she asks, heavy with sarcasm.

"Yes," he confirms.

Tiffany erupts. "Of course it fucking is! Why can't you manipulate the minds of the Potentate and make him call–"

"There is something bigger going on here. If I manipulate their minds now, whoever's pulling their strings will be on to me, and I can't have that, not if I want to solve this. Permanently."

His forehead pinches with the thought. Her arms slump down to her sides in defeat knowing if he is right that this is the only option. Ian continues seeing all the fight has gone out of her.

"I will make it painless, heal you, and wipe all the memories of being tortured from your mind. I do not have to show you this kindness, but again, I'm doing it for her, not you. Time is of the essence, and we must begin now."

"Okay," she replies, her voice strong but wary.

The scene blurs and then quickly comes back into focus.

Tiffany lies nude on the very same type of metal table we used to torture souls on. Ropes bind her to the table, held hostage for all of Inferuna's viewing pleasure. I can't help but take in the few tattoos she has that appear stark against her pale blue skin. Her tail and wings are pinned beneath her, trembling with nerves.

Ian seems to fast forward through the memory, and I feel all of his emotions as he watches with me. He's infuriated at having to do this. Even though the memory of Ian before me is pretending not to care.

I catch sight of my pink hair in the horde of demons and other monsters surrounding the makeshift stage. Pompously, he addresses the crowd, explains the demonstration he is about to perform, walks about the stage, gesturing, and even elicits a couple of laughs from the crowd.

He stops and chuckles darkly, motioning to Tiffany, saying a few more words that I'm not capable of comprehending at the moment.

Panic and bewilderment are building in my chest.

He didn't betray me. How did I not figure this out? Why didn't he tell me he was going to do this?

And I hear a voice in my mind, not part of his memory.

"No, I wouldn't spare a moment longer and risk your safety," Ian says calmly, and I feel the ghost of a hand smoothing down my hair in comfort.

My heart continues to beat wildly.

The scene speeds by. Blood and gore cover the instruments of pain and malice neatly organized on the small trolley tray, similar to those that occupy human hospital rooms but two times the size.

He is meticulous about everything he does, and by the end, my best friend is hardly recognizable. She no longer has hair. Even her eyelashes are gone. There's no flesh left on her body, and she's twitching. Her beautiful wings are missing the membranes and nothing but a skeletal frame remains. However, she doesn't seem to be experiencing the pain of his actions.

How did I not notice that at the time? She told me that repeatedly, but I thought she was just saying that to make me less angry.

The next time I remember seeing her, she was healed.

My worry for her was clouded by my own extreme emotions. I created my own tragedy, and it was all for nothing. He was protecting me.

I feel another emotion that I still refuse to acknowledge. It is attempting to escape my smothering hold. I push it down. That warm feeling has no place in this memory.

Ian is silent in my mind as he replays scenes I didn't know existed.

He picks up Tiffany's mutilated body and carries her to our suite. He heals her with magic, an ability I didn't know he possessed. I can't describe the process, just that she was completely healed.

Tiffany gave him a small, watery smile.

"Well, that sucked," she sighed. "But it was worth it if it kept her safe. Won't they be curious how I'm healed so quickly? That amount of torture would take a while to heal with only Vitasmooth."

Ian doesn't return her smile but responds, "You will stay in our suite for a few days, and no one will be the wiser. They do not care about your wellbeing, so no one will be looking for you."

Tiffany rolls her eyes. "Yeah, yeah, nobody cares about me. Get on with it."

"I will be vancating with Mariax shortly," he says as he slips a cell phone out of his pocket and holds it up before handing it to her.

"How did you even—never mind. There's no service for

this kind of human technology, but I'll take it. Will you use your magic on it to make it work?" she asks, her eyes glinting with mild excitement.

He slips out another phone before stating, "I have already programmed my number. If you need help to get out of here before your time is up, all you have to do is call."

Tiffany pockets the phone and nods in acknowledgement.

The scene blurs again.

Ian's emotions are chaotic and brimming with anxiety. I'm overwhelmed. I can't fully process everything I'm seeing right now.

The memory of Ian desperate to find me. He speeds through time and space, popping up in different parts of Inferuna. He doesn't take the time to mask himself, and he appears, scans the surroundings, and moves on.

We must have searched all of Inferuna by now, and he still hasn't found me. Little does he know I'm in the torture center, the last place he would look. Tiffany must have already found me by now, and I'm guessing I'm close to fleeing.

Absolute terror washes over him as he echoes his emotions in the memory. He can't find me and assumes the worst, that the Potentate had taken me when he was caring for Tiffany. Regret he spared a moment to heal her is strong.

The real Ian's voice speaks in my mind. "You wouldn't have left if I had found you. I could have explained everything…"

"You saved my best friend and protected me, even if it wasn't the right way to go about it." My voice breaks as I continue, "I would never have asked you to do that or have allowed you to use her, Ian."

"I know, but I did it anyway. You can't change the past,"

he says seriously.

"I didn't regret leaving without you at the time." I sigh deeply.

"I never have, and I never will betray you, angel. I admit I sometimes take things a bit too far, but I always weigh all my options. Now, pay attention."

His invisible hand grips my chin and turns my face to view a new memory as it appears.

We finally pop back into the torture center. We are standing in the room I just vancated.

What's left of the soul I tortured is writhing on the table, and bloody instruments are scattered across the floor. The entire room is splattered with blood. The memory of Ian turns on his heel to exit the room just as the instructor walks out of a room further down the hall.

I feel Ian's emotions radiating through me powerfully. A smile filled with vengeance curls his lips. He rushes forward and is before the instructor before he can flee. Ian grips him by the throat and raises him in the air.

"I told you one day you would meet your end by my hand," Ian growls.

It's then that I notice the dead demon close to the entrance of the building, just beyond the instructor. It shows signs of being strangled.

The pattern I left behind on his throat would match my tail, wrapping around it perfectly and then cutting it open. The demon deserved to suffer for attempting to capture me, and strangulation wasn't enough to cool my blood lust, so I also slashed its throat. It was dead before it hit the ground.

My eyes flashed back to the struggling creature in front of Ian.

At this point, Ian admits to himself that I am no longer in the realm of Inferuna. He is fully unhinged as he laughs darkly, describing all the ways he will torture our instructor.

"I will enjoy slowly placing tiny cuts all over your body. Truly showing you, my devoted instructor, everything I've learned in your training. What kind of pupil would I be if I did not display everything I've learned over the years?"

Ian winks at him, and a piece of everything I lost is minutely soothed.

The instructor's skin pales before turning blue from lack of oxygen. Ian releases his throat, only to grab the instructor's hair as he falls to the ground, yanking him upright again. The instructor screams as Ian drags him, using the force of his body, lethal rage fueling his muscles, to move him down the hall to a different torture chamber at the end of the building.

He throws the instructor inside and slams the door behind them both.

In the next moment, I'm back in my own mind.

My entire body is shaking from shock, nerves, and the overwhelming emotions I can't contain. Hunter is by my side already, smoothing a hand down my hair.

I'm pressed between the two of them.

Ian has one arm wrapped around Hunter's waist, pulling him close to us, while his other hand remains lightly pressed to my temple. He slowly trails his hand down until he gets to my waist, pulling me in more securely between them.

"You didn't betray me," I uttered quietly.

"No, I never did."

CHAPTER 38

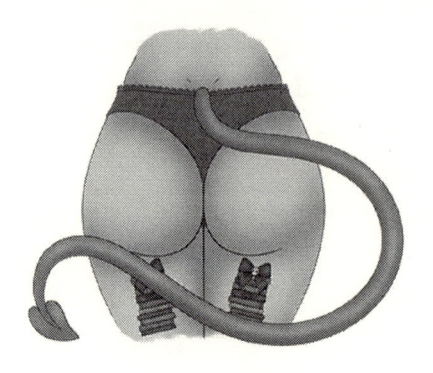

Mariax

The sound of metal-on-metal pierces my eardrums as the female in front of me struggles against her bindings. She is bound to the giant Saint Andrew's cross that is bolted to the floor on the side of the room. My plan is to wear her out enough that she'll be begging me to end her punishment, and then I will continue with more vigor.

I need this. After everything Ian showed me, I need to clear my own head.

She knows what she did to deserve this punishment, and I can see she's nervous about the outcome. However, there's also an underlying current of excitement vibrating off her skin.

She looks like something that belongs in a child's fairy tale, at least on the outside. On the inside lies a predator wanting to draw in the souls to snack on them. This submissive is a siren, but you wouldn't know it at first glance except for the slight shimmer of her skin and the unnatural ethereal beauty of her face.

She's almost too perfect, with an airbrushed quality.

I was surprised when she came to me looking to be a submissive because sirens are generally the complete opposite of a submissive.

They enjoy pain and misery in themselves and inflicting it on others. This one wants to further explore her darker side with her own pain. So here she is in her human-like form with legs and arms, but I learned that if you place her feet in a bucket of water, her tail and scales will reemerge.

With her permission, I began experimenting.

It turns out that scales are exceptionally sensitive, and they grow back. I have never worked with them before, so I had to get creative.

At first, I just began lightly petting them with my tail, watching her response closely.

Certain areas on her body where the scale seemed lighter, like around her breasts, were extremely sensitive. Just the light feather petting in the growth direction sends her nearly into hyperventilation. However, if I ran my tail the opposite way, the scales lifted up, and she would scream in anguish.

We've been in this session for hours, and I am not even close to finishing.

After her last session, the siren decided to lure a human to her right outside my building. Why she thought she could get away with that, I have no fucking clue, but when she came back for her next session, I showed her the security footage. Her skin turned the color of pale rotting seaweed when it's been left on the beach to dry.

Her ass is bare to me, making sure that all of her scales are on display for what I'm about to do.

I tap my shifted tail, currently resembling a cattle prod, and run it up the scales of her back, so they lightly pick up with each bolt of electricity running over her skin. It looks as though they're about to rip off at any second.

She begins shrieking, so I stop and shove a ball gag into her mouth while I berate her for her behavior.

"This is the last time you will ever enter my premises.

No one hunts, no matter the style, in front of my property without reaping the consequences," I hiss. "When your entire body is in endless agony, remember to be grateful you're still breathing."

I lift the bucket of water by my feet, the rim in one hand and supporting the base in the other, before throwing the water at her back as hard as I can. She wanted to know what her hard limits were. I guess we'd found them. It wasn't difficult at all to rid her of those scales, but I'm sure she can find a nice, tasty soul far away from my territory to heal herself.

I shift my tail into a long flat knife and meticulously peel up her scales one by one. Her scales are pink against the floor as her muted screams sound. Blood runs in rivets over her ass, but she hasn't made the hand signal for me to stop her punishment.

I change tactics, preparing to electrocute all the wet, vulnerable skin on her back. Her body seizes up with the first prod, hands gripping around the chains, and her arms are fastened.

There's a sharp knock at the door, and Lauren speaks through the intercom, alerting me to an emergency.

"Fuck off, I'm working with a client," I shout over the zapping of electricity.

Lauren replies, "Mistress, this situation requires your direct attention."

"For fuck's sake," I mumble under my breath.

I drop my tail, and it returns to normal. I grab a cloth hanging on a hook near the cross and wipe off my hands, stomping to the room's exit and flinging it open.

"What is the disaster you can't possibly handle alone?" I question Lauren with the corner of my top lip pulled up in a snarl.

"Mistress, there is a man outside attempting to force his

way through the wards. He is screaming your name and shouting bullshit about the club, Hunter, and you," she quickly explains.

I shoulder past Lauren with an irritated huff and make my way to the main door of the building.

When I step outside, I come face to face with a short, stocky, pissed off male.

His smell hits me before I even get near him.

He reeks of cheap liquor and shifter. His clothes are stained and wrinkled, showing he has been in them for a while. The knees show the most wear. I walk down the stairs and face him through the purple haze of my wards.

He goes to shout at me before halting as he takes in my appearance. In response, his mouth drops open, and his eyes widen. My outfit is still coated in scales and blood, remnants of it ring my fingernails and my wrists.

I smirk at his expression and then unleash my anger on him.

"Who the fuck do you think you are loitering outside of my business? The last creature that dared to cross me ended up in my dungeon missing key body parts," I threaten, flicking some of the scales on my hands at him to show that I'm serious.

I feel my magic skimming my skin and wrapping around me in a thick layer before radiating outwards. I know it reaches him when he stiffens and his eyes narrow.

A smart male would have fled, whereas this one doesn't seem to have all his mental abilities.

"So, you're the infamous Mariax, huh? The reason Hunter won't take me back?" he spits.

"In the flesh," I verify, throwing my arms out wide. "So, you came here to assault me? Insult me? What?"

"I came here to fucking kill you, you disgusting whore. You ruined my godsdamn life!"

"How would I have ruined your pathetic little life?

Hmmm…" I tap my index finger on my chin. "Oh, I know. A certain wolf finally saw you the way you are now? Pathetic, a sniveling excuse for a wolf. If he broke your heart, which I doubt, that has nothing to do with me."

"Wrong. It has everything to do with you. Ever since he met you, he's changed. He's more outspoken. He's been making things happen in the community. He's just better…more, I don't know what, but it should be me getting the credit for it," he says, his voice filled with woe.

Interesting. I pull my phone out from my back pocket and call Hunter. I tap the tip of my boot impatiently. This needs to be dealt with, and it's not my job to handle his pack bullshit.

He answers on the fifth ring.

"Cheetie, is this a booty call?" he asks seductively, the pitch of his voice deep. The warmth of his accent attempts to soothe me.

"You need to come down to The Snuggle Palace right now before I kill one of your wolves," I order.

"What do ye mean, kill one of my wolves?" Hunter questions, his sexy tone vanishing.

"There's a male here threatening to murder me because he claims I took you away from him. He is blaming me for your breakup, and I would rather rip his brain out through his nose, then listen to this shit."

I can hear his eyes are narrowed through the phone. "What does he look like?"

Pack shit needs to stay off my doorstep. My clients don't need this attention. I don't have time to deal with his bullshit. I've got my own problems.

Hunter says again, drawing me away from my thoughts.

"Mariax, please tell me what he looks like."

"Fine," I acquiesce. "He's stocky, about six feet, with mousy brown hair clipped very short. Stubby nose. A scar that runs along his right forearm."

There's silence on the line for a beat.

"Fuck. That's Patrick, my ex. I'll be there as soon as I can."

"Oh, I know. He already told me what a whore I am for stealing you," I say and then hang up on him, shoving my phone into the back pocket of my leather bodysuit.

We stand there, glaring at each other for what felt like an eternity but was probably closer to ten minutes.

I'm impatient, and I want to be done for the day to go relax.

To take a long bath, snuggle up in my little nest in my bed, and finish the Bea Paige book I started. It's not so much to ask. What does a demon have to do around here to get some godsdamn peace once in a while?

But then, the idiot wolf makes a huge mistake.

"Look at you, too scared to face me, hiding behind a ward," he says cockily, pointing a chunky finger at me.

My fury barrels into me full force as I step through the wards.

"I was attempting to keep this civil for Hunter's sake. But hopefully, he won't mind if I break you a wee bit," I say sweetly, holding my pointer finger and thumb a small distance apart in demonstration, mimicking Hunter's accent at the end of my threat to drive him further into jealousy.

I draw my foot back and crash it into his kneecap, the sharp stiletto spike of my boot embedding in his shin. He falls to his knees, blood gushing from his leg when I pull my heel out.

I wipe my bloody heel off on his shirt before placing my hands on my knees and bend to whisper, "Do you want to continue to make threats you will never fulfill?"

Finally, a frazzled-looking Hunter comes sprinting up the sidewalk across the way. He barely checks for traffic as he crosses the street, causing several people to blare their horns. Stomping up to the kneeling Patrick, he punches him in the face.

I step back to give him room and cackle, pleased with Hunter.

Patrick turns to glare at me from the ground.

I shrug and say, "I told you to get the fuck off my property. You didn't, so enjoy your reward for your refusal to do so."

Hunter is seething, his fists balled at his sides. Patrick returns his ire and attempts to spit on Hunter, but it only lands on his own chest.

So pathetic.

Hunter plants a boot on Patrick's abdomen and leans on it with his full weight, resting his arms on his raised leg and staring down. The air whooshes from Patrick's lungs as Hunter applies pressure.

"Didn't I order ye to get the fuck out of Appalachian Pack territory?" He shouts, loud enough to set off the alarm of the car parked on the street next to us.

"You should have never broken up with me. I was the best thing that ever happened to you," Patrick states, rejection filling his tone.

Hunter stands and kicks him in the face; I hear Patrick's nose break. I stand far enough away to keep Hunter focused and be ready to help if he needs it.

The glee inside of me battles to break free. My body is practically vibrating with the need to jump back into the fight.

Hunter looks at me and holds a hand up to tell me to stay.

I catch movement out of the corner of my eye. Another shifter was leaning against a lamppost; it must be Charlie. I've never met him, but he matches the description Hunter gave me.

Before Hunter can do more damage, Charlie pulls Hunter away, leaving the bloodied fool on the ground groaning in pain. Hunter puffs out his chest and stands to his full height.

Hunter's tone drops into an even more menacing timbre to speak to Patrick. "If I ever see yer face again or hear a word ye have been spotted nearby, I'll hang ye by yer entrails until ye bleed out."

Hunter and Charlie each grab a leg and drag Patrick behind them up the sidewalk. The motion causes his shirt to ride up. He starts screaming as the cement of the sidewalk slowly sandpapers his flesh raw.

Hunter turns his head and yells back to me. "I'm sorry for the inconvenience, my wee Cheetie. Let us take out the trash for ye."

I chuckle and blow him a kiss before returning to the siren.

CHAPTER 39

Ian

I watched Hunter and his beta go to several meaningless locations.

That list was intuitive, but they missed all the signs pointing to where I'm standing in a business park. It's dank, gloomy, and exactly the type of place you would expect nefarious activities to happen.

I don't waste time but check out the most promising building on the list. A menacing aura surrounds the warehouse. The signature is barely noticeable unless you're already looking for it. Whoever or whatever created this signature did not intend for it to ever be found.

Hunter and Charlie likely dismissed the warehouse because their source of magic is miniscule.

The shadows embrace me in welcome as I become one of their own, moving quickly along with the growing dusk. The door is most likely unlocked, but I don't care because no space can deny me entrance in this form.

I slip under the crack below the door, remaining in my shadowed form on the other side, and take in the surrounding space.

Immediately, I feel a dark, pulsing aura surrounding the

space. Surrounding the room are some kind of heavy machinery pushed to the sides, bits of debris and trash scattered about. However, in the center of the space, it's completely open.

I move over there and look up, only seeing chains of various lengths hanging from the space above. Attached to the chains are huge hooks.

I return to my corporeal form and continue checking out the space, following the stairs up swiftly. A small secondary level has grates for flooring, and I can see straight through to the ground below.

That's when I see what no one else has yet.

Hiding in plain sight, but cloaked, stands an object that few people know about. It is essentially a one-way ticket to any plane the maker wishes, a door if a name is needed for what is before me.

I step closer, drawn to the dark energy. This is what was manifesting the aura I felt from the street.

It has been tens of millenniums since I have seen one of these. These portals were never common practice. Most supernatural communities and planes of existence have outlawed them as they allow ungoverned travel.

Whoever is housing this object is risking more than just their death.

Many beings think death is the worst possible outcome. But there are so many worse things than death. Death is only the beginning. If you want to be terrified of something, be terrified of what lies between the ether, of what lurks when you close your eyes and what stalks your nightmares come to life.

I've only been truly afraid of a couple of things in my life, and knowing this is to be used on my Angel is one of them. My heart rate picks up rapidly as I think about the danger Mariax is in. Whoever is stalking her means more harm than I imagined.

I squeeze my eyes shut and grip my hair tightly, screaming internally, refusing to let my anguish out. I refuse to stop these useless emotions.

All of a sudden, I feel a different presence. The most natural form of evil.

If I want to save Mariax, I'll have to volunteer myself as bait. Nothing can hurt me with my powers, so there's very little that they could do to me without using this weapon, which I know is not meant for me. They wouldn't waste it on me when they already had their sights set on her.

So, I allow them to come. Allow them to think they have the upper hand. I hear no footsteps, but feel the movement of the air around me. The presence is inches from my back.

Pain so immediate and overwhelming throbs between my shoulder blades. The metal chains rattle and clang together.

The hook shoved into my spine pulls sharply upward, scraping against my vertebrae until my toes skim the grates.

A scream tears through me.

I am in absolute agony, but less than a heartbeat later, something smashes into my left temple. Blackness consumes everything.

ACKNOWLEDGEMENTS

My Kitten, you know who you are. Thank you for being there for me and encouraging me to finally write a fucking book. Also, I always enjoy testing out new scene ideas with you, and I cannot wait to try more.
XOXOXXX

Thank you to my kids for trying to leave your mama-llama alone to work on her book. I love you to the mountains and back. Always.

Queen Bitch Alpha, your title says it all. Thank you for being there for me since day one. You've read all of the versions of MOS and I cannot believe I didn't scare you off.

Kylie, I have so much to thank you for, but first, drink your water you dehydrated hoe. Now, on to business, you have been one of my biggest cheerleaders and I'm so glad we became besties.
To my BETA readers, thank you for reading the rough version of MOS. Your comments and encouragement helped me to make this book so much *more*.

Cake (AKA Vale), thank you for everything you do. I cannot possibly list all the reasons I am thankful for you, but I will list a few. You talked me through many melt downs, whether it was helping to find a solution or simply saying, 'Yeah, that fucking sucks, babe.' You inspire me, and I use the lessons you've taught me daily. You're one of my best friends in life and I love you.

To Becks, you are an inspiration and a force to be reckoned with. I have learned so much from you and I'm proud to call you my mentor and best friend. Thank you for holding my hand and offering me all of the author advice basically every day. The friendship we have built started with books, but it has become so much more than that now. However, I am always happy to teach you in the ways of dark romance and suggest sexy scenes for you to write. Love you!

To Opal, you brought out the monster fucker in me and she is here to stay. As Mariax clearly shows, I am obsessed with your Duskwalker Brides series and I will never get enough of the sexy bone daddies that live rent free in your brain. Thank you for all of your help and for being my boss bitch role model. I would be even more of an anxious puddle without you.

SOCIAL MEDIA

Follow me on social media to keep up with the latest book news!

Facebook:
https://www.facebook.com/groups/3013556378947992

Goodreads:
https://www.goodreads.com/author/show/7859325.C_M_Hutton

Instagram:
https://www.instagram.com/anxioustattooedbookish/

Patreon:
https://www.patreon.com/CMHuttonAuthor

Tiktok:
https://www.tiktok.com/@cmhuttonbooks

Twitter:
https://twitter.com/CMHutton1